THE KING FROM ASHTABULA

Books by Vern Sneider

THE TEAHOUSE OF THE AUGUST MOON

A PAIL OF OYSTERS

A LONG WAY FROM HOME

Vern Sneider

THE KING
FROM
ASHTABULA

G. P. PUTNAM'S SONS
New York

For My Sister

Chapter 1

NORMALLY it would have been bingo night for the little American community sitting high above the ancient capital of Tamabaru, looking out over the East China Sea. But throughout the day the people of the Nakashima Islands had been going to the polls. For the first time in their history they were being allowed to vote. And thus, because it was the eve of their freedom, Brigadier General Matthew Scheick—commander of the United States Civil Affairs Team governing these fifteen small islands—had canceled the game out of respect for such a memorable occasion.

So with the game called off, the evening became more of a private rather than a community affair. Major McCloud of Intelligence, and his wife Agnes, were guests of Lt. Colonel Seymour, of Operations, and his wife Cora. The Captain Carlisles were over at the Captain Cronewetts'. And all along Caroline Drive, named for Mrs. Scheick, the smoke from the barbecue grills rose straight and blue into the calm of the June twilight. The smell of broiling steaks drifted out along the neat white row of poured concrete houses—whose gaily painted doors of pink, and yellow, and aqua faced a black-topped street; and whose picture windows, at the rear, looked out over a cobalt sea. And all along Caroline Drive the officers and their families gathered to share the evening meal and await the returns of the voting.

Only at Cottage 1A, that of General Scheick, were there fewer guests than one might expect on such an occasion. "We'll have the Hendersons in later in the evening," Mrs. Scheick had said to the General, and went on to explain. "After all, Matt, we haven't seen Elwood in seven years. This will give the three of us a chance to become acquainted. And perhaps we'll get some idea as to what's troubling the boy."

It was true. They hadn't seen Elwood, Mrs. Scheick's youngest sister's son, in seven years. Since they had been out here on the Nakashima Islands, he had gone from junior high school to college. And the boy whom they remembered as never wanting to get a haircut, back home there in Youngerville, Iowa; whom they remembered as wearing braces on his teeth and hating them, was now a pleasant-appearing lad with a butch cut and a nice smile.

"I just can't get over how you've grown, Elwood," Mrs. Scheick said as they sat there in the garden chairs, out in the back yard.

It was a statement Mrs. Scheick had made several times since Elwood had arrived, late that afternoon, on a shuttle plane from Okinawa, and he tried to answer it as best he could. "Well, Aunt Caroline," he said, "I'm nineteen, going on twenty now. I'll be a junior in college this fall, so . . ."

"But just the same, you've grown," Mrs. Scheick said once again.

"I guess I have, Aunt Caroline," he replied and looked, a little desperately, at his uncle, over by the barbecue grill.

General Scheick was a fine figure of a man. He had the build and physique of the born soldier. Never, even in his cadet days at the Academy, did anyone ever have to tell "Pug" Scheick to take a brace. He had the natural squareness of shoulders and erectness of trunk so prized by the military. Never, even in his cadet days, did anyone have to say, "Get more authority in your voice, Mr. Scheick." The General could whisper a command and be heard two blocks away. In fact, in athletics, on the parade ground, or in the field of leadership, the General never had a single moment of difficulty at the Academy. His difficulty always had a tendency to come in the classroom.

Over by the barbecue grill now, the General held his hand above the charcoal, tested the heat, then turned. "Elwood," he said, "you'll have your steak rare, won't you?" And when the youth replied in the affirmative, the General nodded in approval, for he liked a man who liked his steaks rare.

Deftly, the General put on the meat, then regarded the youth. "As I was saying, Elwood. It's too bad you're only getting in on the tail end of this operation. I wish you could have been here earlier. I had a tight little command, first-class men; and you should have seen how we brought these Islands along, how we developed them."

Mrs. Scheick gave the General a look, but he missed it. Thus she said pointedly, "Well, we're certainly glad that you could come out and visit us, even though the operation is nearly over. I hope, however, that you didn't have any other plans for this summer, Elwood."

"Well, I guess not," the youth replied. "Our fraternity was having a national convention, but . . ."

"Yes, sir, Elwood," the General continued obliviously. "It's been a fine operation. And it's a good operation to retire on, because, frankly, it's the high point of my career." He flipped the steaks. "If I have any regrets, it would be simply that Washington required us to have this voting in June. My hopes were that we could have it on July 4. Then through the years the Nakashima Islands could celebrate their freedom right along with us."

Mrs. Scheick coughed, and the General, glancing up, caught a glimpse of her face. Puzzled, his eyebrows raised as he tried to figure out what was wrong. Then realizing, he put on his best smile. "But all that's out here and concerns me." He grew confidential. "Tell me, Elwood. How are things back home?"

"They're all right, I guess," Elwood said.

"How's that Landridge girl who lives down the street?" the General asked. "I hear she's turning into a real beauty."

"She's all right, I guess," Elwood replied, and Mrs. Scheick frowned, for it was just as her sister Mildred said it was.

"He's so noncommittal about everything," her sister had written. "Why, we never know what he's thinking. Or if I do manage to pry something out of him, he'll never give an explanation." And it was what his mother had pried out of him that was now the cause of his visit out here in Asia.

"Elwood," she had said one day during Christmas vacation, when he was moping around home. "Why don't you go down to the grain elevator and help your father? After all, you're going to be running the business in a couple of years, so it wouldn't hurt to spend some time there."

It was then that he shook his head. It was then that he said, "I don't think I want to go into the elevator business." And his words caused repercussions halfway round the world.

For the Youngers (Mrs. Scheick's family) had been buying grain and selling grain, milling flour and grinding feed ever since Iowa was settled. It was Great-Grandfather Tobias Younger who had come out from New York State, establishing the mill and elevator, and founding the town of Youngerville. And always there was a Younger at the head of the business.

In a sense, however, the line had been broken, because Mrs. Scheick's father, Owen Younger, had three daughters—Dorothy, the oldest; Caroline, who was Mrs. Scheick; and Mildred, Elwood's mother. But Owen Younger never had a son, so in the course of events it had been a son-in-law who eventually took over as manager. That was Elwood's father—Fred Cummings.

Yet, in reality, it was still a Younger family business. True, Fred Cummings owned ten per cent of the stock, but that was merely a gesture. The three girls had simply reduced their holdings, allowing Fred to buy in to give him incentive. The fact remained, however, that the three Younger girls still owned ninety per cent of the stock, thirty per cent apiece. And it was this thirty per cent that meant the difference.

For Dorothy, the oldest, it meant the difference between her husband working and not working. For Mildred, the youngest, it meant the difference between living in a nice comfortable home on a shaded street, which Fred Cummings could have provided, and living in the Younger family mansion with its great white pillars, and its full square block of land surrounded by a white fence; with its cutting garden of flowers, and its gardener, and its beautiful old carriage house, the carriages replaced now by a couple of the higher priced autos.

And for General and Mrs. Scheick it had, throughout the years, also meant the difference—between whitefish roe or salmon caviar and Beluga; between taking a cottage at some lake while on leave and going on a cruise. And now, with retirement looming on the horizon, it could mean buying an orange grove outright—an orange grove which General Scheick was certain they needed for an active retirement—or buying it on credit. Although Mrs. Scheick was not convinced that they should buy it either way, for as she stated to the General, "Who wants to raise oranges? And who wants an active retirement?"

So when Elwood stated his doubts about going into the elevator business, out in Laguna Beach, California, the nonworking husband of Dorothy promptly had a light heart attack, although the doctors said it could have been a slight case of indigestion. Mrs. Scheick took to her bed for three days, though the General could never remember her having been sick before. And the frantic Mildred, Elwood's mother, had written, "I just don't know what we're going to do if he won't take over."

It was true, too, for what would they do? Dorothy had no children. The Scheicks had two daughters. Thus Elwood was the only male member of the family. The sole remaining possibility was young Alice, Elwood's sister, who was fifteen. Some day she would be married, and there would be her husband.

But as General Scheick explained it, in confidence, to Colonel Henderson, his executive officer, "You only have a fifty-fifty chance with a son-in-law." And the General had his own case as proof. His older daughter was married to an Army captain; so, of course, everything was all right there. But the younger!

"After twenty-two years of living on Army posts," the General would say, shaking his head, "you'd think she would have at least picked out a promising young lieutenant." But what had she done? She had married an insurance salesman from Des Moines.

So it was that Elwood's mother had written to Mrs. Scheick, "Fred says he will run the business for a while yet, but frankly we're going to have to do something, because I just can't understand what has gotten into him. He seems to have lost all interest in things. Why, half the time they can't get him down to the Youngerville Club for a game of hearts—and you know how well he always liked to play cards. So maybe this coming summer if Elwood could come out to visit you, if he could see the discomforts of overseas living, maybe he'd learn to appreciate all the things he has back here. Why, every time I tell him our home is the showplace of the whole county, all he ever says is, 'It needs insulation.' So maybe if he could come out to visit you, perhaps you and Matt could make him come to his senses." And so with the complete assurance of both Mrs. Scheick and the General that they would do just that, Elwood was now sitting in their back yard, out by the East China Sea, waiting for dinner.

The steaks being finished, the General brought them to the table. "Well, here we are, Elwood. Yes, sir, it's certainly good having you with us." He paused, then said slowly, "But I hope you won't get too homesick for Youngerville."

The youth shook his head. "I won't miss the place, Uncle Matt."

"You won't?" General Scheick glanced quickly at Mrs. Scheick. "That's funny. Why, even after all these years of being away from there, I still find myself thinking of it. There's something about the old home town that gets in your system. You know, when Uncle Karl Younger appointed me to the Academy, I honestly didn't know if I wanted to leave or not."

"Your Uncle Matt is right, Elwood," Mrs. Scheick joined in. "There's something about Youngerville . . . well, there's such a sense of security there. Isn't it comforting to know that you have a niche back home, a place in which to fit?"

"No," the youth said. "It's not very comforting. To tell you the truth, it's pretty monotonous just to think of it."

The General looked at Mrs. Scheick. Mrs. Scheick looked at the General. "Well . . ." the General began, then unable to think of anything appropriate, said, "Well . . . excuse me for a second. I want to get my vitamins." He walked over to the barbecue grill and returned with eight bottles, which Elwood regarded curiously. "Did you ever try vitamins and minerals, Elwood?"

"No, not myself," Elwood replied. "But a couple of summers ago I tried some experiments in livestock feeding out on Bean Blossom Road using bonemeal and—"

"Bonemeal!" General Scheick held up a bottle of chalklike pills. "I take it regularly. In fact, I have the whole command taking it. Did you ever try rose hips?"

"No, I never tried anything, Uncle Matt. These were livestock-feeding experiments."

"We'll have to get you on rose hips then. They're a wonderful source of Vitamin C. You know, Elwood"—General Scheick's face grew serious—"with all due respect, I never believed in this business of fading away. If a man puts the right combination of ingredients together, in the form of food, he should be able to go on for at least a hundred and twenty-five years. Now, for instance—"

"Matt," Mrs. Scheick said sharply, "Elwood said he performed some experiments in feeding livestock. They sound fascinating, don't they?"

"Fascinating?" The General's eyebrows arched. "Oh, yes, yes."

"Did they turn out well, Elwood?"

"Pretty well with the hogs and chickens, Aunt Caroline."

"And the cattle?"

"I didn't try any experiments with cattle."

"Well, if you had, I'm sure you would have had excellent results." Mrs. Scheick smiled, paused, then continued. "It seems to me that there would be such a wonderful opportunity for someone, back in Iowa, to develop . . . well, new feeds and

13

things. I'm so glad to hear that you're interested in that type of project, Elwood."

"Oh, I'm not interested in it," the youth said. "It was just something to do to pass the summer."

"You won't have any trouble passing this summer," General Scheick said jovially, then caught Mrs. Scheick's sharp look and added, "Of course, it won't be anywhere near as pleasant as being back home." He glanced tentatively at Mrs. Scheick, who was glaring at him, and went on, "I mean it's really rough out here. It really is, Elwood." Mrs. Scheick's eyes were stormy, so he said, somewhat desperately, "And just to prove it to you, I'm going to get you in on what's left of this operation, Elwood. I'm going to let you see the things that come up."

There was a moment's silence, then Mrs. Scheick said slowly, "You know, I think that might be a good idea. That way you could see for yourself how really difficult it is here, Elwood."

A look of relief crossed General Scheick's face, and Elwood moved forward in his chair. "That sounds pretty interesting," he said.

"It is interesting." The General nodded. "But it's also difficult. Remember that, Elwood."

"Are you sure I wouldn't be interfering?" the youth asked.

"Interfering? Not at all." General Scheick's voice was assuring. "I want you to see everything that comes along."

"Especially the difficult decisions and problems," Mrs. Scheick said.

"Especially the difficult decisions and problems," the General repeated.

"Now isn't that a wonderful opportunity, Elwood?" Mrs. Scheick asked.

"Yes, it is," the youth replied. "I've been kind of lost. I just don't know what I want to do, and this might give me some idea."

"Well, you're going to see there's nothing out here that you want to do," Mrs. Scheick said. "You're going to see how really hard things are."

14

But Elwood barely heard. His forehead was wrinkled in thought, and then he began slowly. "Uncle Matt," he said, "if you're going to take me in on what's left of this operation, maybe I'd better fill myself in on some of the background."

"That's an excellent idea, my boy. What do you want to know?" General Scheick asked.

"Well, for one thing, about the vote."

"Ah, the vote." A certain warmness arose in General Scheick. "The big thing to remember about it is this, Elwood—these people have never voted before in their whole existence. But today, thanks to us, they have gone to the polls to make their choice."

"That's what I want to know about," Elwood said. "I mean what are their choices?"

General Scheick smiled. "First, they are voting as to whether they want to be a protectorate of another nation. Or an independent nation. This is all listed on a printed ballot which I, personally, drew up."

"I see." Elwood considered. "Now suppose a voter decides that he wants the Nakashima Islands to be a protectorate of another nation. What happens then?"

"Then he must decide of whom he wants the Islands to be a protectorate. For instance, number one—he can choose for his Islands to be a protectorate of the United Nations. Number two—he can choose for them to be a protectorate of the U. S. Or number three—he could choose for his Islands to return to Japan, as before the war."

"But Uncle Matt," Elwood said, "that's only three choices. Suppose . . ."

General Scheick grinned. "I know what you mean. Suppose a voter wants the Islands to be a protectorate of some other nation. No, we're not denying them a choice, Elwood. It's just that we had a paper shortage, and so I couldn't list every country in the world on the ballot."

"What does the voter do then?"

"He simply fills in the blank space that I left. All he has to do is write in Norway, or Denmark, or Greece. That's up to him. I don't care. But whatever he writes in is his official vote, and he knows that the United States Government will back him to the limit. I have assured the people of that time after time."

"I see," Elwood said. "Now suppose that instead of wishing to be a protectorate, the people of the Nakashima Islands should vote to become an independent nation. Then what?"

"Then they must make one more choice. They must choose their form of government."

"Could they choose communism?" Elwood asked cautiously.

General Scheick laughed aloud. "Of course they could. In drawing up the ballots, I placed communism first on the list, gave it top billing, so to speak, because I want the whole world to see how it stands up under a free election."

"What other choices were on the ballot?"

"Socialism—it's there if they want it. And then"—the General smiled and the warmness grew in him—"and then there's our own form of government. There's democracy."

Elwood regarded him. "How do you think the voting is going to go, Uncle Matt?"

"Well . . ." the General began slowly, "I wouldn't want to make any public prediction, because if the wrong outfit picked it up, it might sound as if we rigged the vote, or influenced the people. And that's not the truth, Elwood. We have an officer stationed in each township. But his duty is to see that everything is strictly on the up and up. And, of course, we have radio teams standing by, but all they are going to do is send in the returns to me. However, having been out here for seven years, it's only natural that I'd know which way the wind is blowing. And since it's all in the family, I'd say *first* they'll vote to become an independent nation."

"And then, Uncle Matt?"

"And then—" the General beamed—"they'll vote for democracy."

"Independence and democracy, so that's it," Elwood said.

"That's it exactly." The General was emphatic. "It's as I told Washington the other day—what would any people select when they had a free choice?"

16

"Well," Elwood said reflectively, "I guess that doesn't leave much room for any election betting."

General Sheick smiled paternally. "On the contrary, my boy. The betting here in the command is very lively."

Elwood regarded his uncle in surprise. "You mean there might be some other possibility?"

"Oh, no . . . no. The outcome is a foregone conclusion," the General said. "We're betting on what percentage of the population is going to the polls. Major McCloud, of Intelligence, thinks we'll get ninety per cent voting, while Colonel Henderson, my executive officer, thinks ninety-five."

"And you, Uncle Matt?"

"I'm saying ninety-eight per cent."

"That's pretty high, isn't it?"

"High? No, Elwood," the General said. "Not when you realize this is the first time in their history that these people have had an opportunity to vote. They're not going to pass this by. In fact, I'd say we'd have a hundred-per-cent turnout, but there are always a few who are sick or incapacitated and can't make it."

Dinner was almost over now, there being no dessert in the Scheick household. For Mrs. Scheick, who was remembered around Youngerville, Iowa, as being a strapping, big girl, didn't eat sweets herself; and the General, since he had become interested in vitamins and such, looked upon dessert as consisting of something in the nature of wheat germ and unsulphured raisins in soybean milk—a "conglomeration," as Mrs. Scheick called it, which she would not allow to be served at her table.

Dusk was beginning to settle. The lamp in the picture window in Cottage 2A, at their left, was turned on, and Mrs. Scheick, seeing it, said, "The Hendersons will be over in a minute." And because the Nakashima Islands maids were not working on this, their day of voting, added, "I'll just pick up a bit."

"Can I help you, Aunt Caroline?" Elwood asked.

"No. You sit and visit with your Uncle Matt. By the way, would you like a Grasshopper?"

The General, who was about to put his vitamins away,

looked up and hesitated, while the youth questioned, "A Grass-hopper? What's that?"

"It's an afterdinner drink. It's half *crème de cacao* and half *crème de menthe* over crushed ice."

"I don't believe so," Elwood said. "But thanks anyway."

The General finished capping his bottles then and set them to one side, for they were not needed now. The General's theory being that a drink was all right as long as you realized that alcohol used up certain vitamins of the B Complex and Vitamin C. Consequently, he held that when you took a drink, you should take rose hips, brewer's yeast and/or desiccated liver right along with it to compensate for what you were dissipating.

Quickly Mrs. Scheick cleared the table; and Elwood, sitting in a garden chair, heard footsteps as Colonel and Mrs. Henderson came along the side of the house. Then he saw the tall, thinnish figure of the Colonel, and the somewhat matronly figure of Mrs. Henderson in the semidarkness. "Bill, Irene," the General said, a smile on his face. "Come on in and meet Elwood." And the two of them came through the white picket gate.

"Well, Elwood, it's good to have you with us," Mrs. Henderson said. She was a woman of fifty, and for fifty years she had been in the Service. For she came from an old Army family. One of her forebears would have been with Custer if he hadn't been in the guardhouse. Going to Grandma's for Thanksgiving, for Mrs. Henderson, had always meant walking over to the other side of the Post. And it was her father, who was the first sergeant, who straightened out the young Lt. Henderson in the lieutenant's first assignment after graduating from the Academy.

In her fifty years of service Mrs. Henderson had learned many things, and one of them was flexibility. In the last command she had been a redhead, given to drinking martinis, starting at eleven or so in the morning, and playing poker all afternoon. In this command, her hair had gone back to its natural color, black streaked with gray; usually, she settled for a glass of ice water. And since Mrs. Scheick had organized an investment club amongst the officers' wives, Mrs. Henderson had turned from the poker table to the market and was now the club's expert on Steels.

"It certainly is good to have you with us, Elwood," Colonel Henderson said, extending his hand; and automatically, he surveyed the youth's posture. For if there was anything Colonel Henderson was particular about, it was the way a man stood. "There's just no excuse for sloppiness," he often said, causing the overhearer of the remark to regard the Colonel's own posture in appraisal.

Actually, the way Colonel Henderson stood did leave something to be desired. He had been built on the principle of the steel spring, the theory being that you keep the man in a stretched, exaggerated position long enough, and he will not snap back into his original shape, but somewhere in between. The "in between" being considered a sort of ideal shape for the normal course of living.

The Colonel's trouble was that he had not snapped back quite right. As a youth he had always had a rounded back and caved-in chest. So in resnapping, the neck had once again gone forward, while the shoulders were still drawn back in a pinched effect, the whole being a far cry from the plumb line stance. In fact, in his whole four years at the Academy, the Colonel had always been out of plumb. The truth is, he was so left-footed that he gained a certain notoriety, the instructors using him as a landmark, often saying, "The third man behind Mr. Henderson, pull in your chin." So while General Scheick and Colonel Henderson were quite different in physical appearance and temperament, still there was a certain rapport between the two—for in the normal course of duty, the methods and ideas which General Scheick considered to be good, Colonel Henderson always considered to be damn good.

Having surveyed Elwood and finding his posture satisfactory, in a civilian sort of way, Colonel Henderson smiled. "Now that you're here, Elwood," he said, "I hope you'll join in and be one of us."

"He's going to do just that, Bill," the General said. "In fact, he's going to come into Headquarters and see every decision and problem we have to face."

"What an opportunity!"

"That's the way I feel," General Scheick agreed, then turned. "Irene, could I get you a drink?"

Mrs. Henderson, who knew the nature of the General's drinks, said, "No, thank you. I'll just have a glass of ice water a little later."

"You, Bill?"

"Well," Colonel Henderson said, "if it's not too much trouble, I could go for a Barracuda's Milk."

"No trouble at all." General Scheick was assuring. "I was just about to have one myself. Elwood, will you join us?"

"I don't think I know what a Barracuda's Milk is," the youth replied.

"It's just about the smoothest drink there is," Colonel Henderson stated with authority. "And since your uncle invented it, the whole command is drinking them like crazy."

"What's the base?" Elwood asked. "Gin, or whisky, or . . ."

"It's carrot juice," General Scheick said. "Then I add a quarter jigger of cod-liver oil, plus a little coconut milk and blackstrap molasses for flavor, and blend the whole works together. Would you like to try one?"

Elwood thought for a moment. "Well . . . no, thank you, Uncle Matt. I believe I'll wait and have a glass of ice water with Mrs. Henderson."

"All right." The General nodded. "But we're going to have to get you on vegetable juices. They're wonderful." He glanced at his watch. "By George, the first returns should be in in a few minutes. I better step on it."

"Shall I get the ingredients for you?" Mrs. Henderson asked.

"Would you mind, Irene? Caroline's in the kitchen."

"I don't mind at all," Mrs. Henderson replied and started off.

As she left them, Colonel Henderson turned. "You know, Elwood," he said, "some day, somebody is going to write a book about your Uncle Matt and the work he has done out here in the Nakashima Islands."

"Now, now, Bill," General Scheick protested, the smile all over his face.

"It's the truth, Elwood," Colonel Henderson continued. "These Islands are virtually a living memorial to your uncle. And did he ever make them open their eyes back in Washington. Washington could hardly believe all the things he has done. For instance, do you realize that in this whole chain of Islands, not one single person is on welfare?"

Elwood whistled. "Is that right?"

"Yes, it is. It's remarkable, isn't it? And do you realize that the people out here are eating, on an average, 1,473 pounds of food apiece a year?"

"Is that good?" Elwood asked, not being familiar with such statistics.

"Good? It's excellent. The average American consumes slightly more than 1,500 pounds of food per year. And you must remember that physically these people are smaller, so they're eating just as well as we are."

"What kind of food do they eat?"

"Mostly sweet potatoes. It's their favorite. You see, over here a man's social status is determined by the number of times a day he has them. And I'm happy to say that most are eating them at every meal."

"For breakfast even?"

"They've acquired a taste for them. Here a man wouldn't feel right if he couldn't start the day with a couple of boiled sweet potatoes under his belt. Isn't that correct, sir?"

"That's correct," General Scheick said.

"Yes, sir," Colonel Henderson continued. "Your uncle has done a tremendous job, Elwood, and I only hope that some of those congressmen realize it. Your uncle has taken what they had out here and given it refinements. . . ."

Elwood was puzzled. "I don't think I know what you mean by that," he said.

"Well, for instance, they had a good educational system, that is, of its kind. But your uncle introduced English into the curriculum and established scholarships to American universities.

And then take the police. They were a pretty fair outfit. But do you know what your uncle did? He expanded the force, dressed them up in smart uniforms, put them on ponies. And here, in the Nakashima Islands, is the only mounted police force in the whole Far East. Man, you ought to see an inspector's eyes pop when he comes in and finds himself being escorted by a few troops of them. But tell me, Elwood, did you ever hear of the Scheick Code?"

"I don't think so," Elwood said.

"Well, sociologically, it's the greatest thing that ever happened to Asia," Colonel Henderson went on. "Under the Scheick Code there are no more arranged marriages, everyone is free to make his own choice. What do you think of that?"

Elwood considered. "Well, I guess you can't blame anyone else for your own mistake then, can you?"

General Scheick smiled. "You're right there, Elwood. You can't. But seriously, the Code has made a tremendous difference in the lives of the people."

"I would imagine," Elwood said. "But what else has been happening out here?"

"We built them the finest road system in the Far East," General Scheick said. "The old system was adequate enough. But we widened it, improved it, left plenty of space on either side of the roads so we could expand them into super highways when they're needed. And we did it on a balanced budget."

"Gosh," Elwood said. "I didn't realize anything like that was going on. So you took what they had and improved it?"

"We did," Colonel Henderson said. "And in addition to that, we've given them a government to be proud of. We call it the GNI—the Government of the Nakashima Islands. They have their own chief executive, their own representatives, and we, of the military, have always functioned as the senate, so to speak. Now all they have to do is elect some senators to take our place, and they'll have the American system duplicated. That is, as soon as they elect themselves a president. You can see that it's been a tremendous operation."

"Yes," General Scheick said slowly, "it has been a tremendous operation, but I do regret that I was never able to instill a sense of property into the people, a sense of pride in their homes. Take the capital below us. Those houses should be in tiptop shape. I wanted to see white houses down there with trim red tile roofs. And I wanted to see Watanabe Square made into something."

"What's Watanabe Square?" Elwood asked.

"That's a piece of ground, perhaps three acres in size, right in the center of town that they use for a sweet potato market. It's dusty and trampled, with not a blade of grass in sight. In fact, with those half-tumbled stores surrounding it, it looks like a shanty town or a hobo jungle. What I wanted was to have it made into a pretty little park, right, Bill?"

"That's right, sir. All of us in the command did. But these people . . ." Colonel Henderson shook his head. "However, sir, you shouldn't have any regrets. Why, everyone is saying that this is going down in their history as the period of Enlightened Intervention."

Mrs. Scheick, carrying a tray with the ingredients for Grasshoppers, came from the kitchen then. And with her came Mrs. Henderson, carrying a tray with the ingredients for Barracuda's Milk. "Matt," Mrs. Scheick said, "I brought the phone along so you could get the returns."

"Why thank you," the General said, then his eyes fell on the *crème de cacao* and *crème de menthe.* "Do you want some desiccated liver to go along with that?" he asked. But catching her glance, he knew that she didn't. He knew she was just going to dissipate her vitamins without even a thought of making them up, so he could only give her a warning frown. Then taking the phone, he set it on the table and lined up his ingredients for Barracuda's Milk, for Barracuda's Milk is a lot of work.

"You know, sir," Colonel Henderson began, "someday somebody is going to make a fortune by coming up with an Instant Barracuda's Milk."

General Scheick considered. "By George, I think you're right, Bill," he said, and the little group settled themselves as all along Caroline Drive the lamps in the picture windows glowed softly in the Asian night. Reaching over, he picked up the cod-liver oil and was just measuring a jigger when the phone rang. "General Scheick speaking."

On the other end of the line a voice said, "The first report is in, sir. It's from Bamboo Island."

"Good. What percentage of the population voted?"

"Ninety-eight point two, sir."

General Scheick smiled and covered the mouthpiece. "They're really turning out, Bill," he said. "Even better than I thought."

"Well, it's as you said, sir, they're not going to miss this chance."

"Right." General Scheick nodded, then asked, "And what are the final results?" There was a moment's silence, then his smile faded, his face flushed, and he exploded. "Why that's ridiculous! Captain, you get hold of that radio team and tell them that if they don't get accurate reports in here, I'm going to court-martial every blasted one of them. Now recheck and phone me back."

As he slammed down the phone, General Scheick almost knocked over the cod-liver oil. Seeing his face, Mrs. Henderson twisted uneasily while Colonel Henderson brushed at an imaginary fleck of lint on his trousers; and Elwood leaned forward curiously.

"What's the matter, Uncle Matt?"

General Scheick had trouble controlling himself. "Nothing, Elwood. It's just that one of my radio teams got things balled up." And once again the phone rang. "General Scheick speaking."

"Sir," came the troubled voice, "I've rechecked that report. It's true. And here are reports from five of the other Islands. They're all voting the same way."

General Scheick was stunned, the phone almost slipped from his fingers. Then as he hung up, Mrs. Scheick said, "Matt, aren't they holding to the ninety-eight point two per cent turnout that you expected?"

"They're holding to that, all right," the General replied, his face ashen.

The phone rang again. "Yes," General Scheick said slowly.

". . . the remainder of the Islands have reported in? What percentage voted? It's even higher . . . ninety-nine per cent." Apprehensively, he glanced at the group around him. "And the results? Ninety-nine per cent for . . ." He replaced the receiver and looked out at the East China Sea.

"Uncle Matt," Elwood broke the silence. "Didn't they vote to become an independent nation?"

General Scheick regarded him. "Yes, they did that. However, there's been a write-in vote."

"A write-in vote!" Colonel Henderson was startled. "But, sir, democracy was already listed on the ballot."

"I know, Bill." General Scheick could hardly bring himself to utter the words. "But they rejected it."

"They rejected democracy!"

"Yes, Bill. The whole ninety-nine per cent rejected it."

"What did they vote for then, sir?"

"A king. They all want a king." A muscle quivered in General Scheick's throat. "And here I've already told Washington that we had it in the bag."

Colonel Henderson shook his head to clear it. Mrs. Henderson said, "Caroline, I think I will have a Grasshopper, after all." And Elwood rose to his feet. "Boy, Uncle Matt," he said, "you sure do have the difficult problems out here, don't you?" The General could only look at him, and the youth went on, "What do you do about something like this?"

"Do?" General Scheick's forehead was wet. Through his mind raced the thought of Washington. He reached for his handkerchief. "Well, I think the first thing we better do is find out what happened," he managed and began mopping his brow.

Chapter 2

YOSHIMITSU MATSUMOTO, chief of the Nakashima Islands Mounted Police, mainly by virtue of the fact that he spoke English, sat on the straw mats of his living room floor. Tonight, instead of wearing the U. S. style khaki uniform with the yellow muffler tucked in at the throat, his somewhat plumpish figure was wrapped in a blue and white kimono. And in the light of the borrowed American candles (there being no electricity for the civilian population) his moon-shaped face was intent as he leaned over the dachshund-legged table and sorted a new batch of magazines, which the Nakashima Islands janitors, up at headquarters, had saved for him. For while Yoshimitsu Matsumoto was chief of mounted police to the Americans, to the Nakashima Islanders he was their leading literary figure, and a good part of his income was derived from the translation of American stories and articles.

Now, having the new batch arranged by general content, he picked up one of the home type and smiled as he began the evening's search for material. But as he scanned the first article, his smile faded. For the article concerned building or adding a room to bring the family together; and if there was anything Yoshimitsu Matsumoto wanted, it was, as he termed it, an "apart" room. Because some thirty or so years before, Yoshimitsu had married into the Takamini distilling family, who had been manufacturing for the past fourteen centuries a drink called *awamori*, which was a kind of sweet potato brandy. And while the Takaminis were prominent in the Nakashima Islands, and while the Takaminis had money, still none of the Takaminis had ever built or bought a house in Tamabaru, the capital. The whole family lived out in the back country near their distillery with its source of raw material, namely sweet potatoes.

But the Takaminis were always coming to town. The Americans had started it when they introduced the Scheick Code, this business of freedom of choice in marriage. For in the Takamini family there were several girls of marriageable age. In fact, right at the moment, there were three of them soundly asleep on the mats in one of Yoshimitsu's back rooms—three whose names he wasn't quite sure of, because somehow all the Takaminis looked alike. Consequently, he simply addressed them as, "Well, well." Such as, "Well, well, it's good to see you again." Or, "Well, well, how are you this morning?" Yet he did know they were the daughters of Uncle Shoji and Aunt Fumiko, because Uncle Shoji and Aunt Fumiko were also back there, asleep on the mats.

In the old days of the go-between, in the old days of sight being unseen, there would have been no problem for the Takamini girls, Yoshimitsu reflected. The family would have simply arranged a marriage. But in these days when they looked each other over, it was sad but true that the Takamini girls didn't fare too well on the open market. In fact, they didn't fare at all. Still, hope springs eternal, someone has said, and the various branches of the Takaminis were always making forays into town with their marriageable daughters, the trouble being that they always used Yoshimitsu's house as their campaign headquarters.

No, Yoshimitsu reflected, he didn't want a room to get together. He wanted a room to get away, so that he could translate any time in order to keep the table filled with sweet potatoes, instead of having to wait until almost nine o'clock, after the Takaminis had gone to bed.

27

Slowly, he arose to his feet and began pacing on the white straw mats of the floor. But then, maybe all that was needed was to get the law changed back to the old way of the go-between. A frown crossed his face. Yet with the Americans around, just try that! This was one of those cultural differences, Yoshimitsu told himself, and it all depended on how you looked upon the the approach to marriage. In the old way, you started with cold water, and through the years you brought it up to the boiling point. In the new way, you started with boiling water, and you were supposed to keep it boiling.

Which was the easier to do, Yoshimitsu didn't pretend to know; but he did know that the trouble with the world was that there were too many differences. As he paced back and forth, he suddenly began to toe in. That was the way he walked in his student days in the early 1920's, up in Japan at Shimonoseki Normal College. Then he toed out, as wide as his ankles would allow, gave a little spring to his knees and began to waddle like a duck. That was the way the Chinese students walked over at Foochow University, where he had done a year of graduate work in no particular subject. That was the figure-eight walk of the Chinese scholar, so called because the outspread feet bore a resemblance to the Chinese character for eight.

And suppose you tried a middle course? Suppose you walked with your feet pointed straight ahead. Whom did you walk like then? You walked like an American Indian, Yoshimitsu knew from his translation of western stories. Sadly, he shook his head and was just about to cross the room in American Indian fashion when he heard the car draw up to his front gate and immediately realized who it was, because there were no cars amongst the civilian population, and no one amongst the military had a sedan except General Scheick.

Automatically, Yoshimitsu's hand went to his shirt pockets to see if they were buttoned. But then he realized that he was wearing a kimono, and the thought of being out of uniform flustered him. He wondered if he would have time to get back into it and knew that he wouldn't. Then spying the United States Officers' Guide, which Colonel Henderson had given him, he quickly picked up the pile of magazines, and carried them to a back room. He was just opening the Officers' Guide to that section on the Customs of the Service when the banging came upon the door.

Book in hand, Yoshimitsu walked over, slid back the door of weathered boards, which served as a part of the outside wall of the house, looked straight at the three figures standing before him in the dark and said, "Is someone there?"

"Of course there is!" General Scheick thundered. "Who the hell do you think's been knocking?"

Yoshimitsu feigned surprise. "Oh, it's you, Mr. General." He indicated his kimono. "I hope you will pardon me for being dressed like this. I got my uniform out airing. You know how it is when you're around horses."

But General Scheick wasn't interested, so Yoshimitsu turned to Colonel Henderson. "Mr. Colonel, and how are you this evening? See, I've just been reading." Yoshimitsu opened the Officers' Guide to the Customs of the Service and expected Colonel Henderson to smile, because it had been Colonel Henderson who had suggested to the General that in matters of etiquette and so forth the Nakashima Islands Mounted Police be guided by the same code as the United States Army.

Colonel Henderson, however, didn't smile. And so Yoshimitsu looked at Elwood. "Well, well," he said. "It's good to see you."

"Thank you," the youth replied, holding out his hand. "I'm Elwood Cummings, General Scheick's nephew."

"The Mr. General's nephew! Ah, so." Yoshimitsu bowed. "But what can I do for you gentlemen?"

"Do? I'll tell you what you can do!" General Scheick's face was flushed and his jaw was thrust forth. "You can tell me why your people slapped the United States Goverment in the face!"

Yoshimitsu was truly surprised now. "Did we do that?"

"You did. You certainly did."

"Well," Yoshimitsu said, "in that case I think we all better sit down and talk it over." He indicated the low little table. "Please, Mr. General, after you."

They sat on the straw mats of Yoshimitsu's living room. And

29

as a snore from Uncle Shoji Takamini drifted out, Yoshimitsu scratched his head and asked, "Now, Mr. General, how did we slap the United States Government in the face?"

General Scheick looked full at him. "By voting for a king. Don't you realize that a monarchy is the very form of government we Americans revolted against?"

"You did? And when was that?"

"In 1776. You've heard of King George III, haven't you?"

"George III . . ." Yoshimitsu tried to recall. "What was he king of?"

"England."

"Oh, England." Yoshimitsu began to smile. "No, I never heard of him. But I heard of Henry VIII. He was quite a fellow." Beaming, he looked to General Scheick and Colonel Henderson, but instead of agreement, there was only exasperation on their faces, so he went on. "We didn't mean to slap the United States Government in the face though, Mr. General. Didn't you know that we were going to vote for a king? Everyone else did."

"Now wait a minute," General Scheick said. "That's not true. There was absolutely no hint that we were being sabotaged. Even Major McCloud, my Intelligence Officer, had no inkling."

"Sabotaged?" Yoshimitsu turned the word over in his mind. "What has sabotage got to do with it?"

"Everything. You don't think a people would reject democracy of their own free will, do you? Of course there's been sabotage. There's been a pressure group at work here, putting the heat on the people, making them vote for a monarchy. Now isn't that right?"

Yoshimitsu was conscious of the eyes staring at him. And he wanted to oblige. He wanted to say, "Yes, that's right." But he couldn't, so he said, "No, Mr. General, there was no pressure group at work. That's wrong."

"Wrong!" General Scheick refused to believe. "That can't be wrong."

"Oh, yes." Yoshimitsu nodded. "It is."

General Scheick was speechless; and Elwood, seeing his uncle's bewildered look, said, "Mr. Matsumoto, may I ask a question?"

"If you want to."

"Well then, you said everyone knew the people were going to vote for a king. How did they know?"

"Ah, I see. They knew because of Shinerikyu and Amamikyu."

"Shinerikyu and Amamikyu? Who are they?"

"Oh, they aren't now," Yoshimitsu said quickly. "They were a long time ago. Shinerikyu was a boy, and Amamikyu was a girl. Anyway, they came down from the skies to the Nakashima Islands. That was the beginning of things. And here they had six children."

"What's that got to do with it?" General Scheick asked.

"Everything. Because since Shinerikyu and Amamikyu started things around here, they were the ones who said how things were going to be. So of their first son, they said he would be the first King of our Islands."

"Oh, I get it." Elwood smiled. "Because of this your people consider a monarchy their rightful form of government."

"That's right . . . What did you say your name was?"

"Elwood Cummings."

"That's right, Elwood. That, in itself, is one logical reason why we should all vote for a king. Don't you agree, Mr. General?"

"Hell, no, I don't agree," General Scheick exploded.

"You don't?" Yoshimitsu was surprised. "Why not?"

"Because this is a modern day and age. A monarchy, hell's fire, that's an archaic form of government. How do you expect to get along today with a rusty, outmoded system like that?"

"Oh, but it worked very well in modern times," Yoshimitsu said. "And that's another reason the people voted for a monarchy. They know how good things were under old King Gihon."

"Who?"

"Old King Gihon. He was our last King. He died in 1620."

"In 1620! Do you call that modern times?"

"That was only 340 years ago," Yoshimitsu said. "And things

were mighty good under old King Gihon. He built everything up step by step. He got us right up to the edge of a golden age. So the people got to thinking. They said to themselves, 'Aha, let's get the king back. He'll put us over the line.' " Yoshimitsu regarded General Scheick. "You know things are pretty good in a golden age."

"Now wait a minute," General Scheick said, "you say this old King Gihon died in 1620? And that he got you up to the verge of a golden age?"

"That's right. One more step, and we would have had it."

"And you've just been sitting here for 340 years waiting for the final step?"

"Oh, we had to," Yoshimitsu replied.

"Why?"

"Because of the Interruption."

"Now what in hell is the Interruption?"

"The Interruption? Well, after old King Gihon died, the Chinese came in. They said, 'That's the end. No more kings around this place.' Then the Japanese came and kicked the Chinese out. Then—"

"Matsumoto," Colonel Henderson cut in sharply, "don't you dare classify us as a part of the Interruption. We brought you a period of Enlightened Intervention."

"Okay," Yoshimitsu said. "So then you came, but now the Enlightened Intervention is about over. Our King is coming back. He can take the final step. Isn't that good?"

"I don't see anything so damn good about it," General Scheick said. "But who is this king you're bringing back to the throne?"

Yoshimitsu smiled brightly. "Oh, we don't know that."

"You don't know! You mean you voted, and you don't even know who you voted for?"

"That's right."

"But that's not possible. You couldn't have done that."

"Yes, that's possible, because that's what we did."

General Scheick was badly shaken. He ran his hand over his eyes, trying to collect his thoughts; while at the end of the table Elwood leaned forward. "Uncle Matt," he said, "I think what

32

Mr. Matsumoto means is that the people voted for the succession, that is, for the descendant of the first son of Shinerikyu and Amamikyu."

"That's right, Elwood," Yoshimitsu agreed. "We couldn't vote for the King himself, because we don't even know if there is a king."

General Scheick looked up quickly. "What do you mean by that?"

"I mean we don't know if the royal family exists any more or not."

"Do you think that there's a possibility that they don't?" General Scheick asked, a note of hope creeping into his voice.

"Yes, there is a possibility. You see, Yamaguchi Kiei, our leading historian and scholar, has been tracing the royal line, but he's been having trouble. Of course, we know our last king was Gihon."

General Scheick smiled. "Yes, but that was in 1620. You have 340 years to account for."

"No, we don't. Yamaguchi Kiei knows who the King would have been up to seventeen years ago. It's only since then that he's not sure."

"Why in hell didn't you say so?"

"I didn't get around to it yet."

General Scheick drew in his breath, held it, to control his temper, then he began slowly, evenly. "Well, I can tell you this, Matsumoto, the United States Government is never going to accept a royal line without verification."

"That's what Yamaguchi Kiei is trying to do."

"Maybe so," General Scheick went on. "However, as far as I'm concerned, the Government of the Nakashima Islands that we set up is still in effect. The legislature is still in power."

"But there is no more legislature," Yoshimitsu said.

"What do you mean? I didn't disband it."

"I know. They disbanded themselves. Last night they all went home, because what's the use of the legislature sticking around? The King is everything anyway, so . . ."

"Everything! You can't mean he's absolute?"

33

"Oh, sure," Yoshimitsu replied, rubbing his nose which had begun to itch.

"Hell, man, that's a dictatorship!" The perspiration broke out all over General Scheick. "And it was set up under my command." He looked to Colonel Henderson. How in heaven's name was he ever going to explain this to Washington? But they didn't have a king yet. They only had a gap. Fixing Yoshimitsu with a stare, he said firmly, "Matsumoto, you go see this historian, this Yamaguchi Kiei. Find out if he has verification or not."

"But he wouldn't have it yet," Yoshimitsu said, glancing toward the room where he had put his magazines.

"Get down there anyway. Camp on his doorstep until he puts it on the line—you either have a king or you haven't."

"And do you want me to let you know?" Yoshimitsu asked.

"Of course I do. Why do you think I'm sending you?"

"Oh." Yoshimitsu arose, looked thoughtful, then deciding that this was an official mission, said, "I'll go put on my uniform."

As he left the room, General Scheick, Colonel Henderson, and Elwood sat in silence, their faces intent in the candlelight. Then Colonel Henderson spoke. "You know, sir," he said wonderingly, "I can't understand it. I can't understand it at all. Voting for a king! Why, here these people had a chance to be like us, and they turned it down."

34

Chapter 3

USUALLY at around six o'clock or so each morning, the senior members of General Scheick's staff would gather for a walk before breakfast. It was not a compulsory thing, but rather an informal get-together, marked by high good humor. There would be Colonel Henderson, the executive officer; Lt. Colonel Seymour of Operations; Major McCloud of Intelligence; and three or four others. They would meet in front of the General's home, and then go tramping up into the hills.

Sometimes they would wander through the old courtyards of the ancient Castle of Tamagusuku. Sometimes they would follow one of the countless paths that twisted, and turned, and crisscrossed the low ridges. And it all added up to one thing: "A feeling of aliveness," as General Scheick expressed it.

But this morning there was no feeling of aliveness. General Scheick sat at the breakfast table, his eyes red; and Mrs. Scheick, entering the dining room and finding him there, was completely surprised. "Why, Matt," she said, "what are you doing at home? I thought you'd be out hiking."

"I canceled the walk," the General said and, seeing Mrs. Scheick's startled look, added, "I wasn't able to sleep all night."

"You weren't sick, were you?"

"Oh, no, no," the General replied. "It's just the situation."

"Is it that bad?"

"I'm afraid it is."

"What are you going to do?"

"Hope," the General said. "Hope they can't dig themselves up a king."

"But what if they should?"

"I've already written to Mosby," General Scheick said, and Mrs. Scheick nodded.

Because whenever General Scheick was troubled, whenever he needed advice and counsel, he always turned to his old friend and mentor, Major General Mosby Winthrope, now of the Pentagon. For the friendship between Major General Mosby Winthrope and Brigadier General Matthew Scheick was long and close. It had started back at the Academy when Matt Scheick, in his second year, played second-string tackle behind the regular, Mosby Winthrope, then in his last year and an All-American candidate. They had been on the track team together, Matt Scheick being the number-two shot putter, right behind Mosby Winthrope.

And even after graduation their paths had often crossed and their friendship grew. Second Lieutenant Matt Scheick, in his first assignment, served under First Lieutenant Mosby Winthrope, who commanded the company. Together they had set up the first obstacle course at old Fort Bitely. And to this day, if Mrs. Scheick hadn't put her foot down, the older Scheick daughter, instead of being named Alice, would have been named Mosby Scheick.

"I think you were wise to write him," Mrs. Scheick said, then asked, "Is Elwood up yet?"

The General nodded. "He's out in the back yard, staring into space."

Mrs. Scheick smiled. "Matt, it was positively a stroke of genius on your part to let him see the problems that come up. I'm sure he's beginning to realize that things aren't so rosy in this part of the world."

"If he doesn't realize it now," the General said, "he never will."

"Well, I'm sorry all this trouble had to happen," Mrs. Scheick went on. "But as long as it did, I'm glad it happened now so he could be in on it. I think I'll write his mother and tell her that we have him thinking."

Out in the back yard Elwood wasn't actually staring off into space. In reality, he was looking down at the ancient capital of Tamabaru. For far below him, the old city with its five thousand or so inhabitants was coming to life. Along the roads leading into town he could see women, clad in brown banana-cloth kimonos, with reed baskets balanced atop their heads, moving slowly along, bringing sweet potatoes into the market at Watanabe Square.

Turning, he glanced at the little river, called the Tamsui, which came out of the green hills and wound its slow, quiet way beneath countless arched bridges, past a dozen stone quays, then flowed out through the tidal flats to join the East China Sea. And then he looked at the town itself, at the weathered old houses with their faded red tile roofs, and he understood what his uncle had meant. For certainly the town was run down and dilapidated.

His gaze strayed then to the level plot of land immediately below him. This was the vegetable gardens for the American community. Along one side was row after row of compost piles, rotting under General Scheick's personal supervision. And the gardens were still, for the Nakashima Islanders who did the hoeing and weeding, planting and harvesting, had not yet come to work. But then Elwood's eye caught movement on one of the paths leading up from the ancient capital, and he recognized Yoshimitsu Matsumoto.

Quickly, he walked to the house, and called through the screen door, "Uncle Matt, Mr. Matsumoto is coming up from Tamabaru."

In the dining room General Scheick, who was about to take a sip of a blackstrap molasses combination which he substituted for coffee, put down his cup and a muscle quivered in his neck.

Mrs. Scheick, who didn't believe in substitutes, took one more sip of coffee, then followed the General out into the back yard.

Huffing and puffing, Yoshimitsu Matsumoto came up the path. Reaching the wall at the back of the General's yard, he stopped and surveyed it dubiously, and it was evident to Elwood that he was going to have trouble. Quickly the youth stepped forward, extended his hand, and with Elwood pulling and Yoshimitsu scrambling, he came up and over.

As he dropped into the yard, Yoshimitsu bent, brushed his trousers, which were tucked into combat boots, checked the scarf at his throat, straightened his helmet liner—painted yellow out of respect for the U. S. Cavalry—and turned a sweat-streaked face toward General and Mrs. Scheick. "Ah, good morning, Mrs. General." He smiled his brightest smile. "You're up early this morning. I wish I could say the same for my wife. And good morning, Mr. General. How are you?"

But General Scheick was in no mood for small talk. Instead, he came right to the point. "Matsumoto," he said, "did you find out?"

Yoshimitsu nodded. "Yes."

"Which way is it?"

"Good news."

"You mean you weren't able to trace the royal line?"

"Oh, no. We were able to trace it. We found our King."

General Scheick's world shook beneath him. It was like the time in the annual football classic when the Navy team had ganged up on him. It was like the time his grip slipped as he was coming down the debarkation tower, and he fell the last five feet, landing on the base of his spine. He was stunned. But then he managed, "Are you sure? I told you the United States Government would never accept a royal line unless it's been verified, say, by three or four sources."

"Three or four sources?" Yoshimitsu's face was solemn. "Why, we wouldn't even accept that ourselves. Now you take this case, we have verification from fifty different places."

"Fifty?"

"Oh, yes. Yamaguchi Kiei uncovered a whole lot of new evidence. So you can tell Washington that everything is all right."

At the mention of Washington, General Scheick had to struggle to keep from wincing. But Washington was going to want to know about this, so he said, "Matsumoto, who is the King?"

"The King? His name is Kenji Nakamura. Yamaguchi Kiei says that from now on he will be known as King Kenji I. That's because we never had a Kenji before."

"Kenji Nakamura," General Scheick repeated the name. "How old a man is he?"

"Oh, I wouldn't know that," Yoshimitsu replied. "You see, you just asked me to find out if the royal line was verified or not. . . ."

"Didn't you even find out where he lives?"

"Oh, yes. I was kind of interested in knowing that myself. He lives in a village named Little Koza. Yamaguchi Kiei says the records show that after old King Gihon died and the Chinese threw them out, the royal family moved to Little Koza and took up agriculture."

"In other words they became farmers."

"Yes."

"And they've been in Little Koza since 1620?"

"That's what the records show, Mr. General."

"How much education does the King have?"

"I don't know that, Mr. General."

"Well, can he read and write?"

"I wouldn't have any idea. I wouldn't know if he owns his own land. He might just work it for somebody else."

"You mean he might be a tenant farmer?"

"That could be."

"What are his politics?"

"Well, let's see." Yoshimitsu pursed his lips in thought. "Now if he lives in a village . . . and if he is a tenant farmer . . ."

"Yes?"

"Then I don't think he'd be interested in politics. I think he'd be interested in whether he's going to have enough sweet potatoes to last him through the winter."

"Well, it's your own damn fault," General Scheick said.

"You're the ones who voted for this archaic form of government. You're the ones who wanted a king. You voted for him sight unseen. And this is what you get—a sharecropper. How in the devil do you expect to take your place among the nations of the world with a king who can't even read and write?"

"Oh?" Yoshimitsu was surprised. "Can't he read and write? I didn't know that."

"You just said he couldn't."

"No, I didn't say that, Mr. General. You said it. I said maybe he couldn't. You see, when you sent me down to Yamaguchi Kiei's, you just said that I should find out . . ."

"All right," General Scheick said wearily. "All right."

"Why don't we do this, Mr. General?" Yoshimitsu went on. "Why don't we take your car and go out to Little Koza? I'd like to meet the King."

General Scheick eyed him. "Why in hell should I take you along?"

"Because you'll be going out anyway. You're going to have to find out who the King is and what he's like. And how are you going to do it without an interpreter? No one in Little Koza will speak English. And you can see I speak it so well myself . . ."

General Scheick gave him a long hard look, then turned toward Cottage 2A. "Bill!" he called. "Hey, Bill!"

Colonel Henderson looked out of the window of his house. "Yes, sir?"

"Come on, Bill," the General said. "They dug themselves up a king. We better go out and give him the once-over."

According to the customs of the Service, General Scheick's position in the car was in the rear seat on the right side, so that is where he sat. Next to him on his left was Colonel Henderson; while in the front seat Elwood was squeezed in between the corporal who drove and Yoshimitsu Matsumoto, who rode along with his arm hanging out the window.

In the old days, in the days when the royal family was exiled by the Chinese, it had taken them four days to reach Little Koza by horsecart. But now Little Koza was only a half hour away from the capital by car. And as they zipped along Nakashima Islands' Highway Number 3, a broad, wide road—built under the supervision of General Scheick, with ample space on each side for conversion into a superhighway—the farmers in the fields would look up, straighten from their planting of sweet potato slips, smile, and wave to them. And Yoshimitsu Matsumoto, with his free hanging arm, would give them a running salute.

Except for the highway, which had been built by American bulldozers, it was a land created by the hoe. Each field, surrounded by its earthen boundary dike, each terraced plot on the gentle hills, had been patiently cut and leveled until now the Nakashima Islands was not a land of farms, but a land of gardens.

They rolled through village after village, for everyone lived in a village—the farmers simply going out each morning to their holdings. They rolled through cluster-type villages, where the houses were grouped tightly together. They passed through shoestring-type villages, where the houses were strung on both sides of a single main street. They went through scattered-type villages, where small clumps of houses were spread here and there amidst the fields. Until at last Yoshimitsu pointed and said, turning his head, "There it is, Mr. General. There's Little Koza."

Little Koza was a village of the cluster type, its thirty or so houses nestling in a grove of pine. The fields around it were alive with men at work with their planting. And the corporal, driving, had to shift into low, because on the road ahead were several women carrying large clay jars.

"What are they doing, Mr. Matsumoto?" Elwood asked, indicating the women.

"Oh, they're coming to the village well for water. It's on the edge of town there. Did you ever hear of the well at Little Koza?"

"No, I don't think I have."

"It's very famous," Yoshimitsu said. "In the old days the water was known all over—in China, Japan, and even in the islands in the southern seas." He pointed. "See. There it is, Elwood. There!"

41

Stretching in order to see better, Elwood peered past the driver, and saw the well. It was quite an impressive sight, for the well was sunk in a large pit. An ancient stone stairway led down to it. And there on the wet stones, in the shade of the pines, half the women of the village were gathered, visiting in the morning.

"Do you see the well, Mr. General?" Yoshimitsu asked.

But General Scheick wasn't interested in wells. "Where in hell do we go now?" he asked.

"I don't know," Yoshimitsu replied.

"Can't you find out?"

"Oh, sure." Yoshimitsu, seeing a clearing in the pines ahead, indicated it to the driver. "That must be the village meeting hall. Stop there, and I'll ask somebody where Kenji Nakamura lives."

The driver pulled off the road by the clearing, and Elwood spied a black-banged little girl with a boiled sweet potato in her hand, her baby brother strapped to her back, watching them. "Maybe she would know where King Kenji lives," he said.

"Ah, so." Yoshimitsu nodded. "But she wouldn't know him as King Kenji. She'd probably just know him as Kenji Nakamura." He stepped from the car, called to her in Japanese. She listened, then pointed, and Yoshimitsu said, "The Nakamuras live three houses down that street. I'll lead the way." The rest also stepped from the car; and Yoshimitsu, pointing his feet out in the figure eight of the Chinese scholar, gave a little spring to his knees and led them off at a waddle.

The street was really only a path wide enough for a horsecart to squeeze through; and Elwood looked around curiously. Walls of stone rose on either side of him, enclosing the houses. As they passed the first home he tried to peek into the courtyard, but his view was blocked by a small inner wall which served a dual purpose, namely, to keep out the glances of the curious, and also to keep out any evil spirits who chanced to pass that way. They passed the second home; and reaching the third, Yoshimitsu, beaming, stepped aside. "This is it, Mr. General. After you."

General Scheick didn't so much as look at him. With the stride of authority, he simply led on, and with a sweep they rounded the small inner wall and entered the courtyard.

42

The courtyard was much like that of any other home in the Nakashima Islands. It was covered with sand from the seashore, carefully raked. But what caught the General's attention was the fact that this house had a tile roof, while the others of the village had thatch; and the front of this house, instead of being comprised of weathered, sliding doors, was thrown open completely, revealing a series of shelves upon which various articles were displayed.

General Scheick looked at the shelves, then turned to Yoshimitsu. "What the hell kind of establishment is this?"

Yoshimitsu scratched his head. "It looks to me like the village store."

"Didn't you tell me the royal family were farmers?"

"I thought they were," Yoshimitsu replied. "Yamaguchi Kiei said they took up agriculture after the Chinese threw them out. But that was 340 years ago, so maybe, in the meantime, they changed jobs."

There was some kind of a meeting going on within the building itself. A dozen barefooted women sat in a circle on the straw mats, and they were so intent that they failed to notice Yoshimitsu and the Americans.

Briefly, General Scheick glanced at them. "Matsumoto, find out if the King is around anywhere. Tell him I want to talk to him."

"All right, Mr. General." Yoshimitsu walked over to the house front, listened for a moment, then said in Japanese, "Excuse me, ladies, but is Kenji Nakamura at home?"

Eyes turned as the women regarded him; then an aged woman, sitting at the head of the group, spoke quickly, whereupon Yoshimitsu bowed to her and walked back to General Scheick.

"Well?" General Scheick asked. "Is he home?"

"I didn't find out," Yoshimitsu replied. "They have a very important meeting going on, and the aged one asked if we would wait a few moments. She'll talk with us then."

"Who is she?"

"I don't know."

General Scheick felt like exploding, but then he glanced at the

43

aged one. She was, perhaps, in her mid-seventies, clad in a home-woven brown banana-cloth kimono, with gray hair that was pulled straight back from her forehead. A smile was on her bronzed, lined old face as she nodded to the General, and somehow he smiled back.

"You don't mind waiting, do you, Mr. General?" Yoshimitsu asked.

"Well . . ." General Scheick saw that the backs of her wrinkled hands were tattooed in a blue diamond design. For a moment he wached her hands, resting quietly on her lap. "I guess not," he said. "But what kind of a meeting do they have going on that's so important?"

"They're forming a mutual loan society," Yoshimitsu replied.

"A what?" Colonel Henderson questioned.

"A mutual loan society. Haven't you ever heard of them, Mr. Colonel?"

"How would I have heard of them?" Colonel Henderson said. "I don't buy anything on credit any more. Credit only gets people in trouble. Isn't that right, sir?"

"No," General Scheick replied. "I wouldn't say that, Bill. When I retire, unless Mrs. Scheick is willing to put up the money for an orange grove, I might have to borrow myself."

Colonel Henderson swallowed. "What I meant, sir, is that it might get somebody in trouble. Don't you think?"

"That's possible, Bill," General Scheick said, and Colonel Henderson wiped his forehead.

But Elwood was curious. "Mr. Matsumoto, these mutual loan associations . . . I never heard of them either. Are they something new?"

"Oh yes, Elwood, quite new. Old King Gihon introduced them in about 1572."

"You mean he originated them?"

"No. They originated in China, maybe ten thousand years ago."

"How did old King Gihon get hold of them then?"

"Oh, didn't I ever tell you that? Well, you see, when old King Gihon was just a young fellow, the Chinese were already mon-

44

keying around. So one day they said to King Eiso, who was old King Gihon's papa, they said, 'King Eiso, you better send Gihon to school over in China. We'll teach him a lot of things that we think he should know.' So what could King Eiso do? Anyway, Gihon was a pretty smart boy." Yoshimitsu tapped his forehead. "He kept his eyes opened in China. When he saw something we could use, he would store it away. And one of the things he stored away was the idea of the mutual loan associations. That's how we happen to have them."

"I see. But how do they work?" Elwood asked.

"There are all kinds," Yoshimitsu replied. "In this case, though, there are twelve women there, so—"

"You're wrong," Colonel Henderson interrupted. "There are thirteen."

"Yes, but only twelve are forming the association. I listened. The aged one is just presiding. She is witnessing the rules. So each of the twelve women is going to put up ten Nakashima Island dollars every month. They'll do this for twelve months. In that way, each of them will get a chance to borrow one hundred and twenty dollars in some month. They draw numbers to see in which order they will borrow."

"That's a pretty good idea," Elwood said.

"It is," Yoshimitsu agreed. "It wouldn't have lasted ten thousand years if it wasn't."

But Colonel Henderson's eyes narrowed suspiciously. "What about the carrying charges? What about the interest?"

"There's no interest."

"I heard that one before, too," Colonel Henderson said. "The last time I borrowed money, they told me I was paying three per cent. But they didn't tell me it was three per cent a month. And you can't tell me they don't charge interest here. How do they meet the overhead?"

Yoshimitsu, with a gesture, indicated the open-fronted village store. "There is no overhead. The person presiding, like the old one there, never makes a charge for their services. It's an honor to be asked."

45

"Maybe so," Colonel Henderson eyed the group, "but you're never going to get me in one of those things."

"I always say that too." Yoshimitsu nodded. "But every once in a while there I am again."

"But Mr. Matsumoto," Elwood began. "What do the women do with the money they borrow?"

"Oh, they buy a little pig."

"A pig!" The blood rushed to General Scheick's face. "You mean they're keeping me standing here waiting while they finagle around, borrowing money to buy a hog!"

"But you don't know how important getting a pig is, Mr. General. When you got a pig, you really got something."

"Does it really mean that much?" Elwood asked.

"Oh, sure. A pig is your bank account. It means having the money out in the pen to buy what you want."

"Doesn't it mean pork, too?"

"No, when you own a pig you don't eat it. You sell it. And I'll tell you this, Elwood. If you really want to be somebody in the Nakashima Islands, just get yourself about six pigs. Why, you'd be better known than the Mr. General even."

"All right, Matsumoto, that's enough." General Scheick's voice was sharp. "You tell them to break up that meeting."

"Okay, Mr. General. It's breaking up anyway." Yoshimitsu indicated the group who were rising from the mats. One woman, with a hundred and twenty Island dollars in her hand, bowed to the group. They all turned and bowed to the aged one. Then the aged one looked speculatively at Yoshimitsu Matsumoto and the Americans and spoke rapidly in Japanese to Yoshimitsu.

"Mr. General," Yoshimitsu translated. "She would like to know if you want to see her store license? She just renewed it a couple of months ago over at the township offices."

"I don't want to see any license," General Scheick said.

"She wants to know if you are here to collect taxes then?"

"No."

The aged one smiled. "In that case, she says it is a pleasure to talk with you. What can she do?"

"Tell her I'm looking for Kenji Nakamura."

"All right." Yoshimitsu translated, then turned. "Mr. General, she says Kenji Nakamura is not home just now, but she is his grandmother."

"His grandmother!" General Scheick regarded the aged one with the blue tattooed hands.

"Yes, that would make her a queen, wouldn't it? Or at least a queen grandmother."

"I guess it would," General Scheick said thoughtfully, then whispered to Colonel Henderson, "You know, Bill, if she's the Queen Grandmother, she might be a good person to know."

"Mr. General," Yoshimitsu went on, "she would like to know if you or any of the rest would care for a cup of tea?"

"Thank you," the General said. "But I don't believe in stimulants. And neither does Colonel Henderson."

"You, Elwood?" Yoshimitsu asked.

"No thanks."

"I don't think I'll have a cup either then," Yoshimitsu said. "However, the Queen Grandmother asks if we would join her while she has some."

"It would be a pleasure," General Scheick said.

"She says the pleasure is hers."

They slipped off their shoes and stepped onto the clean straw mats covering the floor of the little store. The aged one gestured for them to be seated, and they formed a circle around her. The water was already heating over a small charcoal brazier, and she turned. "Elwood," Yoshimitsu translated, "she says: 'Sonny, would you please hand me that box of tea over on the shelf?' "

"I'd be glad to."

"She thanks you. She would have gotten it, but she's been having trouble with her joints lately, so it's hard for her to get up."

"Trouble with her joints?" General Scheick questioned. "Does she mean they're stiff?"

"Oh, yes. And she wishes she could get some wisteria root. You boil the root and drink the juice. That's a remedy her grandma used to use."

"Well, I don't know about wisteria," General Scheick said. "But personally, I would recommend bonemeal. I take two tablets with each meal."

The Queen Grandmother smiled. "She says if you take it, she, too, would like to try it, because you certainly cast a strong shadow."

"I beg your pardon?"

"She says you cast a strong shadow. You see, here in the Nakashima Islands when someone does not look well, we say he casts a light shadow. But when a person is full of vitality and energy like you, we say his shadow is strong."

General Scheick's chest swelled. "Is that right?"

"Yes, it is. She says she hasn't seen anyone in a long time who looks so well as you. She says just by looking at you a person can tell that you got good joints."

General Scheick beamed. "It's all in putting the right ingredients together in the form of food. Now you tell her not to worry. I'm going to get her some bonemeal."

"Would you?"

"I certainly will."

"Mr. General, she says she would appreciate it. She would truly appreciate it."

The tea was ready now. The Queen Grandmother poured a cup, then leaned forward. "But she hopes you will not think her impolite for drinking alone like this, Mr. General."

"Mr. General ..." General Scheick began. "Did she call me that?"

"Oh, yes. She recognized you immediately because she has seen your picture so often. In fact, she used to have your picture in the store here to sell. A man in Tamabaru got hold of a whole bunch of them, thinking the people might want them in their houses."

"I'll be darned," General Scheick said, since he always used darned instead of damned in the presence of ladies. "I never knew that."

"Oh, yes. She says until the man went broke, she used to carry your picture in stock all the time."

48

"Well, that certainly is a surprise. So they used to sell my picture. I'll be darned."

The Queen Grandmother set the cup of tea before her, picked up another cup, and began filling it. "She says, Mr. General, that as long as she is pouring, she might as well pour a cup for Kenji, too." Then, taking the filled cup, she put it before the vacant place beside her and regarded General Scheick. "But, Mr. General, she would like to know why you, the commander of all the Islands, should come to see her? This is such a great honor that she cannot believe it."

General Scheick smiled. He liked this aged one. She had a way that . . . well, pleased a person. He regarded her, and as he did so, a look of apprehension spread across her wrinkled face, her eyes widened, and he asked, "What's the matter?"

"She says she just realizes that you didn't come out to see her at all, that you came out to see her grandson. She hopes that Kenji hasn't done anything wrong. She hopes he isn't in trouble."

"Oh, no, no," General Scheick said assuringly, "it's not that. It's just that, well . . . I suppose she knows that there has been a vote."

"Oh, yes, Mr. General. She was the first one in line when the polls opened. She voted for the King, just like everybody else."

"Does she know who the King is, for whom she voted?"

"Yes, he is the descendant of the first son of Shinerikyu and Amamikyu."

"But does she know the supposed descendant of the first son is her grandson?"

"No, Mr. General," Yoshimitsu said. "She doesn't, but I will tell her." Slowly, he translated, and General Scheick, Colonel Henderson and Elwood watched the lined old face of the King's grandmother. As the impact of the words struck her, amazement swept across her features, only to be replaced by disbelief and doubt. For a moment she sat motionless, then she shook her head. "Mr. General, she says you shouldn't fool an old lady like her. It isn't nice."

"Tell her I'm not fooling her. Tell her about what Yamaguchi, whatever his name is, found."

49

"I'll do that," Yoshimitsu said, launching into a long, involved discussion in Japanese. The Queen Grandmother listened carefully, questioning here and there, then suddenly she began nodding. "Mr. General, she says she should have known. She says she should have realized a long, long time ago that her grandson would be King."

"Why?"

"Because she just remembers what he did when he was a baby. Do you know about the parties given for children, here in the Nakashima Islands, when they are a year old?"

"No."

"Well, we give a party. And on the little table, which is placed in the center of the room, we put a lot of items. For instance, a sweet potato slip, a stack of make-believe money, maybe an abacus, plus other things. Then we let the child choose from the table, and what he takes first shows what he is going to be. If he takes the sweet potato slip, he is going to be a farmer. If he takes the stack of make-believe money, he is going to be rich. If he takes the abacus, he is going to figure up things. But, Mr. General, do you know what Kenji did?"

"That's hard to tell."

"His grandmother says he didn't take anything. He just shoved everything aside, and climbed up on the low table and sat there. She says she should have known then that he was going to sit on a throne."

General Scheick deliberated. "That might be true," he said. "But that could also mean that he's just a sitter."

When Yoshimitsu translated, Grandma began to smile. "No, Mr. General, she says you are thinking about Kenji's grandfather, not Kenji. And do you know, she says that when Kenji was born, they all just laughed and laughed and laughed."

Briefly, General Scheick glanced at Colonel Henderson, then said, "Do you mean he was that amusing to look at?"

"Oh, no. They laughed so he would be a happy child. And they even carried him around to all the pigpens in the neighborhood."

"So he could see the pigs?"

"No, so the pigs could see him. It's good luck to have the pigs look at you. Anyway, she says it looks as if all the signs are right for Kenji, so—"

"But there's a lot more to it than that," General Scheick said quickly.

"Oh, she agrees with you there, Mr. General. But at least the signs aren't wrong."

General Scheick shrugged. "Maybe so." He glanced at the cup of tea which the grandmother had poured for her grandson. "However, I wonder if we could see the King?"

"He's at school right at the moment, Mr. General."

"At school? Well, at least that's some encouragement. What grade is he in?"

"This is his second year."

"Only his second year? I can see where there could be some complication if he's only a second-grader. What about his father?"

"He doesn't have a father or mother. There was an awful lot of fever around when he was just a baby. The Queen Grandmother is his only living relative. But I think King Kenji should be able to handle it himself."

"I don't," General Scheick said. "A second-grader is too young to be running a country."

"Oh, he's not so young. He's nineteen, Mr. General."

"Nineteen and only in his second year at school?"

"Do you think that's too bad?" Yoshimitsu asked.

"I don't think it's very d—darned good."

"That's funny. His grandma says she has always been proud of his ability as a scholar."

As General Scheick observed the aged one, he could see the pride in her old eyes. "Well," he began carefully, "I guess some learn a little faster than others." Again he glanced at the cup beside her. "But I'm afraid the King's tea is going to get cold."

"She expects it will, Mr. General."

"Oh, does he like cold tea?"

"No. But he's not going to drink it."

"Then what did she pour it for?"

51

"To show that she is thinking of Kenji and remembering him. She always pours a cup for him when she pours a cup for herself."

"Now wait a minute," General Scheick said. "He's at school, isn't he?"

"Yes."

"When do you expect him home?"

"In about two years."

"Why in the devil should it take him two years to get home from school?"

"Because he goes to a place called Cambridge College."

"You mean he's a college sophomore?"

"I don't know what a sophomore means. His grandma says, though, that in about a week from now school will be out, then he will be finished with his second year."

"So he's one of the Nakashima Islands students that we sent out. This puts a new light on things," General Scheick said, then turned to his executive officer. "But we didn't send any university students to school in England, did we, Bill?"

"No, sir, we didn't. Any we sent out went to school in the States. There's a mistake."

"That's right, Mr. Colonel," Yoshimitsu said. "There was a mistake. That's why King Kenji didn't get to school in England. When he won the scholarship at his township high school, they asked him where he wanted to go to school, and he said Cambridge. But then when he got there, he found out he wasn't in England at all. He was at a Cambridge College in a place called Ashtabula, Ohio. Somebody got mixed up," Yoshimitsu continued. "But I think it's a good thing, because all through our history, the King has always gone to school in the country of whoever was running the place. So see, there is another good sign."

Both General Scheick and Colonel Henderson gave Yoshimitsu a look, which he missed, and Elwood asked, "Mr. Matsumoto, how come the King wanted to go to school in England?"

"Oh, his grandma says he didn't especially want to go to school there. It was just that he read a book one time that was printed at Cambridge University. So when they asked him where he wanted to go, he didn't know the name of any other places, so he put that down. But his grandma wants to know, Mr. General, why you think his being in the second year of school at nineteen is not so good? After all, he did win the scholarship at his township high school."

General Scheick was somewhat embarrassed. "I'm afraid there's been a slight misunderstanding."

"It doesn't sound so slight to her."

"Well, it was a misunderstanding anyway," General Scheick said quickly. "However, I'm curious. Didn't she have any idea at all that she was of the royal family?"

"Well, she says now that she thinks back, she remembers that a couple of times her husband told her that he was King of all the Nakashima Islands. But she says if you believed all the things that he used to say, you would have been the biggest fool that ever walked."

"Oh, was he a little on the windy side?" General Scheick asked.

"She says she is afraid he was more than a little windy. Why, he used to tell people he owned anywhere from a half acre to ten acres of land, depending on whether it was the tax collector or some stranger he met. But when she made him sell the land so she could start this store, the truth came out. He owned about an acre. That's the way it was all the time."

"I see." General Scheick regarded her. "So she's the one who started the store."

"Yes. Kenji's grandpa was just a talking farmer."

"And the royal family had been farmers since the Chinese booted them out?"

"That's right."

"Well, you have to give her credit," General Scheick said. "It must have taken a lot of doing to get them out of agriculture after 340 years."

53

"I think it must have, too," Yoshimitsu agreed. "But I was just wondering if this isn't the reason Yamaguchi Kiei had such a time tracing the royal line. As I understand it, he ran into some awfully conflicting stories."

"Maybe so." General Scheick looked at the Queen Grandmother, who was shaking her head, and asked, "What's the matter?"

"She says she just can't believe that her grandson is King of the Nakashima Islands. And she would like to know if you are going to notify him."

"Unfortunately," General Scheick began slowly, "I have to notify my superiors in Washington about this whole mess."

"Will they get in touch with King Kenji?"

"Yes."

"And will they bring him back home?"

"I'm afraid so."

"You're afraid so, Mr. General? The Queen Grandmother would like to know if you're not happy that our King is being returned."

"Of course I'm not happy."

"Oh, and why do you feel that way?"

"For one thing it interferes completely with my personal plans."

"Ah. Ah so." The Queen Grandmother was nodding. "She says she understands, but that is the way things go sometimes."

"What does she mean by that?"

"Well, she says she had some personal plans, too. She had planned that when Kenji returned he would take over the store, and she would become *inkyo*."

"What's *inkyo*?"

"It means turning over the head of the family. It means not having any more duty, or responsibility, or having to look after the welfare of the family. It means turning all that over to another and just taking it easy, and doing what you want."

"I see."

"Yes, that is what she was going to do when Kenji came back to take over the store."

"What about now?" General Scheick asked.

"Well, now she's not sure, Mr. General. She'll have to see, because Kenji isn't coming home to take over a store. He's coming home to be King of the Nakashima Islands, so she doesn't know if she can become *inkyo* or not."

Chapter 4

COLONEL HENDERSON knew that it was his own fault, because he was the one who had suggested to General Scheick that the Nakashima Islands Mounted Police adopt the United States Army Customs of the Service. But you can't blame yourself. And so as he stood on the quayside, with the noise of the crowd rising around him, he looked at the anxious young lieutenant commanding the firing squad which had just pulled the blunder. And referring to Yoshimitsu, Colonel Henderson muttered, "Him and his damn ideas."

For it was in the Officers' Guide that Yoshimitsu had discovered, in that section on military courtesy, that any member of a reigning royal family shall be accorded a twenty-one-gun salute, and he had carried it to General Scheick. "I think when the King comes home from America," Yoshimitsu had said, "we should have twenty-one soldiers lined up with guns. Then when he steps off the plane, they can shoot in the air, and he will be welcomed."

"I don't see why," General Scheick said.

But Yoshimitsu had produced Colonel Henderson's copy of the Officers' Guide, and there it was in black and white, so the

56

most General Scheick could do was hedge. "I'll tell you what," he said. "I'll give you one man and let him fire twenty-one times."

That, however, wasn't satisfactory. The Officers' Guide stated a twenty-one-gun salute, not one gun twenty-one times. The trouble was that in the whole command there weren't twenty-one rifles. They could only muster twenty. For a moment the General was tempted to try to wiggle out of it. But Colonel Henderson had said, "It's a good thing, sir, that he interpreted guns to mean rifles. Suppose he wanted artillery pieces, then what would we do?"

General Scheick didn't even want to think about shuttling in artillery pieces, so quickly he put Colonel Henderson in charge of the detail. And while Colonel Henderson could find no more than twenty rifles, he did find a solution: Major McCloud had a shotgun, which made the twenty-first gun.

"As long as it says that any member of a reigning royal family shall get a salute," General Scheick said, pointing to the Officers' Guide, "I'm going to give the Queen Grandmother one too. She's a nice old lady." And so it was that the firing squad pulled the blunder.

The entire population of the ancient capital of Tamabaru, plus hundreds from the surrounding countryside, were in the quayside area. And they would have crowded the quays, except that troop after troop of mounted police were drawn up there, waiting for the King to fly in on the amphibian plane from Okinawa. Consequently, they were forced back by tail-swishing ponies, and so large was the assembly that it even spilled into Watanabe and Kunigami Squares.

With the exception of the police, who wore American khaki uniforms and the yellow helmet liners and scarves of the cavalry, the crowd was dressed in their workday clothes of faded cotton shirts and trousers for the men, home-woven brown, banana-cloth kimonos for the women—for few could afford more. Yet each person had managed a strip of red cloth, red being the color of joy, and a strip of white cloth, white being the color of peace and contentment, and these were attached to

57

bamboo poles which the crowd waved vigorously from time to time.

A raised platform had been constructed for the occasion. It, too, was decorated in red and white. And it was crowded with Nakashima Islands dignitaries, the chair of the dismounted Yoshimitsu Matsumoto being second only to the chair of the leading historian and scholar, Yamaguchi Kiei. The American community was also there. Mrs. Scheick sat between the General and Elwood, while just behind them sat the senior members of the staff and their wives, all in little hats and white gloves.

As they sat there, suddenly there was a stirring in the crowd, and General Scheick saw his sedan, which he had sent out to Little Koza for the Queen Grandmother, drawing up. Gripping the package which he had brought with him, he arose to meet her. "Matsumoto," he said, "you better come along too. I'll need someone to interpret for me."

"Okay." Yoshimitsu turned. "Mr. Colonel, aren't you going to shoot the guns now?"

"I'll give the command when she gets out of the car," Colonel Henderson replied. And as the General himself opened the door and helped the Queen Grandmother out, Colonel Henderson raised his hand. The young lieutenant commanding the firing squad barked an order, and twenty rifles and a shotgun roared out in royal salute. Then a twenty-second shot filled the air as the second barrel of the double-barreled shotgun cut loose.

Quickly, Yoshimitsu turned, counted the weapons, and said, "Mr. General, you can't give the King only twenty-one guns if you give the Queen Grandmother twenty-two."

"It was a mistake," General Scheick replied.

"But you gave her twenty-two guns."

Wearily, General Scheick motioned for Colonel Henderson. "Bill," he said, "you're handling this. You straighten it out." And turning, he smiled and nodded to the Queen Grandmother.

"Twenty-one guns is the regulation," Colonel Henderson explained, but Yoshimitsu shook his head.

"I like twenty-two guns better," he said. "Just think, the Nakashima Islands are probably smaller than any place else, yet our King gets one more gun than anybody else's. That's nice."

Colonel Henderson turned. "What should I do, sir?" he asked. "It's not regulation."

"Hell, give him twenty-seven guns for all I care," General Scheick replied.

"No, twenty-two is just right," Yoshimitsu said. "We don't want to be hoggish." And Colonel Henderson signaled over the young lieutenant in charge of the firing squad.

"Yes, sir, Colonel," the lieutenant said, "I'll give him twenty-two guns, but I'll need more ammunition."

"What do you mean more ammunition?" Colonel Henderson demanded.

"I'm all right on the rifles. It's the shotgun. Major McCloud only gave me two shells—one for the King and one for the Queen Grandmother. Since we already fired both, I'll need two more."

Overhead, the drone of a plane was heard, and a speck appeared in the sky, coming from Okinawa. "There he is! Here comes the King!" Yoshimitsu shouted in English, and the crowd took up the shout in Japanese. "Are you all ready, Mr. Colonel?"

The perspiration broke out on Colonel Henderson's palms. "Sir," he said to General Scheick, "there's been a little mix-up. However, I'll straighten it out." He beckoned to Major McCloud, up on the platform.

Quickly, the Major hurried down the steps, a squat man with a broad face and gray eyes which seemed to stare absently. He joined the little group at the foot of the stairs; and Colonel Henderson, glancing at the speck in the sky, which was growing steadily larger, said, "Major, we need two more shotgun shells. Will you hurry up to your quarters and get them? And get back here before that plane lands."

"Sir," Major McCloud said, "I'd be glad to, but my wife always takes care of things, and she packed them away somewhere. I don't know where they're at."

Colonel Henderson glanced at Mrs. McCloud, sitting on a chair up on the platform. "Would you ask her to run up and get a couple?"

"Certainly, sir." Turning, Major McCloud called, "Agnes!"

Agnes McCloud listened intently as Colonel Henderson explained the situation. "And would you try to get back before the plane lands?" he asked.

She looked at the sky, and they could all see that it was going to be close. "Perhaps if I could use the General's car," she said. "The police haven't got it blocked in, so I might have a chance."

The drone of the plane was growing louder, and the crowd began pointing and laughing. "Certainly. Take it, Agnes," General Scheick said. "And don't forget. I'm counting on you."

The little group at the foot of the steps watched gravely as the corporal-driver threw the car into gear. They heard the squeal of tires on the stones of the ancient quayside. They could see Agnes McCloud, sitting firm and erect on the back seat, her little hat perched atop her head. And they knew that if anybody could make it, Agnes could.

The Queen Grandmother also was watching. Tugging Yoshimitsu's sleeve, she whispered softly, and Yoshimitsu said, "Mr. General, she feels she is causing you a lot of trouble. But I told her not to worry, because you like to do things right, so it's no trouble at all."

General Scheick eyed him coldly, a fact which did not faze Yoshimitsu in the least, then turned to the grandmother. She was still wearing her same old brown banana-cloth kimono, but she was wearing a new pair of reed sandals, and he said, "Matsumoto, I'm sorry for keeping her waiting. Explain we had a little mix-up. And will you ask her how she's feeling today?"

Yoshimitsu translated, then replied, "Mr. General, she says don't worry about the mix-up. That happens to the best of us. And as far as feeling, she is feeling very excited, because this is the first time she will be seeing Kenji in almost two years."

"No, I mean how is she feeling physically?"

"Oh. She says her joints certainly aren't any better."

General Scheick held out the package he had brought. "Well, here's the bonemeal I promised her. Tell her to take two tablets with each meal. This will fix her up."

"She says, by golly, she'll do that, because she wants relief.

60

She thanks you, Mr. General." The Queen Grandmother bowed. "And now she wonders what you want her to do?"

"Well, we intended for her to sit up on the platform during the program, but if the steps are too steep, why . . ."

"No, she will make them. But what is this program you speak of? Is it some sort of a ceremony?"

General Scheick's face became grave. "I wish we had time for a ceremony. I wish we could have an honor guard and all the rest. But this is a serious situation. I want to get the King up here just as fast as I can and find out what he has in mind for these Islands. And that's what I'm going to do. Just as soon as we give him a . . . a twenty-two-gun salute."

"Ah, yes." Grandma nodded slowly. "She has been thinking a lot, and she is also anxious to know what the King has in mind."

"Good." General Scheick held out his arm. "If I may." The Queen Grandmother took it, and slowly he helped her up the steps.

On the platform the American community, having heard of Agnes McCloud's mission, were whispering amongst themselves and anxiously watching for the General's car to break from the confines of the town and begin its climb up the hill to Caroline Drive. The Nakashima Islands dignitaries, however, were unaware of the situation. They were watching the grandmother of their King. As she came up onto the platform itself, with the package of bonemeal in her hand, they rose to their feet, causing the American contingent to turn, perceive the arrival, and then hesitate, not knowing whether to follow suit.

But General Scheick gestured, brought the Americans to their feet, whereupon the Queen Grandmother smiled up at him. She then bowed to the Americans, bowed to the Nakashima Islands dignitaries and, spying Elwood, waved.

Yoshimitsu had stayed down at the foot of the steps, so General Scheick was without an interpreter. He could only lead her to her chair; and when she was seated, he said, "Okay?"

She understood that. Nodding, she replied, "Hokay."

The General turned then, and like the other Americans, looked to the road leading up the hill. He realized the car was being

61

slowed by the old, twisting streets of the ancient capital, for it was still not in sight. He looked up at the plane, and all American eyes turned with his. The amphibian was circling wide, getting ready to set down on the Tamsui River, there being no airfields on the Nakashima Islands. And the General knew it then. The whole American community knew it. They all knew Agnes McCloud couldn't make it.

For a moment the General stood, the weight of command resting squarely on his shoulders, and all eyes were on him. Then he walked to the head of the steps and called, "Matsumoto, get down to the quay. When the plane pulls in, tell the King to stay aboard until we're ready for him."

"How will I know when you're ready for him?" Yoshimitsu questioned.

"I'll tell you. Now get a move on."

"Okay." Turning, Yoshimitsu pointed his feet out, assumed his best Chinese figure-eight waddle, so all would know he was a scholar, and started to cross toward the quay, whereupon he heard a call, "*Oi*, Yoshimitsu! Over here!"

Glancing toward the crowd, Yoshimitsu saw a whole sea of waving hands and recognized the Takaminis. Not only was Uncle Shoji there, but Aunt Fumiko was there as well. There were also the three daughters. And upon looking closer, he saw Takaminis all over the place. Quickly, he changed directions, and as he joined them, Uncle Shoji asked, "Did you have any luck?"

"No," Yoshimitsu replied. "I wasn't able to manage it. I tried, but I couldn't get you a chair on the platform."

"Ah, so," Uncle Shoji said, and on his face was a certain resignation, borne through the centuries. Because it had always been the same for the past fourten hundred years: there was never a seat on the platform for a Takamini.

"If you had a uniform on," Yoshimitsu said, "I could lend you my horse. Then you could see real good."

"I can see all right." Uncle Shoji thought for a moment. "Well, I guess it can't be helped. But I know what. The King has been away for two years. Now the first thing he's going to want is a good dish of boiled sweet potatoes."

62

Instinctively, Yoshimitsu grew wary.

"So," Uncle Shoji continued, "why don't you invite him to join us over at your house for dinner tonight?"

Yoshimitsu looked at the army of Takaminis. "You mean you're all coming over to my house to eat?" he asked.

"Oh, sure. And if you invite the King and his grandmother"— Uncle Shoji indicated his daughters—"that would give the King a chance to meet the girls, and who knows?"

Yoshimitsu eyed the Takaminis. "Oh, I don't think the King would be able to come," he said quickly. "He'll be tired. Besides, maybe you people will want to go home."

"Now you don't know for sure that he will be tired," Uncle Shoji said.

"I know for pretty sure."

"No, you're just guessing. So you better ask him."

"Well . . ." It was at that moment Yoshimitsu heard a whistle. Looking in the direction of the platform, he saw the Americans frantically waving to him, urging him on. He saw the plane setting down on the Tamsui River and said thankfully, "I got to go now." Wheeling, he hurried off as fast as his figure-eight would permit, and Uncle Shoji's voice trailed after him. "Be sure to ask him," Uncle Shoji called. "Now be sure to ask him."

Agnes McCloud was very late with the shotgun shells. By the time she arrived and turned them over to the salute detachment, not only did they have the King's footlocker unloaded but also the mail for the Americans. And the horses of the mounted police were becoming noticeably restless, in contrast to the people who, having waited for three centuries, were not bothered by a few minutes more.

At length, however, all was in order. General Scheick strode down to the plane; and as he approached, Yoshimitsu, standing in the door, asked, "Are you ready, Mr. General?"

"Ready," General Scheick replied, drawing himself up for the greeting.

"Are you going to shoot the guns now?" Yoshimitsu asked.

"Of course I'm going to shoot them," General Scheick said, signaling to the salute detachment.

"Okay then." Yoshimitsu moved aside, and a hush fell over the crowd as even the mounted police leaned forward in their saddles to see better. "Mr. General," Yoshimitsu said. "Here's the King!" And twenty rifles and a shotgun roared out in a twenty-two-gun salute as King Kenji I of the Nakashima Islands stepped from the plane.

The King was a slightly built youth dressed in khaki trousers, white sneakers, and a sweater to which was attached his fraternity pin. He wore a small cap perched atop his close-cropped black hair. Under his arm were a half-dozen or so phonograph records, while on his face was a dazed expression. But then the crowd began cheering and a smile of sheer delight started, spread, and all his white teeth, made seemingly whiter by the contrast with his bronzed skin, were revealed in a broad grin.

General Scheick was stunned. He had expected a little more maturity. For a moment he couldn't take his eyes from the small cap, then the realization hit him that this was the man to whom the whole future of the Nakashima Islands was entrusted.

"Mr. General," Kenji said. "It is so nice of you to come down to meet me. I thank you very much." His grin broadened and feeling a few more words were in order, he added, "It certainly is a nice day, isn't it?"

"Nice day?" General Scheick managed.

"Yes, and you know, Mr. General, you wouldn't have had to go to all that trouble about the salute. Twenty guns would have been more than enough."

General Scheick was unable to speak. His eyes could only slip to the phonograph records.

Seeing this, Kenji went on, "Oh, do you like music, too, Mr. General? So do I. And I got some good ones here." He extended a record. "Here's one of the latest: 'You Can Feel The Breeze in Your B.V.Ds.' I'll play it for you sometime."

General Scheick could only stare.

"And now what do you want me to do?" Kenji asked.

"Do?" General Scheick struggled to gain his composure. "What I think you better do is come right up to the platform

64

and tell your people what your policy is going to be. Just follow me."

They started across the quayside, and even the police, astride their ponies, were cheering now. The cheers grew in volume as the people who had spilled back into Watanabe and Kunigami Squares joined in. And then the crowd began waving their red and white streamers violently in welcome to their King.

General Scheick was silent as they strode along, and Kenji said, "This is quite a day, isn't it, Mr. General?" He waved to the crowd. "But I certainly never thought anything like this would happen to me. You know, I just can't get over it."

They reached the foot of the platform, and Grandma, in spite of her stiff joints, half rose in her chair to get a better look at her grandson. A smile was on her old face as she watched him. And as he came up the steps, she just couldn't get over the changes that had taken place in him during the past two years. For one thing, she had always worried that perhaps they didn't feed him very well at this place called Cambridge College in Ashtabula, Ohio. But now she could see that they did, because he had filled out and grown a good two inches.

Grandma wasn't even conscious that all on the platform had risen. Her eyes were only on her grandson. Then he was before her, smiling down at her. "Grandma," he started to say in English, forgetting she couldn't understand it, then quickly switched to Japanese. "It is so good to see you again."

"It is good to see you, and good to have you home."

"But I never thought I would come home as the King," he said.

"Nor I either, Kenji." Her voice was low. "Nor I either."

General Scheick was standing over them. "King Kenji," he said, "we better get started."

"All right, Mr. General." Kenji nodded. "Do you want me to tell them my policy now?"

"No. I want to say a few words first. Just have a chair."

As King Kenji, phonograph records in hand, sat down next to his grandma, General Scheick stepped to the microphone.

65

Snapping it on, he blew in it and said, "Can you hear me out there?"

His words were in English, and the crowd was Japanese-speaking. Yet here and there were a few who could understand, so he was answered by scattered "Hokays!"

General Scheick nodded, then began slowly: "Ladies and Gentlemen, once I had looked forward to this day. For seven years I have been waiting for the moment when I could stand up here and say, 'And so to you, the people of the Nakashima Islands, our brothers in democracy, I now declare—you are free!'"

He looked out over the crowd. "But this day has arrived, and now, unfortunately, you are not our brothers in democracy. You have made a mistake, but I want you to know that mistake was made possible through the courtesy of the United States Government."

Up on the platform, the Nakashima Islands dignitaries, most of whom spoke and understood English, began scratching their heads. "By that I mean," General Scheick went on to explain, "it was we who gave you the opportunity to vote. It was you who made your own mistake."

"Ah, so," someone behind General Scheick whispered, and the General turned his head.

The dignitaries, happy that they had caught the General's meaning, nodded brightly, indicating that they were able to unravel it; and seeing this, General Scheick felt that he was striking home. "Now these are trying times," he continued. "In these times a nation needs wisdom, maturity, and experience in government." He glanced briefly at the King. "So just let me briefly review the experience my staff has brought to your government in the past. First, there is Colonel Henderson. . . ." General Scheick stated the Colonel's qualifications, then he went on with Major McCloud and the rest. The named officers sat with heads modestly bowed, and the Nakashima Islanders, having no translation of the speech and not knowing what was going on, followed suit and also bowed their heads.

"I only wish," General Scheick continued, "that these Islands could have the benefit of that wisdom, experience, and maturity in the future. And I only wish I could say, 'You are free!' However, since that is not the case . . ." General Scheick turned. "King Kenji, will you step forward, please?"

Quickly Kenji handed the phonograph records to his grandmother, pulled down his sweater and, cap in hand, stepped up beside General Scheick, who towered over him.

"King Kenji," General Scheick said, and there was no happiness in his voice, "on behalf of the United States Government, I now turn the Nakashima Islands over to you."

There was a hush, a silence; and General Scheick, aware of it, turned to the Nakashima Islands dignitaries, certain that the gravity of their mistake was now becoming clear to them. But then Yamaguchi Kiei, the old historian, whispered, "The Interruption has ended!" and he began applauding. The full meaning of the moment came to the crowd then, too. Way back to Kunigami Square they understood. The cheer was deafening. The streamers waved wildly. The little American community, not quite knowing what to do, even joined in the applause. And Grandma, hearing the cheers and seeing even the Americans applaud, smiled proudly. It was only General Scheick who was ashen.

King Kenji stood before the microphone, then all his white teeth were flashed in a smile as he said in English, "You know, this has been quite an experience." He paused. "But first of all I want to thank the Mr. General and the United States Government for letting us make this mistake. I hope it will be a good one."

It was the eyebrows of the American community that arched now, and Kenji quickly went on: "I don't mean a good mistake. I mean I hope everything will turn out all right, just like it did at Cambridge College when somebody made a mistake and sent me there. Of all the places I could have gone, that was the best.

"So I would like to thank Mr. Hayden, president of Cambridge College," Kenji said. "Do you know what he did? He was on his way over to Chillicothe to kick off the summer alumni fund-raising drive for the new administration building, though, of course, Mr. Hayden says they would never do away with the Old Main, because it has a certain promotional value which is hard to replace. Anyway, he went out of his way to stop by the fraternity house to see me, and he said, 'My boy, do your duty and do your best. And I hope the Nakashima Islands will ever be prosperous.' Now don't you think that was nice of him?"

Since the speech was in English, Grandma couldn't understand a word of it, so she continued sitting proudly. But the American community was exchanging glances.

"And then there was Mr. McQuigley, who taught my class in World Government," Kenji continued. "He feels awfully bad, because he said that if he had known I was going to be King, he would have speeded up the course. He said he would have really covered ground. But the reason he didn't do that is because he never has anyone go into government. In fact, the only one he ever had was Adrian DeSlovar, who became a justice of the peace over in Van Wert. Besides, you can't blame Mr. Mc-Quigley for taking things at normal speed. He was teaching twelve full hours last semester, and he was so busy that he said he was not getting out mornings for coffee until almost a quarter to ten."

The American community was sitting openmouthed now, and Grandma, smiling, turned her head and saw them; then puzzled, she regarded her grandson.

"But Mr. McQuigley briefed me," Kenji went on. "Mrs. McQuigley made some iced tea for us, and we sat out in his back yard, and he told me exactly what he would do if he were King. He said he is Irish, so he admits that he is prejudiced, nevertheless he told me that one of the most urgent problems today is the Insular question, that is, the relationship between England, Ireland, and Scotland. Do you know that the Scotch have a legitimate claim to the throne? And do you realize that Ireland is divided? How do you think that makes them feel in Ireland? So I am going to consider all that, just as Mr. McQuigley said I should."

Complete confusion was now on the faces of the Americans,

and Grandma tilted her head, looked from person to person, trying to discern what was going on.

"Once again I want to thank you," Kenji said. "And again, I hope our mistake is a good one. Now I will translate into Japanese so the people will know what I said."

As Kenji translated and his words drifted out, Grandma also sat openmouthed. Confusion swept over her, too, as it did over the crowd, who regarded their King blankly. On the platform, the Nakashima Islands dignitaries were once again scratching their heads, then Yamaguchi Kiei, the historian, whispered, "Ah, so. It is confusing. Nevertheless, that must be some of the new learning that the King absorbed in America."

"Ah, the new learning." The dignitaries nodded in awe, for learning commanded respect. And then the dignitaries became as cheer leaders. "A hundred thousand years to King Kenji!" they shouted. "A hundred thousand years to King Kenji!" rolled in from Watanabe and Kunigami Squares. And even the horses of the mounted police began to whinny.

Then the program was over, and the Nakashima Islands dignitaries began crowding around their King, began bowing and introducing themselves. General Scheick, rising from his chair, was puzzled, confused, and distressed. The rest of the Americans also arose. Agnes McCloud, who had failed to get the shotgun shells on time, dabbed at her eyes and started toward the General. But Elwood got to his uncle first. "Uncle Matt," he said, his eye on the fraternity pin on the King's sweater, "would you mind introducing me to the King?"

"All right, Elwood," General Scheick said and repeated to himself for the fiftieth time, "Now what the hell do you think he was talking about?"

As they reached the King, the old historian was bowing before Kenji. "Your Majesty, I am Yamaguchi Kiei," General Scheick and Elwood heard him say in English.

"It is so nice to meet you, Mr. Yamaguchi." Kenji returned the bow.

"I thank you, Your Majesty, but I have a question. I am re-

69

cording your return for posterity, so I would like to know what it is you have in your hand?"

Kenji held up the phonograph records. "This is American music."

"Music! Ah, music," the old one said in awe and delight, then spying General Scheick, he smiled. "This is a good sign, indeed, Mr. General. The King brought back music. Old King Gihon did the very same thing when he returned from school in China. In fact, had he not done so we would have no classical music today."

General Scheick looked at the record titled "You Can Feel the Breeze in Your B.V.Ds" and felt that certainly there were no future classics here. Nevertheless, Yamaguchi Kiei was bowing to the other dignitaries. "It is a good sign. The King has brought back music."

"King Kenji," General Scheick cut in, "I have some questions I want to ask you. First, however, I want you to meet my nephew Elwood Cummings."

The two youths faced each other, and the King extended his hand. "I'm glad to know you, Elwood."

"I'm glad to know you, Your Majesty."

Their hands clasped, a look of surprise swept over the King's face as he recognized a certain grip, then he began to beam. "Son of a gun! We're fraternity brothers!"

"We sure are." Elwood grinned at his uncle. "We're both Lambda Beta Thetas. I spotted the King's pin on his sweater."

"Fraternity brothers!" King Kenji couldn't get over it. "Son of a gun. We got to talk this over."

A Nakashima Islands dignitary came forward, bowed and whispered in Japanese. Kenji returned the bow and whispered greeting, then turned. "Elwood, I don't see your fraternity pin. Are you engaged to some girl?"

"No," Elwood replied. "I didn't wear it, because I never expected to run into any brothers out here."

Another dignitary came forward, bowing and whispering. Kenji followed suit, then said, "You know, Elwood, I was going

70

to our national convention this summer. But then I was made King."

"I was going, too," Elwood said, "but my mother got the idea that I ought to come out here."

"What for?"

"Oh, they're trying to talk me into taking over the family business."

"Don't you want to?"

"Gosh, no."

"What do you want to do?"

"I don't know. That's what I'm trying to figure out."

"It's kind of tough, huh?"

"It sure is. It's got me stopped cold."

There was a polite cough beside them as Yoshimitsu Matsumoto touched the King's elbow. "Excuse me, Your Majesty." He introduced himself. "But my uncle by marriage, Shoji Takamini, would like to invite you over to my house for dinner tonight. Could you come? There won't be anybody there except all of my in-laws."

"Well, I don't know," Kenji said. "I haven't even thought about eating."

"Uncle Shoji would certainly like to have you and your grandma, too."

"Excuse me, King Kenji," General Scheick cut in. "I want to make a suggestion. Instead of you going out to dinner tonight, I think the two of us should have a long talk. After all, I've been in command here for seven years, and you're just taking over."

"Well, if you think we better . . ."

"I certainly do, because frankly I'm quite doubtful of certain things."

"Okay. But first let me ask Grandma."

"By all means ask your grandmother," General Scheick said. "In fact, I'd like her to sit in with us." He glanced at the little old lady, who was deep in thought. "She could furnish a maturity that would be of great help."

Kenji spoke to his grandmother, who looked first to Yoshimitsu, then to General Scheick. "Grandma says to thank you,

71

Mr. Matsumoto. She doesn't think we had better come over to your house, however."

Yoshimitsu nodded. "Well, maybe some other time." Turning, he shrugged to the Takaminis who had collected at the bottom of the steps.

General Scheick smiled. "What time would it be convenient for us to meet then? Perhaps seven? Or seven-thirty?"

"Oh, Grandma says we can't meet with you either, Mr. General."

General Scheick was taken aback. "You can't meet? And why not?"

"Because Grandma thinks that maybe she and I ought to have a little visit tonight. She's very anxious to find out about this college in America."

General Scheick was about to protest, but the aged one was drawing her brown banana-cloth kimono about her, was looking at the steps; while King Kenji said, "Mr. General, do you know where I can borrow a horsecart to take Grandma home?"

Indignation arose in General Scheick. He could see here and now that the King was wrong in not taking advantage of his, the General's, wealth of experience. He couldn't agree with the King about not meeting with him; however, he couldn't let the aged one walk, or even ride home in a horsecart. "I'll furnish you transportation, King Kenji," he said. "You're completely wrong, but I'll give you a ride anyway."

"We appreciate that, Mr. General. And we won't bother you any more." King Kenji bowed, then turned. "Elwood, how about riding out with us? Hey, I know. How about eating with Grandma and me? Then we can tell her all about college, and we'll even sing her some fraternity songs."

"That would be a lot of fun, Your Majesty."

"Don't call me 'Your Majesty,' Elwood. Just call me Kenji."

"I don't think I'd better do that."

"But I want you to."

Elwood considered. "Well, how would this be? If anyone is around, I'll call you 'Your Majesty.' When you and I are alone, I'll call you Kenji. Okay?"

72

"Yeah, that's okay if you want it that way. But will you come out to Little Koza with us?"

"Sure."

"Good." Kenji smiled. "If you'll give me a hand, we'll get Grandma down the steps and into the car. Then as soon as I dig up my footlocker, we'll be all set to go."

They started down the steps, and General Scheick had to shake his head. Then he caught sight of his aide at the bottom of the stairway, trying to push through the crestfallen Takaminis.

"Sir," the aide called, quickly mounting the steps, "they've got the mail sorted that came in on the King's plane. Here's one for you. I knew you would want it right away."

General Scheick glanced at the sender's name, and the smile spread across his face. It was the reply to his letter, to his request for advice. It was from his old friend and mentor, Major General Mosby Winthrope, now of the Pentagon. And as General Scheick read the salutation his smile broadened, for it began "Dear Pug," which was his nickname from his Academy days. But as he started to read the letter proper, his face fell. He shook his head to clear it, and began all over:

DEAR PUG:

Do you realize what a situation you have caused? I'm writing this in a letter instead of sending a radiogram, because I don't want anyone but you to see it.

The translations of the Soviet headlines have just hit the streets, here in Washington, and the town is in an uproar. The headlines state: DEMOCRACY BEATEN IN A FREE ELECTION.

Of course, we're being big about it, replying that it's not the system that counts, saying that the important thing is the principle of self-determination. But underneath, Congress is sore as hell, one congressman stating that his great-great-great-grandfather, who was a corporal in the Revolutionary War, must certainly be turning in his grave.

Frankly, Pug, they were all for bouncing you for letting this thing take place. But the Pentagon has rallied behind you, because Congressman McQuirk, at Mrs. Carhart Inglehorn's cocktail party the other night, stated: "If the Islands had been under civilian administration in the first place, this goof-up would never have happened." So naturally we, of the military, closed ranks.

Because of our friendship, I have now been placed in charge of this operation. From now on, you will answer directly to me. Like myself, you are nearing retirement, Pug, and I don't want to see you go out with this blot on your record. In fact, all of us here at the Pentagon want to see you vindicate yourself.

It's too late to do anything about the King. Since they elected him, we're stuck with him. But I'll tell you this: Washington wants him and those Islands in our camp and no fooling around! We have managed to get you one more chance. We will manage to keep you on there as an adviser. And my personal advice to you, Pug, is that you had better make the ripple.

(Signed) MosBy

General Scheick, letter in hand, could only stand and stare off into space. Then he heard a voice addressing him, and he looked down. "General, sir." Agnes McCloud, her eyes red from crying, was standing before him. "May I speak to you?"

"Why of course, Agnes."

"General, sir, I feel awful, and I want to apologize for not getting the shotgun shells here in time. I know I let the command down."

"You didn't do that at all, Agnes."

"But I did, and I want to make up for it."

"And me, too, sir," Major McCloud of Intelligence joined in. "I should have taken care of those shells myself, instead of shoving them off on Agnes to pack away. Isn't there something we can do, sir?"

General Scheick was silent for a moment, then he smiled paternally at these two, who were so loyal to the command. "Well, Agnes." He indicated the letter. "I'm staying on here."

"You are, sir?"

"Yes. And I'm facing the most crucial situation of my whole career."

Colonel and Mrs. Henderson had drifted over, as had Lt. Colonel Seymour and his wife. They stood in a little group and solemnly watched their commander, whose jaw was firm.

"I'm staying on here," General Scheick continued, "and my job is to get this king and these people in our camp. And as all of you know, a commander is helpless without a strong staff."

Agnes McCloud's face lit. "I understand, sir. Well, Henry and I will stay with you. Won't we, Henry?"

"You bet we will, sir," Major McCloud said.

"That's what I wanted to hear." General Scheick smiled.

"Sir." Colonel Henderson edged forward. "I just want you to know you can count on Irene and me. We'll stay."

"Good, Bill. Good."

"And that goes for us, too," Lt. Colonel Seymour said, referring to himself and his wife Cora.

General Scheick knew that he couldn't find a more loyal group anywhere, and he looked off to where the King and his nephew Elwood were walking across the quayside, looking for the King's footlocker. For a moment he watched them, then he turned to Agnes McCloud. "Agnes," he said, "you didn't let the command down. It was I who did that."

"Oh, no, sir. You didn't," the group around General Scheick chorused.

"Yes, I did. I did indeed. I let that Matsumoto talk me into giving the King a twenty-two-gun salute." General Scheick held up a finger. "Now all of you. Listen to me. There's an object lesson here."

The little group around him was intent. "Yes," the General said, looking at Colonel Henderson and his wife Irene, looking at Lt. Colonel Seymour and his wife Cora. "There's an object lesson here. Regulations said a king is to be given a twenty-one-gun salute. I departed from regulations. When you depart from regulations, it leads to nothing but trouble."

General Scheick waited for the impact of his words to sink in, then continued. "We got into trouble. We got out of trouble. Now we're starting with a clean slate. And, by George, we're not going to get ourselves involved again. Right?"

"Right!" the little group said in unison, and Colonel Henderson added for all of them, "We'll help you get that king and these islands in our camp, sir."

75

"Good." General Scheick was thoughtful for a moment, then went on, "And one other thing comes to my mind here. We have a moral obligation to these people."

"A moral obligation?" The group regarded him.

"Yes. We are morally obligated to save these people from themselves."

There was a silence, then Agnes McCloud said, "Well, don't you worry, sir. We'll save them from themselves. And not only will we do that, but we'll do it by regulation."

Chapter 5

THE following morning General Scheick and his staff once again had their walk. But this morning it wasn't marked by the usual high good humor. Although it was the unwritten rule never to talk, or even think of business on such jaunts, still, when a man has got to make the ripple, a certain amount of worry is bound to creep in. Try as he might, General Scheick couldn't keep it away. It showed on his face, and so the staff remained silent out of respect for his feelings. But General Scheick could see their loyalty. It pleased him, and he knew that these men could be counted on.

They came down out of the green hills, and reaching Cottage 1A, General Scheick looked at his watch. "Gentlemen," he said, "we'll synchronize. It is now six forty-seven. We'll meet promptly at eight in my office."

"Eight it is, sir," Colonel Henderson said firmly, speaking for all of them. And saluting smartly, they went off to breakfast.

Mrs. Scheick was already at the table, sipping her coffee and rereading a letter from Elwood's mother, which also had come in on the King's plane. "Good morning, Matt," she said. "Will you have a cup of coffee with me?"

"No. I think I'll have some blackstrap molasses and hot milk," the General replied. "I need the iron this morning."

"That's up to you." Mrs. Scheick rang the little table bell for Haruko, the Nakashima Islands maid.

"Well," the General said, picking up his napkin, "it looks like we're not going to have that orange grove as soon as we expected, Caroline."

"Yes, Matt. And personally I'm glad for this delay. It might give you time to reconsider."

"What's to reconsider?" General Scheick asked.

"A number of things. In the first place, why bother growing oranges? You don't know anything about the business."

"I've been supervising the growing of vegetables for the whole command for the past seven years, haven't I?"

"Yes, but fooling around with smudge pots and all those things . . ."

"I'll tell you this, Caroline. A person needs an active retirement. A person needs to keep going. Otherwise, he just wilts on the vine."

"I don't need an active retirement," Mrs. Scheick said. "I'm tired of doing things. All I want to do is rest."

General Scheick regarded her as Haruko came in from the kitchen and set the hot milk and molasses before him. Slowly he picked up the cup and said, "Caroline, I want to make a suggestion. I think you ought to drink at least two cups of this a day. Frankly, I don't believe you're getting enough iron."

"Don't be ridiculous," Mrs. Scheick said and reached for her coffee.

A silence fell over the room, and General Scheick could see that this was not the moment to talk further of orange groves, so he indicated the letter beside Mrs. Scheick's plate. "What were you telling me last night about Mildred? I'm sorry, I had so much on my mind, I'm afraid I didn't catch it."

"Oh. Well, I wrote Mildred and told her that we had Elwood thinking, and she was very happy to hear it, because she says Fred is really in bad shape. He just lies around the house weekends, instead of going fishing."

General Scheick thought it over. "You know," he said slowly, "it sounds to me as if Fred needs some iron, too."

"Oh, good heavens!" Mrs. Scheick exclaimed.

"It's entirely possible," General Scheick said. "When they get that tired, listless feeling . . ."

"Look, Matt," Mrs. Scheick said. "I own nearly one-third of that elevator. And let me ask you—how would you like it if a man like that was running your business?"

"Oh. Oh, yes. I see what you mean."

"We need Elwood to take over." Mrs. Scheick glanced toward the bedroom where the youth was dressing, and a worried look crossed her face as she said, "But do you know, Matt, he didn't get in until four this morning?"

"He didn't?"

"No. And I don't like this idea of his going out to the King's home village. This King might not be a very good influence on him. He might get ideas of not wanting to go back to Iowa."

"I wouldn't get upset about it," General Scheick said.

"I am upset about it." Again Mrs. Scheick glanced toward the bedroom. "Because I certainly wouldn't want him to get any ideas like that."

When Elwood came in to breakfast, he, too, was wearing a pair of khaki trousers and a sweater, just as the King had been wearing on the previous day.

"Good morning, Elwood," Mrs. Scheick said. "You didn't have to get up so early. I'll bet you're awfully tired, aren't you?"

"I'm not a bit tired, Aunt Caroline," the youth replied. "Good morning, Uncle Matt."

General Scheick acknowledged the greeting, and Mrs. Scheick went on, "I don't believe I've seen you since yesterday afternoon when the mail arrived. Anyway, I heard from your mother. She says that the Landridge girl asked about you."

"Who?"

"The Landridge girl, who lives down the street."

"Oh, Dorothy."

"Yes. And your mother says she's such a pretty thing."

79

"That's nice," Elwood said, reaching for his napkin.

A silence fell over the room. The disappointed Mrs. Scheick sipped her coffee while the General, after a moment or two, began probingly, "Elwood, did you have a good talk with the King last night?"

"We sure did, Uncle Matt," Elwood replied. "We had a real good talk."

General Scheick hesitated. "I know it's none of my business, but just for curiosity's sake, may I ask what you talked about?"

"Oh, well Grandma wanted to know all about college in America."

"Was she interested in that?"

"She sure was. She wanted to know everything, about what Kenji was studying . . ."

"What was he studying?"

"Retailing and Marketing. His faculty adviser thought that since his grandma owned a store, that might be a good thing. Then Grandma wanted to know about Mr. McQuigley and this course in World Government that he taught. And she had a million questions. We even had to tell her about how it was living in a fraternity house, and sweetheart serenades—"

"What's a sweetheart serenade?"

"That's when a fraternity brother gets engaged. We all march up and sing songs to his girl. In fact, Kenji and I even sang Grandma a whole bunch of fraternity songs."

"That was nice," Mrs. Scheick said. "By the way, what did you have to eat out there?"

"Sweet potatoes," Elwood replied.

"And what else?"

"Nothing."

"Nothing? Didn't they even have ham with them?"

"Oh, no, Aunt Caroline. No one out here ever has ham."

"But how in the world did they serve just sweet potatoes?"

"Boiled."

"Boiled! You mean you picked up a boiled sweet potato and ate it?"

"Yes."

80

Mrs. Scheick couldn't help grimacing. "Why, that sounds as bad as some of the combinations your uncle eats."

General Scheick put down his milk and molasses. "Unfortunately," he said, "nature doesn't always put the necessary food elements in the most attractive packages."

"She certainly doesn't," Mrs. Scheick agreed, then went on, "But tell me, Elwood. You didn't like those boiled sweet potatoes, did you?"

"No, Aunt Caroline."

"And you wouldn't want to live, say, out in a village like where the King lives?"

Elwood shook his head. "Gosh, no."

"I'm glad to hear that," Mrs. Scheick said. "It must be terribly monotonous living in a place like that."

"It sure must be," Elwood said, and his aunt smiled.

Haruko brought their breakfasts, and for a moment they busied themselves with their ham and eggs; then General Scheick said, "Do you have anything on the docket today, Elwood? I'm having a very important staff meeting at eight, and I thought you might want to sit in on it."

"Gosh, Uncle Matt," the youth replied, "I'd like to, but I promised the King I'd come out."

"Do you two have something planned?"

"No, Kenji said we'd just fool around."

"Just fool around?" General Scheick put down his knife and fork. "Just fool around, eh?"

"That's what Kenji said. Of course, Uncle Matt, if you want me to go to the staff meeting . . ."

"No. No. That's perfectly all right." General Scheick lapsed into thought. All through his ham and eggs, and all through his second milk and molasses, he sat in silence. And it wasn't until his watch showed seven-forty, that he came back to the reality of the room. "Well, I better be heading for headquarters," he said, putting down his napkin.

"Oh, Uncle Matt," Elwood began, "could I borrow some transportation to get out to Little Koza? It's quite a hike out there."

"Of course, my boy. Come on. We'll walk down to the motor pool and I'll get you a jeep and driver. Tell him when you want to come back, and he'll pick you up, too."

"Oh, Elwood," Mrs. Scheick said, "I forgot to tell you. Today's Thursday. My Investment Club meets at ten. This is going to be a lengthy session, because we have quite a bit of money on hand and we're searching for a new stock to invest it in. So perhaps you had better have lunch with your uncle down at the Officers' Club."

"Thanks, Aunt Caroline," Elwood said, "but I don't know what the King has in mind, so he and I will probably just pick up a bite somewhere."

"If you wish," Mrs. Scheick said, and the three of them arose from the table, each to go his own way for the day.

When General Scheick reached his office at three minutes to eight, the staff was already gathered there. The General's aide was already passing out pencils and paper to the ashen-faced Major McCloud and Lt. Colonel Seymour. Colonel Henderson's stomach was twitching, and it was all a case of tension, he knew. Yet how can you expect a man to keep calm when a whole nation is at stake?

As General Scheick entered, the staff jumped to its feet, but General Scheick waved them back to their chairs. "Please, gentlemen, please," he said and sank into his own swivel chair, behind his desk.

There were still three minutes to go, and the General turned, looked out through the window, stared at the blue, almost cloudless sky that hung over the Nakashima Islands. The staff watched him, their faces apprehensive, and silence hung over the room.

Then there were no minutes to go. It was eight o'clock. Slowly General Scheick swung, in his swivel chair, from the blue Nakashima Islands sky. He faced his staff, looked each man in the eye, and said, "Gentlemen, I have it on good authority that the King intends to just fool around today."

"Just fool around!" Colonel Henderson exclaimed, and the staff was shocked.

82

"Why the damn fool," Major McCloud said. "His first day on the job, and here he is—goofing off already."

Quickly, General Scheick held up a restraining hand. "Gentlemen," he said, "I'm afraid you don't understand."

"Isn't his goofing off a lousy thing to do, sir?" Major McCloud asked, not knowing which way to sway.

"No, Henry. I think it might prove a very useful thing," General Scheick said. "But let me explain. A long time ago I learned something that has proven invaluable throughout my career. And I learned it as a second lieutenant, back at old Fort Bitely.

"At that time," General Scheick continued, "I had the good fortune to be serving under my best friend and mentor. You know him now as Major General Mosby Winthrope, but then he was a first lieutenant. Anyway, in those days physical exercise for the troops consisted of arm waving in the morning. Everyone realized that we really needed something to give the men a workout. You'd hear it everywhere you went—out on the terrace of the Officers' Club, on the polo field, in the swimming pool."

General Scheick half turned in his swivel chair, looked through the window, his mind back on those days when he was a second looie. "We all knew pretty much what was needed. We knew we needed some kind of obstacle course, but nobody was doing anything about it except talking. Then one day General Winthrope got fed up. He said to me: 'Pug, let's show 'em. Let's design 'em a course, and end this gabbing.' And that's what we did. Not only did we design it, but we put it down on paper, every blessed detail; and we got it up to old General Schlosser, the post commander.

"Of course, General Schlosser made some changes. As I remember it, he lowered the climbing walls from ten feet to nine feet six inches; and he widened the water jumps from nine feet six inches to ten feet. But basically it was our obstacle course. Every time Mosby and I saw a man go through it, we knew we were responsible."

General Scheick paused, then continued, "I've never forgotten that lesson of old Fort Bitely. I've used it time after time in my career. Whenever something was needed, I always remembered my friend Mosby saying, 'Pug, let's show 'em.' Then I'd sit down, get a concrete plan on paper, and submit it. Oh, they'd change it around upstairs. But basically, it was always my plan that went into effect. Basically, it was always I, calling the turns. And, gentlemen," General Scheick looked them in the eye, "that's what we're going to do here."

A new awareness had crept into the staff. "I'm getting the drift of it, sir," Colonel Henderson said.

"Good." General Scheick smiled. "Now let's take a look at this situation. These Islands are a new nation. To function, they are going to need a Table of Organization, a T/O. I doubt very much if the King will ever think of this. But we're going to think of it. Get this down on paper now, Bill. I have thought it over, and these are the officials the Nakashima Islands are going to need." And as General Scheick dictated, Colonel Henderson wrote:

Table of Organization (T/O)
for the Nakashima Islands

1. Prime Minister
2. Foreign Minister
3. Finance Minister
4. Defense Minister
5. Minister of Trade
6. Minister of Transport
7. Minister of Labor
8. Minister of Power
9. Minister of Education
10. Minister of Agriculture
11. Minister of Health

"Man!" Colonel Henderson said when General Scheick finished. "Man! That's a tight organization, sir."

"It's mighty tight," Major McCloud agreed, and the staff had to whistle in admiration.

"Thank you, gentlemen." Again General Scheick smiled. "But this is only half of the plan I intend to submit to the King."

84

"Only half the plan?" Colonel Henderson questioned uncertainly.

"Yes," General Scheick said decisively. "Now we're going to staff the T/O with men whom we know, and whom we can trust. I figure if we get a group of, shall we say, pro-Western ministers in here, why . . ."

"I get it, sir," Colonel Henderson said quickly. "If we get a group of pro-Western ministers in here, why it would be like having a first mortgage on the place."

"A first mortgage, indeed," General Scheick said, and he could see there would be no holding his staff now. "Bill, get this down on another sheet of paper," he went on. "For Prime Minister put down Louie Yamaguchi."

"Now there's a real choice," Colonel Henderson said approvingly. "He's amenable to reason."

"You're darn right that's a real choice," Major McCloud joined in. "Why, I remember last Christmas we wanted some eggs for eggnogs and couldn't get any in the whole capital. But Louie managed some. Yep, he's all right in my book."

"Good." General Scheick nodded. "Now for Foreign Minister put down Louie's brother, Henry. Are there any objections?"

"I have none, sir," Colonel Henderson said.

"Henry's all right in my book, too," Major McCloud replied, and added, "You know, sir, the Nakashima Islands are really going to have an outfit here."

General Scheick considered. With men like Louie and Henry Yamaguchi at the helm, the future seemed bright. "You're right," he said. "You're entirely right. Now for the Minister of Finance I suggest . . ."

Chapter 6

BY NOON, General Scheick had the personnel for the Naka-shima Islands lined up, so it was no wonder that lunch was marked by such a feeling of well-being. And after lunch, taking his vitamins plus a hundred extra milligrams of C to fortify himself just in case something infectious was flying around in the air, he said to Colonel Henderson, "Well, Bill, let's drive out to Little Koza and set it up."

"All right, sir," Colonel Henderson said and added, "You know, sir. I really learned something today. That idea of drawing up a plan when everyone is just sitting around gassing, that's terrific."

"Why thank you, Bill." General Scheick smiled with satisfaction, and together they got into his sedan.

The Nakashima Islands was a land created by the hoe, thus it was only natural that the people should be working with their hoes as General Scheick and Colonel Henderson drove through the countryside. This was the season for transplanting sweet potato slips from crowded seedbeds into more open ground. So the farmers were moving along, making slits in the earth with the implements. They would then slip in a sweet potato cutting and with their left heel press the soil around it, quickly moving on to the next, and the next, planting.

But as General Scheick's sedan rolled through the countryside, the farmers would straighten and wave to him. In the corners of the fields they had set up their bamboo poles, with the attached streamers—red for joy and white for contentment. These were the same poles they had carried when the King arrived home from America. And after waving to the General they would point to the streamers, smile, and nod happily.

The streamers were flying in every field on each of the small islands, giving the whole land a carnival appearance, an appearance of joy and festiveness. And within the car General Scheick, armed on one hand with a Table of Organization and on the other hand with a list of personnel to fill it, also felt joyful and festive. He returned each and every wave and smile, even volunteered a few on his own.

They came into Little Koza, passed its shaded old well; and reaching the entrance to the home of King Kenji, they swept around the small inner wall into the courtyard and stopped dead. For the Queen Grandmother's store wasn't open today. The sliding doors of weathered old lumber had been drawn shut and latched, and now the little store stood silent and deserted.

"What the hell?" General Scheick muttered, looking around. "Now what do you think is up?"

"That's hard to say, sir," Colonel Henderson replied. "But if the King intends to just fool around, why maybe they went off on a picnic or something."

"Maybe so," General Scheick said. "But you'd think they'd at least tend to business. That's no way to do, locking up like that."

"Sir," Colonel Henderson said, "why don't we go check with the police? They'll surely know where the King is."

"That's a good idea." General Scheick nodded. "We'll drop into their headquarters and kill a couple of birds with one stone."

"How do you mean, sir?"

"Well, the mounted police are surely going to become the Army. And since we have Matsumoto down as Defense Minister, we might check on him and see what kind of an outfit he's running."

The headquarters of the Nakashima Islands Mounted Police was not prepared for a surprise inspection. The members of the Records Section were all lounging at their homemade desks, having a cup of tea. The members of the Detective Force were stretched out on benches, having an afterlunch snooze. And as General Scheick's sedan drew up, the younger, more energetic members of the headquarters detachment were playing a game. Thanks to Yoshimitsu Matsumoto, their chief's, translation of American stories, they had learned about the fast draw. Six of them were lined up in a row for a test of speed, with an umpire over to one side, his hand raised, ready to give the signal. Not having any weapons, however—the mounted police being unarmed—they were forced to rely on revolvers which they had carved from wood. And so as General Scheick opened the door, the umpire unfortunately dropped his arm in signal, and the General ran into one of the finest volleys of "bang, bang" that ever reverberated through a headquarters.

For a moment General Scheick was too startled to speak; then the blood streamed to his face. "What the hell is this?" he demanded.

Over to one side Jiro Kamakura, executive officer to Yoshimitsu Matsumoto, who was lolling in a swivel chair with the top button of his khaki trousers opened for comfort, quickly grasped the situation. "Tenshun!" he called in English. And as every member in headquarters froze stiff, he hurried forward to apologize. But not being fluent in English, he could not be profuse, and all he could manage was, "Excuse please. We shoot you no. Accident."

"It'd better be an accident!" General Scheick thundered. Then, regarding the flat-faced, bespectacled Jiro Kamakura, said, "And button the top button of those trousers!"

"Top button?" Jiro questioned, then perceived. "Ah, so. Excuse please." He began bowing and added by way of explanation, "Four sweet potatoes for lunch."

"I don't give a damn if you had eight," General Scheick snapped. "You don't go around with your trousers open. And where are your scarves?"

Not a member of the headquarters detachment was wearing his scarf.

"Scarves? Ah, so," Jiro whispered and gave a command in Japanese, whereupon the police rushed to get their yellow scarves. Unfortunately, most were using them as *furoshiki*— the large Japanese handkerchiefs which act as carryalls. And as the police began unwrapping the remains of their lunch from the scarves and began hastily donning them, General Scheick was too shocked to speak, for here was a flagrant insult to the colors of the United States Cavalry.

"Where is your chief?" General Scheick was finally able to demand.

"Chief? Ah, Matsumoto-*san*." Jiro began bowing again and indicated a room to the rear. "Please. You go."

General Scheick went, indeed, and Colonel Henderson stormed along right behind him. There was no door to the chief's office; only a kind of reed stripping covered the opening. Pushing aside the stripping, General Scheick and Colonel Henderson entered; and there, sitting at an improvised desk, deep in the translation of something or other, was Yoshimitsu Matsumoto.

"Matsumoto!" General Scheick roared. "What the hell's going on around here?"

"Huh?" Yoshimitsu looked up. "Oh, hello, Mr. General. Hello, Mr. Colonel. I didn't expect you to drop in."

"That's evident."

Yoshimitsu closed his magazine. "I hope you will excuse me, but I've had to do some extra translation. All the Takaminis were in for the King's arrival, so I've had a lot of expense."

General Scheick wasn't interested in Yoshimitsu's personal problems. "Matsumoto," he demanded, "why aren't those men out there busy?"

"I think it's because there's nothing for them to do," Yoshimitsu replied.

"Well, find something for them!"

"But they've already brushed their horses two times today. And we've already built the compost piles. You should see how nice we piled it, Mr. General. The corners are just as square."

"Have you turned the old piles?" General Scheick asked.

"No, I think we forgot to do that."

"Get them out there then. That'll keep them busy."

Yoshimitsu nodded, called to Jiro in the other room; and when Jiro appeared in the doorway, Yoshimitsu gave the order in Japanese. "Pitchforks," he said.

"Pitchforks," Jiro repeated in resignation and went off to rally the Records Section, the Detective Force, and various and sundry other members lying around headquarters.

"Now then," Yoshimitsu said, falling into his official capacity. "What can I do for you, Mr. General?"

"You can tell me where the King is."

"The King? He's out in Little Koza at his grandma's store."

"Like hell he is," General Scheick said. "I was just out there and the place is closed up."

"It is?" Yoshimitsu appeared to be quite surprised.

"Look." The irritation was evident in General Scheick's voice. "You're supposed to be the police. You're supposed to know what's going on in these Islands. Now where the devil is the King?"

"I haven't seen him today."

"I didn't ask you if you had seen him."

"And I didn't hear where he was either."

"Sir," Colonel Henderson said, "how about getting the Detective Force to track him down?"

"We can't do that," Yoshimitsu said, "because the detectives just went out to repile the piles."

"Forget it. Forget it," General Scheick said, trying to control his temper. "I'll find him myself."

"Oh?" Interest arose in Yoshimitsu. "How are you going to do that?"

"It's none of your business," General Scheick replied. "You just keep these men busy."

90

"All right, Mr. General," Yoshimitsu said; and as General Scheick was about to leave the office he added, "And don't worry. We'll repile the piles real good."

General Scheick gave him a long, hard look; then turning on his heel, he strode through the mounted police headquarters muttering, "The damn fool. The damn fool."

As they reached the General's sedan, Colonel Henderson asked, "Now what do we do, sir?"

"I just remembered," General Scheick said, "that Elwood went out to Little Koza in a jeep from the motor pool. Let's go up and talk with the driver. Maybe we can get a lead."

The motor pool was not prepared for a surprise visit from the General either. The sergeant in charge barely had time to shout a warning to those sitting in on the poker game. "Toss the cards in that muffler," he yelled.

But Corporal Majewski had three sevens in a five-card stud game. "Like hell," he said. "I'm not giving up this hand." And spying a comic book, he slipped his cards in between the pages, then picking up the book he pretended to read. So it was that they were lined up in a row of innocence, backs resting against the wall, comic books in hand, when General Scheick and Colonel Henderson drove up.

"Tenshun!" the sergeant in charge called, and the row of innocence leaped to its collective feet.

"Sergeant, who drove my nephew out to Little Koza this morning?" General Scheick asked.

"I did, sir," Corporal Majewski, of the three sevens, said, stepping forward. And Colonel Henderson, his eyes narrowed, surveyed the row of figures, trying to determine what was missing.

"Did you take him anywhere else after you reached Little Koza?" General Scheick questioned.

"Yes, sir. I brought him, the King, and the King's grandmother back into town. They went over to talk to some old man who lives on the Street of the Blue Lanterns."

"Did you take them anywhere from there?"

"Yes, sir. After they talked to this old man, they got back in the jeep and I took them out to Little Koza again."

"They're not at Little Koza now," General Scheick said.

"I know that, sir." Majewski nodded. "Because when we got back out there, they packed a couple of horsecarts that they had. We loaded the jeep, too. And the King and your nephew drove the carts in while I took the King's grandmother up to the castle."

"Castle? What castle?"

"Tamagusuku." Corporal Majewski pointed to the hills beyond the ancient capital. "Up there."

"What did they go up there for?"

"They didn't tell me that, sir. All I know is that's where the whole bunch of them were heading."

General Scheick turned and regarded the hills, while Colonel Henderson was regarding the men before him, and the Colonel's face was stern. He had it now. He knew what was missing when they drove up. That row of innocence hadn't been reading at all; he could tell because their lips hadn't been moving. "Corporal," Colonel Henderson said, "give me that comic book."

"The comic book, sir?"

"Give it to me." Colonel Henderson took it, and as he did so, three sevens fluttered in the breeze. "So you were playing poker on duty. That's the end. Sergeant, collect those cards."

"Yes, sir," the sergeant said and relief swept over him, for he had been in that hand betting a pair of kings against those three sevens.

"Now give them here." Colonel Henderson took the deck and continued. "From now on I want those men kept busy."

"Yes, sir," the sergeant said. "But we've already washed all the vehicles twice today, sir."

"Well, find something else for them."

"Yes, sir. But I can't think of anything. I'd appreciate any suggestions you might have, sir."

Colonel Henderson was stopped. There are no compost piles to be piled around a motor pool, nor are there any to be repiled. Then an idea struck him. "Sergeant," he said, pointing, "have the men restack those empty gasoline drums." And with a feeling of satisfaction and accomplishment, Colonel Henderson went over to the car and took his seat beside General Scheick.

General Scheick, however, had been oblivious to the goings-on about him. He kept staring at the distant hills; and as Colonel Henderson joined him, he said, "Bill, now why in hell do you think they'd want to go up there?"

"It beats me, sir," Colonel Henderson replied. "Unless there's some kind of symbolism involved. Maybe they have to go up there and tell their ancestors they're reporting for duty or something."

"That could be. Let's go up and find out. Have you got the copy of the T/O?"

"I sure have, sir." Colonel Henderson nodded, patting the folded papers in his pocket.

They were only able to go as far as Caroline Drive in the General's sedan, because from there on the road was no more than a seldom-used cart trail. Geographically, Caroline Drive and the American community were located on a shelf about halfway up the highest rise in the Watanabe Hills. It was on top of this rise, the loftiest in the whole Nakashima Islands, that the Castle of Tamagusuku was built by King Satto I in the third century B.C.

From its lofty position not only could one look out over the main Island of Tamashima, but one could also look out over the surrounding East China Sea, and there in the blue distance squatted the other fourteen small Islands of the chain. This site had been selected because of its commanding position, for throughout its history Tamagusuku had always been a fortified castle, with high stone battlements, and rambling quarters to house the men-at-arms who normally lived there.

In 1620, however, after the death of old King Gihon and the Chinese take-over, the Chinese, in order to erase the royal family from the memory of their subjects, had ordered them to abandon their ancestral seat. Thus Tamagusuku was given over to the elements. And for three hundred and forty years the ele-

93

ments had been battering the ancient walls. As General Scheick and Colonel Henderson walked up the cart trail, it was now a castle in name only.

In order to house the great number of people who usually lived there in the old days, the castle had been constructed in a series of ten circular courtyards which were really terraces that descended, like rings, down the hill. The terrace at the peak had contained the royal apartments, with their gardens and pools. A great stone wall separated this terrace from the one just below, which also contained apartments, and gardens, and pools for the aristocracy of higher rank. And so it was, each terrace was walled, each terrace contained quarters for varying groups, and so it was that in those early days, the higher one lived on the peak, the higher was one's social status.

Wild grass now grew in what had once been the flower gardens. It spread amongst the fallen stones of the buildings, covering them, until all one could see were mounds of green. The walls separating the terraces had fared better, however. They still half stood, enabling the general outline of the castle to be recognizable. And these walls were cool and damp beneath the tall pine trees. The cart trail, leading up to the castle, had once carried royalty, but now it was used only by farmers, who took their goats up to pasture in the courtyards. So as General Scheick and Colonel Henderson walked along, here and there a goat would look up at them, bleat, then go back to its grazing.

The officers passed from one courtyard to another, gradually rising on the peak. Entering the topmost courtyard, they spied the King, the Queen Grandmother, and Elwood, seated on the fallen stones, a brazier before them, with a pile of bamboo to one side of them and a few bundles of rice straw to the other. Curiously, General Scheick regarded them, but then he mentally shrugged, for he had more important things on his mind. "Hello," he called, smiling—for a smile is one of the best approaches when presenting a plan.

The three intent figures looked up. "Hi, Uncle Matt. Hello, Colonel," Elwood called. "Come on over and join us."

"Coming over," General Scheick answered jovially; and approaching, he saw they were taking the rice straw and twisting it between the palms of their hands into strands of rope.

"Well, Mr. General . . . Mr. Colonel," King Kenji greeted them. "I didn't expect to see you up here."

"Frankly, we didn't intend to be up here," General Scheick said. "I see you're weaving rope. That's a nice pastime." He looked at the Queen Grandmother, whose old eyes were twinkling. "And how's your grandma this morning, King Kenji? Are her joints any better?"

"No. Not yet."

"Is she taking the bonemeal I gave her?"

"Oh, yes. Just as you directed. And she thanks you once again for bringing it to her. But she would like to know if you would like a cup of tea? The water comes from the well at Little Koza. We brought it in with us."

"No thank you. But why should you bring water from the well at Little Koza?"

"Because the water from the well at Little Koza makes some of the best tea in the world. It contains just the right amount of calcium to bring out the taste of the tea. And it doesn't contain any iron, or salt, or other impurities to ruin it."

"Who would have thought there's any difference in tea," General Scheick said.

"There's a lot of difference," Kenji went on. "And the first consideration in tea-making is always the water. In fact, Mr. General, I just found out myself that the reason the royal family moved to Little Koza after the Chinese threw them out in 1620 was because of the water there."

"Is that right?"

"Yes. They figured there wasn't much left for them; so they decided that at least they were going to have a good cup of tea once in a while, and they moved near the water that would make it."

"That's quite interesting," General Scheick said. "Incidentally, I had occasion to be out in Little Koza today. I see your grandma has her store boarded up."

"Yes, and Grandma would like to know if you saw anyone around it."

"No. No one was bothering it."

"She didn't mean that, Mr. General. The mayor of Little Koza is trying to sell it for her, and she was just wondering if maybe he had a buyer looking at it."

"I didn't see any."

"She was afraid of that."

"What does she mean—afraid?"

"Well, she wants to get rid of it, but it's so hard to find anyone with the capital to buy things that she's afraid she's going to have it on her hands for a long time."

"That could be," General Scheick said and turned to Colonel Henderson. "Bill, may I have a copy of the T/O, please?"

"Yes, sir," Colonel Henderson replied, and as he handed it over, the quivering started in his stomach. For he knew how much depended on the King's yes or no.

"King Kenji," General Scheick said, and it was an effort to keep his voice even. "My staff and I talked it over this morning, and we feel that if the Nakashima Islands are to function as a modern nation, they are going to need a Table of Organization."

"A Table of Organization?" King Kenji questioned. "What is that, Mr. General?"

"Let's put it this way. You want to take your place amongst the nations of the world, don't you?"

"Oh, yes, we want to do that," the King replied.

"All right. Now this chart that we have drawn up will enable you to do so. See, here you have a Prime Minister. He's your number-one man. Then you have a Foreign Minister, and a Minister of Finance."

"Hey!" the King said. "That would work good."

"That's what we figured. Now read it over carefully."

King Kenji did as directed; and when he had finished, he said, "Mr. General, it was certainly nice of you to do this. I'll have to ask Grandma first, but I think this is exactly what I need."

"By all means ask your grandma," General Scheick said, and

watched as the King explained the list to the aged one. She listened, then began questioning, and a muscle twitched in General Scheick's throat.

"What does she say?" the General asked.

"She says she thinks we'll be able to use your Table of Organization."

"You accept it then?"

"Oh, yes, Mr. General," the King replied.

"Good," General Scheick said, beaming. And Colonel Henderson had to shake his head in admiration, for it was just as the General had said it was: when they're fooling around, you prepare a plan for them, and ninety-nine times out of a hundred they'll accept it. "Bill," General Scheick held out his hand, "would you give me the personnel list, please?"

"Yes, sir," Colonel Henderson replied. And now his stomach was calm, his voice confident.

"King Kenji," General Scheick began. "Now that you have a T/O, our next step is to find the men to fill it. We know that you are busy." He indicated the partially woven rope. "So we have gone ahead and drawn up another list. For Prime Minister we recommend Louie Yamaguchi. Here, look at this. With the exception of possibly one man, I think it can stand as it is."

But now the King shook his head, and now the King said, "I'm afraid I won't be able to accept that list, Mr. General."

"No? Oh, I see," General Scheick said. "You mean you can't accept it as long as any member is questionable. That's all right. We'll just cross off Yoshimitsu Matsumoto. He doesn't impress me either."

"No, I mean I won't be able to accept any of it."

General Scheick was disconcerted. "And why can't you accept it?"

"Because of Shinerikyu and Amamikyu."

"Not those two again!"

"Yes, Mr. General. The first son of Shinerikyu and Amamikyu was the first King. And the second son was the first noble. Isn't that right, Elwood?"

"That's right, Uncle Matt," Elwood said. "And it's always

97

been the custom that the advisers to the King are the nobles. That's why Kenji can't accept the list."

"Who told you all that stuff?" General Scheick demanded.

"Yamaguchi Kiei, our leading scholar and historian," the King said.

"When did you see him?"

"This morning."

General Scheick was indignant. "I thought you said you were just going to fool around today."

"I was. But Grandma thought over all the things I said on the platform when I returned. And she thought over all the things Elwood and I told her last night. And the first thing this morning she said, 'Come on, Kenji. We're going to see Mr. Yamaguchi.' So we did, and it's a good thing too."

"Why?"

"Because I never knew the Nakashima Islands had so many problems. Why, Mr. General, do you realize that the lanterns have gone out?"

"Now what does that mean?"

"Well, in the days of old King Gihon there used to be a great trade network. Mr. Yamaguchi said it extended from Japan, to China, to the southern seas. He says the great junks used to glide by our Islands. And things were so good here that our villages were always aglow in celebration. So the traders, passing in the night, would see the lights; and we became known, through this whole part of the world, as the Land of the Lighted Lanterns."

"So what?" General Scheick said.

"So the lanterns have gone out, and now I have to start making up the ground we lost during the Interruption." The King paused. "Mr. General, do you realize the nobles have all been disbanded, and I have to call them back together again?"

General Scheick could hardly believe it. "You mean in this day and age you are going to re-establish the nobility?"

"Oh, sure," King Kenji said. "But before I can do that I have to fix the castle, so they'll have a place to live."

"Are these jokers going to live here, too?"

"They and their retinues. One of the most important things is to re-establish the Court."

"Re-establish the Court!" General Scheick was shattered. He had read all about the decadence of these courts, both in history and in historical fiction. "But you can't be doing that, man!"

"Oh, but I am," the King said. "And see, Grandma and I are moving up here too. We brought all our things in from Little Koza." Kenji pointed toward a clump of tall pines where two two-wheeled carts, loaded with household goods, stood half hidden in the shade, with two Mongolian ponies, one gray and one brown, tethered to their wheels. "And see, Mr. General, Elwood and I are going to use all this bamboo to make the royal apartments."

"That's right, Uncle Matt," Elwood said. "Grandma is showing us how to build a house like they have out in the villages. We use the bamboo for siding, and we're weaving this rice-straw rope to tie it together with; then we're going to get some thatch for the roof. And after we finish the royal apartments, we're going to build some apartments for the nobility."

General Scheick's eyes narrowed suspiciously. "King Kenji, I want to ask you a question. You say you are going to bring the nobles in here to live—"

"The nobles and their retinues."

"All right, the nobles and their retinues. Now what I want to know is: who is going to pay for the support of these people?"

Kenji smiled brightly. "Ah, Mr. General, that's what I want to see you about. Mr. Yamaguchi says that the King must furnish room, board, and a clothing allowance, but the nobles must supply their own spending money."

"So?"

"So I wanted to see you, because Mr. Yamaguchi says that you controlled the Nakashima Islands tax money under the old government."

"And I suppose you want to dip into the Treasury!"

"Yeah, I was thinking about it."

"That's what I thought," General Scheick said and his face grew solemn. "Look, King Kenji, you're making a mistake. How do you think this is going to look to your people—fixing up the castle as your first official act, and then calling in a bunch of nobles to help spend the money?" He eyed the King. "I just came from the countryside. Do you know what the people have done? They have stuck their streamers in the corners of their fields."

"I know, Mr. General," Kenji said. "I saw them."

"I'm glad you did. Those streamers were put there in the first flush of celebration. And I want them kept flying. I don't want them to come down."

"Oh, I don't want them to come down either," the King said.

"All right. Don't monkey around then. Besides, you can't afford this kind of foolishness. You have the finest road system and finest mounted police force in the Far East to maintain and support. Do you know the trouble we went to, to build that police force? Why, it took my Operations officer a year and a half just to match the ponies and get them assigned to the right troops. You can't let something like that go down the drain."

"Yes, but . . ."

"Let's just forget it then."

"But Mr. Yamaguchi has already started to trace the nobles," Kenji protested. "And he is going to notify them that they should be ready to move to the castle with their retinues when the King calls them."

"Well, cancel it," General Scheick said. "And as far as the castle is concerned . . . Look, King Kenji, what do you want to move up to this ruin for? Cottage 15B is vacant. Come down with us. I'll introduce you to the gang, and we'll teach your grandma to play bingo. She'll get a big kick out of it. Go ahead, tell her what I said."

King Kenji translated for his grandmother, who sat with her tattooed hands folded quietly in her lap. She listened to the whole story, then King Kenji said in English, "Grandma says she didn't understand about the roads and police. She didn't know it cost so much money to maintain and support them."

"Those are your major expenditures of government," General Scheick said earnestly. "Of course, you have a few other items such as the post office system and the educational system, but those are of a minor nature."

"Grandma says she understands. She says to bring in and support the nobles, we could probably raise taxes. . . ."

General Scheick was startled. "You can't raise taxes."

"Grandma agrees with you, Mr. General. She says she certainly doesn't want to pay any more. She's tired of taxes. And she's sure everyone else is, too."

A feeling of relief swept over General Scheick. "That's very wise. Very wise, indeed. If you raise taxes, those streamers will come down from the fields for sure." He turned to the old grandmother. She knew what she was doing, General Scheick told himself. She had an innate wisdom, a sense of the appropriate that enabled her to see the right and wrong position in a situation. Then he went on, "King Kenji, ask her if she doesn't agree with me. Ask her if you shouldn't forget all this foolishness about the castle and the nobles."

"All right, Mr. General. I'll ask her." King Kenji spoke to his grandmother, who then looked at the General, looked at her grandson.

"What does she say?" General Scheick asked.

"She says no, she doesn't agree with you."

"But that's completely illogical."

"She doesn't think it is."

"But where are you going to get the money to support an outfit like that?"

King Kenji's forehead wrinkled. "Grandma says I'm the king. That's something I have to figure out."

"Damn," General Scheick muttered and paused in order to sum up the full weight of logical argument behind him. But Grandma Nakamura had picked up a few strands of rice straw. With a twist of her old hands with the blue tattoo marks, she began weaving it into rope to be used to tie together the bamboo siding of the royal apartments. There was a certain finality in her actions that made General Scheick frown and then hesitate. "Well, you think it over again, anyway," he said, and turning he started for the archway leading from the royal courtyards down into the next terrace, with Colonel Henderson trailing after him.

"Sir," Colonel Henderson said, "isn't there any way we can persuade them to listen to reason?"

"How?" General Scheick asked. "They've got the bit between their teeth."

"What are we going to do then, sir?"

"Well, first of all," General Scheick said, "I'm going to send a radiogram to General Winthrope, explaining the situation."

"And then, sir?"

"And then I don't know." General Scheick turned and looked back at the little group.

The grandmother was calmly weaving while the King and his nephew were deep in conversation. "Elwood," King Kenji was saying, "you know, this is just like being back in college."

"How do you mean, Kenji?"

"Well," the King said slowly, "I always needed money then, too. But just like now, I was always broke."

Chapter 7

BECAUSE the King needed money so badly, it was understandable that he should be nervous as he waited for the Thursday morning meeting of the Officers' Wives Investment Club. He and Elwood stood in the hallway of the Community Recreation Center, a one-story Army building which served for children's birthday parties, bingo games, Saturday night dances, and other festivities. The meeting was scheduled for ten o'clock, but already it was five minutes after, because Mrs. Seymour, wife of the Operations Officer, and the Investment Club's expert on Chemicals, had forgotten her volume charts and had to go home for them.

As they waited for her, Kenji whispered, "Elwood, do you think the ladies will go for the idea?"

"I don't know," Elwood replied. "It works all the time back in Iowa, so I don't see why it shouldn't work out here."

"I don't see why it shouldn't, either. But I hope they'll go for it, because I don't know of anybody else who's got money to invest like those ladies." Kenji listened for a moment to the rustle of voices of the women in the room, just beyond. "You're going to do all the explaining, though, aren't you?"

"Yeah, I'll take care of that," Elwood assured him as Mrs. Seymour, volume charts under her arm, came through the screen doors.

She was a large woman and now she was breathing quite heavily. "Well," she said, "I guess we're ready. If you two will just come in here." With a nervous glance at each other, Elwood and the King who needed money so badly turned toward those who had it. For there were fifteen members in the Investment Club. Each month each member put in ten American dollars. At the exchange rate of ten to one, the collected one hundred and fifty American dollars became fifteen hundred Nakashima Islands dollars. And Elwood had learned from his aunt that the Club hadn't invested the previous month, so the ladies had three thousand Nakashima Islands dollars on hand.

The room where the Club met was set up almost like a schoolroom. At the front was a platform, raised about a foot from the floor, and on it was an American flag, three or four chairs, and a large desk. As Elwood and the King entered, Mrs. Scheick, the club president, was seated behind the desk, papers spread out over its surface; while before her sat the other fourteen club members with charts, financial publications, graph paper, and pads stacked on the writing arms of the chairs.

Mrs. Scheick indicated the chairs on the platform. "Elwood, would you and the King sit up here, please?" And when the two youths took their places, she said, "Girls, we're ready."

A hush fell over the room, and Mrs. Scheick continued, "Girls, we have a very distinguished visitor with us today—the King of the Nakashima Islands. King Kenji, would you stand, please?"

Uncertainly, Kenji arose, forced a smile that showed all his white teeth, and as the ripple of polite applause filled the room he nodded shyly two or three times, and sat down again.

"King Kenji," Mrs. Scheick said, "would you care to say a few words?"

Kenji's mouth suddenly became dry. "I don't think so, Mrs. General," he replied. "Elwood said he would do all the explaining."

Mrs. Scheick smiled at him. "Well, it's nice having you with us anyway, Your Majesty." Then, the preliminaries being over, her face grew solemn. "Girls," she began slowly, "my nephew Elwood has asked for time this morning, because he has an investment which he thinks might interest us. He and I have talked this over, as I have already told some of you." Mrs. Scheick's eyes met Irene Henderson's, for it was Irene with whom Mrs. Scheick had discussed it. "And because of the situation, and because I may be partial, I am going to bow out and leave the decision entirely to you."

Once again Mrs. Scheick's eyes met Mrs. Henderson's, and Irene smiled in understanding. For Mrs. Scheick had told her, "This is too good to be true, Irene. Why, if Elwood helps the King with this business out here, he's just one step away from taking over the elevator back home, and my problem is solved." So now Mrs. Henderson crossed her fingers so Mrs. Scheick could see, and Mrs. Scheick continued.

"Girls, please don't let what I might want influence you in any way in this matter. After all, this is business and we are cold, tough traders." She picked up her pile of papers. "Now I'm just going to sit in the back of the room there, and I'm not even going to vote." She arose. "Elwood, the meeting is yours."

"Thank you, Aunt Caroline." Elwood waited for Mrs. Scheick to take a chair, then he turned to the cold, tough traders, as Mrs. Scheick had called them. "Ladies." He smiled his best smile. "First of all I want to thank you on behalf of the King and myself for giving us a part of your very valuable time. It was kind of you." He looked to the ladies for reaction.

At the very least, he expected slight smiles for the appreciation he was showing, but the ladies simply regarded him with unblinking eyes, and he continued. "Please believe me, ladies, I'm not making one cent out of this. I'm only helping the King. Any money we derive will go to bring in the dukes. That's all he asks for now. He's willing to wait until later to bring in the earls, viscounts, and barons."

Elwood hoped that this statement would at least cause a head to nod in understanding; but there was no nod and he knew that, indeed, this was strictly business.

So he went on: "Ladies, the proposition that the King and I have to offer is known as Contract Egg Farming. One summer, back home in Iowa, I fooled aound with some livestock-feeding experiments, so I'm familiar with it. And I believe it should work better out here than back in Iowa even.

"You see, the product involved is eggs. In Iowa they are plentiful. Out here they are practically nonexistent—everybody eats sweet potatoes. That's why the King and I feel that anyone who gets eggs on the market at a popular price is going to make some money. We hope that will be you, ladies, and, of course, us."

At the mention of the word *money*, Elwood could see definite interest. He looked to his aunt, who was nodding encouragement to him, and pressed on. "Now briefly, ladies, here is the way Contract Egg Farming would work out here. First, there would be the Corporation. Let's call it the Nakashima Islands Egg Corporation. That would be you. You would supply the money to buy chickens and feed.

"The second party would be the King and I. Normally, we would agree to house the chickens, which you furnish, care for them, collect and clean the eggs, and turn these eggs over to you for marketing. However, under the circumstances, if you will supply the money, we will do everything except market the eggs. That is, we'll go out to the villages and buy the chickens and feed for you. And all we ask in return is that you pay us six cents, in Nakashima Islands money, for every dozen eggs we produce." Elwood looked around the room. "Does anyone have any questions?"

"Yes," Agnes McCloud said. "Is the stock of this Nakashima Islands Egg Corporation listed on the big board?"

"No, it's not, Mrs. McCloud," Elwood replied. "You see, we're trying to organize the Corporation now."

"Well, one of our Club rules is that we buy only stock listed on the New York or American Stock Exchanges."

"I see." Worriedly, Elwood glanced at his aunt, who seemed apprehensive.

"Elwood," Mrs. Seymour began, "at what price-to-earnings ratio is this stock selling?"

A frown crossed Elwood's forehead. "I really don't know if you can figure that here. We had planned on marketing the stock of the Corporation at one Islands dollar per share."

"Have you earned anything yet?" Agnes McCloud asked.

"Why, no, Mrs. McCloud. We're just organizing."

"Well, if you haven't earned a cent," Agnes said, "and the stock is priced at a dollar a share, you're selling at over a hundred times earnings. Our rule is never to pay more than fifteen times earnings for any stock."

"But, Mrs. McCloud," Elwood protested, "couldn't that be figured another way?"

"I don't see how," Agnes stated. "Besides, I have another question: What margin of profit does this Nakashima Islands Egg Corporation make on its product?"

"Gosh," Elwood said. "It's never marketed a product yet."

"Well, it wouldn't come within our twenty per cent rule, then."

"I guess it wouldn't, Mrs. McCloud, but . . ."

Agnes shook her head. "There are dozens of questions I could ask you, Elwood, but just from these few I think it's evident that this Nakashima Islands Egg Corporation, which you want us to set up, is really not much of an investment."

From the looks on their faces it was evident that the majority of women were in agreement with Agnes. Desperately, Elwood glanced at his aunt. "Well, I guess it isn't," he said slowly. "I guess the truth is that it's an outright speculation."

As he mentioned the word *speculation*, Elwood was conscious of a little flurry amongst the women. Puzzled, he regarded them and saw a flicker of interest amongst the cold, hard traders. Mrs. Seymour, of Chemicals, bit her lip. Mrs. Carlisle, of Utilities, bit the end of her pencil, and Agnes McCloud asked, "Elwood, is this much of a speculation?"

"I'm afraid it is," Elwood replied. "In fact, I guess maybe it's sort of like a horse race."

107

"A horse race. Then there's a chance of making an awful lot of money out of it, isn't there?" Agnes questioned.

"That's possible."

"Do you think we could make, perhaps, five hundred per cent profit on our money?" Mrs. Seymour asked.

"If this hits, five hundred per cent wouldn't even touch it," Elwood replied. "In a normal market, eggs ought to sell for at least a dollar a dozen. And apart from the feed, you're only paying us six cents a dozen to produce them, so—"

"And do you know," Agnes McCloud cut in, "we could plow back our profit. Buy more chickens. You and the King could handle them for us, couldn't you, Elwood?"

"We'll handle all you can get."

"Elwood, are eggs really so scarce out here?" Mrs. Henderson asked.

"Terrifically scarce, Mrs. Henderson. Just to give you an idea of their value here, the greatest thing that can happen to a family is to have a child born to it. And to announce a birth, the people give colored eggs to their friends. So you can see that eggs are considered very valuable."

"I think that's a very sweet custom," Mrs. Henderson said.

"And I think it should be encouraged," Agnes McCloud added. "And you know, there are so many other things we could do to promote the sale of eggs. For instance, we could have a booklet printed in which each of us includes her favorite egg recipes. These people are probably out of the habit of eating them, so we'll reacquaint them with the many wonderful ways in which eggs can be used."

"That's a good idea," Mrs. Seymour said. "Now take egg salad sandwiches. They would be excellent for the lunch buckets of the farmers and workers."

Kenji raised his hand. He wanted to tell Mrs. Seymour that here, in the Nakashima Islands, no one carried lunch buckets and that there was no bread. So he felt duty bound to warn her that he didn't think egg salad sandwiches would be very popular. But no one was paying any attention to him.

"Girls," Agnes McCloud was saying, "I think we ought to put

108

in an extra twenty dollars apiece, because this sounds like such a good thing. That will give us six thousand Nakashima Islands dollars, and we can buy twice as many chickens."

"I'll be happy to put up the extra money," Mrs. Seymour said. "But first, I think we should organize. Do you agree?"

The Club agreed, and Irene Henderson said, "Well, for the chairman of the board then, I nominate Mrs. Scheick."

"I second the motion," Agnes McCloud said. And as a chorus of "ayes" arose, answering the question "All in favor," Irene Henderson turned to Mrs. Scheick. "Well, Caroline, it looks like you're it."

The chairman of the board was touched. "That's so kind of you," she said, looking at her nephew. "And I appreciate it for more reasons than one. But getting down to business, I, also, would like to make a nomination. I nominate Irene Henderson as president of the Nakashima Islands Egg Corporation."

King Kenji was confused. "Elwood," he whispered, "are they going to invest money or not?"

Elwood was also puzzled. "I don't know," he replied, "but it sounds to me like they already bought it." He glanced back at the ladies, heard Irene Henderson seconded as president, and voted in; heard Mrs. Seymour nominated and seconded as a vice-president, and heard Agnes McCloud become treasurer.

Things were still moving awfully fast when his aunt said, "Elwood, now that we are organized, as chairman of the board I'd like to know when you can get into production."

"You mean you have officially bought the Nakashima Islands Egg Corporation?" he asked.

The ladies glanced at him as if he were backward. "Of course."

"I just wanted to be sure," Elwood said apologetically. "Now for production. When could the treasurer turn the money over to us . . . however much it is?"

"It's six thousand Islands dollars," Agnes McCloud said. "I can get half of it for you now, just as soon as I collect the extra twenty dollars in U. S. from the girls. And I can get the other half, which is our regular investment money, in about five minutes. It's home in the dresser beneath my personal things."

"Good." Elwood rubbed his hands. "In that case, the King and I could start out tomorrow morning buying chickens for you. And let's see, today is June 20 . . . I'd say by July 20 we'll have the flock built up."

"How much does a chicken cost?" Irene Henderson, the president, asked.

"The King says, as he remembers it, a pullet—that's a young hen—sells for about a dollar apiece in the villages."

"So that means we can buy six thousand chickens," Agnes stated.

"No, Mrs. McCloud. You also have to feed them, so you'll have to spend some money on that."

"Oh, darn," Agnes said.

"Besides," Elwood went on, "the King and I want to ask you ladies for a favor. We were wondering if you would lend us, say, a thousand dollars against production?"

"Why?" Agnes McCloud asked.

"Because if Kenji gets the thousand dollars advance he can afford to bring in the dukes."

"I didn't mean that. I meant why should we?"

It was a hard question to answer, and Elwood looked desperately at his aunt, who said, "Girls, that might not be too bad an idea. If Elwood and the King had an advance, it would give them incentive."

"But it means buying a thousand less chickens for us," Agnes protested.

The chairman of the board realized that she was going to have difficulty. "Well, let's see then if we can't work something out," she suggested.

"Like what?" Agnes asked.

Mrs. Scheick thought rapidly. "Well, suppose we give the boys an advance. That is doing them quite a favor, and in return they should do something for us. Suppose instead of charging us six cents for every dozen eggs produced, they lower it to five? How does that sound, Agnes?"

"I don't know," Agnes replied. "How many dozens of eggs will they be producing a year?"

"Well," Elwood said, "suppose we hold back a thousand for feed, and a thousand for an advance. That still gives you four thousand dollars, and consequently four thousand chickens. I don't know how it is out here, but back home in Iowa we can easily get two hundred eggs per chicken per year. If we can duplicate that, that means 800,000 eggs, or about 66,600 dozens."

Agnes' eyes widened as she calculated a savings of $660. "That idea sounds good to me," she said. "I'm for it."

"And the rest of you girls?" Mrs. Scheick asked.

The rest were for it, too.

"Now then, Elwood," Mrs. Scheick went on. "If we advance you a thousand, will you and King Kenji take five instead of six cents a dozen?"

"Mrs. General," Kenji said, "we'll even take—"

"Five is fine," Elwood broke in hurriedly.

"Good." Mrs. Scheick nodded. "We authorize you then to withhold one thousand Islands dollars from the money Mrs. McCloud turns over to you. Well, I guess that's settled," she said in relief. "Does anyone have any questions?"

"I do," Agnes said. "Now 66,600 dozens of eggs a year means about 180 dozens a day. How much a dozen can we sell these eggs for?"

"As I said before," Elwood replied, "a dollar a dozen ought to be a fair price, even with a plentiful supply on the market."

"So that means that every day we're out of production, we lose $180."

Here and there the members of the Club glanced at each other. "That's right, we do, don't we?" Mrs. Seymour agreed.

"We certainly do," Agnes continued. "Now I don't see why it's going to take Elwood and the King until July 20 to build the flock. That's a full month."

"Well, ladies," Elwood explained. "The King and I have to finish the royal apartments. Then we have to construct quarters for the dukes. So if we allow ourselves plenty of time, not only can we do those things, but we can also go around buying chickens for you and build coops for them. We didn't realize you were in such a hurry."

"You'd be in a hurry, too," Agnes said, "if you were losing $180 a day."

Elwood looked at the cold, tough traders, and it was easy to tell that he didn't have any backing in this matter, so he asked, "How long would you say would be an adequate time, Mrs. McCloud?"

Agnes considered. "I think you ought to be able to round up four thousand chickens in a week."

"A week!" Elwood looked to his aunt.

"Why don't we do this?" Mrs. Scheick said. "Why don't we give them until July 4? That's two weeks."

Two weeks was fine with the girls, and although Elwood had his doubts, still he knew it was the best he and Kenji could do.

"But you have to promise," Agnes said, "that you'll give our chickens top priority. I mean you won't put the dukes ahead of them, will you, King Kenji?"

"Oh, I wouldn't do that," Kenji said. "And just to prove it, Mrs. McCloud, I won't call the dukes and their retinues in until July 4. That way there'll be no partiality."

"Good," Agnes said briskly and arose from her chair. "Mrs. Scheick, shall I collect the extra twenty dollars apiece now? Then I can take the boys over home and get the other half. That way they can get started before lunch yet."

Elwood looked at Kenji. Kenji looked at Elwood. Then they both looked at their watches. It was 11:10.

"If you wish, Agnes," Mrs. Scheick said.

"We don't want to lose any time." Quickly Agnes started to make the collection.

"Ladies," Elwood said as Agnes began going from member to member, "I just want to say thanks for your kindness."

"And I want to say thanks too," Kenji joined in. "I sure appreciate it."

"That's all right," Mrs. Scheick, the chairman of the board, spoke for all of them. "I'm sure that this is going to be very profitable for all of us." And she smiled in satisfaction.

Agnes McCloud had a thought then. She stopped, her eyes

wide. "Girls," she began, "I have a wonderful idea. On that booklet of egg recipes we're going to prepare, instead of giving them away, don't you think we can sell them?"

A chorus arose. "Oh, no, we couldn't do that!" the club members protested.

"Well, it was worth a try," Agnes said, and somewhat disappointed, she continued taking up her collection for the King.

Chapter 8

THE Fourth of July had always been a fun day in the command. As the sun rose high, General and Mrs. Scheick had always led the motorcade out from the ancient capital of Tamabaru, out to Big Shamoji Beach. And there, beside the East China Sea, the picnic tables were set up and loaded with the potluck offering of potato salad and baked beans, cole slaw and molded gelatine salads, ham and fried chicken, and every conceivable delicacy the Supply Officer could bring in from the States.

It had always been a fun day, indeed, with firecrackers and games for the little tykes, croquet and softball for the grownups; with three-legged races, and egg-carrying races. And always leading the fun and winning most of the events was General Scheick, bronzed and full of vim, his hair rumpled by the wind and his head thrown back in laughter.

But there was no picnic this Fourth of July. General Scheick had canceled it, and now he sat in his office with the Venetian blinds pulled to shut out the sun. He sat quietly and alone in the semidarkness with a radiogram in his hand, a radiogram which read:

ON THIS GLORIOUS DAY I WANT TO REMIND YOU OF BASIC PRINCIPLES. I WANT TO REMIND YOU THAT ALL MEN ARE CREATED FREE AND EQUAL. AND I EXPECT YOU TO KEEP IT THAT WAY.

(*Signed*) MOSBY

For a long while General Scheick sat there, deep in thought; then, reaching into his desk, he brought out a letter from his old friend and mentor, and now commanding officer. A letter received immediately after he had reported on his failure to place Louie and Henry Yamaguchi as Prime and Foreign Minister respectively. And once again, for the hundredth time, he read it:

DEAR PUG:

I am astounded and amazed. Your plan to place the proper men in government was laudable and your efforts were sincere. But what has happened to you? How in the name of heaven could you be so concerned over the failure of a plan not to realize what you have let happen out there?

Do you realize that by letting those people re-establish the nobility you have slapped the common man in the face? Do you realize that by letting them establish this leprous system of class, you have struck a blow at the very heart of democracy?

Not only am I astounded and amazed, but I am shattered. I have never felt fear before, yet now I am afraid, so much so that we have resolved not to let a word of this out of the corridors of the Pentagon, for I would not want to be responsible for what might happen should this become generally known.

To give you an example. A few nights ago I had occasion to attend a buffet supper given by Mrs. Carhart Inglehorn. During the course of the evening, I had a chance to talk with Congressman Homer Hoplow of Kansas, and I said, "Mr. Hoplow, what would you think of the idea of establishing a nobility in . . ." Here I was being very cagey, so as not to reveal any information. ". . . in America?"

Frankly, Pug, I have never heard such a bitter tirade delivered off the floor of the House of Representatives. "If we ever sank so low as to allow this group of entrenched privilege to gain a foothold here," Congressman Hoplow said, "the sunflower would hang its head in shame. The flag would fly at half-mast in Topeka. No longer would the cry of 'Fly High with Hoplow' ring across the Kansas countryside, for I, personally, would go into mourning. And the great state, which is my home, would, I assure you, secede from the union forevermore."

Congressman Hoplow only said the above by way of introduction, his entire statement being too lengthy to reproduce. But I assure you, he grew more bitter as he went along. So how could you have let it happen, man?

We cannot have a society of class! We must have a classless society!

(*Signed*) MOSBY

General Scheick put down the letter, once again read the radiogram, then slowly turned in his swivel chair. Out past the drawn blinds, out in the Islands of the chain, the dukes were already packing. The class of entrenched privilege was about to descend on the capital. But how could he stop them? Still, he was the one who was responsible for keeping all men free and equal. He ran his hand over his eyes, and his face was lined with worry.

Up in the Watanabe Hills, Mrs. Scheick's face was also lined with worry, although as chairman of the board she did her best to conceal it from the other directors and officers of the Nakashima Islands Egg Corporation. She walked at the head of the little group in their summery dresses, making their way up from Caroline Drive to inspect their flocks of chickens in Tamagusuku Castle, and the chatter behind her was light and filled with enthusiasm.

For as they passed from terrace to terrace they could see the chicken coops—low, squat affairs woven of reeds, with reed runways. "Well," Mrs. Henderson, the president, said, "it certainly looks as if the boys have been working." And all had to agree, for the home-woven coops were scattered everywhere.

They entered a courtyard once used by minor nobility, whereupon the cackling of chickens reached them, a sound which brought smiles to their lips. "My," Agnes McCloud said, "isn't that pretty?"

Again there was agreement by all except Mrs. Scheick, who kept her eyes straight ahead, who led her directors and officers up the path, through the courtyards of the dukes and into the royal enclosure at the very summit.

In the old days, the royal apartments were sprawling, spacious things of gray stone. Today, the royal apartments consisted of a neat little ⊓ shaped bamboo house, with a clean thatch roof. But the ladies weren't concerned with the royal apartments. The ladies were concerned with eggs.

Mrs. Scheick looked about the royal enclosure and could see no one. However, the sound of hammering came from within the apartments; and hearing it, she called, "Elwood! King Kenji!"

Within the apartments, Elwood and the King recognized the voice, paused in their work, eyed each other, then Elwood said, "Oh, Marie! Here they come."

Kenji peeked out through the doorway. "Elwood," he said. "I think on this one we both better do the talking. Okay?"

"Okay," Elwood replied, and together, with hammers in hand, they walked out to meet the ladies.

The King's grandmother also had heard the call. Seeing the ladies, she smiled, waved to them, and hurried as fast as her aching joints would permit along the opened veranda in order to meet them in the center section of the ⊓ .

The ladies returned her smile and wave. "Well, good morning," Mrs. Scheick said, and while her voice was gay, her heart was heavy. "How is everyone this morning?"

Not so good, I think, Kenji thought to himself, but aloud he said, "Well, we're pretty busy, Mrs. General." Grandma, in her old banana-cloth kimono and reed sandals, spoke then, and he added, "But Grandma says it is so nice of you ladies to come up. She wonders if you won't join us on the veranda? She is sorry we have no pillows to sit on, but she says the floor is clean."

The ladies could see that the floor was clean. However, there was the problem of the skirts. "Well," Mrs. Scheick said, "it would be a little more convenient if we sat on the edge."

"Ah, so. Grandma understands." The aged one looked at the

summery apparel of the women, and Kenji went on, "Grandma says your dresses are so bright and so pretty. She likes color and brightness, and she only wishes that we had more of it here in the Islands."

"Tell her," Mrs. Scheick said, "that I think her kimono is very nice." And as a clean, fresh breeze swept in from the East China Sea, causing a windbell to tinkle somewhere within the royal apartments, she added, "And tell her I think this is delightful."

"She thanks you. She, too, likes the breeze." King Kenji pointed. "And she likes to look out there at the other Islands in the blue. But about her kimono Grandma says when you wear the same brown every day, you sure get tired of it in a hurry. But she wonders if she may ask you a personal question?"

"Why, of course."

"Well, she noticed that on the day that I came home all you ladies, sitting on the platform, were wearing pretty hats and pretty white gloves. Now, she notices, you are not wearing them. She is curious about that."

"I see. It's this way," Mrs. Scheick explained. "Hats and gloves indicate a certain degree of formality. A ceremony, such as the King's return, calls for them."

"Ah. And on what other occasion would you wear them?"

"Let's put it this way," Mrs. Scheick said. "We wear hats and gloves when we want to appear *more* dressed up."

King Kenji translated; then said, "Grandma likes that. She likes the idea of giving everyone a sign of your intentions. Would you wear them in the afternoon when you went around visiting friends?"

"Yes, you might."

"Ah, so," Kenji spoke for his grandmother, whose face crinkled in thought.

Agnes McCloud, however, was growing impatient. "Excuse me," she cut in. "King Kenji, where are you storing the eggs that you are producing for us?"

Kenji glanced at Elwood; and Mrs. Scheick, who had been in constant consultation with the two youths on the project, knew it had to be faced. "Girls," she began, "there aren't many eggs to be stored."

"But with four thousand chickens!" Agnes exclaimed.

"I'm afraid we have only two hundred," Elwood said.

"Only two hundred!" Mrs. Seymour gasped, and Agnes added, "Haven't you two been working?"

"Sure, we've been working," Elwood said. "We've been working so hard that we didn't even have time to build quarters for the dukes. In fact, we didn't even have time to finish up the royal apartments." He held up his hammer. "That's what we're trying to do now, because we got to have some place for them to stay when they come in this afternoon; and the only thing we can do is move them in with the King."

"We sure have been working," Kenji joined in. "Every day we've been going around to the villages with our carts trying to buy chickens."

"Yes, girls," Mrs. Scheick said. "I'll vouch for that. They have been working. And I've been going out myself, in the General's sedan, trying to buy chickens too."

"Well, why do we only have two hundred chickens then?" Agnes questioned.

"For the simple reason," Mrs. Scheick said, "there are no chickens in the villages to be bought."

"But I've been through some villages," Agnes said. "I've seen chickens wandering around."

"That's just the trouble." Elwood faced the ladies. "They were wandering around. Believe me, out here a chicken is strictly on its own, picking up what it can find. They don't feed chickens here like they do back in Iowa."

"Why not?" Agnes asked.

"Because they don't have the feed. A chicken needs grain, and the only grain grown here is rice—so little, in fact, that it is never used as everyday food."

"That's right, ladies," Kenji joined in. "We only use a little rice now and then for ceremony, such as on the day of the Festival of the Kites."

"Well, you're the King," Agnes said. "Why don't you encourage these people to grow rice? Then we'd have plenty of chicken feed."

"I couldn't do that," Kenji explained. "You see, if a farmer puts an acre of ground into sweet potatoes, he'll get maybe eight hundred bushels during the course of the year. If he puts the same acre in rice, he'll get maybe twenty bushels."

"Why didn't you think of all this before you took our money?" Agnes demanded. "You certainly should have known what the situation was."

"But I didn't know." The King's face was sober and solemn. "Why, I never even thought about eggs until we went into business."

"And you haven't produced any eggs at all for us?" Mrs. Seymour asked.

"Oh, yes," Elwood said. "We've produced ten dozen to date."

"Only ten dozen!" Agnes exclaimed. "According to my figures, you should have produced two hundred dozen by now."

"I think it's a good thing we didn't produce two hundred dozen," Kenji stated. "You see, first of all rice costs five Islands dollars per pound. It would take about three pounds of rice, or fifteen dollars' worth, to produce one dozen of eggs, which sells, at the moment, for two dollars. So, ladies, by not producing, we have saved you thirteen dollars a dozen."

"You saved us . . . well, really!" Agnes exclaimed. "I think you better give us back the thousand dollars we advanced you."

"But if I do that, how can I support the dukes and their retinues?" King Kenji asked. "Through the kindness of you ladies, they are coming in this afternoon. The people all know it. Everybody knows it. It's too late to call it off."

"That's not our problem," Agnes said coldly. "If you're not going to make a profit, and pay dividends and things, I think we better liquidate."

Kenji regarded the ladies. With the exception of Mrs. Scheick, who seemed extremely worried, and Mrs. Henderson, who seemed uncertain, the ladies had a certain look of determination on their faces which spelled the end. Desperately he turned to his grandmother and a torrent of Japanese poured from his lips as he explained the situation. Then Grandma began speaking slowly. "Grandma says to tell you ladies that she knows exactly how you feel. She ran a store, and she knows how it is to have all your money go out and no profit come in. But she believes that if you can find a way to market eggs at a dollar a dozen and earn a profit at that figure, you're going to make a fortune. She knows because she has seen what the people want in Little Koza, and Little Koza is just like all the villages."

"But how can you sell eggs at a dollar a dozen when feed costs five dollars a pound?" Agnes McCloud wanted to know.

"Grandma says that is the big problem. However, she feels that if you will give us a little more time, why then we could take the eggs, hatch chicks, and build your flock up to the four thousand that you want. And all the time we're building your flock, we'll be working on the feed problem."

"What if you can't solve it?" Agnes asked. "No one has been able to solve it before. If they had, you'd have chickens all over the place."

"Grandma says no one has had a reason to solve it before. You just don't go around solving things for the dickens of it. You have to have a reason."

A silence fell over the group, caused mainly by indecision. Uncertainty was in Agnes McCloud's eyes—on the one hand she could see the Nakashima Islands dollars rolling in; on the other hand she could see them going out. There was uncertainty in Mrs. Scheick's eyes, too. She wanted to keep Elwood in this for the sake of the family business; yet as chairman of the board of the Nakashima Islands Egg Corporation, she had to consider her sister club members and their investment. She hesitated for a moment longer, then determination swept across her face. "Girls," she began, "I think it's worth a try. I think we should give the King and Elwood more time. What do you say, Irene?"

Irene Henderson's years of Army service came to the fore. "I think you're right, Caroline," she said to the General's wife. "I think we should, too. Do you agree, girls?"

The girls agreed with the Executive Officer's wife, and Mrs.

Scheick said, "I think we have made a wise move." Yet she could tell that Agnes was thinking, and when Agnes was thinking it wasn't good, so she added quickly, "Why don't you girls start putting together our booklet on egg recipes?"

"That would be an excellent idea," Irene Henderson picked it up. "Why don't we stop into the Officers' Club and have some coffee and get this project going?"

"Yes, why don't you girls go ahead?" Mrs. Scheick prompted.

"Aren't you coming with us?" Agnes asked.

"I'll join you in a little while. There are a couple of details I want to iron out." Mrs. Scheick glanced at Irene.

"Come on, girls, we might as well go then," Irene said, rising. "Good-by, everyone."

The girls arose, said their good-bys; and as Irene Henderson led them off, Mrs. Scheick breathed deeply in relief. "You know, boys," she said, "we were lucky to get this extension of time."

"We sure were," King Kenji agreed fervently. "And Grandma says we better make good use of it, because there's not going to be another chance. That's why she wants to know, Elwood, how we should go about hatching these eggs."

"Well, we can't build up a flock of four thousand chickens by setting eggs under hens," Elwood replied. "We have to have incubators. If I could get some tin and some sources of heat . . ."

"I believe I could get you tin," Mrs. Scheick said. "I'll phone the Quartermaster. And you want just anything that will give heat?"

"Anything. Then Kenji and I can improvise incubators. Of course, we can't start this afternoon, because we have the dukes and their retinues coming in."

"Well, please start just as soon as you can."

The youths nodded, and Grandma spoke. "Mrs. General," Kenji said, "Grandma wonders if the ladies wouldn't feel better if they had a little money coming in?"

"I'm sure they would, especially Mrs. McCloud."

"Well, she has a suggestion. She remembers when she was just a little girl, she went with her grandma and grandpa to a wedding ceremony over in the village of Goya, that's the chief village in our township. She remembers that they had some of the most wonderful food she has ever tasted. And one of the things she remembers is a kind of egg they had. They called it a hundred-year-old egg. She had never seen it before, nor has she seen it since, so it must have been a tremendous luxury. But it was so rich and good that she can still taste it. And she wonders why we couldn't make these hundred-year-old eggs? Why we couldn't market them and have money coming in? People should be willing to pay a little premium for a luxury. And with a premium tacked on, maybe we could make a profit."

"That's a wonderful idea," Mrs. Scheick said. "But does it really take a hundred years for them to age?"

"No, Grandma feels there must be a process to it."

"Can she find out?"

"She is not sure, but she will ask Yamaguchi Kiei to see if our history says anything about them. At any rate, she says let's put it on this basis: if she can get the recipe or process, whichever it is, how would it be if we hatch half of the eggs from the two hundred chickens we have on hand and make the other half into hundred-year-old eggs?"

"That's fine with me," Mrs. Scheick replied. "And if we can only find some feed for these chickens . . ."

"That is one thing Grandma says we must all put our minds to." The breeze from the East China Sea came then, and Grandma put her head back to catch its coolness. "Mrs. General," Kenji continued, "Grandma wants me to tell you how much she likes the idea of your Investment Club."

"Does she really?"

"Yes, and the thing that amazes her is that no one out here has ever thought of them."

"Well," Mrs. Scheick said, "I believe the idea is comparatively new, even in America."

"But they are so much like our mutual loan societies which old King Gihon introduced. Both have members, and the members put in so much money each month. It is only the time element and the use of the money that differ."

"How do they differ?"

"As for time, a Mutual Loan Association lasts only long enough for all the members to borrow from it. Then it comes to an end. But your Investment Club goes on and on."

"Providing there are no serious differences of opinion amongst the members."

"Ah, yes. As for the use of the money, in a Mutual Loan Association the members loan to each other and share in each other's hardships. While your Investment Club loans to a business and shares in the profit."

"If there is a profit."

"If there is a profit," Kenji said and waited for his grandmother to continue, but she looked out to sea and gazed at the other islands in the distance. Then he went on slowly, "Grandma says she only wishes that she had known about these investment clubs years and years ago."

"Oh?" Mrs. Scheick regarded the aged one curiously. "And may I ask why?"

"It's just that, Grandma says, if she could have gotten her hands on some money, that is, some money which she could have used for a long period of time, she wouldn't have had a store only in Little Koza. She would have had a store in Goya, the chief village in the township. She would have had a store in Tamabaru, the capital." King Kenji gestured toward the blue distance. "And she says she would have had stores out there, too."

Chapter 9

I T WAS always a simple matter to tell at what time anyone was going to arrive at Tamabaru, the ancient capital, whether they be coming from one of the other Islands of the chain or from the outside world, for the only way to get into Tamabaru was by water. At low tide the estuary formed by the meeting of the Tamsui River and the East China Sea was a mud flat with a bare trickle of water, ebbing, flowing back into the sea. But at high tide it was a clear, blue avenue of approach for the sampans that plied between the Islands, or the amphibian planes coming from Okinawa. So one simply calculated high tide by means of the lunar calendar, and one knew.

The tide on July 4 began running at 2:16 P.M. At 1:45 P.M. the unsmiling General Scheick, with the unsmiling Colonel Henderson beside him, stepped from his sedan onto the stone quayside, surveyed the crowd gathered there and said, "Look, Bill, they're flying their damn pennants again."

It was true. The farmers had taken their bamboo poles with the red and white streamers from the corners of their fields and had carried them into town to welcome their dukes, just as they had welcomed their King. But now there was no platform and no mounted police so the crowd had more room, and the people spilled out onto the old quayside, held back only by politeness and respect.

"You know, Bill," General Scheick went on, his eyes on the sea of bronzed faces, "I can't figure this out. Here this . . . this group of entrenched privilege is coming in to take over, and these damn fools seem happy about it."

Colonel Henderson had to agree that they did seem happy about it, for the people were laughing, and grinning, and bowing. "I can't figure it either, sir," he said. "But if you ask me, they should be down on their knees thanking us. If it wasn't for us keeping the King from dipping into the treasury, they'd be paying for all this."

"You're right there," General Scheick said; and turning, spotted Yoshimitsu Matsumoto, chief of mounted police, coming down the quayside, giving directions to Jiro Kamakura, his executive officer, who, in turn, relayed them to two policemen, one carrying a chair and the other a homemade desk.

"Ah, Mr. General, Mr. Colonel." Yoshimitsu began smiling. "It is good to see you again. And it is nice of you to come down to welcome the dukes."

Major General Mosby Winthrope's letter flashed across General Scheick's mind, and mentally he cringed. "I didn't come down to welcome the dukes," he said coldly. "I came down to see that all men remain free and equal."

A puzzled look swept across Yoshimitsu's face, but being unable to fathom it, he shrugged. "Well, that's nice. But won't you join us? We're going to put the desk and chair on the third quay, up ahead, and land the dukes and their retinues there."

"What's the desk and chair for?"

"They're for Yamaguchi Kiei, our leading historian and scholar. He's recording this for posterity, so we want him to have a good seat."

"What do you mean—he's recording it for posterity?"

"He's going to write it down so it will be in the accounts of our history. We keep records on everything. You look in the scrolls and you can read all about King Satto leaving to pay tribute to the Japanese, or King Eiso taking a bride. It's very interesting."

"That's a matter of opinion," General Scheick said. But he could see that if they were going to land the dukes on the third quay ahead, he had better move up. For he wanted a good look at this so-called nobility, these men who, according to custom, acted as advisers to the King, so that he could protect the interest of the common man. Turning, he started toward the quay with Colonel Henderson and Yoshimitsu following.

As he neared it, Yamaguchi Kiei, ink and brushes in one hand, a scroll in the other, saw him and began smiling. "Ah, Mr. General. It is kind of you to join us on this great day. But it is a sad day, too, is it not? Just think, we used to have fifteen dukes, one for each Island. But twelve duchies have passed from existence, including the Duchy of Tamashima, this, the main Island. Now only three dukes remain."

"Only three dukes remain?" General Scheick questioned, a rising note of hope in his voice.

"That is correct. There is the Duke of Tatami Oshima, or Mat Island. It was called that because it was the center of our mat-making industry twenty-two hundred years ago. He is the senior duke. Then next in order is the Duke of Tōfu Shima, or Beancurd Island. They used to make a very famous beancurd there. And the third duke is the junior duke. He is the Duke of Take Shima, the Duke of Bamboo Island."

"So only three are left," General Scheick repeated. "That's very interesting."

The two policemen had come up with the desk and chair, set them down on the quay. Yoshimitsu surveyed their placement, then, just to make sure, he slipped into the chair to assure posterity of a good view. Satisfied, he arose and called, "Mr. Yamaguchi, I think we are ready."

"I thank you." The aged one looked out toward the East China Sea where eight or ten sampans hovered, waiting to come in. "Mr. General," he said slowly, "there is a very good sign here today, a very good omen."

"How's that?"

"It concerns the tide. We never do anything on a low tide, such as move into a new house, or have a ceremony, because a low tide indicates ebb and withdrawal. But the high tide, a high tide indicates increase and fullness. And have you noticed? The dukes are going to land on such a tide."

General Scheick regarded the sea of mud between the quay and the outer harbor. "I don't see how they could get in on any other tide. If they'd try walking in through that stuff, they'd sink over their heads."

The aged one held up a finger. "Ah, but it is the symbolism that counts." Then a troubled look came into his eyes. "I cannot understand one thing, however. The dukes must have small retinues. See, there is only one sampan each from Mat, Beancurd, and Bamboo Islands. Small retinues are not good."

To General Scheick, small retinues seemed like excellent things—the only thing better would be no retinues at all. "Well, personally," he said, "I don't go for all this royal pomp and ceremony."

"But the idea of the retinues was not meant for pomp and ceremony," the aged one said quickly. "Old King Gihon did not have that in mind at all when he established them."

"He didn't?"

"Most certainly not. King Gihon wanted the dukes to comb their Islands for the most intelligent young men and bring them into court so they could observe and learn the latest in music, and culture, and new ideas. Then, when they went home, they would carry all this back to the other people. Do you not think old King Gihon had a good plan?"

As General Scheick thought of it, he had to admit that maybe old King Gihon had something. In fact, he was sorry he hadn't known about this before, because they could have staffed headquarters with some of the youngsters from the outer islands, could have exposed them to American ways and methods. In such a situation, with ideas rampant, the plan would have been outstanding, but now . . . He looked up at the castle and shrugged.

Down at the far end of the quayside a cheer arose. "Ah, here comes the King," Yamaguchi Kiei said. "I must get ready." Going over to the desk, he unrolled the scroll, took up a brush, then raised his head to the blue, cloudless sky, for surely posterity would want to know what kind of a day it was.

The cheer began to spread. The streamers began to wave. And General Scheick saw the King and his nephew coming down the quayside, each leading a little Mongolian pony which was hitched to a two-wheeled cart. "Well, I'll be damned," he said, for seated on a box in the cart whose pony Elwood was leading, was the Queen Grandmother.

As he watched, the Queen Grandmother leaned forward, whispered to her grandson; and the King, deep in conversation with Elwood, looked up and became conscious of the crowd. He began smiling and acknowledging the cheers. Elwood joined him, and they came down the quayside, the three of them, waving and bowing, as the shouts of "One hundred thousand years to our King . . . one hundred thousand years to the Queen Grandmother" arose louder and louder over the ancient capital at Tamabaru.

Quickly, Yoshimitsu Matsumoto stepped forward. "Your Majesty," he said, "we're going to unload them over here. If you please." He gestured.

"Okay, Mr. Matsumoto," the King said, "we'll back the carts around so we can load their baggage." Seeing the aged historian, he bowed. "Hello, Mr. Yamaguchi. And Mr. General, Mr. Colonel, how are you?"

"Fine." General Scheick looked at the Queen Grandmother, who was smiling at him. "And how's your grandma?"

"Not so good. She says we have a saying that going downhill, no one is old. But she has just come downhill, and in a cart, too, and she knew she was old every inch of the way."

"That's too bad." General Scheick pointed. "Incidentally, where did you get those carts and ponies?"

"Oh, Grandma owns them. When she ran the store out in Little Koza, she used to rent them out so farmers could take their sweet potatoes to market."

"I see. Well, has your grandma been taking the bonemeal I gave her?"

"Oh, yes. She's been taking it regularly, and her joints are maybe a little worse."

General Scheick considered. "In that case, I better prescribe something else. King Kenji, will you tell her that I think we're going to have to oil them?"

At the little desk the ancient historian, who was busy writing, paused and looked up. "Excuse me, Mr. General," he began, "but what are you going to do?"

"Oil her joints."

The old historian cocked his head. "Perhaps I had better explain that more fully in the scrolls. I am afraid no one would know what that means, myself included."

"Well"—General Scheick's face was solemn—"the body is like a machine. It, too, gets rusty. So we're going to give her vegetable oil. That works down in and eases the movements."

"Ah, so. Thank you." The old one bent over his scroll and with graceful strokes recorded the General's words.

"Now you tell your grandmother," General Scheick continued, "that I want her to take three teaspoonfuls a day."

"But, Mr. General," Kenji said, "we don't have any vegetable oil."

"Just ordinary cooking oil is all right."

"But there's no cooking oil on the Islands."

"That's right, Mr. General," the old historian joined in. "In the days of King Gihon there used to be whole fields of rape and sesame seeds raised. There used to be mills which did nothing but press oil. But since the Interruption, it has come down to only sweet potatoes."

"Well, tell her not to worry," General Scheick said. "I have a gallon of rice-bran oil on hand for myself, and I'll let her take a couple of quarts."

"Grandma thanks you, Mr. General. She thanks you very much. She doesn't ask to be able to walk uphill. All she asks is that she might be able to ride down in comfort."

The tide was beginning to run; and Yoshimitsu, watching it

and knowing time was passing rapidly, coughed gently. "Excuse me, Your Majesty. I wonder if I may introduce my uncle, Shoji Takamini? The Takaminis have been waiting for quite some time to meet the King."

"Oh, sure," Kenji said and turned to Uncle Shoji.

"Your Majesty." Uncle Shoji bowed. "It is a pleasure. Indeed, we have been waiting for quite some time. It's been fourteen centuries."

"Is that right?" Kenji said. "Well, it's good to see you then."

"Not only is it a privilege for me," Uncle Shoji went on, "but it's a privilege for my daughters, who can hardly wait to meet you. They are such pretty girls, too. Let me introduce them. This is my oldest, Little Springtime."

Little Springtime was not what you would call a small girl, as her name would lead you to believe. Nor was she quite as young as you would believe from her name. In fact, there was something about the line of Little Springtime's neck that suggested the approach of summer. As Kenji bowed to her, she giggled and hid her head behind the small paper fan which she carried.

"And this is Opening Rosebud," Uncle Shoji continued.

Opening Rosebud bore a strong resemblance to her older sister, only her giggle was of a slightly higher pitch.

"And this is my youngest," Uncle Shoji said.

King Kenji looked to the youngest but couldn't see her face because she already had it behind her fan. "Well, it's been a great pleasure meeting you girls," he said, and by way of conversation added, "I hope to see you again sometime."

Uncle Shoji, however, didn't take it as conversation. "We can arrange that, Your Majesty." He smiled. "Why don't you come over to Yoshimitsu's house this afternoon for tea?"

Kenji glanced warily at the girls. "I don't think I can do that. I have to take the dukes and their retinues up to the castle and get them settled."

"Well," Uncle Shoji said, "why don't we come up to the castle and have tea with you, then? I want you to get to know the girls better. They're such nice girls, and they're all single."

"I don't think I could have you up today," Kenji hedged. "I got so much business on my mind." Desperately turning to Elwood, he whispered, "Elwood, help me get out of this. He's trying to fix me up with his daughters. I haven't time for that stuff."

Elwood regarded the three girls, who were gazing up at their King. "Okay. I really do want to see you about something anyway. Come on."

"Thanks," Kenji whispered, and before Uncle Shoji could protest, he made his apologies and broke away. Quickly, he walked over by one of the carts, where Elwood was waiting. "Elwood," he said, "thanks again. I sure appreciate it."

"That's okay, Kenji." Elwood nodded. "But what I really want to see you about is this: if Aunt Caroline is able to get the material for us to improvise incubators, we've still got a dickens of a job on our hands. We'll have to watch temperatures day and night, so would it be all right if I moved up to the castle?"

"Hey!" Kenji's eyes widened. "That would be swell."

"Would you have room for me?"

"We'll make room. But, Elwood, about those sweet potatoes. Aren't you going to get tired of sweet potatoes all the time? We do."

"We can't worry about that now," Elwood replied, and around him the crowd stirred and pointed to the harbor. The tide was coming in fast, and a sampan was already making its way toward the quay.

"Well, here comes the first load," Kenji said. "Mr. Yamaguchi, would that be the senior duke?"

"It is the senior duke," the old historian replied. "I recognize the sampan as the one running between here and Tatami Oshima."

"I better bring Grandma a little closer then."

"Here," General Scheick said, "let me get the cart and bring it nearer." Walking over, he took the pony by the single-rope rein, led him onto the quay; and turning, he said to the Queen Grandmother, "Okay?"

"Hokay." She smiled at him, then pointed to the little sampan, its single sail filled with the cool breeze, and began nodding brightly, trying to indicate to the General that the dukes were coming in and things were as they should be.

General Scheick caught her meaning all right, but he couldn't go along with her, so he simply shook his head, letting her know exactly where he stood in this matter.

"Ah, so," she whispered. But nothing could be done about it. That was the way things were. So she turned her attention to the approaching sampan. Then a puzzled look crossed her face. "Kenji," she said, "I wonder where the Duke's retinue is?"

Kenji looked at the sampan. All he could make out was a single figure and what appeared to be a cage of some sort. "I don't know, Grandma."

The sampan came in inch by inch, and upon the quay all leaned forward in anticipation. It had been three hundred and forty years since a duke was recognized in these Islands, and the people were anxious to see their nobility again, while General Scheick was curious to see what they had dug up.

As they watched, the figure in the boat began waving his arm back and forth. He seemed to have wisps of fiber of some sort clenched in his hand. "King Kenji, what is he waving?" General Scheick asked.

"That is hemp fiber. It indicates obedience."

"That is correct," the old historian agreed, looking up from his scroll. "In the old days when the nobility came into court, they dressed themselves in hemp to show that they would obey the King. Of course, today nobody could afford hemp, so I told the dukes a few strands of it would be sufficient."

The sampan was drawing near. General Scheick didn't exactly know what to expect of a senior duke; but, taking one look, his eyes widened, for he didn't expect to see this. The Duke was about sixty or so, a squat man with a broad face, which was now smiling a full-toothed smile. He was wearing a home-woven, banana-cloth kimono, exactly the same as the Queen Grand-mother wore. Atop his head was perched a battered gray felt hat of ancient vintage. And he certainly didn't look like a member of the entrenched class of privilege. With his bare feet, he looked more like he had just come out of the sweet potato fields.

"Well," General Scheick began, not quite being able to find words. "Well, you'd think he'd at least put shoes on for the occasion. After all, he's supposed to be coming into court."

The lack of shoes, however, had no effect upon the senior duke. In fact, there was a certain look about his feet—calluses here, bumps there—which indicated that here was a man who had never been hampered by clogs, or slippers, or the rubber-soled *tabi*. The Duke wasn't even conscious that the people up on the quay were wearing shoes; all his efforts were going into grinning. And when the sampan docked, he climbed up, using his feet as nimbly as his hands.

King Kenji himself was a little surprised; but hiding it, he stepped forward, saying, "I am the King."

"Ah, the King." The Duke held up his hemp fibers, not so much in a gesture of obedience but as a sign that he had not forgotten to bring them.

"I wish to welcome you home," Kenji went on.

"Home?" The Duke took off his hat and scratched his head. "I don't live here. I live on Tatami Oshima."

"I mean home to the castle."

"Home to the castle. Ah, I understand," the Duke said. "I thought you thought that I lived here. I don't. I've never even been here before."

"You've never even been on the main Island?" Kenji questioned.

"No. None of the family has since old King Gihon told us to go back to Tatami Oshima in 1577."

"That is very interesting," Kenji said, unable to think of anything else. "But I would like you to meet my grandma. Grandma, this is the Duke of Tatami Oshima."

Again the Duke held up his hemp fibers, and they bowed to each other. "It is good to have you back again," the Queen Grandmother said. "And have you brought your retinue?"

"Now what is a retinue?" the Duke asked. "I got the message, but I couldn't figure out that word."

"It means your retainers or attendants," Kenji said.

"So that's it."

"You haven't brought in any young people?" the Queen Grandmother questioned.

"Oh, no."

"What about your wife or family?" Kenji asked.

"They're home taking care of the sweet potato crop."

"I see," Kenji said. "Then you haven't brought anyone."

"Oh, yes. I brought my pig," the Duke said, pointing to a bamboo cage in the bottom of the sampan, where a large black hog lay stretched out, sleeping. "Do you know anyone around here who has a good boar?"

"Not offhand," the King replied.

"Well, we'll just have to look around then," the Duke said. "Now I guess we better unload her. Where do you want her, Your Majesty?"

"Are you going to take her up to the castle with you?" Kenji asked uncertainly.

"Oh, yes." The Duke nodded. "She always goes right along with me."

"In that case," the King said, "we'll put her on the cart." Turning, he called, "Elwood, would you hold that pony? We don't want him to start moving when we load the cage."

Elwood took the pony by the bit and watched as the Duke of Tatami Oshima began gathering an unloading crew. He got the King; Uncle Shoji Takamini; Yoshimitsu, and Yoshimitsu's executive officer, Jiro Kamakura; the crew of the sampan; plus the two police who had brought up the desk and chair—for the hog was a good-sized one, going well over three hundred pounds.

As the group dropped into the sampan, Yamaguchi Kiei rose from his chair. "I must watch this closely, Mr. General," he said.

General Scheick was in agreement. It certainly deserved watching. Here was a so-called duke, a man—who according to tradition was supposed to advise the King—here he was, concerning himself with the moving of a hog.

The pig, all three hundred plus pounds of her, lay stretched out on her side, sleeping contentedly. Carefully they lifted the

135

bamboo cage, slipped it onto the quay. And as they lifted the cage from the quay, the pig raised her head, looked at the King, at the Duke, and at those around her. "Mr. General," Yamaguchi Kiei cried. "Mr. General, see the sign!"

"What sign?" General Scheick asked.

"The pig! She looked at us. It is good luck!"

General Scheick's eyebrows arched, and he watched as they lifted her onto the cart.

It was a job, but they managed it, and gently, too, for the pig didn't raise her head again. "She was a heavy one all right," the freely perspiring Yoshimitsu said as they finally got her loaded.

"She sure was," the King agreed and leaned back against the cart, his arms and shoulders aching from the strain of it. But then he caught sight of the second sampan.

"Kenji," his grandmother called. "The Duke of Tōfu Shima is landing. Quick!"

The Duke of Tōfu Shima, or Beancurd Island, was landing indeed. A lithe figure, he stepped nimbly onto the quay despite his blue and white kimono. He was a distinguished-looking individual of fifty or so. His graying hair, instead of being cropped short in the Nakashima Islands manner, was cut long and combed back in western style. He, too, had a strand of hemp fibers in his hand. And as he stepped onto the quay a spark of interest was in his eyes; but it faded as he surveyed the weathered old buildings of the capital.

"Ah, welcome," Kenji said. "I am the King. It is good to have you back again."

"I thank you." The Duke extended the hemp fibers, bowed, then straightened. "I see the capital hasn't changed any. It's exactly the same as when I came here for the first time as a boy in 1916."

"Do you come in quite often?" the King asked.

"I used to," the Duke replied. "But I've given it up." He indicated the cart. "That is your grandmother, is it not, Your Majesty? I must pay my respects." Extending the hemp fibers, he bowed.

"It is good to have you with us," the Queen Grandmother said.

"Thank you."

"I hope you have brought a retinue with you," she went on. "The Duke of Tatami Oshima brought none."

"I brought none either."

"You didn't?" A startled look spread across the old face.

"No. I figured it was such a bother . . . well, what was the use?"

The Queen Grandmother was troubled now. Anxiously she regarded her grandson, but Kenji failed to notice, for the third sampan was coming in. "Will you excuse me?" the King said. "This will be the Duke of Bamboo Island. So I must greet him."

"By all means. Go ahead." The Duke bowed. "I'll just stand here."

As Kenji turned, he was conscious of a stirring in the crowd. He glanced at Yamaguchi Kiei and saw the old historian rise from his chair. He saw General Scheick lean forward, a puzzled look on his face. And he saw his grandmother, her mouth half-opened, gazing in astonishment.

Cocking his head to one side, Kenji glanced in the direction of their gazes, and then saw the slim figure of the girl stepping onto the quayside. She wasn't dressed in a kimono. Instead, she was wearing red tights and a Bermuda-length kilt, whose tartan was that of Maclaine of Lochbuie. He regarded her sunglasses and her hair cut in the western manner, his eyes widened, and with Yamaguchi Kiei watching and recording for posterity, the King whistled.

The King whistled, and Yamaguchi Kiei almost dropped his brush, because in this land you did not show feelings in such a way. Here the proper thing to do when a girl up and hit you was to pretend not to notice her.

But the King had whistled; and because he did so, a pair of dark eyes behind sunglasses swung to him, a small head tilted, and an aloof voice said in English, "At Letty Linton we consider whistling juvenile."

For a moment the King could only stand there, then a smile

of sheer delight swept across his face. "At Letty Linton . . . do you go to Letty Linton school for girls?"

"It is not a school for girls." He was corrected. "It is a college for young women."

"That's what I mean." Kenji's smile broadened. "So you were going to school in America on a scholarship. I was, too. I went to Cambridge College."

"Where?"

"Cambridge College in Ashtabula, Ohio."

"I never heard of it," the girl said. "But then, most of the people I know go either to Harvard, Yale, or Princeton. You wouldn't happen to know Sherman Chang, would you?"

"Sherman Chang . . . no, I don't think I do."

"That is too bad. He's a wonderful boy, really. His father is a very prominent restaurant man in the East."

"You mean in the eastern part of the United States?"

"Of course. Where else?"

"Oh, I see. Well, I've never been out of the Midwest, so . . ."

"Really? That's too bad. But then Clarissa, my roommate, says culture is gradually creeping westward."

"That's true," Kenji agreed, "because we had an awful lot of culture at Cambridge College."

"How interesting. Do you know Schopenhauer?"

"Schopenhauer." King Kenji's brow furrowed in thought as he repeated the name. "It seems to me I knew a Charlie Schopenhauer. Is he a Kappa Sig?"

"No, this is just Schopenhauer. I don't think he had a first name. He wrote books about philosophy and things."

"Oh, I never read any of those. Did you?"

"No, but I might next year when I'm a sophomore. That is, if I'm not too busy. You see, my chief interests are in social problems and fashion designing."

"That's very nice," the King said.

The girl regarded him levelly. "Do you realize that social problems are the result of social contact?"

"Is that right?"

"Yes, it is."

"I never thought of that," the King said. "By the way, what is your name?"

"At Letty Linton I am known as Debbie Nakasone."

"Debbie? That's pretty. Where did you get it?"

"Clarissa gave it to me. She says I look as if my name should be that. Besides, nobody could remember Shizu."

Kenji surveyed the sunglasses, western hair-do, and the kilt. "You do look as if your name should be Debbie."

"I know. If I go to New York after I graduate and become a fashion designer, I'm going to have to change it again, though."

"What would you change it to?"

"Allyson. Don't you think that's nice?"

"Yeah, that's nice, too," Kenji agreed. "But for now, can I call you Debbie?"

The girl regarded him. "I don't think you had better."

"Why not?" Kenji asked.

"Because," the girl said, "I am the Duchess of Bamboo Island."

"The Duchess of Bamboo Island?" Kenji said. "I thought Bamboo Island had a duke."

"It did," the girl said. "My father was the Duke, but he has decided to go *inkyo*, to turn the head of the family over to me. That's why I came home from America this summer."

"We better tell Mr. Yamaguchi then. We don't want a mix-up in history," Kenji said, wheeling. "Mr. Yamaguchi, did you know that the Duke of Bamboo Island has gone *inkyo?*" And General Scheick, hearing the words, looked quizzically from the King to the historian.

"He has gone *inkyo?*" Yamaguchi Kiei questioned.

"Yes. And he has turned the head of the family over to his daughter Debbie."

"Debbie?" The old man was puzzled. "He has no daughter named that."

"Excuse me," the King said. "I mean Shizu."

"Ah, yes." Mr. Yamaguchi nodded. "The records show his oldest daughter's name is Shizu."

"This is her then," Kenji said.

"Ah, so. Then truly she is the Duchess of Bamboo Island."

139

The old historian bowed to her; while General Scheick, regarding the red tights and the kilt, could hardly believe. First a barefooted duke and now this. What earthly good would she be to the government? How could she fill a position in the Table of Organization?

"Yes," the girl said once again in English, "I am the Duchess of Bamboo Island." She regarded Kenji somewhat coldly. "Could you please tell me where the King is? He has called us into Court, you know."

"Oh, I am the King," Kenji replied.

"You . . . the King!" For a moment the Duchess of Bamboo Island was taken completely by surprise, but then she regained her composure and regarded Kenji's khaki trousers and sweater. "You don't look like a king. I thought you'd be wearing some robes and sitting on a throne, and things. That's one thing I always liked about Sherman Chang—he would be dressed appropriately. He had some of the nicest vests."

"Well, I've been so busy with the chicken business and stuff," the King said, "that I haven't had much time to think about other things, you know."

"If you're the King, then, well . . ." The girl held up her wrist, and Kenji saw that she had looped the hemp fiber around it, somewhat in the nature of a bracelet.

"Oh, I'm the King, all right." Kenji nodded solemnly. "And that's my grandma. Come on. I'll introduce you."

As Kenji and the Duchess of Bamboo Island started toward the Queen Grandmother, all eyes followed them. Yamaguchi Kiei, the historian, was wondering just how he was going to record this. General Scheick, more than a little desperate over the future prospects for the Nakashima Islands, frowned deeply. Uncle Shoji Takamini told himself, "*Shikata ga nai* . . . it can't be helped." And the three Takamini girls, seeing the look on the King's face as he gazed at the Duchess, knew that they had lost another bout.

"Grandma," Kenji said in Japanese, his face a picture of pure delight, "this is the Duchess of Bamboo Island."

"It is nice to have you with us." The Queen Grandmother

smiled, and as the Duchess bowed low, she whispered, "Kenji, is that one of our ancient costumes?"

"No, Grandma," Kenji whispered back. "That is the latest style in America."

"Oh. I thought I had never seen anything like that before." And as the Duchess straightened, the grandmother went on. "But isn't Bamboo Island supposed to have a duke?"

"It did have," the girl said. "However, my father has gone *inkyo*."

"*Inkyo!*" Grandma leaned forward as interest arose within her. "Isn't that nice. And what is he doing with his time now?"

"For one thing, he is sitting and drinking a lot of tea. And he spends a lot of time watching other people work."

"Ah, so."

"That is all he has done so far, but he says he has a great many things he wants to do."

"It must be awfully nice to go *inkyo*." Grandma was silent for a moment, then went on. "I hope you have brought a retinue with you?"

"No, I haven't," the girl replied.

"You haven't?" The Queen Grandmother was more troubled than ever. "How," she asked herself, "are the people going to know of the new ideas at Court if there are no retinues to carry them back?"

"About my luggage," the Duchess said, "is there someone to get it for me?"

"Oh, I'll get it," the King volunteered. "You just wait here with Grandma, and I'll load it on the cart for you. Okay?"

"Okay," the Duchess replied.

Quickly, Kenji started toward the docked sampan, and as he did so, Elwood called, "Your Majesty, could I see you for a second? I wonder if I can borrow a cart? If Aunt Caroline has the material for incubators, I'll have to get it up to the castle some way. And I have my own baggage to get up, too, so . . ."

But Kenji hardly heard him. His thoughts were on the Duchess.

"Kenji, can I borrow a cart?" Elwood asked.

"Huh? Oh, yeah, Elwood. We'll just combine things. Okay?"

Together they went to the sampan and got the Duchess' luggage, and Yamaguchi Kiei, with graceful strokes, recorded it for posterity. They carried the luggage across the quayside and began the combining operation. The pig was too heavy to shift, so they moved the Queen Grandmother onto the cart with the pig. They put the Duchess on the box, next to the grandmother. Then with the King leading the little pony, and a duke flanking the cart on either side, they started toward the castle, high on the hill. And the crowd began waving their streamers wildly and cheering.

"There goes the government, Bill," General Scheick said. Silently he watched them, his eyes swinging from the barefoot Duke, to the kimono-clad Duke, to the Duchess in her red tights. He watched them. Then it hit him. "Bill. Bill, get the staff together," he ordered. "I think I got it."

"Got what, sir?" Colonel Henderson questioned.

"The solution." A smile spread across General Scheick's face. "The solution to our whole problem."

Chapter 10

AT LETTY LINTON the girls always changed for dinner, so when the Duchess of Bamboo Island came out wearing a red and white striped chemise, the Queen Grandmother, boiling the sweet potatoes over a charcoal brazier, had to stop and look, and look, for never had Grandma seen costumes such as these. She watched the girl standing on the veranda of the royal apartments, her head thrown back to catch the breeze blowing in from the China Sea, and even Grandma had to admit that she was a pretty little one.

Evening was beginning to fall, and the court was getting settled in for its stay at the castle. The center section of the ⊓ shaped structure was officially designated as the apartment of the Queen Grandmother. It was referred to as the middle house. The room at the very tip of the left wing, as you faced it, was assigned to the Duke of Tatami Oshima. A bamboo partition separated this room from the next one, which was assigned to the Duke of Beancurd Island. The third and last room, up near the middle house, was given to the Duchess; while over in the right wing of the ⊓ the King and Elwood had their rooms.

Actually, it was the pig of the Duke of Tatami Oshima that

caused the greatest difficulty in housing, for the King wanted to put her in one of the empty chicken coops in the terrace below, but the Duke protested. "She'll get lonesome down there with only those chickens around," he said. "Why, at home she's one of us." So as the Queen Grandmother called the Court for the evening meal, the pig of the Duke of Tatami Oshima was making herself right at home by wandering freely around the royal enclosure, rooting and grunting.

The meal was to be served in the middle house at a low table, which the Queen Grandmother had brought from their home in Little Koza. And as they gathered and sat down, the Queen Grandmother said, "I'm glad that we are all together again. This hasn't happened since 1620, when old King Gihon passed away."

"I'm glad we're all together, too," King Kenji said, looking at the Duchess of Bamboo Island. "This is going to be great." The senior duke said nothing. He simply reached over, speared a sweet potato with his chopstick and began inspecting it. The Duke of Beancurd Island merely sat staring absently. So the King passed the bowl to the Duchess and went on, "Will you have one?"

The meal consisted wholly and simply of boiled sweet potatoes, so the Duchess had little choice. "Thank you," she said. But King Kenji saw the look of distaste on her face.

"As time goes on," he said quickly, "we're going to be serving better meals up here. That is, if I can get my hands on some money."

The senior duke looked up from the inspection of his sweet potato. "There's nothing wrong with this one," he stated, "except it's kind of small."

The King, however, could see that the Duchess was not in agreement, so he asked, "Was the food good at Letty Linton?"

"It was delicious," the Duchess replied. "My roommate, Clarissa, says it was probably the best boarding school food that she had ever eaten. Their specialty was creamed chicken; and creamed chicken was always such a surprise there, because you'd be expecting something else, and there it would be on the menu." She had her sweet potato peeled now. Somewhat disdainfully she nibbled on it, then putting it down, said, "King Kenji—"

It was the first time she had called Kenji by his name, and it brought the smile of delight to his face. "Yes?"

"King Kenji"—the Duchess' eyes swept the reed and bamboo room—"how long do you intend for us to stay here at Court?"

"I don't know," Kenji replied. "All I know is that Mr. Yamaguchi says that here at the castle there must always be a place for the second son to stay any time he wants to. But I forgot to ask how long the second son is supposed to remain." He turned to the Duke of Beancurd Island. "Do you know?"

"I know how it was in King Gihon's time when he was bringing us up to the verge of the golden age," the Duke replied. "King Gihon used to call the dukes in regularly to have them observe and learn of the things that he was doing. Then, when he thought they knew enough, he would send them back to their own Islands so they could teach the third sons."

"And didn't the King used to keep some of them here as advisers?" Kenji asked.

"Yes, but that was up to the King. He kept whom he wanted, and he kept them as long as he wanted."

Quickly the Duchess of Bamboo Island regarded Kenji and said, "Well, I hope you won't keep us very long."

Apprehensively, King Kenji looked at her as the Queen Grandmother raised her eyes from her sweet potato. "Do you have other plans?" he asked.

"Yes, I do."

"Ah, so," the Queen Grandmother said. "So that is why you didn't bring a retinue. You didn't intend to stay."

"That is correct," the girl said. "I want to go back to Letty Linton. The only reason I came home is because my father went *inkyo*, and I had to take over as head of the family. Otherwise, I would have just continued on with my scholarship." As the girl mentioned the word *scholarship*, a sudden thought hit her, and her eyes widened. "King Kenji, we still have the American scholarships, don't we? They are still in effect, aren't they?"

"I don't know," Kenji replied. "I never thought to ask the Mr. General, and he never said anything about them." A fearful look crossed his face. "I was hoping you might want to stay here, though."

"Here? But what is there here?" the girl said. "There are no movies, no television, there's not even a radio. All there is, is *sabishii*."

At the mention of the word *sabishii*, both the Queen Grandmother and the Duke of Beancurd Island stopped eating. Only the senior duke chewed stolidly on, unhearing and grunting a little like his rooting hog. For the word *sabishii* describes a feeling, a kind of haunting melancholy. You feel it in the evening hanging over the villages of Asia. It means a nothingness to do. It means a loneliness. It means an ending day and a dying year. "Yes," the girl continued. "All there is here is *sabishii*. This is no place to be young in. You waste being young here."

King Kenji was silent as his thoughts went back to the days before he had gone to school in America, to the days when he lived with his grandmother in her little store in their home village. He remembered how it was when night began to close in over Little Koza. How darkness would grip the villages and the whole countryside, for the lights had gone out in the Land of the Lighted Lanterns because of many reasons, one being that no one could afford to burn them. And he remembered that there was nothing to do but go to sleep.

"I don't want to stay here," the girl went on. "I want to go back to Letty Linton. Then when I graduate, I'm going to move to New York City and be a famous fashion designer." She looked at Kenji. "You know, there's no *sabishii* in New York City."

"Isn't there?" Kenji questioned.

"Oh, no. I was there three times with my roommate Clarissa and some of the other girls from school. We had such a good time."

The Duke of Beancurd Island was regarding her now, and an eager interest was in his eyes. "What did you do in New York City?" he asked, putting down his sweet potato.

"Everything. You see, Clarissa is a New Yorker. She doesn't

really live there. She lives in Connecticut. But she knows all the things to do."

"I understand," the Duke said. "So she is a New Yorker."

"Oh, yes. If you want French, or Italian, or any other kind of food, Clarissa knows where to go for it. And the waiters know her by name, too."

"Ah, so." The Duke of Beancurd Island nodded, a smile playing on his lips.

"And Clarissa knows all about the stage plays that are on Broadway," the girl said.

"And would she know the restaurants that the actors frequent?" the Duke asked.

"Oh, yes," the girl replied solemnly. "Clarissa knows all that."

"And you want to know all that, too?" the Duke asked. "You want to become a New Yorker?"

"Yes, I do. New York City is a very fine place to live. And as I said before, there is no *sabishii* there."

"There's no *sabishii* in Ashtabula, Ohio, either," Kenji stated solemnly. "Why, my fraternity brothers and I used to drive around in the jalopy I bought for thirty-five dollars, and . . ."

"I wouldn't know about that," the Duchess said. "I'm only familiar with the East. But it really doesn't make much difference to a man if there's *sabishii* or not."

"It doesn't?" the King questioned.

"Oh, no. We girls at college used to talk it over all the time. You see, it doesn't make any difference to a man, because a man is organized."

"I don't think I know what you mean," Kenji said.

"Well let's take you, for instance. Like any man, your education is in keeping with your mental ability and your father's finances. Do you agree?"

"I don't know," Kenji replied. "You see, it was the United States Government that sent me to college in America."

"That is the exception," the Duchess stated. "We girls have agreed it is in keeping with your father's finances. Now because you are organized, do you know the next thing you will do after you finish your education? You will get married."

147

Kenji's eyes lighted. "Do you think so?"

"It is inevitable. And after you are married, you will be expected to have a family . . . provide food, clothing, and shelter for them. Also an education."

"That is, providing the United States Government doesn't do it," Kenji said.

"There you are bringing up the exception again." A touch of irritability crept into the girl's voice. "That's not fair."

"Excuse me," Kenji said quickly. "I didn't mean it. But then what happens to me?"

"You will have a home life. You will have a business life, in your case it's being King. And you will have your responsibility to the community."

"Oh, I already have my responsibility to the community." Kenji nodded earnestly. "For instance, I have to get the chicken business making some money, so I can keep on supporting the dukes. It's going to be a tough proposition to show a profit. I know because I was taking Marketing and Retailing."

"But that's not the point," the girl said. "The point is you have found your identity."

"I have?"

"Yes, because you are organized. Now take me, though. Or take any of the girls at school. We haven't found our identity yet. And it's not easy for a woman to find her identity, because she's disorganized."

With the exception of the senior duke, who was concentrating on his second sweet potato, all gathered around the little table looked at the Duchess of Bamboo Island, and all were just as puzzled as the King. "I don't think I know what you mean by that, either," Kenji said, expressing the general feeling.

"It is so simple, really," the Duchess explained. "I want to be a person in my own right, and to do that I have to become organized."

"Well, instead of going back to America, couldn't you organize yourself here?" Kenji asked hopefully.

"No, I can't, because my problems are social. The big thing is

I need social stimulation. We girls all agreed that if we do not have social stimulation, we are lethargic."

"Is that right?"

"Yes, it is. That is the whole trouble with the Nakashima Islands. We do not have stimuli."

The Queen Grandmother, who had been listening carefully, asked, "What does the word *stimuli* mean?"

"It means . . . well, King Kenji, how would you explain it?"

"I think," Kenji said, "it means something that lifts up your spirits, that gets you going. Isn't that right?"

"That is approximately correct," the Duchess agreed.

"And this is what you think we need in the Nakashima Islands?" Grandma questioned.

"That is it exactly," the girl replied. "There are just no stimuli here."

"Ah, so," Grandma said, and silence fell over the group as they continued to eat the evening meal. They ate without speaking; and when at last they had finished, the senior duke arose from the mats. "Well, I think I'll go and talk to my pig a little bit," he said. Going to the veranda, he began calling, "Sui! Sui! Sui!" And was answered by a series of happy grunts.

King Kenji looked at the Duchess, who had grown even more morose, and said, "Debbie, I have some phonograph records I brought back with me from Cambridge College. They're brand-new ones."

"Really?" The Duchess almost smiled. "Can you do the cha-cha?"

"Oh, sure," Kenji replied. "Can you?"

"I was probably the best dancer in the freshman class."

"Let's look up Elwood then, and maybe we can go down to the General's house and do some dancing."

"Why can't we just play the records here?"

"Because I don't have a phonograph."

"Can't you borrow one?"

"I don't know. But even if I could, we don't have any electricity up here to run it, so . . ."

"See?" the girl said. "That's the way it always is. There's nothing, only *sabishii*." In the failing light of evening her face wore the haunting melancholy that the word *sabishii* implies, then she went on, "King Kenji, would you go down and see the General about the scholarships? Maybe I can leave here right away."

The sadness arose in Kenji. "Well . . ."

"Would you do it right now?"

"If you wish. But would you like to walk down with me?"

"No," the girl said, looking out into the dusk. "I think I'll just lie down, and maybe I can sleep."

The two of them arose, excused themselves. And as the King started off through the courtyard, his grandmother watched his shadow in the half-dark. She and the Duke of Beancurd Island sat for a long time in silence then, and finally the Duke asked, "Do you think the girl knew what she was talking about?"

"I couldn't tell," the Queen Grandmother replied, and her old, tattooed hands were folded in her lap, "because I haven't the education to know. But I do know she wants to leave."

"Yes. And she is right. This is no place to be young in. It's strange, though, that she should want to be a New Yorker. I used to have dreams like that."

"You mean you wanted to be a New Yorker?"

"No, I wanted to be *Edo-ko*."

"*Edo-ko*? Ah, by *Edo* you must mean the old name for the city of Tokyo."

"That is correct. I wanted to be . . . how would you say it . . . a Tokyoite? I wanted to be of the big city, and know all the restaurants and have all the restaurant owners know me. I wanted to know where they served the best *sushi* and what plays were playing. . . ."

"I understand," the Queen Grandmother said. "And what business are you in now?"

"I am a sweet potato merchant."

"How long have you been doing that?"

"Old King Gihon started my family in it. After he introduced the sweet potato from China, he reorganized everything. Are you familiar with that?"

"Yes. I can still remember my father and grandfather telling about the great prosperity that came to the Islands when the people were able to get 800 bushels of food an acre instead of the twenty or so bushels from rice."

"No, I mean are you familiar with the reorganization?"

"I don't believe I am."

"Well, it applied to the nobility. He gave each of us an assignment. In our case, he told my family to go back to our Island and make a market for sweet potatoes, so that the farmers would have a place to sell, when they wanted to sell. So that they would have a place to buy, when they wanted to buy. That is what we have been doing for 380 years."

"Then truly you should know your business by now."

"I'm afraid there's nothing to know. You simply buy and sell. But I wonder what would have happened if the Interruption hadn't come along? I wonder if our kings would have gotten us across the line from the verge of the golden age to which Gihon brought us, to the golden age itself. And I wonder if I wouldn't have become *Edo-ko*. Or maybe even a New Yorker."

"Would you like to become a New Yorker, too?" Grandma asked.

"I'd like to become anything but a sweet potato merchant." The Duke of Beancurd Island looked out from the ancient castle into the distance where the other fourteen Islands of the chain were barely discernible. Only the wake of white water, caused by the East China Sea gently washing their shores, marked their presence. "But I guess that is the way it is," he said. "You don't happen to have any firewood around that you want broken into kindling, do you?"

"I think not," the grandmother replied. "But it is kind of you to offer."

"It isn't kindness, really. It's just that I learned to break boards with my hands. It was passed on to me by my father, who learned it from his father, who in turn learned it from his father. After being in the sweet potato business for over three hundred years, you often find yourself with nothing to do, so we took to breaking up the kindling around the house."

Chapter 11

AS KING KENJI came down from the castle, his face was twisted as he walked in the night. And he could understand how the Duchess felt about Letty Linton, for he felt the same way about Cambridge College in Ashtabula, Ohio.

The thought of Cambridge came to him then, and a smile played on his lips as he remembered his jalopy painted red and white. For it was a happy coincidence that those should have been the colors of Cambridge, because in the Nakashima Islands red indicates joy and white indicates peace and contentment. And that is the way he thought of his two years at college. They had been two years of joy, and peace, and contentment.

He remembered fraternity row, with the lilacs fragrant in the spring rain. He remembered the pep meetings with the bonfire blazing in the autumn night and the smell of burning leaves in the air. Then there was the Sophomore Cotillion when he and Mellie Wong, who came from Canton, Ohio, were the hit of the whole shebang, especially when they started making up their own steps on the dance floor.

Yes, he knew how the Duchess felt, because on that day when he walked out onto the porch of the Lambda Beta Theta House

152

for the last time, when his brothers gathered around him to sing one last song of fraternity, there were tears in his eyes, for he hadn't wanted to leave. He just wanted to stay forever. And truly the Duchess would have felt the same, for what was there here for her; just a darkened land and a sense that her whole life was passing away.

He reached Caroline Drive now, but here there was no darkness, for the lights glowed softly in the row after row of homes as the little American community prepared for another evening in Asia. Over in Cottage 17B, which served as one unit of the Bachelor Officers' Quarters, they were spreading an Army blanket on the dining room table in preparation for an evening of five-card stud. Over in Cottage 4A, that of Major McCloud, the Intelligence Officer, Agnes McCloud, scanning the recipes for the Egg Cookbook which the women had started preparing, grimaced, for the recipe that Captain Carlisle's wife had submitted didn't sound very good to her. So, going to the phone, she picked up the receiver to call the Captain's wife and tell her so. And as the King started down the street, over in Cottage 1A Mrs. Scheick and her nephew were deep in conversation.

"Now are you sure you don't mind, Aunt Caroline, if I move up to the castle?" Elwood was saying. "Frankly, I think it would be a lot better for the Nakashima Islands Egg Corporation if I do. If I'm up there all the time, I know I can keep a better check on the temperature of the eggs we're hatching."

"I think it's an excellent idea." Mrs. Scheick put down her afterdinner coffee. "And I can't wait to write your mother. She's going to be so happy about this. Incidentally, do you know any good books on poultry raising that I might have her send?"

"Not offhand."

"I'd certainly like to get some literature on it." Mrs. Scheick sipped her coffee. "I never realized how little I knew about chickens until I became chairman of the board."

"Why don't you ask Dad to send you some? Maybe the elevator has literature."

"I think I'll do that. I want to become an expert on this poultry thing. I feel I owe it to the girls to protect their interest."

"Aunt Caroline," Elwood said. "Do you think it will be all right with Uncle Matt if I move up to the castle?"

"I don't see why not."

"Do you think I'd better wait until he gets home before moving?"

"I suppose you might. He likes to feel that he knows what's going on." Mrs. Scheick arose. "Will you join me in some more coffee?"

"No thanks."

Mrs. Scheick went to the kitchen, and as she reached it, the front doorbell rang. "Would you get it, please, Elwood?" she asked.

"Okay." Going to the front door, Elwood opened it and was taken by surprise. "Why, Kenji," he said. "I didn't expect to see you. What's up?"

"I have to see the Mr. General. Is he home?"

"No. Aunt Caroline says he's at a staff meeting. He should be back soon, though. Come on in."

"Okay."

The King started through the doorway, and Elwood asked, "Did you see the things we got out in the cart there?"

Kenji looked toward the little Mongolian pony tied to the tree in front of the General's home. "Yes."

"We were pretty lucky," Elwood went on. "Not only was Aunt Caroline able to get a whole bunch of tin from the Quartermaster, but she was also able to get some Coleman lanterns for heat."

The King forced a smile. "That's good."

Mrs. Scheick, coming from the kitchen, was also surprised. "Why, King Kenji, how nice to see you. Will you have some coffee with me?"

"Thank you," Kenji replied. "But I don't think so. I'll just wait for the Mr. General."

Mrs. Scheick noticed that he seemed subdued, and thinking he was worried, she said, "I know we have a terrible problem on our hands about getting chicken feed. And I know it's going to be difficult building our flocks. But somehow I feel that we have made a good start. Don't you?"

"Oh, I do," Kenji said, but his heart wasn't with it. Mrs. Scheick could tell. So could Elwood. And they glanced at each other.

"Well," Mrs. Scheick said, "perhaps we better talk about that some other time." She turned. "Elwood, why don't you and the King load your things in the cart?"

"That's a good idea," Elwood replied. "Kenji, will you give me a hand?"

"Sure, Elwood," the King said absently. And Elwood went to his room, brought his luggage.

Each of them took two bags apiece. Reaching the cart, they began loading it, and Elwood asked, "Kenji, is something the matter?"

"The matter?" For a moment Kenji was silent. "Oh, I was just thinking about when I was at college, and the Duchess wanting to go back to Letty Linton."

"I see. So she wants to go back." Elwood hesitated. "You kind of fell for her, didn't you?"

"I sure did," the King said. "I sure did."

They lapsed into silence, mainly because Elwood didn't quite know what to say, so he pretended to busy himself with the luggage. But from time to time he glanced at the King in the darkness. But Kenji was lost in thought. And finally it was with a sense of relief that Elwood heard voices down at the far end of Caroline Drive. "That must be Uncle Matt," he said, and the two of them looked toward the approaching group.

General Scheick walked at the head of his staff, his face intent, and once again he asked, "Are you sure now, gentlemen, that you can't see any ramifications to this plan that might get us into trouble?" For in the General's mind still burned the thought of his previous error. So concerned had he been over the failure to place the men of his choice in government, that he never realized that the return of the nobility was a slap in the face to the common man. And he was determined now that there were not going to be any more ramifications to upset everything and get Washington boiling.

"I can't see any, sir," the staff chorused, and Colonel Henderson added, "Sir, it's foolproof."

155

A sense of well-being began to creep over General Scheick, because it certainly did sound good. All they had to do was get rid of the nobility and bring in the common man to run the government. That ought to straighten everything out with Washington. And General Scheick could hear Mosby Winthrope, his old friend, mentor, and now commanding officer, say, "Well done, Pug! Well done!"

As the last of his staff left him to go to their homes, General Scheick began to hum. "Pack Up Your Troubles in Your Old Kit Bag," he hummed. And nearing Cottage 1A, he saw the pony cart and called genially, "Hello, there."

"Hello, Uncle Matt," came the reply. "It's me and King Kenji."

"Well, Elwood. So the King's with you, too. Good. He's just the person I want to see."

"He also wants to see you, Uncle Matt. He came down looking for you."

"It looks like we can do business then." Rubbing his hands, the General approached the cart and looked at it curiously. "What's all this?" he asked, indicating the tin.

"It's to make incubators."

"Incubators? Oh, for the chicken business." General Scheick nodded. "I just want to tell you, Elwood, that your aunt is very happy that you're taking such an interest in chickens. Running a grain elevator is a mighty fine profession, my boy. You can't go wrong by going into the elevator business." He noticed Elwood's luggage. "What's that for?"

"Well," Elwood began hesitantly, "I talked it over with Aunt Caroline, and we both decided that it might be a good thing if I moved up to the castle for a while. You see, I'm going to have to watch the temperature of the eggs pretty closely."

"You go right ahead, my boy. We certainly wouldn't want them to get cold, would we?" General Scheick was brimming over with joviality. "And King Kenji—what can I do for you?"

"It's about the scholarships," the King said. "The Duchess of Bamboo Island wants me to ask you if the American scholarships will continue?"

"I hadn't thought about it," General Scheick began slowly. "But I don't see why they should. After all, you voted to become a nation. It seems to me you're going to have to shoulder things like that."

"In other words," the King said, "if the scholarships are to continue, I'm going to have to pay for them."

"Not you personally, but the government."

"It's the same thing," the King said, "because I'm the whole government."

"Well, that shows you one of the disadvantages of an absolute monarchy."

But the King didn't hear him, for the King's mind was on the Duchess of Bamboo Island, and he knew how unhappy she was going to be about this.

"Yes, you voted to become an independent nation," General Scheick continued. "So I think you'd better start getting those advisers of yours organized. You'd better start seeing if those dukes will fit into the T/O."

"Oh, I intend to do that, Mr. General, but they only came in this afternoon."

General Scheick smiled inwardly. "Look, King Kenji, I've had many years experience placing the right man in the right job. I'll give you a hand with this. Now first thing tomorrow morning, we'll get together with those dukes and see what we can do."

"I can't tomorrow morning," the King said. "I have to concentrate on the chicken business."

"Don't you want to . . . to process the dukes?" the General asked. "After all, they're supposed to be your advisers."

"But I don't need advice," the King replied. "What I need is money, so I'd better go out and earn some."

General Scheick was dismayed. "King Kenji, you're going to have to face up to this problem of the dukes sooner or later. Now we have to set a date on this."

"How would a week from Monday be?" the King asked.

"A week from Monday! That's nine days!" General Scheick exclaimed, and he could visualize the queries pouring in from General Winthrope, wanting to know what he, General Scheick, was doing to protect the rights of the common man. "Now see here," he said firmly, "there must be some way we can make it sooner."

"I don't see how we can, Mr. General."

"Damn," General Scheick muttered to himself. How was he going to explain that the common man had to wait while the King fooled around hatching chickens? Yet he knew this was the best he was going to be able to do at the moment. "Very well. We'll make it a week from Monday then. I'll be up first thing in the morning, and we'll take care of those dukes. And if you get a chance, talk things over with your grandma. She'll agree with me that nine days is too long to wait."

"All right, Mr. General," the King said, but his mind was on other things, and he turned. "Elwood, are you all set to go on up to the castle?"

"Are you going up right away?" General Scheick asked.

"Yes, Mr. General."

"Well, look. I promised your grandmother some rice-bran oil for her joints. You can take it to her. I'll get a couple quarts for you. One teaspoon with each meal ought to do the trick."

"All right, Mr. General."

General Scheick walked into the house with his nephew, and Kenji stood alone in the night. He looked up at the stars in the heavens as he tried to figure things out. And when Elwood returned, carrying two bottles of rice-bran oil, he was still standing there, staring at the skies.

"All set?" Elwood asked.

"All set," Kenji replied, then added, "You know, Elwood, I've been thinking."

"About the Duchess of Bamboo Island?"

"Yes. She's going to be awfully disappointed about the scholarships, and I can understand that. But I was wondering."

"Wondering about what?"

"If maybe instead of going back to America, there isn't something I could do to get her organized and help her find her identity out here?"

Chapter 12

IT WAS a long wait, those nine days until the morning of July 13. It was a wait punctured by radiogram after radiogram from General Mosby Winthrope, wanting to know just what was being done out there. And it was hard to explain, for how could you tell your superior officer that the King was busy with the chicken business, and he didn't have any time for government at the moment? So all General Scheick could do was ask his old friend and mentor to have confidence in his, General Scheick's, ability. Thus it was that General Scheick greeted the morning of July 13 with a deep sense of relief as he and Colonel Henderson walked up to the castle to sew it up.

Already the castle was awake and had been so for hours. In the Courtyard of the Viscounts, Elwood, busily hovering over the improvised incubators, carefully watched the temperatures of the hatching eggs. In Baron's Row, as it used to be called, the Duke of Tatami Oshima's pig rooted eagerly in the moist earth, searching for delicacies, while up on the veranda of the main house, the King's grandmother was busy pouring tea for the circle of women gathered about her.

As they entered the royal enclosure, at the very top of the

peak, General Scheick and Colonel Henderson saw the group; and the Colonel, switching the briefcase under his arm, peered closely and said, "Those faces look familiar, sir. Isn't that the same bunch that was forming the mutual loan society the morning we went out to tell the Queen Grandmother that her grandson was being returned to the throne?"

"They do look familiar," General Scheick agreed. "I think I recognize that flat-faced one."

"Yes, sir, that's the same bunch, all right. See the money. Well, it looks as if they're going in hock again."

It certainly did look as if they were going in hock again, for there was a pile of paper money before the Queen Grandmother which, apparently, was to be passed out to the woman who was number one on the loan list.

As they neared, the Queen Grandmother saw them. In one hand she had a teacup and the other hand grasped the handle of the teapot, so she couldn't wave. But she did bow her head and smile her greetings; then turning, she called to her grandson.

Over in the right wing of the royal apartments the King was busy sanding down what looked like a large picture frame. Hearing his grandmother's voice, he got on his hands and knees in order to peek out past the pushed-back wooden door, and seeing the two officers, he called, "Mr. General. Mr. Colonel. Grandma is having an important meeting so we'll have to meet over here. Okay?"

It didn't make much difference to General Scheick where they met as long as they did meet. "That's as good as any place," he said; and walking over, he added, "Well, King Kenji, are you ready for action?"

"I guess so," the King replied. "Please come inside, so we won't disturb the ladies." He indicated the General's and the Colonel's shoes.

Slipping out of their shoes, the two officers stepped up onto the wooden veranda and entered the King's room. It was a room much like a room in any Nakashima Islands house. The floor was covered with the straw *tatami* mats. The walls were composed of woven bamboo and sliding wooden doors; and a smell of new-cut thatch, from the roof, hung over the whole area. But in a Nakashima Islands house there were no decorations of any kind, while here, on the wall, was a red and white pennant bearing the word: CAMBRIDGE. Here, on the wall, were pictures. There was one of all the brothers of Lambda Beta Theta, standing on the porch of their old fraternity house, smiling for posterity to see. There was a picture of the Freshman Hop, and the Sophomore Cotillion, and King Kenji placing third in the 440-yard dash in the intrafraternity track meet. And there was a large picture of Cambridge College from the air.

As the two officers entered, the King laid aside the frame. "Mr. General, it is very nice of you and the Mr. Colonel to come up and help me this morning. I certainly appreciate it. I never had any experience putting people into jobs."

"Well, we have," General Scheick stated and added, "Would you bring on the first Duke please?"

Since he was the senior, the Duke of Tatami Oshima came first. Barefooted, and with battered felt hat in hand, he entered the King's quarters and his face was wreathed in a smile.

"Please tell him to be seated," General Scheick said and regarded the King. "Now, King Kenji, in examining the nobility, in trying to fit them into the T/O, we are using a test from World War II for the screening of candidates for Officers' Candidate School."

"I see." The King nodded. "But excuse me, Mr. General. He is not trying to become an officer candidate."

"You don't understand," General Scheick said. "This test is merely to bring out a man's ability and background. Just as we like a well-rounded officer, I'm sure you would like a well-rounded Prime Minister, or Foreign Minister, wouldn't you?"

"Well, if you think that's what I need, why . . ."

"Of course that's what you need," General Scheick went on. "Now we have five ratings—Superior, Excellent, Very Satisfactory, Satisfactory, and Unsatisfactory. Each of us—you, Colonel Henderson, and myself—will give him a rating."

"If you say so, Mr. General."

"All right. Let's try him out for Prime Minister." General Scheick faced the smiling Duke. "What is his occupation?"

"Farmer."

"What education has he had?"

"He doesn't think he's had any."

General Scheick glanced at Colonel Henderson. "Doesn't he know?"

"Well, Mr. General, he says he thinks he remembers going to school one time, but he's not sure."

General Scheick considered. "We don't want to be unfair about this, so let's give him the benefit of the doubt. Now then, what does he do in his spare time? You see, King Kenji, this will give us a good idea of his energy level and his desire to improve himself."

"Mr. General, he says he doesn't have any spare time."

"Let's put it this way. What does he do when it rains and he can't work in the fields?"

"He sleeps."

A sense of guilt began to rise in General Scheick. "King Kenji," he began slowly, "I hope you don't think the questions we're throwing him are too tough, do you?"

"Oh, no," the King replied. "When you test them, we have to ask them something."

"That's right," General Scheick agreed. "Let's see if we can find out a little more about what he's like. Please ask him what his hobbies are."

Kenji translated, then said, "He doesn't have any hobbies."

General Scheick regarded the smiling Duke. "Well, surely he must like to do something?"

"Oh, yes, Mr. General. He says he likes to grow big sweet potatoes. Each year he tries to grow the biggest sweet potatoes on his home Island."

General Scheick coughed. "Well . . . well, that's nice." He looked at the King. "King Kenji, I don't think there's much need for us to go on here. You know, it's an awfully fast track today, and you're going to need top-notch men to fill the T/O, so . . ."

The King understood. "You don't think we'd be able to use him, Mr. General?"

"I'm afraid not. Perhaps you better tell him."

It was a delicate thing to explain. For a moment Kenji hesitated, then began translating, phrasing it as gently as possible. And General Scheick and Colonel Henderson, watching, saw the Duke's smile broaden, saw him nod brightly.

Even Kenji was surprised as the Duke spoke, and General Scheick asked, "What does he say?"

"He says this is just like in the old days."

"What does he mean by that?"

"Well, along about 1580 or maybe it was 1575, old King Gihon reorganized his government. He says the King tried and tried to find a job for his great-great-grandfather, fourteen times removed, who was then the Duke. But King Gihon just wasn't able to place him. By golly, he says, you know it's funny how things go sometimes."

"I wouldn't exactly say it was funny," the General said. "Isn't he a little upset about it?"

"No. He says that's the way it is, and we'll worry about to-morrow's wind tomorrow."

"Oh."

"And now he wonders if you would excuse him. We're not going to get anywhere anyway. So he thinks he'll take a walk out to Tobaru village. He heard a rumor that they got a good boar out there, and he wants to take a look."

"Is that all right with you, King Kenji?" the General asked. "After all, it's your government we're setting up."

"I think it would be as good as anything under the circumstances," the King replied.

When he received permission from the King to leave, the Duke arose, bowed, and smiled. And as he left the King's quarters with a wave, General Scheick said to Kenji, "I'm afraid, Your Majesty, that the line has grown a little thin in this case."

In all honesty, the King had to agree that perhaps it had.

"But you have to give him credit," the General went on. "He's made peace with himself. Now then, what do you say we try the Duchess? Let's see what we can do with her."

The King hesitated. "Do you think we should?"

"Why not?"

"Well, she's so upset," the King said. "When she found out there were no more scholarships, and she couldn't go back to Letty Linton, why . . ."

"I'm afraid," General Scheick said, "she's going to have to learn to take disappointments, like the rest of us."

"Well, if you think I should then . . ." Hesitantly, Kenji turned and started for the doorway to get the Duchess of Bamboo Island.

The Duchess of Bamboo Island certainly was upset. When she came into the King's quarters in her Bermuda shorts and ruffled Spanish-type shirt, she was pouting. "Will this take long, King Kenji?" she asked.

"I don't think so," the King replied. "Will it, Mr. General?"

General Scheick, who had risen to his feet, saw the pout. "Not very." He gestured. "But let's make ourselves comfortable. We just want to ask you a few questions, Duchess. You see, we are trying to fit the nobility into the Table of Organization."

"Really? And what, may I ask, is the Table of Organization?"

"This is it," the General said, handing over a typed list. "It's the list of all the jobs that are needed to run the government."

The girl surveyed the list, then said, "But what is all this questioning for?"

"It's to discover your abilities and capabilities. We want to know about your personality, and—"

"My personality! Oh, I have taken the Wisconsin Polyphasic. Everyone at Letty Linton takes it just as soon as they enter."

"What's that?" General Scheick asked.

"It is a test," the Duchess replied. "To determine how your personality is, and there is nothing wrong with mine." She raised her firm little chin. "And as far as my capabilities are concerned, I have taken a whole series of aptitude tests at school."

164

"You did?" The King smiled.

"Yes. And all the tests revealed that I was very apt."

Kenji's eyes were filled with admiration. "Mr. General, there's no need to ask the Duchess any questions at all then."

"Now wait a minute," General Scheick said. "Don't you think we ought to try one or two at least?"

"No," the King stated. "You yourself can see that the Duchess has a superior personality. And if she was apt in everything, she gets a superior there, too. So we'll just have her look over the T/O and pick out any job she wants." And before General Scheick could protest, Kenji added, "Do you see anything that looks good, Debbie . . . I mean Duchess?"

The Duchess of Bamboo Island read the list, then reread it. "Prime Minister, Foreign Minister . . . it seems to me that all of these sound dreadfully political in nature."

"Well," Kenji said, "when you deal with jobs running the government, why you can't help but be political."

"In that case, I wouldn't be interested." The Duchess put down the T/O. "I'm only interested in fashion designing and social problems."

King Kenji's face fell. "Wouldn't you even want to consider being the Minister of Finance? You could handle the Treasury."

"Money . . . what's money?" The Duchess of Bamboo Island arose. "Will you excuse me, please? I want to finish writing a letter to my roommate Clarissa, and have her send all my things back."

"Oh, sure," King Kenji said, scrambling to his feet, and the two officers also stood up. With head erect, the Duchess stepped from the room onto the open veranda. Slipping into a pair of reed sandals, she started across the courtyard. And the sadness was on King Kenji's face as his eyes followed her.

But General Scheick breathed easier, for she just might have stepped right in there and taken over as almost anything. However, she was out of the way now, so he said, "King Kenji, it looks like we're not batting so well. That's two out of two shot."

"I guess it is." The King's eyes were still following the Duchess.

"We might as well bring in the last one, then. Will you call the Duke of Beancurd Island?"

As King Kenji stepped to the door to summon the Duke, Colonel Henderson whispered, "I think we got it made, sir."

"I think so, Bill, unless this one can fill the whole T/O by himself."

"Do you think the King realizes yet that this damn nobility isn't going to be of any use to him?"

"No," the General replied. "He hasn't caught the ramifications."

"Are you going to point it out to him, sir?"

"I'll have to." General Scheick gestured, for the Duke of Beancurd Island was coming across the courtyard, and the two of them lapsed into silence. But a jovial feeling began to rise in General Scheick, because with only one more to strike out, they were just a step away from a government by and for the common man. So when the Duke entered, the General held out his hand. "Well, well, good morning," he said, his voice cheerful. "And how is everything with him this morning, King Kenji?"

Kenji translated, then said, "He says he is fine."

"Oh?" The General looked at the Duke; and whereas before the Duke seemed tired and drawn, now there was a new air of aliveness about him.

"In fact, he says he is very good," the King went on. "And he wants you to know that he has been looking forward to this meeting ever since I told him about it."

General Scheick smiled. "Tell him I've been looking forward to it, too. He doesn't mind if we ask him a few questions, does he?"

"Not at all. Not at all, because he's very interested in some of these jobs on the T/O."

"Let's see what we can do for him then. First, has he had any education?"

"He's had the classical Chinese education."

"What does that mean?"

166

"Oh, he says calligraphy, Confucius, and that sort of thing."

"That's rather interesting," General Scheick said. "But how did he get a classical Chinese education? The Japanese were in power when he was growing up, weren't they?"

"Yes, but that was his father. He believes that had the Chinese been in power, then, no doubt, his father would have given him a classical Japanese education. His father liked to reverse things. He wanted his son to see both ways. From his everyday living he could learn of things Japanese. From his schooling he could learn of things Chinese."

"That's a very good idea," General Scheick said. "I feel that way myself. In fact, I've always liked an officer who has a wide range of experience—staff work, some infantry, some artillery, perhaps a little military government. A man like that can grasp the big picture. He's not narrow and restricted. But tell me, what does he do in his spare time?"

"He breaks boards, or firewood, or whatever is handy."

"So he chops wood. That's excellent."

"Oh, no. He doesn't chop wood, Mr. General. He breaks it with his bare hands."

"With his bare hands?"

"Yes. He's been doing it for many years." The Duke held out both hands. "See the calluses on the knuckles. Sometimes he just takes his fist and smashes it right into a board. Or sometimes he uses the edge of his hand. He can break a hoe handle hitting that way."

"Break a hoe handle!" General Scheick's eyes were wide. "What a form of defense. Tell me, is this thing hard to learn?"

"No, but it takes time."

"What else does he do?"

"He does a lot of physical conditioning. His family have done that for generations. In fact, they have developed a whole series of exercises."

"Could I see a couple?" General Scheick asked.

"Certainly." The Duke arose. "Now the first thing he asks you to remember is that all these exercises are designed to tone the muscles, to keep them fit. So you have to offer the muscles resistance."

"I get it," General Scheick said. "He lifts weights."

"Oh, no. He might use something that offers light resistance, but no weights. Please feel his forearm."

The Duke extended it, and General Scheick, grasping it, whistled, for it was like a steel cable.

"Now to get a forearm like that," Kenji continued translating, "all you need do is squeeze a piece of toweling, say, twenty-five times each morning, and your arm will get harder and harder. But see, there are no weights involved. Only light resistance."

"That's very interesting," General Scheick said. "Ask him to show me an exercise."

"All right. Here's one. His mind will offer resistance to his muscles." The Duke bent, pretended to lift a heavy weight, and General Scheick saw the muscles of his neck tense, saw them quiver. And it was the same with the Duke's back, and chest, and shoulders. Almost every muscle of the body was brought into play as the make-believe weight was lifted higher and higher.

"You know," General Scheick said, "he's really got something there. Let me try one of those."

"He'll be happy to show you one. If you will stand up, please."

General Scheick arose, husky and ruddy, an eager look on his face.

"This one is a tug of war. Now if you will stand here, Mr. General." The Duke placed him. "He will stand opposite you and be your opponent."

"Don't we use a rope?" General Scheick questioned.

"That would spoil it. You only pretend to use a rope. You tense your muscles as if you were using one."

The fire of competition was in General Scheick's eyes. "Okay, let's go."

The Duke crouched opposite him. "He's ready, and—" Suddenly the Duke straightened, regarded the General and began smiling. "Mr. General, he says before we start this, he thinks he better get himself some help. Mr. Colonel, please, would you pull behind him there? He knows he's going to have his hands full."

The smile started on General Scheick's face, spread, and turned into a full-fledged beam as Colonel Henderson took his place behind the Duke and grabbed the imaginary rope. And it was two against one.

"Go!" the King said, and the three of them began pulling. The muscles stood out on their necks, their hands clenched tightly around the make-believe hemp fibers, and every muscle of their bodies was brought into play as they tugged and grunted. It was two against one, but General Scheick was up to it. Inch by inch he began dragging them across the floor. He gave ground now and then, but always he came back stronger, dragging them along. They were putting up a good battle, but they just didn't have the stuff; and finally, with a mighty heave, General Scheick sent them sprawling on the mats.

"Man," Colonel Henderson said, rising to one knee. "You really gave it to us, sir."

"But you two put up a good battle." General Scheick could feel his muscles tingle and the blood course through his body. "You know, Bill, if we combine this with our vitamins, we've really made a find."

"I know I just used muscles I haven't used in twenty years," Colonel Henderson declared.

"And the nice thing about this system is that there's no chance of rupturing yourself," General Scheick said and turned. "King Kenji, I wonder if I may ask you a favor. Would you put the Duke on detached service?"

"You mean you want to borrow him?"

"Yes, I want to introduce this system to my staff, and I'd like to use him as an instructor."

"Well, I'll ask him." The King translated the English, and when he did so, the Duke was startled. "He wants to know, Mr. General, if you want him to show you how to break boards?"

"Of course."

"Oh." The tired look once again came over the Duke of Beancurd Island. He nodded listlessly. "Yes, he will show you if that is what you wish."

"Good. Good." General Scheick beamed as he stood tensing his muscles. And so intent was he that he failed to notice that the meeting in the main house had broken up, and that the women, in walking by, were peeking in at him. But then the door was pushed farther back, and the Queen Grandmother entered, carrying two quart bottles of rice-bran oil.

"Well, well." General Scheick smiled. "Look who's here. And how's Grandma today?"

Grandma returned his smile. "In one way, she feels awfully good, Mr. General. Do you know what? She just sold her store out in Little Koza."

"Is that right? So the mayor was able to swing it for her."

"No. She sold it herself. She got some of the ladies together from out there and showed them how they could buy it."

"I hope she got cash."

"She certainly did, but it took a lot of doing. Some of the ladies had to join mutual loan societies before they could raise the money to form the Corporation. They managed it, though, and now they own everything but the two ponies and the carts."

"Fine." General Scheick hesitated for a moment, then went on, "I know it's none of my business, but what is she going to do with the cash that she received?"

"She knows what she would like to do."

"Like to do?" General Scheick was curious. "What's that?"

"Well, when the nobility failed to bring in retinues, they put us on an awful spot, because the young people of the retinues were supposed to carry back the wonderful ideas they learned at court. But since there were no retinues, we had to search out another way to get the ideas back, and we went to see Mr. Yamaguchi. He looked it up in the scrolls and found out that old King Gihon, in addition to using retinues, used the *Kamishibai* men."

"The what?"

"The *Kamishibai* men. *Kami* means paper. *Shibai* means show. So it's the paper-show men. Here, let me show you how it works, Mr. General." King Kenji went over and picked up the frame which he had been sanding when the officers arrived. Then he brought out a tripod-like affair about four feet tall and fastened the frame to it. "Now see, Mr. General," he said, "the audience all sits or stands before the frame."

General Scheick nodded.

"Then the paper-show man, who stands to one side, slips a picture onto the frame. He tells a story to his audience, and this picture represents a scene of the story he is telling."

"In other words," General Scheick said, "the paper-show man is a storyteller."

"That's right," the King said. "And he has to be a good story-teller. Because he has to make his audience forget that they are watching a paper-show. He must make them think that they are right there when the story is happening. He must make them laugh, or wonder, or cry . . . whatever the story needs."

"I'll be damned," General Scheick said. "What do you think of that, Bill?"

Colonel Henderson looked at the frame. "Do you know what it reminds me of, sir?"

"What?"

"Television. Look, you got the same screenlike affair. Of course, it's not electronic, but you flash pictures on, you talk, you tell a story. It's practically the same."

"Say, it is." General Scheick's eyes widened. "So this was the original television. King Kenji, when did old King Gihon introduce this?"

"Some time before 1600."

"And he thought of this all by himself?"

"Oh, no, he picked up this idea in Japan one time when he was on a visit."

"Well, I'll give him credit," General Scheick said. "He was a pretty foxy old duffer. This is a perfect way to get what you want to say out to the people. It's a wonderful medium for propaganda."

"Oh, but King Gihon didn't use it for that."

"He didn't?"

171

"No. Mr. Yamaguchi told me that old King Gihon liked to kill two birds with one stone. So whenever he did anything, you should always look for two reasons."

"What were his two reasons here?" General Scheick asked.

"Well, his first reason was this: he knew there wasn't much going on out in the villages. He knew it wasn't much fun just hoeing sweet potatoes all day. So he wanted to get the people some entertainment. His second reason was: he had many ideas that he wanted to get out to the people. Ideas that would help them."

"Such as?"

"Such as how to reduce fever."

"How do you do that?"

"By drinking the juice made by boiling the core of willow wood. That's the kind of ideas old King Gihon wanted to get out. So whenever he came across something new, he would have the paper-show men announce it in the villages."

"It seems to me," General Scheick said, "that he overlooked a good bet. But that was 1600. I suppose they weren't familiar with political indoctrination in those days." He regarded the Queen Grandmother. "So, she's going to put her money in paper-shows?"

"Oh, no, Mr. General," Kenji replied quickly. "That is what she would like to do, but she can't swing it, so she'll have to pass it along to someone else." The Queen Grandmother held out the two bottles she was carrying. "But she wants to know if you would like this rice-bran oil back?"

"No, I want her to take it."

"Mr. General, she's afraid she can't do that. It doesn't agree with her. She tried it and had the worst indigestion, so she had to cut it out completely."

General Scheick pursed his lips in thought. "Aha," he began, "so that's it."

"So that's what, Mr. General?"

"It's the gall bladder. It can't handle the oil." He considered. "I guess I'm going to have to change the prescription, King

Kenji. I still want her to get oil, but I'm going to give it to her in a little different form."

"You are?"

"Yes. I'm going to start giving her sunflower seeds. You know what they are, don't you?"

"Oh, yes," the King replied. "There used to be a party store just off campus, and they sold toasted and salted sunflower seeds."

"That is not the way to eat them," General Scheick said indignantly. "They should be eaten raw. Now I'm going to give her a few pounds from my own supply. I suppose she knows what they are?"

"No, she doesn't. They don't grow over here. But I'll explain to her."

"Please do. And tell her I want her to eat as many as she can a day. Tell her to carry them around in her kimono pocket. If she gets a little hungry, she should take a handful, nibble on them."

"She says she'll do it."

"Fine," General Scheick said, "and we'll see how we come out on this."

Over to one side the Duke of Beancurd Island arose and began bowing. "Mr. General," the King said, "do you wish to ask him any more questions?"

"No, why?"

"He asks to be excused then. He thinks he'll go and break some kindling wood."

At the mention of breaking kindling wood, Grandma turned to the Duke, a look of concern in her eyes, but General Scheick smiled and said, "So he's going to get in a little practice, eh? That's good. Tell him I'll expect him down at headquarters in the morning."

"He says if you wish." Once again the Duke bowed and started for the door.

They watched him leave . . . the smiling General Scheick and the smiling Colonel Henderson. And when he had gone, Grandma spoke in Japanese. "Mr. General, Grandma has asked me how we made out. She is very concerned over filling these positions on the T/O."

"I don't blame her, because certainly you need help in running the government."

"That's what she says. It is too much for the King to do everything."

"I'll agree with that." General Scheick regarded the Queen Grandmother. "But we have to tell her the truth."

"Yes. I know." The King nodded, and he told his grandmother how the Duke of Beancurd Island was going on detached service; how the Duke of Tatami Oshima just didn't quite have what it takes; and how the Duchess of Bamboo Island was only interested in social problems and fashion designing, not politics. Grandma listened, then began shaking her head. "Mr. General, she was afraid something like this might happen. She was hoping the dukes, and of course the Duchess, would step right in."

General Scheick saw her wrinkled forehead. "Well, I'm afraid that's the way it goes."

"Yes, but Grandma wants to know what we're going to do."

"There's only one thing to do. As my very close friend General Winthrope says . . . we must look at the ramifications of the situation. Now on one hand we can't use the dukes and the Duchess." General Scheick paused to let it sink in. "Do you agree?"

There was silence and Colonel Henderson bent anxiously, watched the King; and it was with relief that he heard the King say, "We agree, Mr. General."

"Okay. And do you agree that those positions on the T/O have to be filled?"

"Yes." The King nodded solemnly; and Colonel Henderson mentally shook his head in admiration, for the General was handling this beautifully.

"All right," the General continued slowly. "The problem is: who do we get to fill those positions? Let's look around. You have fifteen populated Islands. Why not use the common man?"

"I see what you mean, Mr. General." Turning, the King interpreted for his grandma.

"It's as simple as that," General Scheick went on. "Now offhand a couple of names come to mind. Do you know Louie and Henry Yamaguchi?"

"I heard you mention them before," the King replied.

"Well, they're not nobility," the General said, "but those two are a couple of bright boys. You get men like that in your government and you got something. Please tell your grandma that."

The King did, then said, "Mr. General, Grandma thinks your plan is excellent."

"Thank you." General Scheick beamed.

"And she says she would certainly like to use it, but she's afraid you overlooked a ramification."

General Scheick tensed. "What does she mean by that?"

"Well, we have tried to place the dukes and Duchess. They are the highest order of nobility. But then we have a lot of other classes. We have earls, viscounts, barons."

"Now, wait a minute!" General Scheick said. "Does that whole bunch get a crack at the T/O?"

"Oh, yes. After the dukes come the earls, so they get the next chance at it."

"And before you get around to Louie Yamaguchi you have to run through the whole list of nobility?"

"Yes, Mr. General. That is the way it has always been done."

General Scheick's eyes clouded. "How long is this list?"

"About as long as my arm."

General Scheick swallowed hard. He could see that he was going to have to fall back and regroup. "King Kenji." He frowned. "I think we better start processing these people right away. We better get them in here and find out who we can use, or can't use. Ask your grandmother if she doesn't agree."

"Oh, Grandma agrees, Mr. General. But we can't afford to bring them in, because I have to furnish the nobility with room, board, and a clothing allowance. I don't have the money for that. I'm having enough trouble supporting the dukes. In fact, that's why Grandma can't take her money from the store and go into the paper-show business. She has to hold it in reserve in case we need sweet potatoes."

"Damn!" General Scheick muttered. He ran his hand through his hair. "But who's going to fill these positions then?"

"It looks like no one," the King replied.

"No one?" General Scheick's eyes widened as the implication sank in, then the blood drained from his face. "My God," he said, "that means you have a vacuum in government!"

"It sure looks that way," the King agreed.

General Scheick was ashen. "But a vacuum in government!" He looked to the King, who was staring out across the courtyard. He looked to the Queen Grandmother, who was running her hand over the sanded paper-show frame, and he added, "How in the devil am I going to explain this to General Winthrope?"

Chapter 13

THE Queen Grandmother had never been in an American home before, so she was understandably curious as Elwood, carrying the wooden legs and frame for the paper-show, opened the aqua-colored door of Cottage 1A and called, "Aunt Caroline, we're here!"

"Oh, good," Mrs. Scheick, who was sitting in the living room, said; and folding the letter that she had just received, she arose to meet them.

Automatically, Grandma slipped out of her reed sandals, but Kenji said, "They don't take off their shoes in the house, Grandma." And she could see that things were different here, indeed.

As she slipped back into her sandals, she looked up, saw the friendly smile of Mrs. Scheick, and she, too, began smiling. "Mrs. General," the King spoke for her, "Grandma says it is so nice of you to receive us, and she hopes we aren't interfering with your afternoon."

"You certainly aren't," Mrs. Scheick replied. "In fact, ever since Elwood told me that you wanted to see me, I've been looking forward to this."

"That is kind of you," the King translated. And Grandma, looking about her at the little entryway, with its mirror and bouquet of flowers, only wished that here in the Nakashima Islands they had the same custom that the Americans had. She only wished that she could have worn a nice hat and a pair of nice white gloves, thereby letting the Mrs. General know that she had dressed up for the occasion. But, unfortunately, they didn't do things that way in the Nakashima Islands. You simply wore what you had, and, in Grandma's case, it was her old brown kimono.

"Won't you please come in?" Mrs. Scheick said.

Slowly, Grandma entered the living room, and she had never seen anything like it. The living room wasn't bare, as in the Nakashima Islands houses. Instead it was filled with things, like pictures, and upright things containing glass bulbs. Nor were the walls composed of sliding wooden doors which, when pushed back, revealed the outside. Here was a great pane of glass that you looked through, instead, to see the out-of-doors.

Mrs. Scheick gestured. Nodding and smiling, Grandma hobbled over to the low little table, and King Kenji whispered quickly, "No, no, Grandma. That is what they call a coffee table. We do not sit on the floor around it. We sit on chairs."

"On chairs?" Grandma's eyes were wide.

"Yes. And the Mrs. General has asked you to take this one." The King indicated a small lounge chair. "She says it is the most comfortable."

"Ah, so." Grandma bowed to Mrs. Scheick and regarded the chair, for never in her seventy-some years had she ever sat in one. At the village meetings she had sat on wooden benches, but they certainly were not like these, so she did not know what to expect. Thus, she was a little tense as she eased herself into it, but then she could hardly believe as she felt the softness of it.

"The Mrs. General would like to know if you are comfortable?" the King asked.

Grandma leaned back. "Tell her, Kenji, that I have never been so comfortable sitting down in my whole life. When you're young, you don't mind the floors. But as you get older, they keep getting harder and harder."

When Kenji translated, Mrs. Scheick smiled. "Well, please tell her just to be comfortable, then. Excuse me for a moment. I'll get us some iced tea, and then we can talk."

"All right, Mrs. General." Kenji smiled and added, "Grandma is certainly going to be surprised. Here she's been drinking tea all her life, but I'm sure she's never had it iced before."

When Mrs. Scheick brought the tray with the tall, cold glasses, Grandma certainly was surprised. "What is it we are drinking, Kenji?" she asked; and when the King told her, she stared in wonder at the cubes floating in the drink. She had seen ice before. Sometimes in December in the Nakashima Islands it gets fairly cold, and in the early morning, before the sun rises, you can see icicles hanging from the eaves. But ice in July! She shook her head. "How do they manage it?"

"They have something called a refrigerator," the King replied. "It keeps things cold. It makes ice, too."

"Even in summer?"

"Even in summer."

Grandma looked at Mrs. Scheick, began speaking, and Kenji said, "I told her about refrigerators. And she says with chairs, and a room like this . . . why, she just didn't know there were so many new things in the world."

"I only hope she likes them," Mrs. Scheick said.

"Oh, she does, Mrs. General." Grandma sipped her tea, felt its cooling freshness. "She says this is nice. Very nice."

"Good." Mrs. Scheick regarded the King and Elwood. "And how are things going with you two?"

"Pretty fair," Elwood replied. "We have about six hundred eggs in the incubators. But we haven't been able to work out anything on feed."

"I was afraid of that." Mrs. Scheick indicated the letter on the coffee table. "Incidentally, I've just heard from your father, Elwood. I wrote him, asking him if the elevator didn't have some literature on chicken feed, as you suggested."

Elwood put down his glass. "Did he have any?"

179

"No. All he said was, 'Oh, we wouldn't have anything like that.'" Mrs. Scheick grew thoughtful. "You know, I just can't understand it. It seems to me a mill that wants to sell feed would be putting out all kinds of literature."

"It would be a good idea. Things like the latest information from the agricultural schools, and so forth."

"Exactly. It seems to me they would be getting ideas out to the farmers just as fast as they could."

"Well, maybe Dad is satisfied with the volume of business the way it is."

"Do you think that?" Mrs. Scheick frowned. "Well, I certainly . . . oh, never mind." She turned to the King and said, "I understand your grandmother has a business proposition that she wants to see me about."

"That's right." The King nodded. "Grandma says it's a good one, too. You know, Mrs. General, Grandma formed an investment club among the women out in Little Koza and sold her store to them. And she says she would like to invest her own money in this venture, but she has to hold it back in reserve. So she wants to pass this along to your Investment Club."

"May I ask why?"

"Well, as you know, we are processing the hundred-year-old eggs, Mrs. General, but even those take ninety days to get on the market. And with the chickens hatching and everything, it's going to take a long time before any money starts rolling into the Nakashima Islands Egg Corporation."

"That's true."

"Anyway, Grandma figures that with no money coming in, the ladies are getting upset."

"They certainly are. In fact, the only thing Mrs. McCloud can talk of these days is liquidation."

"But Grandma doesn't want you to liquidate, Mrs. General. She wants you to stay in business so eggs will go out on the market. She knows, however, for you to do that you must have a profit. And she figures if she passes this along you will make that profit and perhaps you will keep the Egg Corporation going."

"Is there a chance for immediate gain in this venture?"

"Oh, yes. And see, if you start this new business you wouldn't have all your eggs in one basket, so to speak."

"I'm certainly for diversification," Mrs. Scheick said. "But just what is the nature of this?"

"Well, in a way you might say it involves show business."

"Show business?" Mrs. Scheick's eyebrows flew up. "That doesn't sound like a very stable thing. I've heard how people lose money in those Broadway shows."

"But, Aunt Caroline," Elwood said quickly. "This isn't like that at all. Here, let me show you." He arose, set up the wooden tripod and frame. "Now you see, Aunt Caroline, it's sort of like, well, Colonel Henderson has called it the original television."

"Really?"

"Oh, yes." And Elwood went on to explain how the paper-show man slipped in the pictures, how he told a story.

"It is a little like television, isn't it?" Mrs. Scheick said. "I don't understand, though, how our Investment Club would fit into this."

"Well, here's the way we figured it," Elwood said. "Now, first of all you ladies would organize the Nakashima Islands Paper-Show Corporation."

"I see. And that would be a division of the Nakashima Islands Egg Corporation?"

"That's right, Aunt Caroline," Elwood replied. "Now we have had Mr. Yamaguchi search the scrolls for us, and we have found that old King Gihon set up the paper-show business on a very sound basis, so we figure that we'll use his methods."

"Oh, and how did he have it set up?"

"First of all, he established what is called the paper-show headquarters. Then he licensed one hundred storytellers to work out of this headquarters. He limited the number to that, and he assigned each one of them a territory in the Nakashima Islands. In the outlying districts, the territory was comprised of ten villages. So every ten days the storyteller would play to the same village; and since everybody lives in villages, all the people had a chance to see a show once every ten days. But in

181

the larger towns, or the capital, there were districts instead of territories."

"I see." Mrs. Scheick nodded.

"Next, the paper-show headquarters was divided into a number of departments. First, there was the casting department. They hired the storytellers. They gave them tryouts, and, I understand, there were always a lot of young fellows interested in going into the business. They also kept tab on the regular storytellers to see that they were on their toes. Secondly, there was the booking department."

Mrs. Scheick regarded her nephew. "You mean old King Gihon even had that?"

"He did, Aunt Caroline. The booking department would shift the storytellers around so that the people didn't have the same one all the time. Then, of course, they would book them into districts according to talent and ability. The young ones they would keep out in the back country. Then, as they got better and better, they would keep bringing them in closer to the capital."

"And do you know, Mrs. General," the King said, "the best district of all was Watanabe Square, here in Tamabaru. That used to be the center of things. When a storyteller got booked into there, he knew he had it made."

"Is that so?" Mrs. Scheick looked at the Queen Grandmother, who nodded solemnly. "And what other departments were there?"

"There were three more," Elwood said. "The paper-show men had to have stories to tell, so there was the story department, which made them up. They had to have pictures to put on the frame, so there was the art department, which painted them. And last of all was the business office."

"I suppose they handled the admissions," Mrs. Scheick said.

"Oh, no, Aunt Caroline." Elwood shook his head. "The paper-show doesn't charge admissions."

"No admissions! How in the world do they make any money then?"

"They sell sweet potato taffy to the audience. After the paper-show man sets up his frame, he gets out his boxes of candy. The more pieces you buy, the closer you can sit to the front. And when enough is sold, he will start the show."

"But aren't there some people who go without buying a thing?" Mrs. Scheick asked.

"We were wondering about that too, Mrs. General," the King said, "so we had Mr. Yamaguchi look it up in the scrolls."

"And that was in the scrolls, too?"

"Oh, yes. We have complete records. Mr. Yamaguchi found that from time to time there were people who would attend without buying taffy. However, King Gihon figured that now and then everybody was bound to be down on their luck and that's when they needed a show most, so if they didn't have any money, it was all right. They could come anyway. They were welcome, and next time maybe they could buy a little more taffy."

"That's certainly intriguing," Mrs. Scheick said. Then her eyes narrowed calculatingly. "King Kenji, I want to ask your grandmother something frankly. I want to know if she thinks my Investment Club could make, let us say, a fair amount of money on this venture."

"Mrs. General, Grandma says she doesn't think you will make a fair amount of money. She thinks you will make a lot of money, because look at it this way: You will have a hundred paper-show men. That means you will have a hundred shows playing every night."

"Oh, my goodness," Mrs. Scheick said.

"Then, Grandma says, at each show you would have practically the whole village, or practically all the people from the district where it is playing."

The possibilities of the venture began to come to Mrs. Scheick. "A hundred shows a night and all with full houses."

"Yes." The King nodded. "Now here is the way the money from the sale of the sweet potato taffy is split. The paper-show man gets anywhere from twenty to forty per cent for telling the story."

"Just a moment." Mrs. Scheick picked up a pen and notebook. "Twenty to forty per cent. What determines that?"

"The area into which the paper-show man is booked. Watanabe Square is good for forty per cent, while the northern villages are good for only twenty-five per cent. But the districts and the percentages are all listed in the scrolls."

"I see. So the paper-show headquarters would get the remaining percentages then—anywhere from sixty to seventy-five." Mrs. Scheick made a note, then looked up. "Who pays for the sweet potato taffy?"

"The headquarters."

"Now wait. Wait just a minute." She turned a page, and in her eye was the look of a trader on the market who has come across a real buy. "Now suppose," she said, "our Investment Club should go into this business. Exactly what would we need?"

"Well, Grandma says you just can't beat old King Gihon's organization, so she says we'll use that as a model. Number one, you would need a building to house your headquarters."

Mrs. Scheick wrote the word EXPENSES in her notebook. "So that means rent."

"Yes. But Grandma says that would be practically nothing. Why, those old stores surrounding Watanabe Square haven't been occupied in years and years. For five Islands dollars a month you could get all the space you need."

Mrs. Scheick thought for a moment. "Aren't they awfully run-down though?"

"Yes, they are. However, Grandma says you ladies know how to fix things so nice. Why, take this room."

"Those stores could be an interesting challenge," Mrs. Scheick stated. "Is there anywhere out here we could get paint?"

"I'm afraid we don't have anything like that, Mrs. General."

"Hmmm. Well, what else would we need?"

"You would need someone to look after the whole operation."

"Oh, dear. How would we manage that? I wouldn't know anyone among the population."

"We can arrange that," the King said quickly. "In fact, Mr.

Yamaguchi has already suggested our leading literary figure, Yoshimitsu Matsumoto, the chief of mounted police. He would be invaluable, because not only does he speak English, but he knows all the classical stories which could be dramatized. And he's always translating modern stories, so you would have a good man there."

"We'd need one," Mrs. Scheick said. "After all, he'd have to co-ordinate the whole thing. He'd have to hire his department heads and storytellers, watch the quality of the art work and stories themselves. And I imagine he'd even have to watch the quality of the sweet potato taffy. Isn't that right?"

"That's right, Mrs. General, except for the candy. Grandma personally knows the best sweet potato taffy maker in the Nakashima Islands. It is a Mrs. Shiroma, a very good friend of hers who lives in Goya. Now Mrs. Shiroma wouldn't be equipped to supply you at the moment. But Grandma will form a little Investment Club among the women of Goya to back Mrs. Shiroma. Then Mrs. Shiroma could hire some girls and maybe rent an empty house, and it wouldn't take more than two weeks before she could supply the whole paper-show business."

"Excellent." Mrs. Scheick smiled. "Excellent." Then a thought struck her and her smile faded. "King Kenji, I think this has tremendous possibilities, but please tell your grandmother that I have a problem."

"What is that, Mrs. General?"

"Well, setting up this Nakashima Islands Paper-Show Corporation is going to cost money. We're also going to need money to carry us along while we organize, train storytellers, get pictures painted, and scripts written. Now to raise that money I have to face the girls. Remember, you and Elwood told them they were going to make a lot of money in the chicken business."

"But I think they might, Aunt Caroline," Elwood said quickly. "Just ask Grandma. She'll agree."

"I'll agree that we might. But Mrs. McCloud isn't interested in that. She's interested in what we are doing now, and what we are doing is losing money. Suppose I stand up there again. Suppose I say, 'Oh, we're going to make a lot of money.' This time I think Mrs. McCloud and the girls are going to want proof. Please tell your grandmother that."

The King translated, and as the words were put into Japanese, his grandmother, sitting in the lounge chair, with one blue tattooed hand resting in her lap, the other grasping the glass of iced tea, listened carefully. Then she looked full at Mrs. Scheick and her grandson put her words into English. "Mrs. General, Grandma wants to know if you, personally, believe the paper-show business will make money?"

Mrs. Scheick returned her look. "I do. I certainly do."

"Grandma says that is all that's necessary. Perhaps then we can find a way to get the ladies interested."

The two of them sat there a moment regarding each other, then they began smiling, and Mrs. Scheick said, "Getting this paper-show business started means a great deal to your grandmother, doesn't it, King Kenji?"

"Yes, it does, Mrs. General, because Grandma wants to get an idea out to the people. She would ask one favor of you ladies in return for turning the paper-show over to you."

"What is that?"

"A little time at the end of each performance in which the paper-show man can tell the people what the King has to say. In the future there may be other ideas. But for now she just has one. That is the idea of your Investment Club."

"Our Investment Club!" Mrs. Scheick was surprised. "I had no idea she thought so much of investment clubs."

"She does. Ever since she has heard of them, she has been thinking and thinking. You see, when old King Gihon introduced the idea of the Mutual Loan Association, it changed everything here in the Nakashima Islands. It got fishing boats built, and pigs bought, and people married. It was an idea that revolutionized everything."

"And does she think the idea of the investment club could revolutionize things in this day and age?"

"Grandma says she is sure of it. She's lived in the villages all her life, and she knows how hard it is to raise capital. But look

—the investment club idea has sold her store for her. And you just let this idea get out to all the villages. You just let the ladies out there get to thinking about making money, and what they can do! She says that if I, King Kenji I, can introduce the investment club just like King Gihon introduced the mutual loan society, then she is sure we can make up all the ground lost during the Interruption. She is sure we can bring the Nakashima Islands up to the verge of a golden age, just like old King Gihon did."

"Well," Mrs. Scheick began thoughtfully, "if that's the case, I'll certainly do all I can to help."

"Grandma thanks you."

"She is welcome. But to get down to the business at hand. How are we going to convince the girls, and especially Mrs. McCloud, that they should put up more money?"

"Mrs. General," Kenji said, "I just happened to think. When Mr. Yamaguchi was going through the scrolls, he found a record of the weekly receipts for old King Gihon's paper-show business covering a period of more than thirty years."

"Thirty years?"

"Yes. Now you know, of course, the paper-show business was traditionally slack in the summer, the farmers being in the fields in the evening and all. But even in the worst summer week, the profits—after all headquarters salaries were paid—were never less than the equivalent of four hundred Islands dollars in today's money."

"Four hundred dollars," Mrs. Scheick said. "Why, that kind of money could carry our Egg Corporation along nicely."

"We know," the King said. "And Grandma wonders if that wouldn't impress the ladies?"

"It would impress Irene Henderson and some of the others," Mrs. Scheick said. "But I don't think it would mean much to Mrs. McCloud."

"You don't?"

"No. Mrs. McCloud doesn't think that way. She likes to see something tangible, like a dividend."

"Well, it's kind of hard to pay money out in dividends when you're not earning any," the King said.

"Yes, it is," Mrs. Scheick agreed. "How can you pay out any money . . ." She stopped and her eyes widened. "But does a dividend have to be in money?"

"Gosh, Aunt Caroline, what else could it be in?" Elwood asked.

"Why couldn't it be in stock?"

"I don't get it," Elwood said.

But King Kenji was nodding. "That's right, Mrs. General. It can be in stock. I came across that in economics."

"Yes, indeed, it can be in stock," Mrs. Scheick went on, her eyes intent. "Now suppose the Nakashima Islands Egg Corporation should declare a hundred per cent stock dividend."

"I came across that, too, Mrs. General," Kenji said. "Up in Japan they call that an octopus dividend, because it's like the hungry octopus eating its own legs."

"But this would be for Mrs. McCloud's own good," Mrs. Scheick continued. "And if we should give Mrs. McCloud two shares of stock for every one we have now . . ."

"Two for one, do you think she would go for that?" Kenji asked.

"I'm sure she would," Mrs. Scheick said. "Why, with a hundred per cent stock dividend in eggs, you just couldn't keep her from putting money into the paper-show."

Both Kenji and Elwood whistled.

"And why couldn't we do this?" Mrs. Scheick continued. "If the paper-show is the original television, why can't we sell advertising space? Just think of the additional revenue that would bring in."

"Gee, it would, wouldn't it?" Elwood said.

Kenji could hardly sit still. "Wait until I tell Grandma, Mrs. General," he said. "Why, she won't be able to believe." He turned to translate, and as he did so, Mrs. Scheick stopped him.

"Just a moment," Mrs. Scheick said. "I happened to remember something. About the paint for those stores down in Watanabe Square. Tell Grandma I'll see the Quartermaster. I'm sure there must be some of that yellow, or pink, or aqua left that I had him get to paint our front doors on Caroline Drive."

Chapter 14

AS GENERAL SCHEICK sat at his desk looking over the strength report he was appalled, for show business had gotten into the blood of the Nakashima Islands Mounted Police. Not only had Yoshimitsu Matsumoto, the chief, resigned to head the Paper-Show Corporation, but they had had try-outs for storytellers and sixty-seven police had left, including Jiro Kamakura, the executive officer, who was so good at telling tales that he had drawn the best district of all, Watanabe Square, and had promptly changed his name from Jiro to the more theatrical-sounding Todi Kabuki.

"And after the way we worked to build up that organization and match those ponies," General Scheick muttered. Then he arose from his chair to go down to the improvised gym which the Duke of Beancurd Island had set up. He was finding that there was nothing like exercise to help ease a man's worries.

Taking a small handful of sunflower seeds to munch on the way, he closed his desk drawer. And as he did so his aide, radiogram in hand, came hurrying in.

"Sir," the young lieutenant said, "it's come."

General Scheick looked at the radiogram. Indeed it had come.

"Thank you," he said, steeling himself, and opening it, began to read.

A VACUUM IN GOVERNMENT. HOW IN THE NAME OF
HEAVEN COULD YOU LET IT HAPPEN, MAN! DON'T YOU REALIZE
THAT NOTHING REMAINS A VACUUM? DON'T YOU REALIZE
A VACUUM IS ALWAYS FILLED? AND CERTAINLY YOU ARE
AWARE OF THAT ELEMENT WHICH THRIVES ON JUST SUCH
A SITUATION.

WE HAVE TO KEEP THIS ELEMENT OUT. SINCE THEY ARE
SUPPORTED BY THOSE WHO HAVE BEEN DENIED, WE MUST GIVE
DENIAL OUR UTMOST CONSIDERATION.

DO YOU KNOW WHAT HAPPENS WHEN YOU DENY A PEOPLE?
YOU HAVE A NATION OF HAVE-NOTS. AND WHEN YOU HAVE A
NATION OF HAVE-NOTS, YOU'RE JUST WAITING TO BE PICKED.

NOW WHAT WE MUST DO IS TURN THESE PEOPLE INTO A
NATION OF HAVES. WE MUST FIND OUT WHAT THEY WANT
AND DO SOMETHING ABOUT IT. I EXPECT YOU TO COMPLY IM-
MEDIATELY.

I DON'T KNOW HOW MUCH LONGER WE CAN KEEP ALL THIS
A SECRET WITHIN THE PENTAGON. I'M AFRAID WE'RE GOING
TO HAVE TO LET IT OUT OF THE BAG. THAT, HOWEVER, IS OUT
OF MY HANDS NOW. I'M MEETING WITH THE BIG BRASS THIS
AFTERNOON, AND THEY WILL MAKE THE DECISION.

(*Signed*) MOSBY

When General Scheick finished, he looked out through the window, looked down at the ancient capital of Tamabaru which lay below him. In Watanabe Square workmen on bamboo ladders were spreading pink and aqua paint on a string of old stores, but he didn't notice, for his eyes were on the farm women in their shabby banana-cloth kimonos, lined up with their sweet potatoes before them. The full impact of Mosby's words hit him then, because certainly there weren't many "haves" down there.

He glanced once again at the radiogram, reread it, and realized Mosby, as always, was right. Striding to the door, he threw it open and started down the hall. As he passed the improvised gym on the first floor, he looked in. Over to one side Lt. Colonel Seymour, the Operations Officer, was lifting an imaginary weight; and since, in his imagination, it weighed in the vicinity of a ton or so, he was straining mightily. In the middle of the room Colonel Henderson was engaged in an imaginary tug of war, his opponents being Major McCloud of Intelligence and the Major's assistant, Captain Carlisle. While over to one side the Duke of Beancurd Island, who supposedly was supervising the whole program, sat staring out the window, his face a study in boredom.

"Bill," General Scheick called.

"Yes, sir." Colonel Henderson straightened, leaving his opponents still in an imaginary pulling position.

"Look after things, Bill," the General said. "I have to go up to the castle and talk with the King and his grandmother." And he set off at a brisk pace which was almost as good as the Duke's exercises for easing the mind.

He passed Caroline Drive, halfway up the hill; and when he started up the narrow cart trail leading to the castle, he noticed, for the first time, that a touch of autumn was in the air. The wild, sumac-like growth bordering the trail was beginning to turn a fiery red, while overhead the green of the trees was beginning to take on a tinge of gold. He walked along the shaded cart trail where old King Gihon used to take his morning constitutional; and arriving at the lowest of the courtyards was surprised to find Elwood, a frown on his face, standing in the center of the wild grass.

"Elwood," the General called, "what's going on?"

"Oh, hello, Uncle Matt," the youth said. "I'm trying to figure out some chicken runs."

General Scheick walked over to his nephew. "What?"

"I have problems. We have a batch of chicks coming in every other day, and we can't afford to feed them rice. So I'm trying to figure out some way so that they can scratch for themselves."

"Oh." General Scheick noticed, also for the first time, that his nephew was taking on a bronzed, outdoor look. "I don't see much of you any more. How have you been?"

"All right, Uncle Matt. I've been wanting to talk with you

and Aunt Caroline. I've been thinking the situation over, and I'd like to drop out of school."

"Why, you can't do that," the General said quickly. "How are we going to stay ahead on the international scene without education? Our future depends on you fellows going to college."

"But it only would be for a semester."

"If it's only for half a semester, it's still a mistake."

"Gosh, Uncle Matt," Elwood said. "I can't walk out on the King at this point. I have to look after these chickens. I have to figure out a way to get some feed for them. Then there's the paper-show business. I want to help get that rolling."

"Well," the General said after a moment, "come down to the house and we'll discuss it. In fact, why don't you go down now and talk with your aunt?"

"Okay, Uncle Matt. I'll drop into Paper-Show Headquarters and see her."

"You do that. And you'll see. She'll tell you exactly what I did." General Scheick looked up at the top of the hill to the royal courtyard. "Is the King home?"

"Yes, he's up there."

"Good. I'll be in touch with you. In the meantime, talk with your Aunt Caroline."

As General Scheick entered the royal courtyard at the very top of the peak, he heard the grunt of the Duke of Tatami Oshima's pig. Nearing the main house, he caught sight of the Duchess of Bamboo Island. She was sitting just inside the door of her apartment, staring out at the East China Sea; and so lost in thought was she that she failed to notice him, the sea itself, or the other Islands of the chain. He was about to call to her when he saw the King and his grandmother over by one of the ancient walls, apparently inspecting something on the ground, so he strode toward them.

It was the Queen Grandmother who noticed him first. She smiled and tugged her grandson's sleeve; and King Kenji, looking up from his kneeling position, began to grin. "Mr. General," he called, "come and see what we've just done."

General Scheick walked over, and glancing down at the base of the wall, he saw the little area of new-turned earth, saw the slip of green that had been placed in it, and asked, "What's that?"

"It's ivy," the King replied.

"Ivy?"

"Yes, I was explaining to Grandma about it. You see, I've just received a letter from Mr. Hayden, the president of Cambridge College. He put my name on the alumni list, and for the fall fund-raising promotion the college is sending out sprigs of ivy from the Old Main." Kenji gestured toward the Duchess of Bamboo Island. "You know, I think this will make Debbie feel better. She's still awfully upset about the scholarships being canceled."

At the mention of the Duchess of Bamboo Island, Grandma's eyes stole to the General; for a moment the two of them looked at each other, then Grandma shook her head.

"Besides," the King went on, "it's going to make me feel good, too, just to see it growing here."

General Scheick stared at him in disbelief. Here they were, just waiting to be picked, and the King was concerned with ivy.

"I only wish," Kenji continued, "that I had some money to give to the college, because things are pretty bad. Why, do you know that the Varsity is going to have to wear the same game uniforms they've been wearing since 1924? Mr. Hayden says that's not good for morale, because it gives the team an awful complex when they have to come trotting out on the field with those old-fashioned nose guards. And you should see the list of the things the college needs."

"That is exactly what I want to see you about," General Scheick said sternly.

"You do?" Kenji's eyes widened. "I know the college needs help, Mr. General, but I'm kind of broke, and—"

"I'm not talking about the college needs." General Scheick was trying to be patient. "I'm talking about the needs, the wants of your people. Tell your grandma what I just said."

"Okay." Kenji translated, and the Queen Grandmother

looked up quizzically. "Grandma would like to know—what about the needs of our people, Mr. General?"

"It's simply this: tell her that if you, as King, don't supply their wants, you're going to have an awfully unhappy bunch around here. So what are we going to do about them? What are we going to do to turn your people into a nation of haves?"

"Well, I don't know." Kenji consulted with his grandmother, then said, "What do you recommend that we do, Mr. General?"

It caught General Scheick by surprise. "I'll tell you this—you damn well better do something."

"Is that so, Mr. General?" Grandma's eyes were on her grandson now. "But Grandma says she has never quite thought of it in those terms before."

"What terms?"

"In terms of fulfilling the wants of our people. Grandma says now when she thinks about it, however, she realizes that is what old King Gihon was always trying to do. She realizes that we reached the verge of a golden age because the people had what they wanted."

"Exactly," General Scheick said.

"In that case then, Grandma says truly we must do something about these wants. But what?"

General Scheick pondered for a moment. "First of all, if you're going to fill them, you're going to have to find out what their wants are, aren't you?"

"That sounds logical," the King agreed.

"All right. And to find out what their wants are, you have to investigate."

"Ah, I understand. We go around asking them."

"Right. For instance, we might form a joint committee." General Scheick turned and looked at the Duchess of Bamboo Island sitting listlessly near the door of her room, and the Duke of Tatami Oshima sitting in the shade, visiting with his pig. "But you don't have anyone to put on a committee, do you?"

"No."

"That's all right," General Scheick said quickly. "This is much too important to reduce to the level of a committee anyway.

194

You and I had better handle this ourselves, King Kenji. Of course, when I say 'you,' I'm including your grandma."

"I know that."

"Fine. Let's conduct an independent investigation then. We'll each draw up a list. See what Grandma thinks of that."

"Grandma thinks it is a very fine idea, and she is for it."

"Wonderful. Now I'm going right down," General Scheick continued, "and look up Louie and Henry Yamaguchi. I'm going to lay it right on the line. I'm going to say, 'Boys, exactly what do you want?' And I expect you to be doing the same thing."

"I didn't know you were in such a hurry, Mr. General."

"We have to be in a hurry. We can't waste a moment."

"Oh." Kenji told his grandmother, who seemed puzzled. "But why must we rush so?" she asked.

"That is the way the Americans like to do things, Grandma. My history professor used to say that the patron saint of America is St. Vitus."

"What does that mean?"

"It's hard to explain. But maybe we had just better be in a hurry, too."

"If you think it best."

Kenji switched to English. "Mr. General, we'll be happy to hurry like the dickens."

"Good. I'll leave you then. And don't forget, King Kenji, we have to make the grade."

They watched the General stride off, determination in his step. They watched him head down toward town to look up Louie and Henry Yamaguchi, and Grandma said, "I like that, Kenji."

"What, Grandma?"

"About the wants." Her eyes fell on him as she said slowly, deliberately, "Just think, we can bring the Nakashima Islands to the verge of a golden age just like old King Gihon did. See, the General clarified the method."

"Didn't the scrolls mention that?"

"Not in those words. They tell what Gihon did, but you have

195

to draw your own conclusions as to the way he achieved things." Grandma paused, waited for the impact of her words to reach her grandson.

Her grandson didn't seem to understand, however. Instead, he said, "Well, Grandma, I'd better get down and find out what the people want."

"Why do you have to go through all that?" Grandma asked. "Don't you remember how it was out in the store at Little Koza? Don't you remember how people used to come in and ask me for things?"

"Yes."

"Well, the things we have to be concerned with are the things I only had sometimes, or the things I never had."

"I don't understand."

"Look, Kenji, someone could make a lot of money by supplying things we never had. It would be a great business opportunity. So if we're going to hurry, why not save ourselves a step or two?"

"How, Grandma?"

"By means of the paper-show. After the show, when the paper-show man explains all about how to form an investment club, we will have him make an announcement. We will have him announce that any investment club that is looking for business opportunity should come up to the castle, and we will tell them what the people used to ask for and what I couldn't supply."

"Do you mean, Grandma, they could go into business then, supplying it?"

"That is right. Then we could also announce that anyone who has an idea on how to supply things but doesn't have any money to go about it, should also come up. We will try to find an investment club to back him."

"In other words, Grandma," Kenji said, "the castle will be kind of a clearing place for ideas and business opportunity."

"I see it that way. You know, I had Mr. Yamaguchi read me some of the scrolls, and now that I think of it, I believe old King Gihon would have done it this way too."

"Do you think so?"

"Yes, because I noticed that old King Gihon liked to keep his hand in things. This will give us an opportunity to do just that." Grandma reached into the pocket of her kimono, felt about, then said, "Oh, my goodness."

"What's the matter?" Kenji asked.

"I'm out of sunflower seeds," she replied. "And do you know, I think they're helping me."

"Maybe you should have asked the Mr. General for more," the King said.

"That's what I intended to do." Grandma nodded. "But everybody was in so much of a hurry that I got to hurrying, too, and I forgot all about it."

Chapter 15

IT WAS quite an opening night for the paper-show down in Watanabe Square. It was decided that it would be much more effective to have it after dark, rather than in the light of evening. So as Todi Kabuki—formerly Jiro Kamakura, executive officer to Yoshimitsu Matsumoto, ex-chief of mounted police—set up his wooden frame in the heart of the Square, the August Moon was rising, full and golden, in the east. The rays of flashlights cut the soft darkness as the crowd began to assemble. And what a crowd it was!

The King and his grandmother were there, as was the Duke of Tatami Oshima. The whole Investment Club, led by Mrs. Scheick, was there with each member carrying a spare box of sweet potato taffy. From the old capital itself came Yamaguchi Kiei, the ancient historian, plus scores of the prominent and not so prominent. Uncle Shoji Takamini was there with his three unmarried daughters, as was Haruko, the Scheick's little Nakashima Islands maid. And even the General came down from headquarters, leading Colonel Henderson and the other members of his staff. While at the back of the crowd, standing glum-faced and hoping for the worst, were other paper-show storytellers, who had been assigned to other areas and who were just waiting to get a chance at this, the best district of all.

But Todi Kabuki had them, else he never would have drawn the Watanabe district in the first place. He had them right in the palm of his hand. Wearing his yellow police scarf, now turned into a yellow and black diamond-shaped check by means of the *sumi* ink, he passed among them selling his sweet potato taffy, nonchalantly accepting—as each box was emptied—the new box handed him by the women's Investment Club. He even sold General Scheick a half dozen pieces, with the staff following suit. And when he was sold out completely, he stepped to the paper-show frame, with all eyes following him.

After much discussion, Mrs. Scheick, the board of directors, and Yoshimitsu Matsumoto had decided that for opening night they should have a classical love story, a Romeo and Juliet story, which can be found in every language and every culture. But they knew it would be no good under the white glare of a flashlight shining upon a series of painted pictures. So Elwood had worked out a system of lighting for them. By means of rubber bands, he fastened colored cellophane over the flashlights. And with himself handling the red, with the casting director, the head of the art department, and the other members of the paper-show staff handling the other colors, they stood ready to help Todi Kabuki.

And Todi Kabuki was good. In soft tones he brought on the girl, so beautiful that she could only exist in the imagination of the artist who drew her, but as Todi spoke, the three unmarried Takamini girls were seeing themselves up there, as was Haruko, the little maid. And even the Investment Club stirred. Although they didn't understand Japanese, yet they recognized the tone.

Then Todi, in the glow from the colored flashlights, brought on the hero, upright, noble and handsome. And with Elwood giving him a full red spot, Todi then flashed the picture of the girl's father, the menace in the play, and there was another stirring in the audience. For while this was a classical story, and while the menace was clad in classical Japanese robes, to General Scheick he bore a strong resemblance to Owen Younger, Mrs.

Scheick's father; whereas to Colonel Henderson he somehow resembled First Sergeant Taylor, whose daughter the Colonel had married.

Still in the blood-red spotlight, Todi showed another picture of the menace in his home stamping grounds, ruling the roost, and General Scheick and Colonel Henderson began to remember. General Scheick remembered the frosty receptions he and his now brother-in-law Fred Cummings used to get when they called on the Younger girls at the Younger family mansion. He remembered his now brother-in-law Fred being dubbed "Good-Time Charley"—while he, the General, was referred to as "The Blockhead." Owen Younger stating at the time for all to hear that if he, Matt Scheick, was so much as made a corporal, he, Owen Younger, was going to burn his Liberty Bonds. While Colonel Henderson remembered the statement made by First Sergeant Taylor about the then Lieutenant Henderson. "I wouldn't trade you a private first class for the bastard," the First Sergeant had said, shifting his chew. And as they sat there, staring at the menace in the blood-red spot, apparently memories were stirring in others, too, for Yamaguchi Kiei, the ancient historian, shook his head and whispered *"Baka Yaro"*—which only means "foolish fellow" in Japanese, but which are fighting words nevertheless.

Todi Kabuki had his ingredients now, and he began stirring them. With a word here and a picture there, he lifted the crowd from Watanabe Square and took them to a world that existed a long, long time ago. He had them laughing. He had them crying. And by the time that true love won out, every storyteller in the back row knew that this was going down as a famous moment in paper-show history.

So it was no wonder that after Todi explained about investment clubs, and after he explained that anyone searching for business opportunity should come up to the castle—it was no wonder that they had a celebration at Paper-Show Headquarters. As the teacups clinked, Agnes McCloud, company treasurer, counted the take, and it was nothing short of phenomenal. "Imagine," Agnes said, "what we will make if we can only find someone to advertise, like on television." And the teacups were raised in toast to the paper-show, although there was a bit of complaining. For the storytellers from the outlying districts said sure Todi could do it, because he was working with colored flashlights while they had to perform in the early evening by the light of day. And Todi himself had a complaint. Scarf around neck, puffing a cigarette, he stood beside Yoshimitsu, who explained, "He says, Mrs. General, he can't see why Paper-Show Headquarters should get sixty per cent and he only forty. He thinks it should be the other way around."

"But that was the agreement," Mrs. Scheick said.

"I know." Yoshimitsu nodded. "However, I thought I could get him a little more."

Mrs. Scheick's eyes narrowed suspiciously. "Why should you be interested in getting him more?"

"Because I represent him. I get ten per cent of what he gets. As they say in the movie magazines, I am his agent."

Mrs. Scheick was shocked. "And are you representing all of the other storytellers, too?"

"Oh, sure," Yoshimitsu replied.

"Well that's the end of that then," Mrs. Scheick stated. "You're not going to head the Paper-Show Corporation and represent the storytellers, too. It's not ethical."

"I was only trying to pick up a little spare money."

"I realize that. Now you're going to have to make up your mind. Are you going to head the paper-show, or are you going to represent them?"

When put in such a manner, Yoshimitsu hardly had a choice. He had to stay with heading the paper-show, yet the thought of losing the extra income sank him into gloom.

But it was a night to remember. All the way home to the castle Elwood and King Kenji, leading the pony, and Grandma, riding in the cart behind, talked about it. "I hope, though," Grandma said, a trace of worry in her voice, "that everyone did not get too carried away with the show. I hope they heard our announcement at the end, because that is what is so important."

Grandma, however, need not have worried. For the following morning the King had just finished breakfast when, looking up, he saw Yoshimitsu himself. "Why, Mr. Matsumoto," Kenji said. "What can I do for you?"

"Well, last night," Yoshimitsu explained, "you had Todi Kabuki announce that anyone who was looking for business opportunity should come up here. So here I am."

"And you're looking for that?"

"Oh, yes," Yoshimitsu stated. "You see, it's getting awfully hard to make an extra dollar around this place, so if you have a little spare-time opportunity . . ."

"Well." The King smiled. "Wait until I tell Grandma. She was quite worried that no one would come up, so she'll be real glad to see you."

Grandma certainly was glad. Coming from the kitchen with a pot of tea for Yoshimitsu and herself, she expressed her happiness several times. Then pouring the tea, she settled down on the veranda. "Kenji," she said, "let's see what opportunity we can find for Mr. Matsumoto, even if it is only on a spare-time basis."

"All right, Grandma. Shall I tell him about the things people used to ask you for, and you didn't have?"

"Yes. Let's try that."

"Okay." The King grew solemn. "Mr. Matsumoto, when Grandma ran her store out in Little Koza, people were always coming in to rent tools, so there is an opportunity—"

"Just a moment, Kenji," Grandma cut in. "You see, Mr. Matsumoto, I had a few hand tools to rent out, things like hoes and sickles. But there was always a demand for larger things like hand cultivators and harrows, and even for carpenters' tools. I never had the capital to buy those things. So if you could form a little investment club, raise some money, and buy a lot of these tools . . ."

"I wouldn't have time to go out to the villages and rent them out," Yoshimitsu said.

"You wouldn't have to rent them out yourself. You could arrange with the village stores to act as your agent. They could rent them to the farmers for you for a certain percentage. The renting of tools is an excellent opportunity, because the farmers never have money to buy all they need."

"Well, I don't know," Yoshimitsu said.

"All right, if you don't want to rent tools, I'll pass that idea on to another group. Instead, perhaps your investment club could start a little shop and hire blacksmiths to make tools which someone else, in turn, could rent out."

"That sounds all right," Yoshimitsu said, "but I'm a city boy, and I don't know about this farm stuff. Why, until I became head of the mounted police, I hardly knew what a pitchfork was. Do you have some other opportunity?"

Grandma turned. "What else do we have, Kenji?"

"They were always asking you for salt, Grandma, and a lot of times you wouldn't have it. So that ought to be a good opportunity, Mr. Matsumoto."

Grandma set down her teacup. "I think we better explain that to Mr. Matsumoto. Now the salt pits are all along the seacoast. The problem is to transport it inland. So if someone would get horsecarts, buy from the saltmakers, set up a regular route and sell to the stores, why they could turn a very nice profit."

"I can see that," Yoshimitsu agreed, "but I had my fill of horses."

"Ah, yes," Grandma said. "What else do we have, Kenji?"

"Golly, I don't know."

"What about products which Mr. Matsumoto could make?" Grandma prompted. "The *kairobai* charcoal, for instance."

"Oh," Yoshimitsu said, "to burn in the pocket warmers during cold weather."

"Yes," Grandma said. "People were always asking for the *kairobai* charcoal. It gives them such comfort to be able to put their hands in their pockets and warm them on a winter's day. But, Mr. Matsumoto, I never was able to get enough of the charcoal. It's made by a special process. They bake the calyx of eggplants into it, then pulverize it. That's what makes the powdered charcoal burn so slowly and so well. Now if someone could start a little place to make this charcoal . . ."

"I don't think I would be interested in that."

"I see." Grandma glanced at her grandson. "Kenji, perhaps Mr. Matsumoto would be interested in other products."

"Like what kind, Grandma?"

Grandma could see it then; she could see that Kenji had been too young to understand about not having things at the store in Little Koza. "Never mind," she said slowly. "Perhaps Mr. Matsumoto isn't interested in products at all." She looked full at Yoshimitsu. "Mr. Matsumoto, what do you want?"

"Well, I want to make some money."

"I understood that. That is why you came here. Then what?"

Yoshimitsu thought it over for a moment. "And I would like to get all the Takamini girls married off so I don't have to feed them when they come into town looking for husbands."

"Ah, so." Grandma held up a finger. "You see, Kenji? People sometimes want things other than products."

"But most of all," Yoshimitsu continued slowly, "I think I would like to get rid of the Scheick Code." His eyes widened. "Hey, maybe you could change it, Your Majesty."

"Change it? You mean change things back to the arranged marriage?"

"Yes, Your Majesty."

"But that wouldn't give anyone a chance to look around," the King said.

Yoshimitsu shook his head. "That's where the trouble comes in. They take one look and you never see them again."

"No, I don't think I'll change the law," Kenji stated. "I like it this way."

"But you don't know the social problems it creates," Yoshimitsu protested.

"Social problems?" King Kenji's eyes widened.

"Yes. Now take Uncle Shoji's three daughters. In the old days Uncle Shoji would have said to a go-between, 'Fix things up with somebody.' And the go-between would have approached a good family with marriageable sons, and everybody would have been happy, except maybe the groom. However, he would get used to it. But now! The girls are unhappy. They nag Uncle Shoji, and he is unhappy. They move in on me half the time, so I'm unhappy. You see, Your Majesty, it creates dreadful social problems."

Grandma looked to her grandson, expecting him to at least sympathize a little with Yoshimitsu. The King, however, didn't seem the least bit sympathetic, for the King was smiling broadly and saying, "You know, that's good."

"Good?"

"Kenji," Grandma said quickly, "you didn't understand. Mr. Matsumoto says it creates dreadful social problems."

"That's why I said it's good, Grandma, because I'm glad we have some social problems."

"You are?" It was hard for Grandma to believe.

"Yes. Next to fashion designing, social problems are one of the Duchess of Bamboo Island's chief interests. I better get her. She knows all about these things. She'll solve your problem for you, Mr. Matsumoto. Besides, this might help her find her identity. Just wait a minute." Kenji arose and stepped out onto the veranda. Over by one of the ancient walls of the castle, he saw the Duchess in her red tights and short kilt and called, "Hey, Debbie, are you busy right now?"

The Duchess was looking at the sprig of ivy which the King had planted and which had now started to catch, sending out new runners of green over the old stones. "Why?" she asked.

"Because I got a job I think you might like. It concerns social problems."

"Really? Who has them?"

"Mr. Matsumoto. Come on. He'll tell you all about it."

As Yoshimitsu explained, the Duchess of Bamboo Island listened gravely; and the King watched her proudly. "So you see, Duchess," Yoshimitsu said, "if I can get Uncle Shoji's three daughters taken care of as a starter, then I can work on the rest of the family."

"I understand." The Duchess had taken on a professional air. "Well, the problem is not unusual. At Letty Linton this exact situation was always a big item of discussion."

"See, Mr. Matsumoto?" Kenji said happily. "I told you the Duchess knew all about social problems."

"Thank you," the Duchess said. "Now first, Mr. Matsumoto, are these girls competitors or non-competitors? By that I mean would they offer another girl competition?"

"In that case," Yoshimitsu said, "I think we can call them non-competitors."

"That makes it difficult to do away with the competition then, because you would have to do away with everyone." The Duchess considered. "We'll have to try a different approach. Now then, what is their proximity to men?"

"If you mean are there any men around them, there aren't. There's no one around the distillery, so that's why they keep coming to town all the time."

"Aha," the Duchess said. "That's the whole trouble. There is no one in the proximity. That is bad enough for a competitor, but for a non-competitor it is deadly. Do you agree, King Kenji?"

"Oh, I agree with that a hundred per cent," the King said.

The Duchess turned. "There you are, Mr. Matsumoto. There's your problem."

"I know that." Yoshimitsu scratched his head. "But what do I do about it?"

"It's really very simple." The Duchess waved a hand. "All you need do is bring them into the proximity."

"That's a very good idea," Yoshimitsu agreed. "But how?"

"They handled it very neatly at Letty Linton for the freshman class," the Duchess said. "They had a mixer."

"What's that?" Yoshimitsu questioned, and even Grandma leaned forward.

"It is a great big party where everybody mixes and meets everybody else. At Letty Linton they invited the freshmen boys from the surrounding men's schools. In fact, that's where I met Sherman Chang, though of course I never would have had any trouble even if they didn't have a mixer." The Duchess regarded the King. "Did they have a mixer at your school, too?"

"They sure did," Kenji said. "We had a wonderful freshman mixer."

Yoshimitsu rubbed his hands. "Say, this sounds pretty good.

206

So the places where you went to school acted as a go-between, bringing people together?"

"Yes." The Duchess nodded. "In a way the school did act as a go-between."

"Well then, do you think there's any possibility that we might have one of those mixers here?" Yoshimitsu asked hopefully.

"I don't see why we couldn't," the Duchess replied.

"I don't either," the King added, and Grandma saw the enthusiasm that was rising in him. "All we have to do is find someone to sponsor it."

"Kenji," Grandma began slowly, "if you had one of these mixers or whatever you call it, what would it involve? I mean, what do you do at those things besides meet other people?"

"We danced at ours," the King said. "How about you, Debbie?"

"We did, too."

"So that means you would have to have music," Grandma said. "And what else happens?"

"Well, we had something to eat. They had a whole lot of sandwiches."

"At Letty Linton we had creamed chicken."

"Ah, yes." Grandma nodded. "I have heard you speak of creamed chicken before. And are sandwiches food also?"

"They are," the Duchess said. "You have to have food at a mixer."

"And decorations, too," the King said. "We had paper streamers all over the gym."

"Ah, so." Grandma regarded the young ones. "Perhaps we should have one of those things out here."

"I think it would be a good idea, Grandma. But who would sponsor it?"

"If anyone is going to act as a go-between in the Nakashima Islands," Grandma said, "I think the King should."

"But I don't have the money to put on a mixer."

Grandma turned. "That is where Mr. Matsumoto could help out."

"If it means furnishing food," Yoshimitsu began, "I don't want any part of it. I've had enough of that."

"Now let's see if we can't turn this into a business opportunity," Grandma continued. "Now then, suppose Mr. Matsumoto should form an investment club. This club would put up the money for the original outlay of cash."

"But how would we get our money back?" Yoshimitsu asked.

"By selling tickets for it. Of the cost of the ticket so much would be allotted for the expenses, and the rest would be profit for the investment club."

"The profit part sounds real good," Yoshimitsu stated. "But do you think we could sell any tickets for this thing?"

"I think you could," Grandma replied. "After all, it would be under the sponsorship of the King."

"Could I tell everybody that?"

"I'm sure the King would allow it, wouldn't you, Kenji?"

"Oh, yes, Grandma, that would be fine with me."

"Hey!" An idea struck Yoshimitsu. "Do you know what we could do? The Mrs. General and the other ladies want to get some advertising on the paper-show. We could advertise there. That way everybody on all the Islands would know about it."

"That would really bring them in," the King said. "But where could we have it?"

"At Letty Linton we had it out on the lawns," the Duchess said. "And it was so pretty with the lights strung all over."

"Lights?" Grandma questioned, one eye narrowing.

"Paper lanterns."

"Paper lanterns! Ah, paper lanterns!"

"Yes. They were strung all over, and the moon was out—"

"Why don't you have it out of doors then?" Grandma said quickly. "Perhaps you could have it in Watanabe Square."

"But that's so run-down, Grandma," Kenji protested.

"I'm sure the Duchess could do something about that with these decorations you talk of." Grandma smiled.

"Oh, yes," the Duchess agreed. "I could fix it very, very attractively."

"See, Kenji?" Grandma said. "That is no problem. And Sonny could help you, too."

"Yes, Elwood could."

"And the three of you"—Grandma shook her head—"why, I'm sure that the three of you could put on a wonderful . . . what do you call these things?"

"Mixers."

"Ah, yes, mixers. You could put on a wonderful one, couldn't you, Duchess?"

"We certainly could," the Duchess stated. "All in all, I think it probably would be the best ever put on in these parts."

"There you are." Grandma smiled, then turned her attention to Yoshimitsu. "Now as I see it, this is going to be a nice source of additional income for you, Mr. Matsumoto. And it won't take up much of your time. It won't take you away from the paper-show business, because the Duchess, and the King, and Sonny will handle all the plans."

"They will?"

"Oh, yes. Now as to raising money to finance this."

"There is a problem." Yoshimitsu's forehead wrinkled.

"Do you think so, really?" Grandma was silent for a moment. "But what about this Uncle Shoji of yours? The Takaminis have done very well in the distilling business. He has a great deal at stake here, so surely he might be interested in joining a little investment club."

Chapter 16

"KENJI," Grandma called from the veranda, where she was sitting in the twilight. "Here comes Sonny now."

"Good." The King stepped out from his quarters and watched Elwood come up the path from the courtyard below. "I wonder how he made out?"

"I was wondering myself," Grandma replied. "But I think he must have made out well. See, he is grinning."

Elwood was grinning—from ear to ear—and Kenji called, "Hey, Elwood, how did it go?"

"It was a struggle," Elwood said. "But I made it."

"Did the Mr. General object very much?"

"He sure did. He said it was the biggest mistake of my life to drop out of school for a semester."

"Oh, and what did the Mrs. General think?"

"She thought it was a good idea."

"Ah." Kenji smiled. "So you're dropping out of school then."

"That's right. Aunt Caroline is going to write my mother and fix things up."

"That's swell," the King said. "I'm sure glad you can stay.

Wait until I tell Grandma." Kenji translated. "And Grandma says she is glad you can stay, too."

"Thank you."

"But Grandma would like to know if you thanked the Mr. General for the sunflower seeds he sent her?"

"Oh, yes. He apologized because they weren't hulled. He says there was a mix-up in the order."

"Grandma says she's glad they weren't hulled, because now she won't have to bother the General any more."

"Oh?"

"She's planted four or five rows of them down at the lower end of the courtyard. So from now on she ought to be able to grow her own supply. She says they're wonderful things. Why, she hasn't felt this good in a long time."

"I'm glad to hear that." Elwood glanced at his watch. "Gosh, I'm sorry I'm so late, but they got to talking after dinner and I couldn't break away. Are you ready to start the meeting?"

"Yeah. I'll call Debbie."

The Duchess of Bamboo Island came from her apartment, and tonight she was wearing red toreador trousers with a white blouse. She walked along the veranda, her reed slippers making a soft sound, and as she approached, Elwood said, "Hi, Debbie. How's it going?"

"Very well," the Duchess replied. "I have it almost all planned. Where shall we meet, Kenji?"

"Let me ask Grandma." Kenji translated then said, "Grandma suggests we meet on the veranda before my quarters."

"Is Grandma going to sit in with us?" Elwood asked.

"No, she says if she does that, I would have to translate back and forth. This way we can speak English. So she thinks she will just sit and enjoy the breeze, and I can tell her about it later."

It was beginning to get dark now. The outer Islands of the chain, stretching in the distance, began to fade and merge into the blackness, marked only by white water breaking on their shores. But even that began to disappear as night closed in over the Nakashima Islands. Only here and there did a rare pin point of light appear in some far village; and because the castle, too, was bathed in darkness, Elwood turned on a flashlight.

"Debbie," the King said, "why don't you take over the meeting? You know more about this than we do."

"I would be very happy to." The Duchess placed her notes on the floor by the flashlight. "Now then," she stated solemnly, "the first thing we have to do is organize this mixer; and in organizing it, the first thing we need is a general chairman to look after the whole thing."

"I'll agree with that." The King nodded. "So how about you taking it?"

"Well, if you insist."

"We do insist," Kenji said.

"In that case, I'll be glad to take over." The Duchess bowed, her Nakashima Islands training coming to the fore. "Now as general chairman," she went on, "I am going to need certain committees to help me, such as: tickets, publicity, decorations, refreshments, music, entertainment, and reception. So to start, who should we get to head the ticket committee?"

"How about Mr. Matsumoto?" Elwood suggested. "It's his business. All he'll have to do is set up ticket-selling booths at the entrance to the Square."

"That will work very well," the Duchess said. "Now who will handle publicity?"

"I'd like to take a crack at that," Elwood said. "I get a kick out of fooling around with the paper-shows, and since we're going to be advertising on them, why . . ."

"All right." The Duchess nodded. "You take it then."

"Swell." Elwood thought for a moment. "You know what we could do? We could arrange for the paper-show men working the villages to handle tickets, too. That is, people could buy their tickets right from them, and we could keep pretty good track of what kind of a crowd to expect."

"I like that," the King said. "That would get some money rolling in, too, so we'd have more capital to operate with. Will you work that out with Mr. Matsumoto, Elwood?"

"Sure. I'll take take care of it. What's next, Debbie?"

"Next comes decorations, and since this is one of my strong points, I think I had better handle that," the Duchess said. "And you don't have to worry, because I will do an extremely good job."

"Oh, we know that." The King nodded solemnly.

"Very well then. Now for refreshments. Who wants that?"

"I'll try that," the King said. "I used to pick up some extra money at Cambridge College by waiting on table, so I know something about food."

"We'll make you head of that committee then." The Duchess consulted her list. "Now for music."

"Why don't you take that, Debbie?" the King suggested. "You're up on the latest songs and everything."

"That's true," the Duchess agreed. "I think I will take it. As for entertainment, I'd suggest you for that, Kenji. Do you know what you could do? You could put on an exhibition of American dancing. And since you're the King and everything, I think it would go over very big. Of course, I'd help you. We could do a cha-cha, and a polka, and anything they want."

"I'm for that," the King said. "And do you know, if anybody wants to learn the dances, why couldn't we do this? Why couldn't we train a whole bunch of, well, sort of instructors? Then when people come up, the instructors could help them. We'll have everybody doing the cha-cha in no time. What do you think of that, Debbie?"

"I think it would be entirely feasible, and I think it should add a lot of enjoyment to the situation. So we will do it."

"And do you know what else you could do?" Elwood said. "Over at the sides of the Square you could have some paper-show men, each with a different kind of story . . . adventure, comedy, love. There would be a lot of people who'd get a kick out of stopping and watching a show. If you want me to, I'll also suggest that to Mr. Matsumoto."

"You better do that." The King nodded. "Besides, think how happy it will make the women's Investment Club. It will give them a chance to do a lot of extra business."

"All we have left then is reception," the Duchess said. "We'll

213

give that to Mr. Matsumoto. It really won't be much of a job because we'll have everyone wearing cards with their name, home village, and home Island—that's what we did at school—so everyone starts to mix right away. Okay?"

"Okay," the King and Elwood agreed.

"Well, there we are," the Duchess said. "We're organized. Now for a date. How would three weeks from today—September 1—be? There isn't too much work to be done, and that would give us plenty of time to get the announcements out to the villages."

"Fine," the King said. "We'll make it September 1. By the way, Debbie, how are you going to decorate the Square?"

"Oh." The Duchess pursed her lips. "Let's see, since the main activity will be at night, I think I'll do it like they did at Letty Linton. I'll string paper lanterns all over the place. You see, the paper of the lanterns will be of different colors, and it will be quite romantic. Besides, the lanterns will give such a feeling of fun and life to the place."

"That will really knock their eyes out," the King said.

"It certainly will," the Duchess had to agree. "And if all the girls come dressed in pretty kimonos . . ." She looked up suddenly. "We'll have to suggest that when we announce the mixer on the paper-show, Kenji, because kimonos go so well with the lanterns."

"Okay. But, Debbie, isn't it going to take an awful lot of lanterns? I mean if you're going to string them all over Watanabe Square?"

"It will take quite a number."

"Where are you going to get them?"

"Ask your grandmother. Having run a store, she probably knows all the makers."

"All right." Kenji turned toward the aged one, who was sitting on the veranda in front of the middle house, looking out into the darkness. "Grandma," he called, "who did you use to buy your lanterns from out at the store?"

"I never sold lanterns," the Queen Grandmother replied.

"Oh. Well, who makes lanterns around here?"

"No one makes them."

"But, Your Majesty," Debbie said, "someone must make lanterns. I've seen them at home."

"They were very old ones then," the Queen Grandmother replied.

"Old ones?" Kenji questioned.

"Yes," Grandma began slowly, "don't you remember what Mr. Yamaguchi told you—how we used to be called the Land of the Lighted Lanterns, but through the years the lanterns have gone out?"

"Oh, yes." Kenji nodded. "Oh, yes. Now I remember."

"Well, how in the world are we going to have a mixer if we haven't lanterns to string around?" the Duchess asked.

Kenji hesitated. "I don't know, Debbie. And I happened to think of something. How did they light the lanterns at Letty Linton?"

"With electricity, of course. Why?"

"Well, we have no electricity here."

"Darn!" the Duchess said in English, and quickly Kenji explained to Elwood.

"Gee, that's tough," Elwood said. "But how do people light their houses?"

"They don't," the Duchess said testily. "They just sit in the darkness or go to bed."

The King cleared his throat. "Maybe we better come back to that. Let's go on with the music situation. Now we're going to need an orchestra."

"And whose orchestra do you suggest?" the Duchess asked.

"Well . . ." The King was stopped cold, for there were no orchestras in the Nakashima Islands.

"How about making it a record dance?" Elwood cut in.

"This is supposed to be a party," the Duchess said. "A record dance wouldn't be any fun."

Again the King cleared his throat. "Let's go on to refreshments. Now what would you think of some sandwiches?"

"And where are we going to get bread for sandwiches?" the Duchess questioned. "Perhaps at the same place we get the orchestra. Either that or we can serve boiled sweet potatoes."

"Boiled sweet potatoes?" Kenji said, and a feeling of sadness began to rise within him.

"Yes. Boiled sweet potatoes. See," the girl's voice carried a note of hopelessness, "what's the use of trying to do anything here? It's just as I said before. There's nothing here but *sabishii.*"

The King had to admit it then. He had to admit that *sabishii* was here with its combination of melancholy, loneliness, and a sense of all the good things in life just passing by.

The girl stirred. "Why don't we just forget about having a mixer?"

Kenji started to reach out to touch her, but quickly drew back his hand.

"If you'll excuse me," the Duchess went on, "I think I'll just go to my quarters, and—"

"Wait, Debbie," Kenji said. "Maybe we can have the mixer. Maybe we can get the things we need." He turned and called in Japanese, "Grandma, do you think there would be a market for lanterns here in the Nakashima Islands?"

"Why?" the aged one asked. "Are you thinking of making them?"

"I don't know, but perhaps this could be a business opportunity for someone."

Grandma smiled in the night. "How do you mean?"

"Well, we would need a lot for our mixer. And if there would be an outside market for them . . ."

"Perhaps there would be an outside market. After all, the traders did call us the Land of the Lighted Lanterns."

"Why couldn't we organize an investment club then, and have them set up someone in business?" the King continued. "We could start a little workshop, use the old lanterns as models, and we wouldn't have any trouble at all getting lanterns for the mixer. What do you think of that, Debbie?"

"Well," the girl began slowly, "that puts a different light on the situation."

"Elwood." Kenji switched to English. "I think we're beginning to get somewhere. Now as for music, why couldn't we dig up some musicians in the capital? A lot of people play the samisen, and why couldn't we start training a combo of, say, piano, bass, and drums?"

"That is a very good suggestion," the Duchess said.

"Why don't you train them then?" the King suggested. "You're good at music, Debbie."

"Yes," the Duchess admitted. "That is another one of my strong points. Now what I could do is this: If we could get some electricity, maybe I could get a phonograph and get them listening to records so they would know what I want. And I could even train a whole orchestra, too."

"I know you could," the King said solemnly.

"But what about refreshments?" Elwood asked.

The King thought for a moment. "Maybe we shouldn't serve refreshments."

"But it wouldn't be a mixer without refreshments," the Duchess protested.

"Oh, I know we have to have something to eat," the King said. "But I think this could be another business opportunity. Why can't we just let them buy their own? That way, all we have to do is get someone to start food stalls around the Square."

"What kind of food stalls?" Elwood asked.

"Maybe noodle stalls," the King went on. "Noodles are very popular over here because they're so rare. Nobody grows wheat or buckwheat. Then maybe we could get a *sashimi* shop going."

"What's that?"

"It's raw fish. You serve it with horseradish. And maybe we can get other kinds of fish, too. Now there is a real business opportunity. We can talk with the fishermen and see what they have to offer." Kenji was getting warmed up. "And do you know, Elwood, those food stalls could stay in business all the time in Watanabe Square. I mean they wouldn't just be opened for the mixer. They could catch the sweet potato market crowd. Then there's the bunch who work in the Paper-Show Headquarters. And they could catch the crowd who go to the paper-shows at night."

"I think you've got something," Elwood said.

"And it shouldn't be hard to set up," the King said. "When the people hear the announcement on the paper-show and come up looking for opportunity, like Mr. Matsumoto did, I can just tell them about all these things. What do you think of that, Debbie?"

"That? Oh, that's fine," the Duchess said, yet her forehead was wrinkled. "But, Kenji, these lanterns. They are made out of paper. Where would the lantern makers get paper, or candles to burn in them?"

"I better ask Grandma." Kenji spoke rapidly. "Grandma says things like that always came from Japan. She says how could anyone make them here? We haven't the materials."

"And Kenji," the Duchess went on, "I was just thinking. Where are the girls going to get cloth for their pretty kimonos?"

Kenji was about to say "Just a moment. I'll ask Grandma," but he refrained, for he knew that the only cloth made here in the Nakashima Islands was the drab brown fabric woven from the textile banana. The others all came from Japan, too.

"Well, we certainly have to have pretty cloth for kimonos," the Duchess continued slowly, "because who would want to go to a mixer in their old, worn clothes?"

Chapter 17

THEY couldn't keep it in the Pentagon any longer. They had to let the situation out of the bag. And out in the Nakashima Islands, on the receiving end of it, General Scheick read the radiogram from Major General Mosby Winthrope.

THERE IS ONLY ONE THING LEFT TO DO. IT IS AS CONGRESSMAN HOMER HOPLOW OF KANSAS SUGGESTS, "WE MUST PUMP IN THE AID. WE MUST INDUSTRIALIZE THEM IMMEDIATELY." AND SO THE POWERS THAT BE WANT AN INVESTIGATION. THEY WANT TO KNOW HOW MANY MILLIONS IT WILL TAKE TO KEEP THE SHIP FROM SINKING. NOTIFY ME AT ONCE.

(*Signed*) MOSBY

Thus it was that General Scheick took himself to the castle. And as he walked along, he noticed that there was something a little different about the cart trail leading up. At first, he couldn't put his finger on it, then he realized what it was. An electric wire had been strung, apparently from the Army lighting system below. It was carried on makeshift poles, and it led right into the heart of the castle.

"Now who in hell gave permission for that!" he said, half aloud, as he followed the wire through the courtyards and up into the royal enclosure.

219

It was only about nine or so in the morning, but as he entered, the blare of music from a phonograph rose up and hit him. It was a kind of wild, screaming music. And for a man who was brought up on "Paradise" and "The Waltz You Saved for Me," it was alarming.

He looked toward the royal apartments, and then he saw what was happening. On the veranda in front of her quarters was the Duchess of Bamboo Island. Before her the electric phonograph blared forth. And around her were seated eight or ten Nakashima Islands youths, samisens in hand, a half-dazed look in their eyes as they listened.

"My God," he whispered, "the whole place is going to pot, and here they are—sitting around listening to records." Rapidly he strode toward the veranda.

"Oh, hello." The Duchess smiled at him. It was the first time he had ever seen her smile. "How are you this morning?"

General Scheick was in no mood for small talk, however. "Where's the Queen Grandmother?" he asked.

"She rode down into town with Elwood," the Duchess replied.

"Rode down?"

"In the pony cart. She wanted to see Yamaguchi Kiei. And since Elwood was going down for the drums anyway, she thought she would ride along."

"What drums?" General Scheick demanded.

"The ones the motor pool made for us out of old oil barrels."

"I didn't give the motor pool permission to do anything like that," General Scheick said.

"No, your wife did," the Duchess said. "We told her we needed them, and she found out that the motor pool sergeant was very familiar with calypso music. He knew all about steel drums, so he made us some. But would you like to see the King? The music kind of interferes with his work, so he went back into the pine grove."

"What kind of work is he busy with?"

"All kinds. But he wouldn't be too busy to see you."

"He'd better see me"—General Scheick's voice was cold—

"or he's going to wake up one morning and find that somebody's walked off with his country."

Turning on his heels, General Scheick rounded the royal apartments and started toward the pine grove at the end of the royal enclosure. As he did so, he saw the crowd of women—there must have been at least a hundred of them—stretching in a line from the edge of the grove to a little desk, behind which the King sat.

"King Kenji!" he called; and the King, deep in conference with two men and a dozen women, looked up.

"Oh, hello, Mr. General. I'll be right with you." The King spoke a few words in Japanese, pointed to General Scheick, arose from the desk and walked over, the perspiration standing out on his brow.

"What's going on?" General Scheick asked.

The King indicated the group of women. "They're giving me a bad time."

"Who in the hell are they?"

"The wives of some fishermen who live down in the capital. You see, over here, Mr. General, the fishermen just catch fish. The wives market them. And when you do business with those ladies you have your hands full."

"What kind of business are you talking about?"

"It started out this way, Mr. General. Now that tall, thin man was looking for some opportunity, and I was looking for someone to start a fish stall in Watanabe Square. That is, a little stand-up restaurant where you could get yourself a snack. He liked the idea real well, so we got the fishermen's wives together to see about buying fish."

"What happened?"

"That's when we ran into the trouble. They wanted this man to buy all the fish their husbands catch, not just what he needs. Well, how can he do that? So I got an idea. There was another man looking for opportunity. I told him about this surplus fish and suggested that he process it into fish cakes, fish paste, and stuff like that. He was all for it. But the ladies liked the idea too, and decided that they wanted to go into the fish-processing business themselves. Now they won't sell anybody any fish unless they can have the processing business."

"So what?" General Scheick said.

"So how am I going to get a fish stall opened in Watanabe Square? And look at all those people waiting to see me. Gosh, I have to get a noodle stand opened too, and I don't even know how to start that, because we don't have anything to make noodles from."

"Now just a minute," General Scheick said, suspicion arising in him. "I want to ask you some questions. First of all, where did you get that electric phonograph?"

"Mrs. McCloud loaned it to us."

"And where are you getting the power to run it?"

"From the Army generators."

"Who gave you permission to tie in?"

"The Mrs. General. Wasn't it nice of her? Of course, she and the other ladies are anxious to get the business."

"What business?"

"The advertising business. With rice at five dollars a pound, and with all those chickens Elwood is hatching, the ladies have sure got to scramble. Why, even the sale of taffy at the paper-shows is hardly enough to keep them going."

"And what exactly are you going to be advertising on this paper-show?" General Scheick asked.

"The mixer."

"Now what the hell is a mixer?"

"Oh, don't you know, Mr. General? You see, I have decided to keep the Scheick Code in effect."

"I should hope so!" General Scheick exclaimed.

"But it creates a lot of problems." The King was solemn. "A lot of girls aren't finding husbands. So as King, I am acting as the big go-between for the Nakashima Islands. I am going to bring all the boys and girls together, and maybe they can work out something for themselves."

General Scheick was staggered. "Work out something for themselves! King Kenji, you can't mean that."

"Oh, I mean it." Kenji nodded. "That's why I already set up

the paper-lantern-making business. And that's why I'm trying to set up food stalls in Watanabe Square."

"But, King Kenji, can't you see what you're doing? My God, man, you're starting a marriage mill."

"I am?"

"You certainly are. You're cheapening the Scheick Code!"

"I never thought of it that way."

"I can see that. Now look, you're facing a serious situation, so serious that one of these mornings you could wake up and find yourself without a country."

"I don't understand that, Mr. General."

"Then just take my word for it. And what are you doing? Fooling around with a marriage mill, fish stalls, and noodles. We have to pull you out of this, man. Suppose I was able to arrange for you to get your hands on some money. What would you do with it?"

"How much would it be?"

"Oh, several million as a starter. How would you use it?"

The King's mouth flew open. "I don't know, Mr. General. I never had more than a hundred dollars before in my whole life."

"Surely you must have some idea."

"Well, I think I'd buy a good farm in Ohio to raise buckwheat for noodles and grain for chicken feed."

"You couldn't do that. You can't buy land in another country. That wouldn't be legal."

"That's the thing I need most, though. But if I couldn't buy land, then maybe I'd just buy buckwheat and chicken feed. And then I'd want to buy some cloth for kimonos—"

"That's exactly what I thought you'd do."

"Isn't that a good idea, Mr. General?"

"Absolutely not. All you'd be doing is consuming. You wouldn't be producing one blessed thing. Now I'm going to lay it right on the line. If you want to save this place, you're going to have to forget about this marriage mill."

"But Debbie is an expert on social problems, and she said—"

"I don't care what she said. You're going to have to forget it.

223

And then you're going to have to turn this country into a producer. Do you know how you do that?"

"No."

"By industrialization. You want cloth for kimonos. All right, take a few million and set up weaving plants. Of course, you'd need power to run them, so take a few million more and build dams. Or maybe you should have steam-generating plants. If you had a Minister of Power he could look into this."

"I sure wish I had a Minister of Power," the King said. "I need candles for lights, so maybe he could look them up, too."

"Candles!" General Scheick ran his hand over his eyes. "Your Majesty, you don't realize the urgency of the situation. I was talking with Louie and Henry Yamaguchi, and I said, 'Boys, tell me frankly, what do you want most of all?' And they replied, 'Opportunity.' Don't you understand, you can't keep denying these people. You have to give people like Louie and Henry a chance or there goes the ball game."

The King's face twisted, he started to speak, then shook his head and remained silent.

"Now what we have to do," General Scheick continued, "is turn you into a nation of industrialists. I'm going to help, because we have no time to lose. In fact, I'm going right down now and organize things. We have to know how much money you need, so I'm going to send Colonel Henderson out looking for dam sites. And I'm going to send Major McCloud out to find locations for textile mills."

"But, Mr. General," the King started to protest.

"There're no buts about it," General Scheick said. "Just believe me, King Kenji. We have to move and move fast." He extended his hand. "We're partners in this, and we're going to help you pull it off." Grasping the King's hand, he gave it a firm shake, then turned and started toward the royal apartments and the path leading down to Caroline Drive.

Standing in the pine grove, King Kenji watched him go, and the King was puzzled and upset. He surely hadn't thought of the mixer as being a marriage mill. He hadn't thought about how when you industrialize you become a producer, and not just a consumer. But then he heard the obvious coughing behind him, and turning, saw that it was coming from the fishermen's wives.

"Oh, yes, ladies," he said in Japanese. "I'm coming." He walked over to the desk, seated himself, and doubts began to creep in. Was all this just a waste of time? Was it any use trying to start a fish stand in Watanabe Square?

The ladies, however, had other thoughts. "Your Majesty," their spokesman said, "we have been thinking. As to this gentleman who wants to go into the fish-processing business, we will give him an opportunity. We will let him finance us."

"Never!" the would-be fish processor said, and the King let out his breath wearily.

"In that case—" the spokesman began but was interrupted by a call from over near the royal apartments.

"King Kenji," Yoshimitsu called. "Your grandma wants to see you right away. She and the Mrs. General are at the home of Yamaguchi Kiei, and they sent me for you. It is very important."

King Kenji turned, regarded the fishermen's wives, regarded the line of women waiting in the shade, looking for business opportunity. "Ladies," he said, "would you excuse me? You have just heard Mr. Matsumoto. My grandma wants me."

The ladies bowed, but the King could see the looks cast in his direction.

"I'll be back just as soon as I can," he said, and he knew then that he needed some help. Maybe he ought to have a Minister of Business Opportunity, or something, to look after things like this when he had to go away.

Chapter 18

A S KENJI turned into the Street of the Blue Lanterns, he was struck with surprise. For in the past the street's name had been only a figurative thing, but now blue lanterns actually were hung everywhere. They were old ones, Kenji knew, because while he had set up a lantern-making corporation, and while the lantern makers were receiving orders by the hundreds, they hadn't, as yet, gone into production. The bamboo was available over on the Duchess' home Island. But there was no paper to stretch over the thin framework. And, of course, there were no candles to burn within them.

But there they were, hung on the stone walls before every house. And King Kenji, walking along, watching them swaying gently in the breeze, found his mind filled with doubts. Now that he thought of it, it seemed that the Mr. General was more and more right. It seemed that industrialization might be the thing to strive for, not a mixer.

Coming to the home of Yamaguchi Kiei, he stopped for a moment; then hearing the laughter of the old man rise, he entered the gateway to the courtyard and saw the ancient historian seated on the veranda by the Queen Grandmother. The old man laughed again, then his laughter gave way to a constant chuckling, and Kenji called, "Grandma, Mr. Matsumoto said you wanted to see me."

"Yes, Kenji. But we have to wait for the Mrs. General. It concerns her, too. She is having a board of directors' meeting and it will be a few minutes before she gets here."

"Oh."

"Come in and sit down, Your Majesty," the old historian said, then added, "Did you notice the lanterns as you came along? It is like the olden times. Of course you are aware that we used to be called the Land of the Lighted Lanterns."

"Yes, I knew that, Mr. Yamaguchi."

The old one shook his head. "Your Majesty, I never thought I would see the day when the lanterns came back; and especially the day when the blue lanterns returned to this street. You know of the blue lanterns, of course."

"I don't believe I do."

"Well, this was the street of scholars. They felt that blue was the color that was easiest on their eyes as they read at night. So they all began using blue lanterns, and that is how the street was named." The old man began chuckling. "But I was just telling your grandmother about the paper-show in Watanabe Square last night. Did you see it?"

"No, I didn't," Kenji said, and he thought he saw his grandmother grimace.

"Oh, that Todi Kabuki was good," the old man went on. "It was a comedy. Now there was this fellow . . ."

Grandma was definitely fidgeting now.

". . . and just to look at him," the old man chuckled. "Why, his kimono was all baggy, and his reed sandals were too big, and one of them had a hole in it . . ."

Grandma coughed.

". . . so one day when he was walking down the street . . ."

"Excuse me, Mr. Yamaguchi." Grandma was apparently unable to stand another telling. "Perhaps we shouldn't wait for the Mrs. General. Perhaps we should tell the King what we discovered."

227

"Discovered?" It took the aged one a moment to come back to reality. "Oh, yes, yes." He chuckled once again. "But if Todi Kabuki brings that show back, you want to see it."

"I will," Kenji promised and looked expectantly at the old historian.

"Ah, yes," the old one began slowly. "Thanks to your grandmother, King Kenji, we have indeed discovered something. Your grandmother came to me and asked, 'Mr. Yamaguchi, who owns the land at the side of the roads?' Now that was an interesting problem, because until the Mr. General came, there was never any land at the side of the roads. The fields came right up to them. So it was of no use consulting the scrolls."

The old one wet his lips. "Thus, I said to myself: 'Let us take this step by step. Now who owned the land before the Mr. General built the roads and made provisions for widening them into superhighways?' I asked myself that. And, of course, it was the farmers. But the Mr. General, as head of the Interruption Government, bought the land from the farmers. So the roads and the land belong to the government. Now you are the government, King Kenji. It is crown land."

"Crown land?"

"Yes. And your grandmother discovered it."

"Why, there must be hundreds of acres of it," the King exclaimed. "This is ten times better than owning a farm in Ohio." He whistled. "Just wait until the Mrs. General hears! She'll think it's almost too good to be true."

Mrs. Scheick did think it was almost too good to be true. "King Kenji," she said as she sat on the veranda with them, "this solves the problems of the chicken business."

"I know, Mrs. General." The King nodded.

"I'm certainly glad of that," Mrs. Scheick continued. "The girls are getting awfully edgy about that investment. But tell me, how do you intend to work this?"

"We were talking about that while we were waiting for you. Grandma suggests that I, as King, rent the crown land to the farmers at a very, very low rate—perhaps not more than a few pennies from each person, which they could afford. But with so much acreage it will give me a good income. And in return for this low rent, the farmers must grow what I specify. Now first, I want a lot of chicken feed raised. That will bring the price down so that you chicken raisers can make a profit and get eggs on the market."

"I'm for that," Mrs. Scheick said.

"And I also," the old historian cut in. "In fact, I would like to see the hundred-year-old eggs come back."

"Oh, we've been processing them for several weeks," Mrs. Scheick said.

"You have?" The old one was surprised.

"Certainly. I believe the Queen Grandmother got the recipe from you."

"Yes, I remember. But I thought she was merely curious."

"And the batches are coming along real good," Kenji said. "Grandma thinks it won't be long before we can market them."

"I cannot believe," the old one stated. "They were such a luxury, and imagine having luxuries in the Nakashima Islands."

"Now what else do you intend to raise on the crown lands, King Kenji?" Mrs. Scheick asked. "Perhaps wheat and buckwheat?"

"Yes, because I want to get a noodle stall going."

Mrs. Scheick's eyes narrowed shrewdly. "Why limit the sale of noodles to a stall in Watanabe Square? Why not have someone make them on a large scale and sell them in the village stores?"

"Noodles," the old historian said. "They would be good. It has been years since any noodles have been available."

"Frankly," Mrs. Scheick said, "I'm interested in getting an advertising account for the paper-show, and if we had a large company manufacturing them, why . . ."

"You have a good idea there, Mrs. General," Kenji said. "And Grandma thinks so, too. She says noodles should sell like the dickens, because people will be so anxious to get away from sweet potatoes. So I'll put the manufacture of noodles down as a business opportunity for when people come to see me."

"Good." Mrs. Scheick nodded. "Now then, Your Majesty. If the farmers are going to raise wheat, buckwheat, and grain for chickens, they are going to need seed. It so happens that my sisters and I own an elevator in Iowa, right in the heart of the American grain country. We deal in seed, and we could get you anything you want."

"You could?" The old historian's eyes were wide.

"Yes."

"That would be great," Kenji said. "It sure would help me."

Mrs. Scheick smiled. "It would be to our mutual benefit. If you wish, I'll write my brother-in-law, who's managing the business, and sort of alert him."

"Please do," Kenji said.

The old historian began shaking his head, and in his eyes was a look of awe and wonder. "Your Majesty," he began slowly, "I wish to congratulate you for the way you are making up the ground that we lost during the Interruption."

"Do you think I am doing that?" Kenji asked.

"Truly you are. Here hundred-year-old eggs are returning. And noodles also. And you are even starting festivals, just like old King Gihon did to break the monotony of everyday living and to fight *sabishii*."

"Festivals?" the King questioned. "What festival are you referring to, Mr. Yamaguchi?"

"The one your grandmother informed me of. The one for the unmarried. The Festival of the Unattached."

"Oh," Kenji said. "You must mean the mixer."

"I beg your pardon?"

"The mixer."

"I am not familiar with that word. But this Festival of the Unattached. It is a wonderful thing. We have a festival for the little boys, and a festival for the little girls. However, grownups also need festivals. And who has ever thought of the unattached before? Ah, this is going to be very popular."

"Do you think so?" Kenji asked hopefully.

"I know so, because this—if you will excuse me, Mrs. General, for saying so—this Scheick Code has created more unattached

230

than we have ever had in our whole history. And it is wise of you, King Kenji, to attack the problem."

"But I never thought of it as a festival."

"Your grandmother did. However, she and I have agreed that we think you have selected the wrong date. We think it should be after the harvest, and a little closer to winter, because the un-attached, being alone, know what it is to have winter approach."

"It would be a break for me to have it later," Kenji said.

"Do so then. October 27 would be good. The days are still warm and golden. And it must run for more than one day, be-cause, as your grandmother says, she wishes the unattached to come from all the Islands. She wishes them to have a few days of happiness here in the capital. And then, when October ends, when November comes, it is through. Do you agree?"

"Oh, yes. And besides, having it more days than one is better for business," the King said; and as he did so, a thought struck him, and he twisted uneasily. "Mr. Yamaguchi, if we have this Festival of the Unattached, do you think it would look all right?"

"Certainly."

"But selling tickets and all . . ."

"What's wrong with selling tickets? Take old King Gihon. He started the Festival of the Kites. He did it because he wished all the little boys to be happy. But he also wanted to sell kites. I can show you in the scrolls. He needed money badly because he had to pay for the Experiment." The old historian turned. "It would look all right to you, would it not, Mrs. General?"

"I don't know," Mrs. Scheick began. "When I first heard about this mixer, I had doubts. I didn't even know if we should advertise it on the paper-show. But since you are calling it the Festival of the Unattached, it puts an entirely different meaning on it."

"But it is more than a matter of words," the old one insisted. "As the Queen Grandmother said, in the old days under the old system a girl never thought of getting married; because she knew that when the proper time came, her father would take care of it and she would have a husband.

"But under this system," the old one continued, "all they can think of is getting married. They worry that they will not be married. Why, we are becoming a nation of upsets. So if our King starts his Festival of the Unattached, the people will know that the King is watching, just as their fathers did. They will know that truly he is the first son of Shinerikyu and Amamikyu, for he is looking after the other children, and the girls can have peace of mind once again."

Mrs. Scheick was silent, then said slowly, "Mr. Yamaguchi, I didn't understand, but I do now. And I'm all for this Festival."

"I am very happy for that," the old one said.

"Me, too," King Kenji joined in. "And Grandma feels the same, because she values your opinion, Mrs. General."

"Please thank her. And I value hers."

Kenji started to glow. "Not only are we going to have the Festival of the Unattached," he began expansively, "but we're going to make a real festival out of it." And both Grandma and Mrs. Scheick smiled maternally at his enthusiasm. "And do you know what I'm going to do? I'm going to figure out a way for the girls to buy pretty cloth for kimonos, just like Debbie suggested. And I'm going to work it out so that the fellows can buy clothes too."

"Oh? And how are you going to do that?" the old historian asked. "Clothing always has been a great problem on the Islands."

"I think," the King replied, "I'm going to start a weaving industry."

"Industry? What does this word *industry* mean?"

"It really means making things, Mr. Yamaguchi. It means having big factories like the Mitsukoshis and the Mitsuis do, up in Japan. Won't that be nice?"

"But that is not possible," the old one said.

"It's not?" the King questioned.

"No. There's no place for industry here."

"Are you sure, Mr. Yamaguchi?"

"Of course. King Gihon himself said so. Wait, I will read you his words." Going to a cupboard, the old one took a scroll, unrolled it, ran his finger down until he found the proper place, then went on, first in English, then in Japanese: "Here it is. King

Gihon made a study of this very situation, and he said, 'This is a land of plants, of stone, and of water. This is a land of agriculture. There is no material to make things.'"

On hearing the words, Kenji looked to his grandmother. "That can't be right," he said in Japanese so she would understand. "That can't be right at all."

"But it is right, Kenji," Grandma said. "What material do we have here?"

"I don't know, Grandma. The Mr. General told me, though, that I have to industrialize. Without industry, how can we have industrialists?"

"Have what?" the old historian questioned.

"Industrialists," the King said. "They are the men who run the industry. You see, that would give the people a lot of opportunity."

The old man shook his head. "There is no place in our scheme of things for an industrialist either. Here, I will show you." He pointed to the scroll with his finger. "Now there is the first son. He is the King. The second son is the noble. The third son is the farmer. Then there are the twins—the artisan and the craftsman. But an industrialist! There is no industrialist. You must tell the Mr. General that."

"But . . ." King Kenji started to protest, then looking once again to his grandma, he saw her nod in agreement. And he knew that truly there was no place for an industrialist in their scheme of things.

Chapter 19

I T'S a long trip from Washington, D.C., to the Nakashima
Islands; and as the amphibian plane began to circle for the
landing on the Tamsui River, Major General Mosby Winthrope
thankfully stretched his legs. He was a big man, and though a
good many years had passed since he had been at the Academy,
still there was the same ruggedness about him, the same physical fitness that had marked his cadet days when he had been
Army's regular right tackle and an almost all-American.

Looking out through the plane window now, he surveyed the
little chain of islands below him. They looked so good from the
air, looked so good on the surface. But beneath, he knew, they
were going to pieces. For a moment his face creased in worry;
then that worry gave way to determination, for he was out here
to salvage what he could, and Major General Mosby Winthrope
never yet had failed in an assignment.

General Scheick was waiting for him on the quayside; and
Mosby, seeing his old friend and protégé saluting there, felt a
twinge of sadness. How long had they known each other? Since
that golden autumn afternoon at the Academy when Mosby
Winthrope, coming from varsity football practice, stopped by to
watch the plebes, and seeing the rookie Pug Scheick miss a block,

stepped in to show him how to take out the end who was giving him trouble. Yes, it had been a long time. And then there had been that business at Fort Bitely. They had pulled that off together. And then there was now.

Quickly, Mosby returned the salute of his old friend, managed a smile, and held out his hand. "Pug," he was about to say, "how is it going?" Thankfully he caught himself, because it wasn't going. It wasn't going at all.

General Scheick also managed a smile. Grasping the extended hand, he said, "Mosby, by George, it certainly is good to see you." That was the wrong thing to say, too. Both of them realized it, for this was the ax. They stood in embarrassed silence for a moment; and struggling for words, General Scheick arrived at "How's Gertrude?"

"Still kicking," Mosby replied, and added by way of qualification, "Of course, that's only a figure of speech. How's Caroline?"

"Just fine," General Scheick said. "I'm sorry she's not here to meet you, though. She and my nephew Elwood went up to Japan a couple of days ago."

"Oh, a little vacation?" Mosby inquired.

"No. She's in some kind of a hassle with her brother-in-law, Fred Cummings. I don't know what it's all about, except that it has something to do with seed for chicken feed."

"Seed for chicken feed?"

"I think that's it. Or maybe it was buckwheat. Anyway, she sent Fred an order, and he replied that the elevator wouldn't be equipped to handle anything like that. So she got sore and went up to Japan to buy it instead."

"Well, I hope she has a good trip," Mosby said, and the civilities being over, he turned and surveyed his surroundings. The harbor of the old capital was busier this morning than it had been in years. Sampan after sampan was coming in loaded from Bamboo Island, and on the quays, workers were piling the bundles of bamboo onto carts for transfer to the lantern-manufacturing company. For while the lanterns hanging before the houses near the quays were old ones, and while there was still no paper available for the manufacture of new ones, still the orders were pouring in, and the company was busy in the manufacture of bamboo framework, over which the paper eventually would be pasted.

Mosby, however, failed to notice the sampans or the lanterns. His eyes were on the troop after troop of mounted police drawn up in welcome. They were certainly an impressive sight, with their matched ponies, and he said, "Pug, I'm glad to see that we have an outfit like this to rely on. We'll be needing them. Have there been any signs of civil unrest?"

"No."

"But there will be. It's just a question of time. Tell me, are the police up to full strength?"

"We were," General Scheick replied. "Lately, though, we've been losing policemen right and left."

"So they're even getting at the police. That's a typical maneuver, striking at your strength and weakening it. What kind of inducements are they offering them to resign?"

"Oh, there hasn't been any activity along those lines. We first lost police to the paper-show business, and now we're losing them to the lantern company. It seems they all want to get a distributorship in the outlying islands."

Mosby regarded his old friend and protégé for a moment, then shook his head. It was evident that the man was missing the situation, missing it completely. Yet, of course, that is what he had been doing all along.

"Mosby," General Scheick said, "would you like to go up and rest a bit? Of course, you'll be staying with us."

"Thank you, Pug." Mosby's eyes swept the mounted police. He certainly would have liked to rest a bit; but since they were getting in even here, in the police, there was no time for that. "Is the King around anywhere?"

"He's up at the castle."

"You better take me right up there then," Mosby said. "We don't have a minute to lose."

As the car started on the first leg of the drive, from town up to Caroline Drive, General Winthrope, sitting in the right-hand corner of the back seat, stared straight ahead; and General Scheick, seated in the lesser position to the left, looked anxiously at him. "Mosby," he said, "Washington understands how it is about this industrialization, don't they?"

"No, Pug, they don't," Mosby replied. "That's obvious, or else I wouldn't be here."

"I realize that," General Scheick pressed on, "but they understand what we're up against, don't they? For instance, take this old King Gihon. Three hundred and sixty years ago he made a survey and stated that there is no place for industry here. He said this is just an agricultural land. In their scheme of things, Japan must be the industrialist. And I think he might have been right. I sent my staff out, and they couldn't find one blessed thing either."

"Pug, the thing to understand is that industrialization is our only hope. Originally, we had intended giving them the slow treatment. We were going to explain, then industrialize them. But you botched things up so that we had to swing over to the fast treatment. We decided to industrialize first and explain later. Now even the fast treatment has been jeopardized. As Congressman Homer Hoplow of Kansas says, 'How many countries can we let get away from us like this! The first thing you know, we'll be standing alone, like a scarecrow in a gooseberry patch.'"

"I see," General Scheick said, and they fell silent.

At Caroline Drive they dismounted from the sedan and prepared to start up the cart trail to the castle. The cart trail once had been little more than an overgrown path, but now there were workers chopping at the underbrush. There were other workers turning under the wild grass at the sides of the trail. And waiting to pass through were half a dozen pony carts loaded with large stones.

"What's going on, Pug?" Mosby asked, surveying the activity.

"The King came into some money," General Scheick replied. "So they're starting to fix things up. In the old days this was known as the King's Road. They tell me Gihon used to walk here in the morning. Now they're going to make it just as it used to be, prune the tree branches to overhang the road, string lanterns down it, and all that kind of thing."

"What are the stones for?" Mosby indicated the carts.

General Scheick hesitated for a moment, then said, "They're starting to rebuild the castle."

"Rebuild the castle!" Shock was on Mosby's face. "You mean they're starting to live it up?"

"I'm afraid so. The King did come into this money, and . . ."

"And you're letting them get away with it?"

"I tried to tell them, Mosby, that a thatch-roofed house was good enough for any king, but no. They have to rebuild it with stone, just like it used to be."

"Where did the King get this money?" Mosby demanded.

"They cooked up some deal and called it the crown lands."

"What?"

"The crown lands. The King declared that all the land along the roads belongs to him, and he's renting it out to the farmers."

"At exorbitant rates, I suppose. How extensive are these holdings?"

General Scheick swallowed. "We think it runs about five per cent of the total acreage on the Islands."

"Five per cent! Pug, how in the name of heaven could you let him pull a deal like that?"

"I didn't know it was happening."

"I can't believe that," Mosby said. "Why, any time you start letting them jiggle the land around you run into trouble, and here the King walks off with five per cent. My God, man, this situation is just ripe for a revolution. Can't you see this is just what the communists want!"

Again they fell silent. As they walked along, the workers on the road would look up, smile at them, and nod brightly. And Mosby, seeing the bright nods, grew more alarmed by the minute, for it seemed as if every man along the road was a comrade, smiling over the situation and just waiting for the signal to pull a coup.

Reaching an inner courtyard of the castle, Mosby saw a fig-

238

ure half bent in the tall grass. "Just a minute, Pug. What's going on over there?"

"I don't know," General Scheick replied.

"Does it look like sabotage to you?"

General Scheick peered closer. "I don't think so, Mosby. That's only the Duke of Tatami Oshima. He's the senior duke."

"What's he up to?"

"That's hard to say."

"We'd better investigate. Follow me."

They walked through the tall grass and reaching the Duke, Mosby said, "What's going on here?"

The Duke, seeing them, straightened, and recognizing General Scheick began bowing. "He doesn't understand English, Mosby," General Scheick explained.

"Well, what do you think that is?" Mosby indicated a reedlike cage.

"I think I know, but let me find out for sure." General Scheick pointed and said to the Duke, "Oink? Oink?"

The Duke began nodding. "Oink. Oink."

"What does that mean?" Mosby asked.

"Look." General Scheick directed Mosby's attention to the Duke who, putting a finger to his lips, tiptoed over, parted the tall grass, and there—all three hundred plus pounds of her—lay his pig sleeping contentedly. "You see," General Scheick went on, "he's building a pigpen."

Mosby put his hand on the reedlike cage. "It does look like a pigpen, doesn't it?" he agreed. "But you have to investigate, Pug. You can't be too careful." They continued on their way up to the royal enclosure, and as they did so, another thought struck Mosby. "So that was the senior duke. I don't know much about nobility, but I can't say I'm very impressed."

"Well, he does leave a little something to be desired," General Scheick said.

"In other words he's deadwood."

"I'm afraid he is, Mosby."

"Why in the name of heaven didn't you clean house right from the start, then?"

"Well, I . . ."

"Pug." Mosby, his face solemn, looked at his protégé. "How do you think we can stand up against them with deadwood?" He pointed back at the senior duke. "The first thing I'm going to do is clean the shanty of people like that."

General Scheick nodded morosely, and they walked on. As they neared the royal enclosure, they heard the sound of music, and Mosby demanded, "Now what the hell is that?"

General Scheick was perspiring. "That's the Duchess of Bamboo Island's combo."

"What is a combo?"

"I had to ask that myself," General Scheick said. "It's a kind of small orchestra. In this case, it consists of a bass, a steel drum, and a piano."

Mosby glanced about at the wild grass. "Now where would you get a piano out here?"

"The King bought it from Agnes McCloud, the wife of my Intelligence officer."

"So the Duchess has her own orchestra, eh? So she's up here playing while Rome burns."

"Actually," General Scheick said, "she's rehearsing them and training a bunch of dance instructors for the marriage mill they're going to start."

"Marriage mill!" Mosby's mouth almost flew open.

"Yes, they're having a big shindig, selling tickets for it, trying to get everybody hooked up with everybody else. I tried to stop the King, but he wouldn't listen."

"And I suppose when the revolution comes, he'll be wondering why it happened. Come on, Pug. I want to see what kind of nonsense this young idiot is up to now."

They found the King on his hands and knees, over by the castle wall. He was holding a little sprig of ivy and his eyes were filled with sadness.

"King Kenji," General Scheick said, "this is General Winthrope, my commanding officer. He's come out from Washington to try to pull you out of your troubles."

"Well, that's nice of him," the King said. "Have you heard

anything from Elwood and the Mrs. General? I mean when they're getting back from Japan?"

"No. What are you doing?"

"I was just looking at the ivy that Mr. Hayden sent me from Cambridge. It came from the Old Main, itself. And now the Duke of Tatami Oshima's pig has rooted it up."

Looking at the King, Mosby saw that he nearly had tears in his eyes; but try as he might, he couldn't sympathize with a man who concerned himself over a sprig of vegetation while his country was going to hell in the proverbial hand-basket.

"But I guess I got here just in time, even though I couldn't save the ivy," the King went on. "Why, she was just about to start on Grandma's sunflowers." He gestured to where a long row of sunflowers were growing along the wall.

Mosby, however, was not interested in sunflowers. Instead, he indicated a group of workers spading under the wild grass. "What are you doing there, King Kenji?" he asked.

"Oh, I'm restoring the royal gardens."

"That sounds like a nice, expensive undertaking."

"It's going to cost me plenty," the King agreed, "but I think we're going to enjoy it."

"You better enjoy it while you can," Mosby said and again pointed. "What's going on there?"

Kenji glanced at another group of workers. "They're looking for the old walls of the castle. We're going to restore it, too, just as it was. However, I am going to put in plumbing and central heating."

"Naturally," Mosby said. "And while you're doing all this, what are you doing in government?"

"I'm bringing in the earls to give me a hand."

"And they will be living up here, too, I suppose, enjoying the plumbing and central heating?"

"Oh, sure. Only I have to fix up a special courtyard for them. It's the third one down. The dukes and the Duchess have the second."

General Winthrope shook his head. "Pug," he said, "I wish you had gotten out of this. I wish you had just retired when

241

the going was good. But since that's not the case . . ." He extended his hand as he prepared to bring out the big broom. "I want you to know there's nothing personal in this."

General Scheick clasped the hand. "I know that, Mosby."

"And, of course, we'll still be friends."

"We certainly will," General Scheick vowed.

"Well . . ." Mosby stiffened. "King Kenji, I hope you realize that you're about to be overthrown."

The King scratched his head. "I am?"

"You certainly are. And I'd say the blame rests partly upon your shoulders, and partly on"—Mosby glanced at General Scheick—"the shoulders of others. But it's too late for that. Now we have to adopt emergency measures."

The King was puzzled. "Excuse me, Mr. General," he said. "But who is going to overthrow me?"

"Why the communists, of course."

"What communists?"

"The ones here. They're all over the place."

"Mr. General," the King began. "I don't think that's right. If they were all over the place, how come everyone voted for the return of the King instead of communism?"

It was a good question, one which carried a lot of logic behind it, so much logic that General Scheick had to say, "By George, Mosby, the King's got something. How come they didn't vote for communism?"

Even General Winthrope was stopped cold, and he cast around for an explanation. "On the surface," he said, "you'd think they would have, wouldn't you? However, maybe they had something else in mind here."

"Oh, you don't have to worry about that," the King said. "Why, we'd never go back to communism."

"Go back," both the generals said in unison, and Mosby added, "Aha. So you were communistic!"

"That's right, Mr. General. Back in 1563."

"Now wait a minute," Mosby said. "No one knew about communism then."

"King Gihon did. You ask Mr. Yamaguchi to show you the scrolls. It's under the section called 'The Experiment.' "

"What Experiment?"

"The one King Gihon tried in 1563. Each village was given all the land surrounding it. That is, the land belonged to all the people of the village. There was no more private ownership."

"What happened?"

"That's what King Gihon wanted to find out. First, he tried the equal shares system. Since everybody owned the land, everybody would get an equal share of the produce. Only that didn't work, because nobody wanted to do the farming. They just wanted to collect. And that was the source of the old Nakashima Islands proverb which says, 'If you want to be there for the harvest, you'd better be there for the planting.' "

"I'll be damned," Mosby half whispered. "Then what happened after the equal shares system failed?"

"King Gihon tried assigning everyone a plot of ground. Now since some land is better than others, he arranged for a reassignment every three years so all would get a chance at the good soil. But that didn't work either, because no one would care for the land assigned to them. Why should they? It was only going to be reassigned to someone else, not passed on to their sons."

"Well, I'll be damned," Mosby repeated.

"And besides," the King went on, "the land was being ruined so badly that if it kept on, everybody knew they would starve to death in another generation. So Gihon stepped in. He gave the land back to the original owners. And that was enough of communism for everybody, especially King Gihon."

"Why Gihon?"

"Because he had to compensate the owners for the damage done during the experiment. It took him years to pay off."

"Well, that sort of puts a new light on things," Mosby said, and it was just like getting what you wanted for Christmas. In fact, this was a dozen times better than any present. Then he grew cautious once again. "But what about the pinks? Surely you must have some pinks around somewhere."

"Oh, no, Mr. General. We don't have any of those either."

243

"Not even a few?"

"No. After the experiment in 1563 . . . well, we consider communism an archaic form of government. The monarchy is the modern form."

"But suppose the people should decide to try the experiment again," Mosby said. "Then what?"

"Oh, we couldn't go communistic now, not with these women's investment clubs springing up all over the place. They're starting businesses right and left."

"Who's starting businesses?"

"The ladies. They're organizing corporations. They're in everything from fish processing to charcoal making."

"Why, that's free enterprise!"

"I know." The King nodded. "And just let the communists try monkeying around with the investment clubs. Let them try taking those businesses away from the ladies. As you say in America, you'd see the fur fly."

"No communists." A smile was on Mosby's lips. "And free enterprise. I'll be damned. Wait until I radio Washington about this. Why, this is everything they want." He regarded the King; and now that he looked at him he could see that here was a fine boy, perhaps a little young and inexperienced, but nevertheless a fine boy indeed. Then seeing the sprig of ivy in the King's hand, he reached out. "Here, King Kenji, let me take a look at that. Maybe we can do something."

Carefully, Mosby took the sprig; and General Scheick, having seen the smile on his C.O.'s face and realizing that, by George, this was free enterprise after all, felt an overwhelming sense of relief sweep in.

"Pug," Mosby said, "how does it look to you?"

"To me?" General Scheick was wallowing in his relief. "Oh, the ivy." Quickly he bent, examined it. "I'm afraid it's gone. Look, that damn pig ruined the whole root system."

"Wouldn't you know it." Glancing up, Mosby saw the Duke of Tatami Oshima coming toward them. "There's no excuse for this. King Kenji, you ought to really chew him out."

"But he didn't do it," Kenji said. "His pig did." Reaching the

King, the Duke began bowing. "And see," Kenji went on, "again he says he is sorry."

Mosby regarded the Duke. "Man, you're really saddled with something here, King Kenji. By the accident of birth his family are dukes, and now everybody has to put up with it."

"But his family weren't always born dukes."

"You told me this nobility thing was hereditary," General Scheick cut in. "You yourself said they all descended from the second son of whatever their names are."

"Of Shinerikyu and Amamikyu. That's true, except there is a kind of symbolism, Mr. General, just like we have the symbolism of the high tide and letting the pigs look at you for good luck. As far as we know, Shinerikyu and Amamikyu have no true sons. All of their descendants are adopted, so to speak. For instance, when someone did something for our Islands, the King would reward him. As an example, suppose somebody got a job in government, and suppose he did real well at it. Then the King would make him a noble."

"Oh," General Scheick said. "So that's why the King's advisers were always nobles. They were just people who worked their way up to the nobility."

"That is correct, Mr. General."

"Ah, so that's it." General Scheick turned. "You know, Mosby, that's quite a system. If somebody shows that he's got the old juice, what the King does, in effect, is commission him."

"He does, doesn't he?" Mosby conceded. "That is quite a system. When the King gets a good man, he simply knights him into the fold, just as we put bars on him."

"Oh, the King doesn't necessarily knight him," Kenji explained. "The King might make him an earl, or viscount . . ."

"We have different ranks, too," Mosby said. "But how did the family of a man like this"—Mosby indicated the Duke—"ever make the grade?"

"It all goes back to his grandfather, thirty-three times removed," the King said. "In the year 966 an expedition set out from China looking for the land of the happy immortals, and they landed here, thinking this was the place. Well, for a while everything was fine. We had big feasts and banquets. Then the Chinese discovered that, instead of being immortals, we were just people, and all kinds of the dickens broke loose. In fact, it became so bad that it looked as if it were the end of the Nakashima Islands."

"Oh?"

"Yes. So the Duke of Tatami Oshima's grandfather, thirty-three times removed, decided that this couldn't go on. He was the commander of our army, so he rallied our forces and drove those Chinese back, right onto their junks and out to sea again. His grandfather, thirty-three times removed, saved our Islands; and as a reward the King made him a duke. That's why this Duke is the Duke today."

For a moment both General Scheick and General Winthrope were silent. They eyed the present Duke, then General Winthrope said slowly, "So his grandfather, thirty-three times removed, was in the Service, eh?"

"Oh, yes." The King nodded solemnly. "He was a big general, just like you gentlemen."

The Duke saw them eying him, and then both of them smiled at him, so he smiled back.

"King Kenji," Mosby began slowly. "About that ivy. You know, accidents will happen." A thought struck him. "By the way, do you have any kind of a pension plan for a man like this?" He indicated the Duke. "You know, if it weren't for his grandfather, thirty-three times removed, why you'd probably be eating chop suey right now."

"The castle is the pension plan, Mr. General," Kenji said. "When the King made his grandfather, thirty-three times removed, a duke, the King guaranteed that there would always be a place at the castle for any Duke of Tatami Oshima. He could come whenever he wanted to, and stay as long as he wished. That's why I'm trying to fix things up now."

"Oh, I see," Mosby said, looking at the workmen, busy there in the royal enclosure; and General Scheick looked, too.

"Tell me, King Kenji," General Scheick said. "What chance does a man have of making 'Duke' today? I mean is there any

246

chance of anyone getting in on this deal at the present time?"

"Oh, yes. Traditionally there always have been fifteen dukes, or duchesses, one for each Island."

General Scheick's eyes widened. "And there are only three now. That means twelve dukedoms are open. By George, Mosby, there is opportunity here after all." His hand swept the courtyard. "And if they had a modern castle up here, just think of the incentive it would offer."

Mosby considered, then nodded thoughtfully. "Pug, you've got something there. King Kenji, is there anything else open besides dukedoms?"

"Oh, yes." Kenji nodded and his eyes stole to a plane coming out of the northeast. "There are a lot of openings—earls, viscounts, barons. The King can create as many nobles as he can afford."

"As he can afford? Ah, yes," Mosby said. "That puts a good check on things. The King isn't going to pass out titles indiscriminately, not when he has to provide fringe benefits like room and board at the castle, and things."

"That's right," Kenji said, then asked, "Mr. General, that's the Japan-Hong Kong plane, isn't it? I hope Elwood and the Mrs. General are on it. I can hardly wait to find out how they made out."

"How they made out?"

"Yes, with the cloth for the kimonos. Debbie designed a whole bunch of Nakashima Islands originals to be produced in Japan."

"What did she do that for?" General Scheick asked.

"So the girls will have pretty kimonos to wear to the Festival of the Unattached."

"Now wait a minute." General Mosby Winthrope held up his hand. "The Festival of the Unattached . . . what in the name of heaven would that be?"

Chapter 20

HIGH TIDE on September 4 was at 2:16 P.M. So shortly after the old amphibian plane came lumbering out from Okinawa; and on the quayside at Tamabaru, King Kenji wiped his forehead, for it was a blinger. Not only were the Nakashima Islands sweltering, but the whole Far East was wrapped in the September heat. Up in Japan on the trains they were stripped to their underwear. Down in Taipei, Formosa, you couldn't budge them from under the fans at the Friends of China Club. In Hong Kong they were wishing they were somewhere else. And here . . . even the Duchess of Bamboo Island had substituted a thin, sleeveless dress for her long, red tights. Still she was uncomfortable as she stood next to the King, watching the plane.

Inside the plane they were also sweltering. "Well, here we are," Elwood said as they edged into the quay.

But Mrs. Scheick didn't answer. She merely dabbed at her flushed face with her too small handkerchief; then, handkerchief in hand, she walked to the door which the Air Corps sergeant had opened, and she was about to step out when she heard the King. "Mrs. General," the King called. "Mrs. General. Just a moment. I'll give you a hand."

Looking up, she saw Kenji's face, wreathed in a smile in spite of the wilting heat. She saw Debbie smiling too, and she said, "Hello, King Kenji. Hello, Duchess."

King Kenji had expected a little more enthusiasm and disappointment swept through him, but he quickly pushed it aside, for he knew how it was in this weather. Then he extended his hand for Mrs. Scheick, who made it on her own, however. And turning, the King saw Elwood. "Why, Elwood," he said. "You old son of a gun. How are you?"

"Hot," Elwood replied and added, "Hello, Debbie. How's your combo coming?"

"They're the coolest," the Duchess said, shifting her attention to Mrs. Scheick.

But Mrs. Scheick didn't notice. Mrs. Scheick was looking about. "Heavens," she said, "can't we get out of this sun?"

"Would you like to step into the shade of those buildings?" Kenji indicated the structures lining the quayside.

Mrs. Scheick realized it was the only shade available. But then she realized something else. "Where is the sedan?" she demanded. "Didn't the General send it for me?"

"I haven't seen it," the King replied.

"He knew I was coming. I sent a radiogram from Okinawa."

"I know, Mrs. General," the King said. "That's how we found out you would be on this plane."

"Where is the sedan then?"

"I don't know."

"Oh, really! This is the living end!"

Elwood caught a glimpse of his aunt's face, and quickly stepped in. "Aunt Caroline," he said, "why don't you go over in the shade there with Kenji and Debbie? I'll run up to the motor pool and get us some transportation."

"I don't want just transportation," Mrs. Scheick said. "I want the sedan, and tell them I want it right away!"

"All right," Elwood said. "Kenji, take Aunt Caroline over to the shade. I'll be back in a few minutes."

It was almost as hot in the shade as in the sun. They stood in silence. Mrs. Scheick simply stared ahead, while the King and

249

Duchess watched. But then the King's eyes stole to the Duchess'. Their looks met. And the King began hesitantly, "Mrs. General, how did things go up in Japan?"

Mrs. Scheick wheeled, then said quickly, "I'm sorry. Don't pay any attention to me. It's just this heat." She paused. "But to be fair with you, King Kenji, it just didn't go at all."

"It didn't go at all!" The words escaped Kenji. He looked to Debbie, saw the fright in her eyes. "But it has to go, Mrs. General. We've been counting on it."

"So have I," Mrs. Scheick said. "I think that's evident or I wouldn't have made the trip."

"But the seed, Mrs. General, to raise the crops for the chicken feed. You were able to get that, weren't you?"

"No, not a single pound."

"Didn't they have it?"

"Yes, they have it. They have enough to plant the crown lands a thousand times over. But, King Kenji, in plain, everyday words, your money is worthless."

"It can't be."

"I'm afraid it is. Instead of going up there with Nakashima Islands paper money, I might as well have gone up with a ream of typing paper. I should have known better. I took it for granted that because our money was good anywhere, yours would be, too."

"And you weren't able to get my originals produced?" the Duchess of Bamboo Island asked.

"I wasn't able to get anything—cloth, candles, paper for lanterns, musical instruments for your orchestra."

The Duchess shook her head. "I don't understand that."

"It's this way," Mrs. Scheick explained. "Every businessman up there wants to deal with you. In fact, they'd even sell you Tokyo if you had a sound currency. But all you have is paper. Printed pieces of paper."

"That's all anyone's money is," the Duchess said.

"Look at it from the Japanese viewpoint," Mrs. Scheick went on. "You want them to give you manufactured articles. In return you would give them your paper money. Now what could they do with your money? They couldn't buy anything here. You have no products."

The Duchess began to understand then.

"And could the Japanese convert your money into Hong Kong or United States dollars?" Mrs. Scheick continued. "Of course not. Why should anyone in the U. S. or Hong Kong want pieces of paper which they couldn't exchange for anything?"

The Duchess turned. "But, King Kenji, about the Festival of the Unattached. We can still have it, can't we?" she asked.

"I don't see how we can, Debbie," the King said slowly. "There won't be any cloth for kimonos, and there won't be any decorations. The lantern-making company will have to go out of business, because they have no paper. And you couldn't have an orchestra without instruments. You'd have to get along with just your combo of the piano you bought from Mrs. McCloud, the steel drum the motor pool sergeant made, and a samisen."

"Oh." There was a crushed look in the Duchess' eye.

But something else was bothering the King. "Mrs. General," he said. "About your Investment Club—you'll still carry on with the chicken and paper-show businesses, won't you?"

"I'm afraid there's no point in that," Mrs. Scheick replied. "We'd only be working for paper, too. The Finance Officer would never convert our profit into U. S. dollars."

"I see," the King said sadly. "And there wouldn't be anything else to exchange it for, would there? I am sorry, Mrs. General."

When Elwood arrived with the General's sedan, he found the three of them standing silently in the shade. As he stepped from the car, he faced the King; and seeing the hurt in the King's eyes, said, "We tried, Kenji. You know that, don't you? But there was nothing we could do."

"I know, Elwood." Kenji regarded him. "I guess this is the end of the chicken business, isn't it?"

"I'm afraid it is."

"I guess it's just the end of everything," the King continued, then glanced at the Watanabe Hills. "Are you coming up to the castle now, Elwood?"

"I thought I'd go up to Uncle Matt's first. I'd like to take a shower."

"Gosh," the King said. "We don't even have showers."

"Well, maybe I'll take one later," Elwood said quickly. "Come on, let's go up to the castle and have some tea."

"Do you want to?" the King asked uncertainly.

"Sure," Elwood replied. "Let's go, Debbie."

"Okay," the Duchess said, and her voice was subdued.

The King faced Mrs. Scheick. "I want to thank you, Mrs. General. I certainly appreciate all you have done."

"I'm afraid it hasn't been much."

"But it has. It has," Kenji said, and the three young ones, their faces grave and sober, started for the Watanabe Hills.

As Mrs. Scheick watched them go, regret welled up in her. She wished she could have done something for them in Japan, but what could she do without a currency that had value? Then regret gave way as once again the September heat came pressing in, and she said to the corporal-driver, "Why weren't you here to meet me?"

The corporal shifted uncomfortably. "I would have been, ma'am, but the General didn't tell me you were arriving."

"He didn't tell you!"

"No, ma'am," the corporal said, and he could see then and there that the Old Man was certainly going to get chewed.

Cottage 1A was cool and dark as Mrs. Scheick entered, and she called, "Haruko!" But there was no answer; and knowing how the maids along Caroline Drive liked to get together to visit, Mrs. Scheick turned her attention to the mail on the hall table that had piled up during her absence. Sorting through it, she came across a letter from Elwood's mother, opened it, and began reading.

There was a nice breeze through the house, and Mrs. Scheick was beginning to feel more comfortable. But as she read, her face became more flushed by the minute, her eyes blazed, and she said, "That Fred Cummings! This is the living end." Throwing the letter back on the table, she started for the bedroom; then hearing the whistling of "On, Brave Old Army Team" coming from the kitchen, she called, "Matt!"

"Why, Caroline." General Scheick looked in, a smile all over his face. "When did you get back?"

"Just when I said I would in my radiogram. Why didn't you have the sedan there to meet me?"

General Scheick snapped his fingers. "Darn. I knew I forgot something."

"Well, really!" Mrs. Scheick exclaimed. "Letting me stand in that hot sun . . ."

"But I've been awful busy, Caroline. By the way, did you find your mail? There's a letter from Mildred."

"I saw it," Mrs. Scheick snapped.

"Is there something wrong?"

"There certainly is. That Fred Cummings! I sent him a letter asking for literature on chicken feed and he said, 'Oh, we wouldn't have anything like that.' I sent him another letter asking him if he could furnish the seed for hundreds of acres, and he said, 'Oh, we wouldn't be equipped to handle anything like that.' And now"—Mrs. Scheick was almost shaking—"now do you know what he's going to do? He's going to buy a convertible because he thinks it might do him good to ride around with the top down and get the fresh air. A convertible! Honestly! And to think that's the way he's been running the elevator all these years and I never knew it."

"Now, now," General Scheick said, "it's just hot."

"And to think of the way Papa worked to build up that business," Mrs. Scheick went on. "And here Good-Time Charley is, riding around in a convertible."

"Now, Caroline," General Scheick said. "You'll feel better when you get your girdle off."

But Mrs. Scheick hardly heard him. "This is the end! I'm sick and tired of that Fred Cummings."

General Scheick realized he was getting nowhere. "All right, Caroline." And he added by way of diversion, "Mosby has arrived."

"And I'm sick and tired of hearing about the obstacle course at old Fort Bitely, too."

"Of course," the General said. "But do you know what? I have good news. Mosby and I see eye to eye on this whole operation. We drafted his report to Washington together, just think of that!"

Mrs. Scheick thought of it.

"But come on out in the back yard," the General went on. "He's anxious to see you."

"Let me at least get a cold drink of something. Where's Haruko?"

"She's busy at the moment. Mosby and I are having a conference with the Duke of Tatami Oshima, and she's acting as interpreter. I just came in to get us four more carrot juices. Let me get you one, too."

"Oh, heavens, don't bother," Mrs. Scheick said. "I'll make myself some iced tea."

"All right." Together they went to the kitchen; and General Scheick, taking a gallon of carrot juice from the refrigerator, said, "You know, Caroline, the Duke is giving us a bad time out there. Both Mosby and I want him to retire. But no, he wants to stay in harness."

"And that's the big conference that made you forget to send the sedan for me?" Mrs. Scheick asked.

"Now you don't realize the importance of this, Caroline. His grandfather, thirty-three times removed, was in the Service. He saved these Islands. As Mosby said, if it weren't for him, these people would probably be eating chow mein right now. Or did he say chop suey?"

From Mrs. Scheick's glance, the General could see that she wasn't much interested in the problem of the Duke of Tatami Oshima, so they prepared their drinks in silence, then started out for the back yard where the little group was deep in conversation.

"Now you tell him, Haruko," Mosby was saying, "that's part of the system. His grandfather, thirty-three times removed, earned a good rest, and he's got to take it easy."

"Hokay." The little maid interpreted, then shook her head. "He say . . . take it easy, can no."

"Can yes. Damn it," Mosby snapped.

"Hokay." In that instant Haruko caught sight of Mrs. Scheick. She leaped to her feet and began bowing profusely.

"Why, Caroline." Mosby rose from his chair. "Caroline, how are you? It's certainly good to see you again." He took her hand. "Why, it seems like only yesterday that we were all together at old Fort Bitely. Remember?"

"Fort Bitely is hard to forget," Mrs. Scheick said.

"And do you remember how Mosby and I pulled it off there?" General Scheick joined in.

Mrs. Scheick wasn't able to direct a glance at him, because Mosby was looking full at her, and Mosby was smiling. "We're going to pull this one off, too, Caroline," he said. "To be frank about it, I came out here with hatchet in hand, and I don't mind telling you that it was one of the most difficult situations I've ever faced, because you know how close Pug and I have been through the years."

"But you didn't have to use the hatchet, Mosby," General Scheick said quickly. "And we have this thing beat."

"We certainly have. You just keep your eye on Pug and me, Caroline. We'll show them. Why, do you realize there isn't a single communist in these Islands?"

"I'm sure of that," Mrs. Scheick replied.

"But Washington isn't. Washington doesn't know. However, Pug and I straightened them out. We sent them a complete report."

"That's fine," Mrs. Scheick said.

Mosby, a smile on his face, shook his head. "Well, it certainly is good to see you again, Caroline. And I hear you're becoming quite an entrepreneur."

"Entrepreneur?"

"A businesswoman, so to speak. I've heard about how you girls have your hand in things." Mosby held up a finger. "That's free enterprise."

"I'm afraid that's all over," Mrs. Scheick said.

"So you're selling out and taking your profit."

"No. We'll probably just let the businesses go."

Moby's jaw sagged. "Let them go? What for?"

"Because there's no point in continuing," Mrs. Scheick said, and went on to explain about her trip to Japan and the worthlessness of the Nakashima Islands currency.

"But you can't just let them disintegrate," Mosby said. "We need you girls to keep things going."

"That's right." General Scheick was in agreement. "How are Mosby and I going to pull this off if you don't keep things running for us?"

"But we'd only be working for worthless paper," Mrs. Scheick said. "However, why don't you see the Queen Grandmother? Perhaps she could make arrangements for some Islands business corporations to take over. At least they're local. At least they could buy sweet potatoes with their paper money."

It was a cinch they had to keep things running. "Pug," Mosby said, "we better see the Queen Grandmother. We better see her right away. Caroline, I don't like to run off like this. However, I wonder if you would excuse us if . . ."

"You go right ahead," Mrs. Scheick said, the thought of the comfort of slipping out of her girdle coming to her. "Please go right ahead, Mosby."

The Duke of Tatami Oshima went up to the castle with them. The three of them walked along the old royal road beneath the overhanging branches, but the activity had stopped now. No longer were workmen busy cutting out the wild growth along the sides, widening the road. Instead, the workmen, hoes in hand, were coming down from the castle. The carts, which had carried building stone up, were coming down, too. And it was obvious from the dejection of the workmen, even from the slow gait of the ponies, that the last load had been carried up and there would be no more.

Reaching the royal enclosure, they found the King and his grandmother, the Duchess of Bamboo Island and Elwood, all sitting on the veranda before the main house. The little group had a pot of tea before them, but they weren't sipping. They were merely sitting in silence.

"Ah, there you are," Mosby said. "I'm glad I found you all together." He swept the courtyard with his hand. "King Kenji, you're not stopping work on the castle, are you?"

"There is nothing else I can do," Kenji replied.

"But what about the Duke here? The King made a promise to his grandfather, thirty-three times removed, that there would always be a place here for him. And what about the other nobility? They served their country. Your kings made promises to them too. You can't go back on them now."

Kenji indicated the little thatched house. "I'm afraid this is the best I can manage."

"But, King Kenji," General Scheick said, "this just isn't good enough. If the castle is going to be the incentive"—he shrugged—"well, who's going to work his head off to become a duke when the only reward is a grass shack on the top of a hill? He can get the same in any village."

"That's right," Mosby said. "General Scheick and I have talked this over. The heart of your system is the castle, and you have to build it up, make it really something. Maybe put in swimming pools and hanging gardens and fountains."

The King looked at him. "That's what I intended to do, Mr. General. That's what Grandma told me I had to do. But how can I? Haven't you heard about our money? I couldn't even put in"—he glanced at Elwood—"showers, because I can't buy showers anywhere. And we don't make them here, you know. And how can I make this the Land of the Lighted Lanterns again? We don't even have paper to make lanterns."

"Now look, King Kenji," Mosby said. "You're just discouraged, but we can't let that throw us. And we can't let this whole thing fall apart. You have to continue. You have to have the Festival of the Unattached. Why, do you know that Haruko, General Scheick's maid, has already bought her ticket? She showed it to me, and the Festival isn't until the last of October.

And do you realize that every maid along Caroline Drive has bought a ticket too? You have to go on. Ask your grandmother. See if she doesn't agree with me."

"Oh, Grandma agrees with you, Mr. General," Kenji said. "She wants to go on too. But she doesn't see how we can, because we need so many things from some place else. And to get them we have to have something to exchange for them. It's the same old problem."

"The same old problem? What do you mean by that?"

"Oh, after the Mrs. General returned from Japan and we learned that our money was no good, we went to see Mr. Yamaguchi, our leading historian, to tell him about it."

"And what did he say?"

"He said it was the very thing that old King Gihon faced when he took over the throne in 1566. Gihon was young, like me, then. And he had an awful lot of ideas. He wanted to get some sweet potatoes so he could introduce them to the Nakashima Islands. He wanted to get some samisens, too, because he liked the music he had heard in China when he was a student. Besides, he thought if he brought in samisens, he could get the people to singing and fight *sabishii*. Most of all, though, he used to see the junks of the great trade network glide by our Islands, carrying spices and ivory from Malacca, carrying the good rice of Korea and the lacquer ware of China. And Gihon thought, Boys, if we're going to get anywhere, we have to be a part of that trade network. Yet when he tried to join it, they told him exactly the same as they told Elwood and the Mrs. General up in Japan. They said, 'Your money is no good.' "

"And all this happened in 1566?" Mosby asked.

"Yes, Mr. General," Kenji replied. "So you can see it is not exactly a new problem. And you can see why Grandma says she doesn't see how we can continue."

"Now wait a minute," General Scheick said quickly. "What did Gihon do when he found out that your money was no good?"

"Oh, well he thought it over and realized that to join the trade network, he would have to have a product to trade."

"In other words," General Scheick said, "something they wanted in China, Japan, Malacca, and Korea."

"That's right. So he began to look around for a product that we had that others might want, and he had to look and look because we had so little. Then he hit on something. He knew the Japanese, the Chinese, and the Koreans liked tea. And we had the well at Little Koza."

"I don't get it," Mosby said.

"It's this way," the King continued. "To make good tea, first of all, you need good water. The water cannot contain too much iron. Iron ruins the taste. But then it must have just the right amount of calcium. Calcium brings out the best taste of the tea. And the water from the well at Little Koza was just right. It made some of the best tea in the world. So Gihon said, 'Aha!' And he began sending it out in great big jars. They bought it like crazy in China, and Japan, and Korea. That's how we got sweet potatoes and samisens. And that's how we were able to join the great trade network."

"I'll be damned," General Scheick said. "What do you think of that, Mosby?"

"Tell me," Mosby began shrewdly, "is that well still out in Little Koza?"

"It sure is," General Scheick replied quickly.

"Why don't we start exporting water again then?"

General Scheick whistled. "Say, that's an idea. Look, King Kenji, we'll send it up to Japan. We'll build you up a credit there, so you can buy everything you need. You can go right ahead with your program. Build up the castle. Carry on with the Festival of the Unattached."

The King shook his head. "No, Mr. General. Grandma and the rest of us have talked it over. And old King Gihon was right. He said that the water from the well at Little Koza was only a temporary thing."

Mosby considered. "I'll admit that water to make tea is a pretty shaky product on which to base an economy."

"King Gihon knew that," Kenji said. "Why, 394 years ago he said it wouldn't last, and see, it didn't. It's as Grandma said,

'What's the use? Who, today, is interested in water to make tea?' "

General Scheick looked to the Queen Grandmother. She sat with hands folded in lap, and he knew she was right. General Winthrope, however, was deep in thought, then once again he began shrewdly, "King Kenji, we have a precedent here. Now Gihon said, in effect, that you needed a product to trade. All right, let's get a product. Let's grab ourselves a slice of the sports car market in America. We can turn out a little car, maybe call it the Winthrope-Scheick. We'll be glad to lend our names to it. And just think . . . your American dollars would be good anywhere. See what Grandma thinks of that."

"Well . . ." Kenji translated, then said, "Grandma says old King Gihon never mentioned making sports cars."

"Of course not," Mosby said. "They weren't even invented then."

"Grandma says in that case, we had just better go along with old King Gihon. And I agree with her, Mr. General. We can't make sports cars. We have nothing to make them out of."

"Wait a minute." Mosby held up his hand. "What do you mean you had better just go along with old King Gihon? Is there another precedent here? Did he discover a product?"

"Oh, yes. He thought for fifty years. He searched for something that always would be wanted, and one day he found it."

"You mean a product on which to build a stable economy?"

"Yes."

"What was it?"

"The pig."

"The pig?"

"Yes. Gihon said prices might fluctuate, but nevertheless there would always be a market for the pig. He said it would last. And see, it has."

"By George, Mosby," General Scheick said, "you know, Gihon might have had something there. Back home, in Iowa, they did pretty well with hogs."

Mosby pursed his lips. "So Gihon said the product on which to base your economy was the pig, eh? All right, let's start exporting hogs then. Let's start sending them up to Japan and get the things we need for the castle and the Festival of the Unattached."

"I wish we could," the King said.

"Why can't you?"

"Because we don't have the pigs. You see, that is the thing old King Gihon was never able to figure out."

"What?"

"How to get pigs out to all the people. How to arrange it so that everyone had pigs to raise and pigs to sell. The water from the well at Little Koza was a wonderful thing. With it old Gihon was able to bring us up to the verge of a golden age. But if he had been able to solve the problem of the pig"—Kenji regarded the generals—"why then we would have had the golden age itself."

Chapter 21

WHEN the radiogram arrived from Washington, Generals Winthrope and Scheick were down in the improvised gym of headquarters. The imaginary rope was drawn taut between them. And while it was a struggle, still General Winthrope, the senior officer, was not only pulling General Scheick across the floor in a tug of war, but General Scheick's whole staff as well. Major McCloud tried to dig in with his heels, and the veins stood out in Colonel Henderson's temples, but they were no match for General Mosby Winthrope. He inched them along, then with a mighty tug he pulled them off balance and nearly sent them sprawling.

"Weeee . . ." Mosby said, straightening, his chest heaving. "You know, Pug, I think the Duke has something in these tension exercises."

"I thought you'd like them," General Scheick said, and both of them looked at the Duke of Beancurd Island, who listlessly stared out of the window. "Would you like to try some weights now, Mosby? We could start with about four hundred pounds."

"Fine, Pug." Mosby nodded. And they were just about to bend, just about to pick up the imaginary weights, when General Scheick's aide entered and handed Mosby the radiogram.

"Thank you." Mosby opened it, began reading, then muttered, "I'll be damned. Well, I'll be damned."

"What is it, Mosby?"

"They don't believe us, Pug. Washington doesn't believe our report that there are no communists on the Islands."

"They don't?"

"No. They say these Islands have to be going communistic. There's no two ways about it. And they want me to radio at once, telling them what we're doing to fight this menace."

General Scheick considered. "Well, it's kind of hard to fight a menace, especially when it isn't there. So what can we do?"

"Damn, if I could only dig up a few pinks, but . . ." Mosby thought for a moment. "This is tough, Pug, but we have to keep them happy." His eyes widened. "Say, how would this be? Suppose we sent in a request for twenty million or so in immediate aid."

"What for?"

"Well, that would make them think they're fighting something, and—Pug, by George, here's the solution to the King's problem. We get him aid, and he can go ahead with the castle. He can get showers and swimming pools."

"Say . . . and he can go ahead with the Festival of the Unattached. He can get musical instruments and paper for lanterns."

"This is it, Pug! This is it!" Mosby said. "Get a radiogram off at once. Tell them we need the money right away. And get your car over here. We have to go up and tell the King his worries are over."

The King and Elwood were sitting on the veranda of the royal apartments, and around them the old castle of Tamagusuku lay bathed in silence. They sat quietly, staring out at the other Islands, and then, as the breeze came, King Kenji, his voice low, asked, "And what did your aunt say we should do with the incubators, Elwood?"

"She said since we got the tin from the Supply Officer, we should just give it back to him."

"And what about the chickens?"

"She said she didn't care."

"Would you want to try selling them out in the villages?" the King asked. "I'll help you."

"I don't know, Kenji. Why don't we just give them away? The Investment Club has written the whole thing off as a loss."

"Maybe that would be best," Kenji said, then shook his head. "Gee, Elwood, I thought we were getting somewhere. I thought we were really starting to roll."

"So did I, Kenji. And gosh, I'm sorry that Mrs. McCloud took her piano back."

"Me, too," the King said. "But you can't blame her. Why should she give it to me for just some pieces of paper?"

"Yes, I know, but . . ." Looking up, Elwood saw his uncle and General Winthrope coming through the old stone archway into the royal courtyard.

"King Kenji," General Scheick called, spotting them. "Hold tight. We have good news."

The generals strode rapidly, their faces beaming; and reaching the King, Mosby extended his hand. "Congratulations, Your Majesty," he said. "Congratulations."

"Thank you," Kenji replied. "But what for, Mr. General?"

"Because we just solved your problem. We got you twenty million U. S. aid dollars."

"Twenty million dollars!" The blood drained from Kenji's face. "There isn't that much money in the world."

"There isn't?" Mosby grinned. "Do you want to see it?"

"You mean it's available right now?"

"I would think so," Mosby replied. "The radiogram had a good half hour to clear. And just think, King Kenji, you can buy anything you want anywhere. U. S. dollars are good all over."

"But twenty million . . ." Kenji shook his head to clear it, then turning, called, "Grandma, Grandma. Come quick!"

The Queen Grandmother was down by the sunflowers that she had planted along the wall. They were starting to head now and she wondered how long it would be before there were seeds to eat, for she was running a little low. On hearing her grandson's call, she started toward him. Approaching, she saw the two Generals smiling paternally at him. But it was the look on Kenji's face that caused her to regard him quizzically, for when she left him to go down to look at her sunflowers, he had been dejected and depressed, just as she. Now, however, he was almost dancing with an excitement that bubbled up from within him. "Yes," she said. "What is it, Kenji?"

"Grandma," he replied. "Our troubles are over. We have it solved."

"Oh?"

"Yes." And Kenji went on to explain about the twenty million in U. S. aid.

Grandma listened, and the generals smiled more paternally than ever. They nodded when she looked up at them, wonder and awe in her eyes, and at length her grandson translated her words. "She says, Mr. Generals, she never has heard of anything like this in her whole life."

"Well." Mosby beamed. "Just tell her we're glad to do it. You can buy anything you want, anywhere. We'll have it air-lifted in. . . ." He turned. "Say, Pug, that's an idea that ought to please Washington. An airlift adds a nice sense of urgency to the operation. Yes, sir, we'll just fly the whole works in. Tell your grandma that, King Kenji."

"All right." Kenji translated, and Grandma began bowing. "Mr. Generals, she thanks you. She thanks you very much. But she would like to know one thing—what will happen to us when this twenty million is all spent?"

"Oh, I'm sorry," Mosby said quickly, "I should have explained. That twenty million is just a figure. When that's gone, we'll get you more."

"And when that, too, is gone?"

Mosby held up a reassuring hand. "Now don't you worry. We're going to get you right on the regular aid list."

Again Grandma bowed. "Mr. Generals, she says this is a wonderful thing. It would be nice for now. However, she says it would be like the water from the well at Little Koza."

"What does she mean by that?" Mosby asked uncertainly.

"She means it would be only a temporary thing. It wouldn't last for, say, a thousand years."

"A thousand years!" Mosby stirred uneasily. "That's an awful lot to ask of the American taxpayer."

"Oh, Grandma agrees with that. And she hopes you will convey our appreciation to the American taxpayer. However, under the circumstances, she thinks we'll just have to refuse."

"Refuse! You can't do that," Mosby protested. "Why, we already sent in a request for aid. The money is probably on deposit somewhere right now. Don't you want help?"

"We could certainly use twenty million."

"Well, be a sport about this then."

"Oh, I want to be a sport," the King said.

"So you'll take it?"

"No, Mr. Generals, Grandma and I are sorry. But it's as she says. We cannot depend on something like that. We have to depend on the pig, just as old King Gihon said."

Mosby was unable to speak. His mouth was dry. In desperation he and General Scheick looked at each other, then he managed, "King Kenji, you have to take it. If you don't, you're going to ruin things for everybody. Why, half the nations of the world will be mad at you."

"I don't want anybody mad at me."

"All right. Take it then."

"But I can't."

"Well, if you won't take it in cash, take it in pigs."

"Pigs?"

"Sure. Get yourself twenty million dollars' worth of hogs. We don't care what the hell you buy. Give them out to everybody. Free. For nothing."

"To everybody!" Kenji exclaimed. "Why, that's what old King Gihon was never able to do—get pigs out to everybody."

"See?" Mosby said. "That just goes to show you. You do as we say, and you'll have old King Gihon beat seven ways from Sunday. Everybody could raise pigs."

Kenji whistled and explained to his grandmother, who whispered, "Why just think, Kenji. The people could then sell the pigs in Japan for yen. Ask the Mr. General if that isn't right."

"Of course it's right," Mosby replied. "And what you could do is convert the yen into a lot of different kinds of money and buy all over the world."

"That is exactly what old King Gihon was trying to do," Kenji stated.

The generals let out their breaths sharply. "I guess that's it then," General Scheick said. "See what Grandma says."

But Grandma was troubled. "She wants to know," the King said, "how we would pay you back for these pigs?"

"Why, you don't have to pay back," Mosby replied.

"Grandma says but you do have to pay back. Whenever you join a mutual loan society to buy a pig, you always pay off."

"But we don't work on that principle." Mosby smiled.

"She says she does. Why, she says if she didn't pay off her debt to a mutual loan society for a pig, she couldn't hold her head up—"

"Look, King Kenji," General Scheick cut in. "You went to school in America. You know how we operate over there."

"Oh, sure." Kenji nodded. "But I was never able to understand it. Now in my course in marketing, they taught us that everybody had to pay for the products they sold. Nobody ever got their products for nothing."

"But this is different," Mosby said. "You see, in America we have a surplus of everything. Tell your grandma."

"Okay, Mr. General." Kenji translated.

"What does she say?"

"She says what a happy situation."

"It's not so happy when you're in it, I'll tell you that. Now you see we have to get rid of this surplus, so we send it overseas. If you try giving things back, you'd louse up the whole works. We'd just have to get rid of it again."

"Yes, but . . ."

"King Kenji," Mosby went on, "this is your big opportunity. Why, it's your chance to pull off a golden age."

"I realize that, Mr. General."

"Don't let it go down the drain then. You and your grandma think this over carefully. Will you do that?"

"We will, Mr. General, because Grandma says no king in the whole history of the Nakashima Islands ever, ever had an opportunity like this before."

"That's true."

"But Grandma says we also have to be able to hold up our heads."

"Well, just think it over," Mosby said quickly.

"Do that," General Scheick joined in. "And if you want to make it forty million instead, let us know. We'll fix you up."

The King, the Queen Grandmother, and Elwood watched the generals leave. They watched them pass through the archway into the Courtyard of the Dukes, then Kenji, his face solemn, said, "Elwood, what a chance this would be."

Elwood nodded. "But you couldn't take the whole twenty million in pigs, Kenji. You'd have to take some of it in seed to sell to the farmers so they could raise feed on the crown land they rent from you."

"I know. And I'd want to use some of it for cloth, and musical instruments, and other stuff for the Festival of the Unattached."

"Sure. And you'd want to get showers for the castle."

"And plumbing, too. Then I'd like to give some money to Cambridge College, and maybe bring my jalopy over." Kenji shook his head. "Elwood, I can't let this get away from me."

"I agree," Elwood said. "But how would this be: instead of giving the pigs out free, as they suggested, why couldn't we charge people for them? What does Grandma think of that?"

"Grandma doesn't think it would work. The people can afford to rent the crown land because I only charge a few pennies. But pigs cost big money, so only a very few would be able to buy them, and most of the people would be missing the opportunity. Gihon intended for all who wanted it to have the opportunity of raising pigs."

"Does she think we could finance this out of taxes?"

"She doesn't think so. Not everyone will be raising pigs, and

why should those who don't, help pay for those who do?"
Elwood's forehead wrinkled, and then he saw Grandma rise.
"Elwood," the King went on, "Grandma says we better get out
the pony cart and go down and see Mr. Yamaguchi. She says
maybe there is a precedent for this kind of thing."

The three of them sat quietly on the straw mats in Yamaguchi Kiei's living room as the old historian searched the scrolls.
He read through the reigns of King Satto and King Eiso. He
read through the reign of King Gihon, then suddenly he looked
up and said, "King Kenji, I just realized. There would not be a
precedent for anything like this because no one ever tried to
give us anything before."

"Oh. I guess I'm on my own then," Kenji said.

"I'm afraid you are. And I hope you will be able to work out
something, Your Majesty. Not only because we need so many
things, but also for another reason."

"Another reason?" Kenji questioned, and the three of them
regarded the old man.

"Yes, because if we had pigs to sell in other places, we must
have someone to sell them," he explained in both languages.
"Someone who, in turn, would buy the products of the other
places and bring them back here. Thus, we would have the
trader."

"Ah, so." Both Grandma and the King began nodding. Only
Elwood was puzzled. "What do you mean by the trader, Mr.
Yamaguchi?"

"It is this, Elwood. The children of Shinerikyu and Amamikyu are: 1. The King. 2. The Noble. 3. The Farmer. 4. The
twins—the Artisan and the Craftsman. And 5. The Trader. The
trader completes our society." He paused. "I am afraid I can't
help you, Your Majesty, but you have to succeed for all of us."

King Kenji was silent, and Elwood said, "Boy, a few thousand Chester Whites would make all the difference in the world,
wouldn't they?"

"Chester Whites?" the old historian questioned.

"It's a breed of hogs. I like them."

"Chester Whites, eh?"

Elwood put his hands on his thighs, ready to rise. "Kenji, let's go over and see Aunt Caroline. She's a pretty sharp business-woman. Remember she kept the Egg Corporation from going to pieces."

"That was smart, figuring out the hundred per cent stock dividend, giving the ladies two shares for one," Kenji said.

"Let's see her then. Maybe she'll have an idea."

"I think we better." The King nodded. "Because any idea might be of help to us."

They sat in the Scheick living room, and as they sipped their iced tea Mrs. Scheick said, "Of course my Investment Club will stay in the chicken business, King Kenji. They'll stay in the paper-show business, too, providing one thing: that any money we earn can be converted into U. S. dollars."

"Yes. I understand that, Mrs. General."

"Now as far as organizing your pig business," Mrs. Scheick went on, "why not set it up just as we did with chickens: or-ganize a corporation, sell shares in it, and buy pigs in the U. S. That way you wouldn't have to worry about paying back, be-cause you're not buying on credit. You're paying cash."

"But, Mrs. General. First, our money is no good anywhere, so how could I buy pigs from the American farmers?"

"Oh, that's right."

"And second, even if our money was good, we could never raise enough to buy all the pigs we need."

"I see."

"And third," Kenji went on, "if I formed a corporation and bought pigs, for the corporation to get its money back it would have to sell them to the farmers. Then we're right back to the same situation. The majority of farmers are too poor for that. That's why old King Gihon said the pigs have to be given out free."

Mrs. Scheick put down her teacup. "But, King Kenji, how can you get pigs from the United States, give them out free to the farmers, and still pay the United States back? Especially when, as you say, your money's no good."

The King looked out through the picture window. "I don't know," he said. "I don't know, Mrs. General. But I have to figure it out."

It was nearly time for the evening meal, so Grandma arose from the veranda of the royal apartments and said, "Kenji, I am going to put the sweet potatoes on now."

"All right, Grandma," Kenji replied and looked out at the other Islands of the chain. Out there, too, they were putting the sweet potatoes on to boil, just as they had been doing for over three hundred years. In all the homes of all the villages, the King knew, there was simply another evening of sweet potatoes in store. "All right, Grandma," he repeated. "I think Elwood and I will go on and see what we can do."

Nodding, Grandma turned and began hobbling along the veranda to the main house.

They watched her go, then Kenji began, once again, "Now as I see it, Elwood, there are only two things I can do: 1. Pay cash for the pigs. 2. Or get them on credit from the U. S."

"And since your money is no good, you can't pay cash. That leaves only credit."

"Yeah. And as I see it, there are only two ways I can pay the U. S. back: 1. In cash. 2. In pigs."

"Gosh," Elwood began slowly, "if you start shipping hogs to the United States, Kenji, I'm afraid you'd just about ruin the Department of Agriculture."

"Okay. I'll pay them in cash then. But our money is still no good. We'd have to have our traders sell pigs in Japan for yen, and convert that into U. S. dollars."

"We're okay to there," Elwood said. "But then what?"

"Yeah, then what? We're right back to where we started." They lapsed into silence, and the King was lost in thought. Then he began, "Elwood, if we had pigs and put them out, it seems to me the farmers could do only two things, just like us: 1. Pay cash for them. 2. Or get them on credit."

"Cash is out. You said they couldn't afford it."

"I know. But I'm trying to put my finger on something here. Suppose pigs were free to the farmer. That is, if we gave him a pig and through no fault of his own he was unable to raise it to market size."

"You mean he wouldn't be financially responsible."

"Yes. So suppose we put the pigs out on credit. In a sense that's putting them out free. It would get the farmers started for nothing."

"How would the farmers who did raise their pigs to market size pay back?" Elwood asked.

"Just like we'd pay back the U. S. In cash or pigs. But cash wouldn't be good. They're always short of it."

"Okay. So we put out pigs, and they pay back in pigs."

"That would be good for them," the King said. "Real good." He thought for a moment. "But it wouldn't be so hot for us, because we're going to have an overhead. For instance, in putting these pigs out we'd have to keep track of where they go, and all that. It's as they always pointed out in Marketing: you have to have a mark-up, or you lose money."

"But when you put out pigs and get back pigs, how can you have a mark-up of, say, ten per cent? How could they give you back one and one-tenth pigs?"

"You couldn't," Kenji said. "You'd almost have to have a hundred per cent mark-up, wouldn't you?" He drifted into thought, then suddenly his eyes widened. "Hey. Hey, now, wait a minute, let me think. When your aunt had the stock dividend, they got two for one, didn't they?"

"That's right. Two shares of new for one of old."

"Why couldn't we do the same thing then? Suppose we gave these pigs out to the farmers and didn't charge them, like King Gihon said. And suppose we gave them lady pigs."

"Oh?"

"Yeah, then in return for the lady pig, they give us two lady pigs back."

"I get it," Elwood said eagerly. "Then we could put the two out and get four back—put the four out and get eight back."

"Sure." Kenji's eyes were like saucers. "Just think, Elwood. That way not only would all the farmers have pigs to sell, but I'd have pigs, too. I could sell them in Japan and use the money to pay the United States back for the loan."

Elwood rose to his knees. "You sure could. You could sell your excess pigs, and keep the others for breeding stock."

"That's right." The King also got to his knees. "I put out one, and I get back two."

"You put out two, and you get back four. All the time it keeps doubling."

"And just think what I could buy with my profit." Over in the main house Kenji spied his grandmother, bending over the sweet potatoes. His face lighted, and he arose to his feet. "Grandma," he called. "Grandma! We got it! We got it!"

Chapter 22

EVEN old King Gihon never would have recognized the ancient capital of Tamabaru. Out past the mouth of the Tamsui River, out in deep water, lay two ships—one from America, and one from Japan. And while the sampans plying between the ships and the old stone quays hadn't changed, still the cargoes they were unloading would have made old King Gihon's eyes light in wonder. For coming from the American ship was crate after crate of Chester Whites; and coming from the Japanese ship was crate after crate of manufactured articles which hadn't even existed in old Gihon's day.

But the harbor was crowded with other sampans, too, arriving from every Island in the chain; because not only was this the afternoon before the first evening of the first Festival of the Unattached, but this also was the first day of the pig distribution. And as the lanterns, strung before all the houses, fluttered in the golden October afternoon, and as the windbells tinkled in the breeze, Yamaguchi Kiei, carrying a scroll in one hand and a writing brush in the other, turned to his companion. "You know, Elwood," he said, "we haven't had so many people in town since the Chinese landed an army here in 911."

"It's sure jammed, all right," Elwood agreed, and as a sampan from one of the other Islands pulled in he added, "Here comes more."

"Ah, yes." The old historian nodded, and together they watched the sampan unload. There were giggling girls in bright kimonos, unnoticing youths with eyes on greener pastures, bare-footed farmers, and solemn-faced women. "Ah, yes," Yama-guchi Kiei repeated, and a young man, just off the sampan, stepped before him.

"Excuse me, Grandfather," the young one said in Japanese and bowed, "but I have never been here before. I wonder if you would direct me?"

"I will." Yamaguchi returned the bow. "Are you looking for the Festival of the Unattached? That is over in Watanabe Square."

"Oh, no," the young one replied. "I am already attached. I have seven children."

"Ah, so," the old historian said. "Well, surely you want the hog market then. That is in Kunigami Square. We are going there, so please just follow us."

"I thank you." The young one bowed again and called to his compatriots. And as Elwood and the old historian started to-ward Kunigami Square a little group of already attached fell in behind them.

"Elwood," the old one said as they walked along, "next year we are going to have to do something about this housing situa-tion. Things are very, very bad."

"Maybe you could get somebody to start inns."

"I think that is what we must do. There were some excellent inns in King Gihon's day, but there has not been much doing in the last three hundred years or so. Naturally, they went out of business."

"Some good inns ought to make a go of it," Elwood said. "Of course, the Festival of the Unattached is only four days a year. Yet the hog market will be going on every day." Some-thing caught his eye, and he pointed. "Look, Mr. Yamaguchi."

Coming toward them were the three daughters of Uncle Shoji

275

Takamini, dressed in bright kimonos with name cards attached. The three Takamini girls were giggling, and laughing, and looking over their shoulders as they walked along, for a couple dozen of paces behind them were three carded youths, following them, grins all over their faces.

"Ah, yes," the old historian said. "I can see that this is going to be quite a festival."

They were entering Kunigami Square now, and old King Gihon would never have recognized this either. In his day it had been a trampled area, used only to collect any overflow crowd that might gather in the main square, named after the Watanabe Family who had been the Dukes of Tamashima, the main Island. But now Kunigami Square had come into its own.

Under the direction of Elwood and King Kenji, Nakashima Islands workmen had set up poles all around the four sides of the Square; upon these poles had been placed latticelike frames of bamboo, thus forming shaded booths. And there in the shade, on three sides of the Square, the Chester Whites slept contentedly in their pens, oblivious to the farmers who constantly filed by, making their selections.

There were also three U. S. Army pyramidal tents in Kunigami Square, their sides rolled up, and each pyramidal tent bore a sign in Japanese and English. One read: THE KING'S OWN LIVESTOCK COMPANY. A second read: THE CROWN LAND COMPANY. And the third was: THE ROYAL SEED COMPANY. So there it all was. The incoming farmers would check in at the Crown Land Company and rent themselves a piece. Next they would go over to the Royal Seed Company, and from the display of Japanese seeds set out in flats beneath the bamboo on the fourth side of the Square, they would make their selections. And then they would go over to the King's Own Livestock Company to select their hog to take home, being limited to one per customer for the time being until more hogs could be brought in from the States.

As Elwood and Yamaguchi Kiei approached the tent of the King's Own Livestock Company, the old historian glanced briefly at the line of farmers before it, then asked, "Elwood,

276

are the earls that the King brought into Court performing satis-factorily?"

"They certainly are, Mr. Yamaguchi. They stepped right into their assignments and took over the three companies just as if they'd always been running them. In fact, I'd say they just about took the load off the King's shoulders."

"That is good." The old one smiled. "Well, I want to get this hog contract that you drew up for the King down in the scrolls. Not only will this be one of the most important documents in our history, but some day there might be another Interruption and the King might have to reconstruct again. This way he will have a precedent."

"Okay, Mr. Yamaguchi."

The old historian pointed to the center of the Square, for in addition to the King's three companies other businesses had sprung up. There were at least a half-dozen cartage companies which would haul by horsecart the pig of your selection from Square to sampan. And there were a good two dozen food stalls, straight down the middle of the Square. "Let us go over there and have a bowl of noodles."

"All right." A familiar figure caught Elwood's eye. "Mr. Yamaguchi, there's the Duke of Tatami Oshima over there look-ing at the hogs."

"Ah, the Duke. I will ask him to join us." Yamaguchi called and the Duke—barefooted, in his old banana-cloth kimono, and battered felt hat perched atop his head—turned, recognized them, and started toward them.

As he approached, a grin was spread all over his face; and pointing, he said in English, "Chester White."

Elwood smiled. "Chester White, eh?"

"Yes, Elwood," the old historian said. "He claims those are the prettiest pigs he ever has seen."

"I'll be darned." Elwood looked at the senior duke. "Chester White."

"Chester White," the Duke repeated, nodding happily; and they went over to the center of the Square to one of the noodle stands that had been constructed there.

The noodle stand was a reed and bamboo affair. It, too, had a latticelike canopy around it; and under the shade of this canopy were a dozen or so rough, homemade tables and chairs. The old historian placed their order, then taking a piece of scratch paper from within the scroll, said, "Elwood, on this hog contract, now if you will give me a few details . . ."

"I'd be glad to, Mr. Yamaguchi. Now first of all, this contract is between the King and the individual farmer who signs it. In Article 1 the King agrees to turn over a sow that has been vaccinated and bred to a pure-bred boar."

"You mean for now, the King will turn over only one sow. Later on, when more are available, a farmer can get any number. Is that not right?"

"That's right. In Article 2, the farmer agrees to take this sow home and take good care of her, that is, in the way of feeding, shelter, and so forth."

"And if he does not?"

"The King can take back his pig. Then in Article 3, the farmer agrees to return to the King two pigs—either gilts or boars—of the King's choice. These pigs shall be no more than eight months old, or weigh less than two hundred pounds, whichever comes first."

"So the King has the pick of the litter."

"That's right. Article 4 covers the demise of any pig before she farrows. If it is due to no fault of the farmer, the King will bear the cost of the pig, and the farmer the cost of the food lost."

"But if it is due to, shall we say, marketing?"

"Then they are subject to arrest and fine."

"Ah, so." The old one nodded. "That is a wise provision, because there is always someone who will try to sell off the pig."

The proprietor came with the noodles then. Setting them before his customers, he stepped back and waited for their approval. Yamaguchi Kiei was the first to pick up his chopsticks. Lifting the noodles, he was about to put them in his mouth when they slipped off. "You know, Elwood," he said, "it has been so long since I have eaten noodles that I have forgotten how." He

278

tried again, succeeded; and after savoring a mouthful, nodded to the proprietor. "Good. Very, very good."

They were good, so good that the little group fell into silence, forgetting the hog contract and concentrating solely on their food. And it wasn't until General Scheick called, "Hello, there," that they saw him and General Winthrope approaching them.

"Ah, Mr. Generals," the old historian said; and like the Duke of Tatami Oshima, he beamed his greeting. "It is good to see you. What brings you down here?"

"A couple of things. First, General Winthrope and I came down to let the pigs take a look at us. It's good luck, you know."

"That is true," the old historian agreed and indicated the Square. "The King is certainly doing a good business in pigs. That, too, seems to augur well for his venture."

"He certainly is," General Winthrope said; and both he and General Scheick regarded the signs marked: THE KING'S OWN LIVESTOCK COMPANY; THE CROWN LAND COMPANY; THE ROYAL SEED COMPANY. "By the way, have any of you seen the King?"

"He was up at the castle a couple of hours ago," Elwood replied, "adjusting the carburetor of his jalopy. Somewhere in the trip over from Cambridge it got out of kilter. But he should be down soon. He and the Duchess were going to do some rehearsing on the dances they're demonstrating tonight at the Festival of the Unattached. Did you want to see him, General Winthrope?"

"Yes. We're having a devil of a time with Washington. They claim they're not equipped to handle any money anyone might want to pay back. And we received a stern warning from the Secretary of Agriculture himself about trying to send back pigs."

"Golly." Elwood frowned. "But that was the agreement. Kenji and his grandma said they wouldn't accept pigs in the first place unless they could pay full value for them."

"I know, Elwood. But your uncle and I stuck our necks out

on that. We're the ones who said it was all right, not Washington. Now I don't know what we're going to do."

The Duke of Tatami Oshima was whispering to the old historian, and Yamaguchi Kiei said, "Mr. Generals, the Duke says since you're here, he would like to ask you a question. He sees everyone else getting themselves a pig and taking it home, so he would like to know what you would think about him doing the same thing?"

"Why, he can't do that," Mosby said. "Why does he think the King is bringing in all this stuff from Japan? Why does he think we're building the castle? It's so the nobility can take it easy."

"But he would like to do something."

"Well, he's the senior duke," General Scheick cut in. "Tell him to take it easy and set a good example for the rest of the nobility. I can't understand this restlessness. It's the same with the Duke of Beancurd Island. Now he's not satisfied with showing us how to break boards. He has to get ambitious." He regarded Elwood. "Elwood, do you think the King will be coming down here to Kunigami Square?"

"No, I think he'll probably head right over to Watanabe Square. I know he wants to look over the arrangements for the Festival."

"We better be getting over there then." General Scheick looked at the Duke of Tatami Oshima. "Now you take it easy," he said; and turning, he and Mosby started off.

They walked along the streets, alive with people and horse-carts. And they had just crossed the Street of the Blue Lanterns and turned into the Lane of Partial Stability when they ran into Agnes McCloud. "Why, Agnes," General Scheick said, looking at her red face. "What's the matter?"

"Darn!" Agnes exclaimed. "Do you know what happened?"
"What?"

"The Nakashima Islands Egg Corporation is running out of hundred-year-old eggs. And the Festival doesn't even start until tonight!"

"That's too bad," General Scheick said. "What are you going to do?"

"Find that Mr. Yamaguchi and see if there isn't a shorter way to process them. It seems to me ninety days is much too long a time to make hundred-year-old eggs."

"We just left Mr. Yamaguchi," General Scheick said. "He's with Elwood in the first noodle shop in Kunigami Square."

"Thank you, General, sir."

"How's business?"

"It couldn't be better. But I don't have time to talk." And Agnes hurried off in the direction of Kunigami Square.

For a moment they watched her go, then General Scheick said, "Mosby, do you suppose Mr. Yamaguchi is any relation to Louie and Henry Yamaguchi?"

"I wouldn't have any idea, Pug."

"I'll have to ask him. You know, there's going to be a great future here for Louie and Henry. Why, I wouldn't be a bit surprised if one of them didn't become the Duke of Tamashima. That's what I like about this system. If you really got the old juice, like those two, there's no stopping you. But on the other hand, if you're just a plugger, why you can still be a baron or something."

"It certainly has a lot of built-in incentive," Mosby agreed.

They had reached the head of the Lane of Partial Stability now, and like all streets running into Watanabe Square, the Lane had been roped off. At the rope was a ticket taker who in return for a ticket gave each one entering a card to attach to their person, bearing name, home village, and home Island. Seeing the Generals, the ticket taker began bowing and called in Japanese to Uncle Shoji and Yoshimitsu Matsumoto, who were deep in conversation.

"And these three boys have been following the girls all afternoon," Uncle Shoji was saying.

"Well imagine that." Yoshimitsu shook his head. "Where are they from?"

"From Goat Island. I saw their cards."

281

"From way out there. Now isn't that nice. And how are the girls taking it?"

"I never saw them giggle so much in all my life. Do you think we could arrange a match?"

"We can't rush it too much," Yoshimitsu replied. "But if they're following them in the daylight, why I think we have a good chance."

"Mr. Takamini! Mr. Matsumoto!" the ticket taker called.

Yoshimitsu looked up. "Well, Mr. Generals, it is good to see you."

"How's everything going?" General Scheick asked.

"Good." Yoshimitsu eyed Uncle Shoji, who didn't understand English. "By golly, I think I'm getting my problem solved."

"I mean how are the tickets going?"

"Oh, that. I'm making money at it, too. We sold nine thousand so far. Mr. General, the Scheick Code is the greatest thing that ever happened to the Nakashima Islands."

"Why thank you."

The Generals surveyed the Square, saw the paper lanterns strung all over, saw the food stalls occupying what had previously been empty buildings, saw the raised platform in the center for dancing, and General Winthrope said, "The King and the Duchess certainly did a good job of fixing up things, didn't they?"

"I think so too," Yoshimitsu said. "And so does Uncle Shoji. He says he never made such a good investment in his life as when I talked him into sponsoring the Festival of the Unattached. He says he only hopes I will let him in on it every year. But we will have to see."

A shout arose in the distance, and General Scheick said, "What's that?"

Yoshimitsu listened a moment. "Ah, that is the King and the Queen Grandmother. They are coming."

"Good. Good," Mosby said. "We're looking for them."

They could tell the King's progress from the shouting, for the cries of "Long Live the King! Long Live the Queen Grandmother!" arose on all sides. First they heard it from the quay-side section, then they heard it from the hog market in Kuni-gami Square, then the Street of the Blue Lanterns, and then they heard the shouts arise in the Lane of Partial Stability; and look-ing down the Lane, they saw the red and white jalopy turn in. The King sat behind the wheel, steering with one hand, wav-ing to the crowds with the other; while beside him sat his grand-mother, smiling and bowing, and Mosby said, "I'll be damned. That car reminds me of when I was in high school. Only we had the rear wheels set in so when a bunch piled in the back seat the front end would fly up, like in the circus."

"Somebody in my class had one like that too," General Scheick said. "I remember how we all used to ride out to foot-ball practice."

They watched the King bring the jalopy up the Lane of Par-tial Stability. Then Grandma, in her old brown banana-cloth kimono, spotted them and began waving as the King swung the vehicle to bring it beside them.

"Well, look who's here," General Scheick said, and both he and Mosby smiled. "It's good to see you, King Kenji. Did you and your grandma come down to let the pigs take a look at you?"

"Oh no. It's the other way around. We came down to take a look at them. Besides, Grandma wants to see where the Festival is being held, so I'm showing her around. But do you know what, Mr. Generals?"

"What?" Mosby asked.

"The shuttle plane just came in from Okinawa, and I received a crate of ivy."

"A crate of ivy?"

"Yes, from Mr. Hayden, president of Cambridge College. I wrote and told him about how the Duke of Tatami Oshima's pig rooted up the sprig he sent before. Then I told him how I was in the hog business, the seed business, and how I have the crown lands."

"Oh, yes." General Scheick glanced at Mosby. "We saw your signs down in Kunigami Square."

"But I told him I wasn't operating at a profit right at the moment," the King continued. "I told him I had to lend some of the aid money to the traders so they could get started buying things in Japan and bringing them here. And I told him it was going to be some time before I, personally, started exporting hogs. But I said as soon as I started showing a profit I was going to send a nice contribution to Cambridge. That's when he sent me the crate of ivy, and the latest thirty-six-page booklet listing the needs of the college."

"Thirty-six-page booklet!" General Scheick exclaimed. "It sounds to me like they need a whole new physical plant."

"No, Mr. Hayden says he thinks they can still get by with the same athletic field, though they may have to resod it. But just think"—the King was beaming—"a whole crate of ivy! They even got it packaged in little bunches. There's some from the Old Main, some from the Lambda Beta Theta house, and they even got some from the college water tower. Boys, I'm going to plant it all over the castle wall."

"That's nice," General Scheick said, then began slowly, "King Kenji, about those signs down in Kunigami Square. We're quite concerned about them. Now there's the King's Own Livestock Company, the Royal Seed Company, and the Crown Land Company."

"Oh, do you think I own too much?" Kenji asked. "Does it sound as if I have a monopoly?"

"That's not it. What we want to know is, are you, the King, owning these as the government or as a private individual?"

"Does it make a difference?"

"It certainly does. If you're owning them as the government, it's socialism. But if you're owning them as a private individual, it's capitalism."

"Oh, I see," Kenji said. "In that case, I'll own them as a private individual. I'll be a capitalist."

General Scheick held out his hand. "Thank you, my boy. I can't tell you how this relieves our minds."

"That's all right," the King said. "And don't worry about a monopoly. When things get going good and everybody has money, I'm going to sell out." He glanced at his grandmother. "But, Mr. General, I wonder if I could see you a moment? Would you mind stepping over there?"

"Certainly not."

"Good." The King led him over to one side, and with another glance at his grandma, who was standing with General Winthrope, Yoshimitsu, and Uncle Shoji, he whispered, "Mr. General, you know in all the rush, I forgot to tell the traders to bring in gasoline. There's not a drop on the Islands."

"There isn't?"

"No. So I was wondering if I could borrow a tankful from the motor pool? You see, I'm awfully low and tonight during the Festival maybe Debbie . . . I mean the Duchess of Bamboo Island and I might want to go for a ride, or something."

"Why, of course. Tell the motor pool sergeant I said you could have what you want. And if you need oil, help yourself."

"I sure appreciate that," Kenji said. "And don't worry, Mr. General. I'll pay it back. You just put it on the bill with the twenty million I already owe the United States Government."

General Scheick winced. "You're not serious about paying back, are you, King Kenji?"

"Sure I'm serious," the King replied. "And Grandma is, too. Why, we wouldn't have it any other way."

"You wouldn't?"

"Absolutely not, Mr. General. We told you that before."

"Oh."

"But you won't say anything about me borrowing a tankful of gas, will you? I mean you won't say anything about me and the Duchess going for a ride? You know, they're awfully old-fashioned over here."

"Oh, no. No I won't."

"Good." They walked back to where Mosby and Grandma were visiting, with Yoshimitsu acting as interpreter, and Kenji said, "Well, Grandma, I got a couple of errands to do."

"Ah, is that so?"

"Yes, I was wondering if . . ."

"Ah, yes. In that case," Grandma said, "I think I will stay down here and look things over. You can stop for me later."

"Are you sure you don't want to go along?"

"No. I will stay. You go ahead."

"Well, if you say so." Kenji backed over to his jalopy, smiling and waving, then he climbed in over the door. And as he started down the street, General Scheick turned. "Matsumoto," he said, "tell the Queen Grandmother that he's a mighty fine boy."

"Mr. General, she says she will agree with you."

"And Matsumoto," General Scheick continued, "ask her what she thinks of all this activity." He indicated Watanabe Square.

"She says she cannot believe. Why just think. Old King Gihon, our greatest King, could only bring us up to the verge of a golden age. But now that Kenji has solved the problem of the pig, she is sure we are going to have the golden age itself. Everyone is saying that."

"I'll go along with you there," Mosby said, and General Scheick agreed. "From now on there shouldn't be any stopping you people."

"That's what Grandma believes. But she would like to know if those sunflower seeds that you gave her couldn't be used for pig food."

"They certainly could. Why?"

"Well, she just wants you to take a look at her. Do you know what she did yesterday? She walked all the way down from the castle to the drive where you live."

"She walked down to Caroline Drive!" General Scheick exclaimed.

"And what's more, she walked back. Uphill."

"No!"

"Yes. So she figures that if sunflower seeds could straighten her out with the shape her joints were in, just think what they could do for the pigs. Why, we'd have the healthiest pigs in the world."

"By George." General Scheick's face lighted. "There's an

286

idea. Do you know what you could do? You could press the sunflower oil for cooking. You couldn't find a healthier oil anywhere, and you could feed the residue to the hogs."

"She's all for that."

"By George," General Scheick continued, rubbing his hands, "we'll revolutionize agriculture in this part of the world. We'll have sunflowers growing all over the place. Incidentally, Matsumoto, she planted some down along the castle wall, didn't she?"

"Oh, yes. She has a nice patch planted. But she would like to know if there aren't some other things she can take, not that she needs them, because she already feels so good. She just wants to take them for protection."

"There're lots of things. For instance, brewer's yeast."

"Brewer's yeast?" Yoshimitsu questioned.

"Certainly. It comes from distillleries."

"From distilleries." A certain light crept into Yoshimitsu's eyes. "And this would be good for her?"

"It would be one of the best things she could take."

"Aha." Yoshimitsu nodded. "I will tell her."

He translated, then the Queen Grandmother spoke, and suddenly Uncle Shoji Takamini began bowing. He began bowing so energetically that General Scheick said, "What the hell's the matter with him?"

"I just fixed him up," Yoshimitsu replied, and Uncle Shoji's eyes were like saucers. "You know, the Takaminis have been trying for fourteen centuries to get a foothold in at Court, and I finally was able to swing it for him."

"What did you do?"

"I got him the job of supplying brewer's yeast to the Crown." Yoshimitsu considered. "By golly, I think I ought to be able to get myself a partnership out of this."

"That's your problem." General Scheick rubbed his hands. "Now tell the Queen Grandmother that in addition to brewer's yeast, we could manufacture multiple vitamins. We could advertise them on the paper-show and get them out to all the people."

"She knows a better way to get them out, Mr. General, by simply using the old medicine peddlers. They could go around to every house and leave a supply of these vitamins. And six months later they would go back and the people would pay for what they used."

"Now that's an idea," General Scheick said.

"That's psychology," Mosby corrected. "You get them in every home on sort of a semi-giveaway basis. You get the people using them, and they'll use more than they would have if they had paid cash for them."

"That is psychology," General Scheick agreed. "Matsumoto, tell the Queen Grandmother we're going to make this the healthiest nation in the world. Tell her we're going to catch the kids when they're young. We're going to give them vitamins and minerals."

"She is for that, Mr. General, and she hopes that you two gentlemen will be successful."

"It's not just General Winthrope and me," General Scheick said. "It's her, too."

"No, Mr. General, she doesn't think she can take part in it. Oh, she's all for health. But she has decided that now is the time for her to retire, to become *inkyo*."

"But she can't go *inkyo* now," General Scheick protested.

"Absolutely not," Mosby joined in. "She can't step out of the picture. We're just starting to roll into the golden age. The King is going to be needing the same kind of advice and guidance she's been giving him all along."

"No, Grandma says the King is nineteen, going on twenty. He was able to solve the problem of the pig, which even old King Gihon was unable to do. So she figures she's got him at least three-quarters of the way up Fool's Hill. What's the difference now if he does make a few mistakes?"

"Yes, but—"

"No, Mr. Generals. She says she is going *inkyo*. Oh, she'll take over once in a while to help the King out. But do you know what she is going to do? She's going to get a hat and gloves like the American ladies wear and go visiting in the afternoons. Then she's going to get one of those great big wide windows like you have in the American houses . . ."

"Picture windows?"

"She doesn't know what you call them, but she's going to get one. And she's going to have it put in the castle so she can sit and look out, and at night she thinks she's going to put a nice paper lantern in it."

"Well," General Scheick said, a little astounded. "Well."

Mosby, however, was nodding. "She's got a point there, Pug. The three of us could really make this place jump, but why shouldn't she go *inkyo?* She worked hard all her life."

"I know she has."

"Let her enjoy herself then." Mosby faced Yoshimitsu. "Matsumoto, tell her that I think she has an excellent idea there. Tell her I'm all for it, and I hope she enjoys her *inkyo,* or retirement, or whatever you call it."

"She thanks you, Mr. General. And she hopes that both of you will enjoy yours. Now she wonders if you would like to walk around the Square a bit and see the sights?"

"If it's all right with General Winthrope," General Scheick said, "I think we better be getting along." He gave Mosby the high-sign. "There are a couple of things we have to talk about."

"So he insists on paying back," Mosby said once again as they neared Cottage 1A.

"He does," General Scheick replied. "And I'm afraid, Mosby, if some provision isn't made for him to return the money, he'll call the whole works off. Then we'll be right back where we started."

"I see." Mosby considered. "Well, let's go sit in the back yard, Pug, and have a cup of energy broth. Maybe we can figure something out on this."

As General Scheick entered the house to fix the hot soup, he found Mrs. Scheick in the living room. "Why, Caroline," he said, "how are you? We've just been down at the Festival, and Agnes McCloud says you're running out of hundred-year-old eggs."

"I know," Mrs. Scheick said absently.

"Is something wrong?" General Scheick asked.

Mrs. Scheick indicated the letter on the coffee table. "It's that Fred Cummings. I've been trying to get a report out of him on how much the elevator made through the September quarter. He says he wouldn't know that. They just wait until the end of the year and figure it up. Now I ask you—is that any way to run a business?"

"I wouldn't worry about it," General Scheick said.

"Of course I'm worried about it. Why, that elevator isn't doing anywhere near the business it could."

"Well, why not just go along with it for now? Then when Elwood takes over, things might be different."

"I don't think Elwood should take over, Matt."

"Who else is there?"

"Me."

"You?"

"Why not? After all, I have been running the Nakashima Islands Egg Corporation. And I did organize the paper-show business, didn't I?"

"Yes, but . . ."

"Well, I'm going to have to tell Elwood that I think it's my place to handle things. I'm certain that Dorothy will back me, too. That will give me at least sixty per cent of the stock."

"But, Caroline, I thought we might just go *inkyo*."

"What's *inkyo*?"

"That's an expression they have out here. It means turning over things, going into retirement. After all, I've got in a lot of service, and there's been this business with Washington. I've just about had it. I don't even want an orange grove. I just want to sit on a porch and take it easy."

"Well, I'm not going to let the elevator business get away," Mrs. Scheick stated. "My place is back in Youngerville. By the way, do you remember the old Garfield home on Strawberry Street?"

"Yes."

"All right. We can buy that. It has porches on two sides. You can sit there all day if you want to."

"But what would I do with myself?"

"You're the one who said you just wanted to sit."

"I didn't mean all the time."

"Well, Matt, I'm going to tell you this. It would be very pleasant back there in Youngerville. And I'm not going to let Fred Cummings ruin that business any more. I'm going to talk with Elwood and find out if he really minds stepping out, then I'm going to send Mildred a radiogram."

There was a certain determination in Mrs. Scheick's voice that made the General shake his head. And he was still shaking it as he carried the energy broth to the back yard. "Mosby," he began, passing the tray, "what are you going to do when you retire?"

"Why do you ask?"

General Scheick told him about Mrs. Scheick.

"Do you have any objections to going back to Youngerville?"

"No. Actually, I think I would enjoy it there."

"What are you objecting to then?"

"I don't know."

Mosby considered. "Could it be this, Pug? Could it be that instead of going *inkyo*, you want to go semi-*inkyo?*"

"I don't think so. For a while I thought I wanted an active retirement. But now I want to step out completely."

"But, Pug, I'd hate to see you spend all your time just sitting on the front porch."

"I don't want to, Mosby. I'd like to sit there mornings, but in the afternoons I want to be up and about."

"Well, it seems to me, Pug, that men like you and me have had too many valuable experiences to let go to waste. We ought to be passing on the benefit of our wisdom to others. Maybe we ought to find ourselves some nice little college somewhere. Get on the faculty part time . . ."

"That sounds good, Mosby. We could do that and still become *inkyo*. That would be a hundred times better than getting mixed up in that elevator business."

"Now, Pug. You're not mixed up in it, yet. Caroline hasn't

even talked with Elwood. The boy hasn't stepped out of the picture. Maybe he has his heart set on the job."

"Maybe so."

"Well, let's not anticipate." Mosby took a sip of energy broth, and he could almost feel new strength coursing through his veins. Then he continued, "Now about paying Washington back. Let's see if we can work out something."

Chapter 23

THE night belonged to the Unattached, and all nature seemed to know it. The October moon sailed high and white overhead. The breeze off the China Sea was cool and gentle. And a touch of melancholy, a touch of loneliness, betokening a dying year, seemed to hang in the autumn evening.

It was not quite eight o'clock. The Festival had not started yet, but already the Square was jammed. Over by the small dance floor both the combo and the orchestra were tuning up. At various points around the edge of the Square the paper-show men were setting up their frames. But mainly it was the Unattached who crowded the Square. Beneath the swaying lanterns, eyes sparkled and hearts beat faster as eyes met; and then the haunting loneliness was banished as the warm flicker of hope arose.

But Elwood felt the loneliness. He felt the melancholy of the autumn. Hands thrust deep in pockets, he walked about the Square, watching and looking. For a moment the thought of home came to him, but quickly he pushed it from his mind; and seeing Agnes McCloud over by one of the food stalls, he started toward her.

"Hello, Mrs. McCloud," he said, reaching the stall. "How are things with you tonight?"

Agnes was busy checking the supply of eggs on hand. "Well, it's a shame we ran out of hundred-year-old eggs, but I think these tea-steeped eggs are going to go almost as well."

"Good." Elwood indicated the various food stalls. "Your Egg Corporation ought to be making some money."

"We will if these darn fool stall operators don't let themselves run out of stock. You know, I have to keep checking them all the time. Incidentally, your aunt wants to see you. She's over at Paper-Show Headquarters."

"Thanks. I'll go right over." Slowly Elwood crossed the Square, and entering Paper-Show Headquarters, found it filled with activity. The business staff was setting out tray after tray of sweet potato taffy, for the storytellers would be telling stories as long as anyone remained at the Festival. The story department was placing the illustrations in neat piles so that as soon as one story was finished, the storytellers could bring in the used illustrations, pick up another batch, and get started again. And so busy were they that no one paid any attention to Elwood when he entered.

Slowly he worked his way through the crowd, waved to Todi Kabuki, who was standing before a mirror, adjusting his scarf before going on; and reaching the back offices, he found Mrs. Scheick and Yoshimitsu deep in conversation.

"I'll be with you in just a moment, Elwood," Mrs. Scheick said and returned to Yoshimitsu. "Now the King is going to open the Festival at eight with a little welcoming speech. Then he and the Duchess of Bamboo Island are going to give an exhibition of western dancing immediately after, and also at ten and twelve o'clock. So all performances of the paper-show have to be ended in order that everyone can watch the King."

"We'll have them ended, Mrs. General," Yoshimitsu guaranteed. "But I still think we ought to work in a few adventure stories."

"Not on an occasion like this," Mrs. Scheick said firmly.

"Yes, but people get awfully tired of love stories."

"Well, Mr. Matsumoto, if these people were tired of love stories, they never would have come to the Festival of the Unattached in the first place."

Yoshimitsu thought a moment. "That's possible. Maybe you only get tired of love stories after you've been attached a while."

Mrs. Scheick gave him a sharp look. "Regardless of what you think of the situation, Mr. Matsumoto, I want the storytellers to concentrate strictly on love all during the Festival."

"If you wish, Mrs. General." Yoshimitsu arose. "We'll do that. Anyway, they got the rest of their lives for adventure." Bowing, he left the office, and Mrs. Scheick checked off his name on her list of conferences.

"How's it going, Aunt Caroline?" Elwood asked.

"Just fine." Mrs. Scheick indicated a chair. "Now what I want to see you about is the elevator business back home."

Elwood's face fell. "Oh."

"I hope you won't take this wrong, but I'm seriously considering taking over the business myself."

Elwood brightened. "That's swell, Aunt Caroline. I was afraid you were going to try to talk me into it."

"You wouldn't want to?" Mrs. Scheick asked.

"Gosh, no."

"That makes up my mind for me then. I thought after becoming involved in the chicken and hog business out here, you might have decided that the elevator was what you wanted."

"Those things decided me all right," Elwood said. "But it's not the elevator I want. I want to go home, finish college, and then go into the Foreign Service."

"The Foreign Service." Mrs. Scheick smiled. "How nice. You go into that, and I'll take over the family business."

"It's a deal." Elwood also smiled. "And you know, Aunt Caroline, I think you're going to do a terrific job with the elevator."

"Why thank you. That settles everything. I'll send a radiogram to your mother immediately."

"Good. I'll let you get back to work then."

Elwood arose, went to the door, and was just about to leave

when Mrs. Scheick said, "Elwood, I hope you don't think I'm pushing your father out. But as you know, he hasn't realized the possibilities of the business, and . . ."

"I think Dad wants to get out. And I think he should," Elwood said. "That will give him a chance to enjoy his convertible."

"I'm glad you feel that way."

"I do, Aunt Caroline. Please don't worry about it." With a wave Elwood turned, walked back through Paper-Show Headquarters, and re-entered the Square. The crowd was cheering now, for the King had just finished his speech opening the Festival and wishing them all well. Standing there listening to the cheers, a sense of comfort, a sense of well-being, came over him. The Foreign Service was the place for him. The Foreign Service offered something new. It was a challenge. But then, noticing the crowd around him, noticing the eyes searching, and the eyes meeting, the feeling of loneliness once again returned.

Up on the dance platform the King, his face a picture of sheer delight, listened to the response to his welcoming address. Then raising his hand for quiet and taking the microphone once again, he said in Japanese, "And now the Duchess of Bamboo Island and I will give an exhibition of dancing. Afterwards, we hope all of you will come up and dance, too." He pointed to the group of young people standing by the orchestra. "The Duchess has trained a lot of instructors, and they'll help anyone who wants to try it. So here we go."

The music started; and as Kenji turned, the Duchess of Bamboo Island came across the floor toward him. And even there, before all those people, he could only stand for a moment and stare, for never had he seen anyone so beautiful. Her eyes sparkled in the glow of the paper lanterns, her kimono rustled softly, and as they began a slow, gliding waltz, Kenji whispered, "Boy."

They danced in silence. The Duchess smiled up at him, and Kenji's heart beat faster. "Boy," he said once again as the orchestra went into a fox trot, and she followed him smoothly, expertly. Then they were doing the samba, then the cha-cha; and King Kenji forgot the crowd. He could see only her, dancing with him in the beauty of the October night. Once again the orchestra went back to the waltz, and once again, with her gliding in his arms, he said, "Boy."

She looked up at him, her eyes soft. "Boy," she whispered. "Is that all you can say?"

There was no chiding in her voice. It was only that this was the moment to say something. This was the moment for the right words; Kenji knew it, so he said, "Boy, you know, you dance twice as good as Mellie Wong."

"Mellie Wong?" The mood of the waltz was gone. "Who is this Mellie Wong?"

King Kenji was aware that he had not chosen the right approach. "Oh, didn't I ever tell you about her? She was just a good friend of mine."

"Really?" The Duchess' eyebrows arched.

"Well, maybe she wasn't such an awfully good friend," the King said desperately. "But she was a good kid."

The Duchess eyed him.

"I mean we just used to date once in a while. You know, like the Sophomore Cotillion. And one time I went over to her house in Canton for a Chinese New Year, just things like that."

"Just things like that! You went to Canton?"

"Oh, this was Canton, Ohio—not Canton, China."

"But you went over to her house."

"Yeah. This was New Year's though. She thought I might like a change from American food."

"I see. So she was quite a thoughtful girl."

"She was," Kenji agreed. "I thought it was darn nice of her to ask me home."

"Oh, so you did. Well, really!"

"Yeah, but . . ." The music stopped. The dance was over, and the cheers from the crowd arose. Together they bowed, and the King turned, extended his hand for the Duchess to take a bow alone. But she didn't bow. Instead she wheeled, walked from the dance floor, leaving him there. The crowd continued cheering. For a moment he stood, then walked to the microphone and said in Japanese, "Well, that was quite a dance. Now, let's all of you dance. Here are the instructors." With a gesture he brought them on the floor, kimono-clad girls and long-haired Nakashima Islands youths wearing almost a uniform of khaki trousers, white sneakers, and sweaters. "Please, won't you come up?"

There was a moment's hesitation, then Haruko, General Scheick's maid, bravely came forward. An instructor stepped to the edge of the floor, extending his hand to her, and the rush was on. They began swarming up on the floor, outnumbering the instructors, but that didn't bother them. They began dancing with each other, improvising, and laughing. The King watched them, a smile on his face; then satisfied that everything was beginning to go all right, he turned his head and saw the Duchess of Bamboo Island walking away. Quickly he stepped from the floor, his smile fading, and he began to follow her.

He caught her just as she neared the rope by the Lane of Partial Stability. "Hey, Debbie," he said, "just a second. I want to tell you something."

She hesitated.

"Yeah, I want to tell you all about Mellie Wong."

She gave him a cold look. "I'm really not interested."

"Yeah, I know. But I just wanted to tell you that she was at least a foot taller than me."

"Oh?"

"Or maybe a foot and a half even. She was way up there."

"Was she?"

"Oh, sure. Why, she could look right over the top of me. And we used to have an awful time when we danced the Lindy. Why, when she'd go to twirl under my hand, she'd bump her head."

"Are you sure she was that tall?"

"Oh, yes," Kenji replied solemnly. "At least that tall." And he could see that the Duchess was thawing a bit. "By the way," he said casually, "how would you like to take a little ride? I got a full tank of gas."

"Well, I don't know."

"But it's such a warm evening. It would cool us off."

"Yes, it is a warm evening," the Duchess agreed, as the paper lanterns swayed in the chill of the October night.

"Besides," Kenji went on, "we don't have to do another exhibition until ten o'clock."

"It would give us a wonderful chance to relax."

"You'll go then? I got the jalopy parked just over there, in the Lane of Partial Stability."

"I might go for a short one."

Kenji's face lighted. "Good."

Together they started toward the rope and had just reached the ticket taker at the entrance when the three figures came out of the Lane of Partial Stability, and Kenji heard the voices.

"King Kenji," General Scheick called, and he was full of jollity and good will. "By George, there you are. You're just the person we want to see."

"Oh, hello, Mr. General," Kenji acknowledged the greeting.

"We certainly do want to see you," General Winthrope joined in, his face wreathed in a smile; and even the Duke of Tatami Oshima, who was with them, grinned brightly.

"Do you want to see me now?" Kenji asked, hoping they didn't.

"Yes, we have good news for you," General Scheick said.

"That's nice." Kenji nodded and sneaked a glance at the Duchess, who was walking ahead, over toward the jalopy.

"First of all," General Scheick continued, "we've placed the Duke of Tatami Oshima. We were talking with him this evening at the Officers' Club, and do you know what we found out?"

The King didn't know.

"We found out that back in the old days, King Gihon had the same trouble with his grandfather, fourteen times removed, as you had with him, King Kenji. That's right. King Gihon did everything to find a job for his grandfather but just couldn't place him. Then one day, shortly after he introduced the sweet potato, Gihon had an idea. He called in the grandfather and said, 'I'll tell you what. You just go home and grow the biggest sweet potatoes on your Island.' And that's what his grandfather did, and that's what the family has been doing for over three hundred and fifty years now."

"Is that right?" Kenji said, feeling something was expected of him.

"It certainly is. Do you catch the idea?" General Scheick asked.

"I don't think so," Kenji replied.

"It's this way," General Scheick went on. "Instead of sweet potatoes, now we have hogs. All we have to do is give the Duke, here, a few Chester Whites, and we got his family taken care of for at least the next three hundred and fifty years or so. Yes, sir, why he'll raise the biggest hogs on all of Tatami Oshima. Right, Duke?"

The Duke of Tatami Oshima, gathering that they were talking about him, nodded and smiled expansively. "Chester White," he said.

"Chester White," both Generals Scheick and Winthrope said in a bond of comradeship, whereupon General Winthrope continued, "And we placed the Duke of Beancurd Island for you, too, King Kenji. Do you know how the first Duke of Beancurd Island got his title?"

"I don't recall offhand."

"Well, you remember how the first Duke of Tatami Oshima got his title, don't you?"

"Oh, yes. He beat the deuce out of the Chinese expedition that was looking for the land of the happy immortals and that was raising all kinds of the dickens around here."

"Right," Mosby said. "But after this Chinese expedition was beaten they fell back and regrouped. In fact they enlisted the aid of a whole slew of Japanese pirates and this time it looked like the end, because the Nakashima Islands Army could never stand up against them." Mosby held up a finger. "Now this is where the first Duke of Beancurd Island came in—of course he wasn't a duke then, he was made that later for his work. But he went out, got in good with the Chinese, got in good with the Japanese. And the first thing you know he had them squabbling among themselves, and by George, they wiped each other out. So there you are. The Duke of Beancurd Island is a natural."

"A natural for what?" Kenji asked.

"Why, for Foreign Minister. Hell, man, what a diplomat he'll make. And is he ever anxious to get started. Why, already he's asking us about the restaurants in Washington."

"Yes, sir," General Scheick joined in. "You don't have to worry about filling that spot on the Table of Organization. We have that taken care of for you."

Kenji glanced anxiously at Debbie, who was waiting by the jalopy. "That was awfully nice of you. I thank you very much. Now if you gentlemen will just excuse me . . ."

"Wait a minute," General Scheick said. "That's only the half of it."

"You mean there's more?"

"Certainly," General Winthrope said. "We've figured out a way for you to pay back for the pigs."

"That was never any problem," the King said. "After I start shipping pigs to Japan and selling them, I'll just turn over the Japanese money to the United States Government."

General Scheick glanced at General Winthrope. General Winthrope glanced at General Scheick. "Ah, yes," Mosby said carefully, "but I think we figured out a better way. You know how it is, King Kenji. The U. S. Government is loaded, and they wouldn't want to fool around with twenty million or so."

"But, Mr. Generals—" Kenji started to protest.

"Now just a moment, Your Majesty." Mosby held up a restraining hand. "Wait until you hear our idea. We figure there are other people who could use twenty million much better."

"Other people?" Kenji questioned. "Who, Mr. General?"

"Well, for instance, the place where you went to school."

"Cambridge College?"

"Certainly. If it takes a thirty-six-page brochure to list all their needs, we're sure they could use a few dollars. So instead of giving the money back to the U. S. Government, why don't you give it to Cambridge?"

"Would that be okay?" the King asked.

"I don't see why not."

The King whistled. "Hey! I could buy new game uniforms for

the Varsity." He eyed the two Generals. "And you're sure this would be all right with the Government?"

"I'm positive," Mosby replied. "In fact, I think it would be quite a surprise for them."

"Well . . ." The King's eyes grew wide. "And just think, I could give Cambridge a new Administration Building. Would that ever make Mr. Hayden happy." Kenji looked up. "But I'd put a card on it saying 'Compliments of the United States Government.'"

"That would be fine, King Kenji," Mosby approved. "And you could even give some money to the Duchess' school."

"Letty Linton! Wait until I tell Debbie."

"And you'd still have money left," Mosby went on, "so you could re-establish the scholarships. We talked this over with your grandmother, and she is all for it."

"She is?"

"She certainly is. She says the retinues were all right in the old days. Then it was all right for the young people to come into court to learn. But today . . . Well, she says if you hadn't gone to school in America, you never would have known about mark-ups. And if you hadn't known about mark-ups, you never would have been able to solve the problem of the pig."

"That's right. But I think if King Gihon had had a course in Marketing, he might have been able to solve it, too."

"Maybe so. At any rate, your grandma wants the scholarships re-established, for as she says, 'It takes two from here and two from over there to make four.'"

The King nodded. "I agree with that."

"In that case, re-establish the scholarships. For instance, the Duchess there—she could go back to school in America."

"Go back?" Kenji's face fell.

"Certainly. You could establish scholarships for all colleges, not just Cambridge."

King Kenji looked over at Debbie.

"Wouldn't that be great?" General Scheick asked.

"Oh, sure."

"Let's go over to one of those food stalls and see if we can get a carrot juice," General Scheick said. "And we'll talk it over."

The King hesitated. "Mr. Generals, I wonder if you would excuse me. Maybe we can talk this over some other time. I would like to get a little air now . . ."

"A little air," Mosby said. "Well, I suppose if you wish, Your Majesty. Could we get together tomorrow though?"

"Tomorrow? Oh, sure."

General Scheick regarded the King. "Until tomorrow then. In the meantime, are there any other problems we can work out for you, Your Majesty?"

"Other problems?" A certain sadness was in the King's eyes. "I guess not, but I thank you anyway." He half nodded. "I'll be seeing you, Mr. Generals." Turning, he walked over to the jalopy, where the Duchess of Bamboo Island was standing with her head thrown back in the night. As he approached, she smiled at him. "I guess we're ready," he said.

She did not reply, but merely waited for him to open the jalopy door. Then he went around, cranked the car and slipped in behind the wheel. "Let's ride out by Big Shamoji Beach," he said. "Is that okay?"

"If you wish."

Swinging the wheel, he started the jalopy up the Lane of Partial Stability, skirted the old stone quays; and as they started out Highway Number 3, they were silent, there in the moonlight. They passed through the village of Tobaru, which was aglow with paper lanterns. They drove atop the old sea wall, through Maebaru and Takaesu, where the lanterns also glowed softly. And reaching Big Shamoji Beach, King Kenji swung the jalopy off the road, faced it into the steadily rising moon, and cut the motor. For a long moment they sat there, then King Kenji, looking up into the heavens, said, "You know, this is quite a night, isn't it?"

The Duchess had to agree. "It certainly is."

Kenji glanced at her. She was looking straight ahead at the path of moonlight on the gentle sea. The sadness welled up in him then, and he began slowly, hesitantly, "Debbie . . ."

"Yes?" She turned to him.

303

"I have some good news."

"Oh?" Her face was filled with a certain expectation.

"I just talked with the Mr. Generals, and do you know what?"

"What?"

"I'm going to re-establish the scholarships."

"The scholarships?" A look of distress crossed her face.

"Yes. So you can go back to Letty Linton next semester if you want."

"Oh, how nice," she said, but her voice lacked conviction.

"And you can go on and be a fashion designer, and you can go to New York when you graduate."

"That certainly is fine." She forced a smile, and they lapsed into silence.

Then the King went on. "But I was thinking. You know, I'm going to need some designing out here. For instance, I don't have any robes."

"That's right, you don't," the Duchess said.

"And I think maybe I ought to stop wearing sweaters and sneakers. I think the King ought to be dressed up a little bit more. So you can see I need a whole new outfit. Of course, I need a good designer to design it."

"It would certainly be an interesting challenge," the Duchess said.

"And I've also been thinking," the King continued, "that the Mr. General made a mistake."

"A mistake?"

"Yes, when he drew up the Table of Organization. He had a Prime Minister, and a Foreign Minister, and all that. But do you know what?"

"What?"

"He forgot to include a place on the T/O for a Queen."

"A Queen?"

"That's right, so I'm going to have to revise it. And I think being Queen might be quite an interesting job. For instance, you . . . I mean the Queen . . . could kind of look after the social problems going on around the place."

"That's right, the Queen could."

"And the job wouldn't have to be political. I mean . . . you know, just in case the Queen wasn't interested in politics."

"I see."

"So I was wondering," the King continued slowly, "if you might not be interested in the job? I was wondering if you wouldn't be the Queen?"

"Do you really want me to?"

"I sure do."

"Well," the Duchess said. "This is quite a surprise."

"But you don't have to be Queen if you don't want to," Kenji said. "I mean if you'd rather go to New York."

"Well, New York is all right, but . . ."

"Yeah, but if there's some other guy, like this Sherman Chang, why I understand."

"Oh, Sherman Chang," the Duchess said. "He was an awful drip. You know, you'd go out to maybe a Chinese restaurant, and he'd want to eat with chopsticks, just to show off. Really!"

"Yeah, but if . . ."

"No," the Duchess said. "I think I'll take the job."

"You will!" King Kenji was overwhelmed.

"Yes, since you asked me, I'll be the Queen."

Kenji couldn't believe. He could only sit dazed, then he began, "Do you know, Debbie, from the minute I saw you get off the sampan I knew that was it. I wanted to turn cartwheels. . . ."

"And how do you think I felt?" the Duchess asked.

"Did you feel that way, too?"

"I guess I did. The minute I saw you I said to myself, 'And who is that?'"

"You did?" Kenji's eyes were glowing and his heart was pounding in the night.

"Yes, but my goodness, I couldn't show it. You know how we can't show our feelings in the Nakashima Islands, that is when we meet someone who up and hits us."

"That's right. We can't, can we?" Kenji said.

"We certainly can't. But then I found out you were the King."

"And what did you say then?" Kenji asked, his voice filled with eagerness.

"What did I say? I said to myself, 'Boy,' I said. 'And how would you like to sit next to him on the throne!'"

305

Chapter 24

YAMAGUCHI KIEI, the ancient historian, bent over the scroll spread out on the low little table of his living room; then dipping his brush in the coal-black ink, gracefully he wrote, *And so it was on the first night of the Festival of the Unattached, the first one to become attached was King Kenji I.*

"Ah, yes," the old one murmured, surveying the scroll with satisfaction, for there it was for all posterity to see. Then putting down his brush, he flexed his fingers and pursed his lips as a thought struck him. What kind of an attaching ceremony would the King have, he wondered; and rising from the straw mats, he went over to see what history had to offer.

He checked the reign of King Eiso and found that King Eiso had had the conventional ceremony of the half-drained cup—one-half the cup had been drained on the day of the Attaching Ceremony and the other half on the day of Attachment. He checked the reign of King Gihon and found that King Gihon was so eager to get married that he did away with the half-cup ceremony altogether and simply drank a full cup on the day of Attachment. Then he checked the reign of King Satto. "Now there is the reverse case," he told himself. For so reluctant was

King Satto to become attached, and so long did he stretch out the ceremony of the cups, that he had come down through history, known even to this day as King Satto the Sipper.

So it was pretty much a case of what the King wanted, Yamaguchi Kiei could see that. Putting his scrolls away, he arose and started for the ancient Castle of Tamagusuku to find out for history just what the King was going to do. And it was quite by accident, as he was passing along the quayside, that he saw the King and Elwood driving along in the red and white jalopy, and he called, "Your Majesty! Your Majesty! Just a moment."

Hearing him, the King waved and pulled over. "Oh, hello, Mr. Yamaguchi," he said. "How are you today? Can we give you a lift?"

"A lift?"

"A ride."

"Well, I do not know," the old one said, eying the jalopy. "I have never ridden in such a vehicle before. But first, Your Majesty, I must ask a question. What kind of Attaching Ceremony are you having? I would like it for the records."

The King smiled. "Ah, I see. Well, I am going to have a Sweetheart Serenade."

The old one scratched his head. "I do not believe I have ever found that in the scrolls, Your Majesty. Could I have missed a reign somewhere?"

"Oh, it wouldn't be in the scrolls," the King said quickly. "You see, Mr. Yamaguchi, what I am going to do is give the Duchess of Bamboo Island my fraternity pin, just like we do it at Cambridge College."

"So that is it." The old one considered. "I do not think I understand."

"Well, we're getting ready for it now, Mr. Yamaguchi," Elwood joined in, pointing to the back seat of the jalopy. "See, there are the candles. We just picked them up from Mrs. Fukahara at the Ahn Ho Trading Company."

"So you burn candles. Then this Sweetheart Serenade must happen at night."

"We have it in the evening, just after it gets dark," the King said.

"Aha."

"But we have an awful problem," the King went on. "We don't know where to get a balcony."

"What would you need that for?"

"The Duchess stands on it. And I just don't know how we're going to rig one up."

The old one eyed the jalopy again. "Where are you going now?" he asked.

"We have to go up and see Elwood's aunt and uncle," the King replied.

"Ah, so." Yamaguchi Kiei drew his kimono around him. "In that case, Your Majesty, perhaps it would be best if I went along and observed these proceedings." He held up a finger. "You know, we could have a great deal of confusion in history here."

General Scheick, General Winthrope, and the Duke of Tatami Oshima, a general thirty-three times removed, were sitting out in the Scheicks' back yard when the King, Elwood and the old historian came around the side of the house. "Well, gentlemen, gentlemen," General Scheick said, rising, "this is a pleasant surprise."

"I hope we're not interrupting anything, Uncle Matt," Elwood said.

"No, not at all. The Duke, here, just stopped in to say good-by —that is, I think that's what he stopped for. Haruko, our maid, has gone to visit her boy friend's parents over on Chrysanthemum Island, so we're without an interpreter. But if we read his gestures right, he's got himself a hog and he's going home. However, would you check on that, Your Majesty, just to make sure?"

"That's correct," Kenji said. "He asked me for permission to go back and I gave it. He says he is going to grow the biggest pigs of anybody, anywhere."

"That's a noble ambition." Both Mosby and General Scheick

looked at the Duke, smiled, and General Scheick said, "Chester White."

"Chester White," the Duke repeated in English, nodding brightly as usual.

"But of course," the King said, "he won't be leaving until after I'm engaged."

"And when is that, Your Majesty?" Mosby asked.

"That is what we want to see you about," the King said. "We're having an awful problem with singers."

"Singers?"

"For the Sweetheart Serenade, Uncle Matt," Elwood said. "We should use the nobility, but they don't know any English. Besides, they probably never even heard of a fraternity song. So we were wondering if General Winthrope, and you, and some of the officers would help us out. We need a sort of chorus to take the place of our fraternity brothers."

"Well, we never had fraternities at the Academy," General Scheick said.

"But, Pug," Mosby cut in. "There's always been a fair amount of singing around the piano in the Officers' Club. I think we could raise a few."

"I would sure appreciate it." Kenji glanced about. "And is the Mrs. General home too? You see, the girl usually has her sorority sisters around her acting as a chorus, too, and I was wondering if the Mrs. General and her Investment Club would help us out."

"She's not here right now," General Scheick said. "In fact, she's meeting with her Investment Club at the moment."

"Oh?"

"Yes, she's turning the reins over to them."

"The reins?" Yamaguchi Kiei, the old historian, questioned. "What is the meaning of that, Mr. General?"

"It means she's turning the business over to them."

"The business. The business. Ah, I understand."

General Scheick regarded his nephew. "By the way, Elwood, we just had a letter from your mother. She also thinks your father should retire."

"Dad will be glad to hear that."

"But he isn't glad. In fact, instead of buying a convertible, he's going to buy a business coupé."

"How come?"

"Well, as I see it, there's a proxy fight shaping up here, and I think your father figures if he can put on a spurt, maybe drum up some business, the girls will back him. But he might as well face it. They're going to stick together, and he's got ninety per cent of the stock against him."

"Personally," Elwood said, "I think this would be a good chance for Dad to get out. Aunt Caroline can run the business."

"Well, I'm not getting involved," General Scheick said. "If Fred wants to end up as assistant manager, that's his lookout."

"I'm not getting involved either," Elwood said. "I'll just stick to the Foreign Service."

"I wish I had something to stick to," General Scheick said; then seeing that the old historian was shaking his head, he asked, "What's the matter, Mr. Yamaguchi?"

"I could not help overhearing," the old one replied. "I see your system is the same as ours."

"In what way?"

"The trader . . . the sixth child of Shinerikyu and Amami-kyu."

"Oh, was their sixth son the trader?"

"The sixth child was not a son. She was a daughter. Just like in your system, our trader is a woman, too."

"Ah, yes." General Scheick said. "Ah, yes. I guess you're right."

The King was rising to his feet now. He regarded the two Generals. "And you will help us out then, gentlemen?"

"Of course we will," Mosby promised.

"And I don't like to rush you," the King went on, "but could you do it right away? I mean, could you line up the singers just as soon as possible? You see, I'm kind of anxious . . ."

"We'll go to headquarters immediately and see what we can find," Mosby assured him.

"That's good," the King said. "And while you're doing that,

we'll go down and see the members of the women's Investment Club." He turned to the old one. "Are you ready, Mr. Yamaguchi?"

"I am ready," the old one replied, rising from his chair, and General Scheick looked at him.

"Say, I have an idea," the General said. "Perhaps I can get you a couple of singers. Mr. Yamaguchi, are you any relaton to Louie and Henry Yamaguchi?"

"Louie and Henry?" The old one thought for a moment. "There are no Yamaguchis named that. But surely that must be Juro and Yoichi. Yes, they are my grandnephews."

"Your grandnephews?"

"That is correct. And do you know, Mr. General, it is too bad about those two."

"Too bad?" General Scheick was solicitous. "Why, did something happen to them?"

"No. But sometimes we almost wish it would. You see, they are the black sheep of the family. Why do you inquire of them?"

General Scheick coughed. "Oh, I just happened to think of their names in passing. It's nothing. Nothing at all."

"Well, we will be on our way then."

The three of them started to leave, and the Duke of Tatami Oshima began to follow. "Is he going with you, too?" Mosby asked.

"Oh, yes," the King replied. "He says he's been looking at my jalopy. And he says he wants to get at least one ride in it before he goes home, so this is his chance."

"Will we be seeing him again?" Mosby questioned.

"He doesn't know for sure," the King said. "But he'll be at the Sweetheart Serenade."

"Well, just in case we miss him," General Scheick said, "tell him to raise big ones."

"He says he will, Mr. General." And the Duke gestured with his hand, indicating that he was going to raise wide ones, as tall as Shetland ponies.

The two Generals stood in the back yard, watching the little group round the side of the house, then General Winthrope said,

311

"Pug, you know that nephew of yours is a mighty fine boy."

"He is," General Scheick agreed. "But in all honesty, Mosby, I really don't think he would have had the stuff to make the grade at the Academy."

"Maybe so," Mosby said. "But that shouldn't stop him from being a success in the Foreign Service."

"I guess it shouldn't," General Scheick conceded. "Well, what do you say if we go down to headquarters and see if we can dig up a chorus?"

They took the back path down the hill and through the vegetable gardens of the Americans. And as they passed the compost piles, General Scheick said, "Mosby, I'm going to hate to leave those."

"Maybe that would be a nice hobby for you," Mosby said. "Maybe you could build compost piles."

"That's a possibility. But I think I ought to have a little more to do than that."

"Well, don't worry about it, Pug. Something will come to you, and the whole thing will straighten itself out."

"I hope so," General Scheick said, and they walked in silence down the hill to headquarters.

Reaching the front door, General Scheick opened it, stepped aside for Mosby to enter; and as General Scheick did so, his aide came hurrying up the hall. "Sir," the aide said, "I was on my way up to your house. A radiogram just arrived from Washington for General Winthrope. Here it is, sir." Nervously he handed it over, for he already had read it.

Slowly Mosby unfolded it, began to read, then the blood rushed to his face and he began to mutter. "Why, those damn fools!"

"What's the matter, Mosby?" General Scheick asked.

Mosby was having trouble controlling himself. "Those damn fools! Listen to this." He read aloud, "Haven't you people, out there, ever heard of economy? You know we're not going to get any of the money back that we're pouring in. So why do you have to put a swimming pool on every level of the castle? Why can't you put a swimming pool on every other level? And as to

Chester Whites, that is the wrong breed of hog. You should be using black hogs. They don't sunburn as easily. And regarding—" Mosby took the radiogram in his hand and wadded it up.

General Scheick's face also was flushed now. "A swimming pool on every other level, why that's ridiculous."

"It certainly is," Mosby said. "Do you know, Pug, if you and I had been born out here we'd probably be dukes."

General Scheick agreed this undoubtedly would be true.

"Well, I'll tell you this," Mosby went on. "If I were a duke, I wouldn't want a bunch of earls hanging around my swimming pool. Not that there's anything wrong with an earl. But it seems to me they ought to keep their place."

"I'll go along with that, Mosby," General Scheick said.

"The damn fools!" Mosby repeated. "Here we have this country on a hog economy. We have a good, capitalist king—and there's none of this business of changing every four years. He's in for life. We have a picture window going into the castle, and ivy growing on the walls." In his eyes was the same fire that had glowed back at old Fort Bitely when everybody was talking about an obstacle course, and no one was doing anything about it. "Pug," he said, "let's show them."

General Scheick saw the fire. "You mean draw Washington up a plan, Mosby?"

"Exactly. Let's show them how to handle a situation like this, how to get a country on its feet. What do you say?"

For a brief moment the fire also flared in General Scheick, but then it died and he shook his head. "No, Mosby," he said. "I'd rather not."

"You'd rather not! Why?" Mosby asked.

"It's like this," General Scheick began slowly, and the gesture of his hand encompassed the whole of the Nakashima Islands. "The way I figure it is that we've got Washington about three-quarters of the way up Fool's Hill on this. From now on let them make their own mistakes."

Mosby reconsidered. "By George, Pug, you're right," he said and shoved the wadded radiogram in his pocket.

313

Before them, the young aide fidgeted nervously. "Sir," he said, "do you want me to get off a reply?"

"Not at the moment," Mosby said. "We're too busy."

The aide's eyes opened wide, for never before had he seen anyone too busy for Washington. "Yes, sir. But is there anything I can do, sir?"

"Yes," General Scheick said. "Will you call my staff together in the gym? I think the acoustics would be best there."

"Yes, sir," the aide said, and he was completely at a loss. "And what kind of a meeting should I tell them it is?"

"It's not a meeting," General Scheick said. "Tell them we're organizing a glee club."

"A glee club?" The words escaped the aide.

"Certainly. We need singers."

"Yes, sir." For a moment the aide could only stand there, then he turned, walked away, but he had to look back, just to make sure, and as he did so, he heard General Winthrope's voice.

"Pug," Mosby was saying, "remind me to get a camera, will you? I'll send some snapshots of the sunflowers growing along the wall to Congressman Homer Hoplow of Kansas. They should get him to go to bat for us."

Chapter 25

AS THE night began to fall and the moon began to rise, Yamaguchi Kiei, the old historian, walking in the shadows of the ancient Castle of Tamagusuku, looked about him just to make sure that all was in readiness. The nobility was there, lining the path which would be the avenue of approach. Up in the gap in the castle wall, which was to contain the Queen Grandmother's picture window but which now was serving as a balcony, he could see Mrs. Scheick and the members of her Investment Club, all dressed in white, standing quietly, waiting. He regarded the single candle up there on the improvised balcony, then nodding in satisfaction, he went over to take his place beside the Queen Grandmother and some of the major nobility.

"Will it be long now, Mr. Yamaguchi?" the Queen Grandmother asked. She was dressed in a banana-cloth kimono, but now she was wearing a little American hat and a pair of white gloves, for certainly she wanted to be dressed up on this occasion.

"No," the old one replied. "As we rehearsed it, it should begin in a moment."

"What happens first, Mr. Yamaguchi?" the Viscount of Kunigami, who had just arrived at court, asked.

"First, the Duchess of Bamboo Island will step up to where the picture window is going to be."

"Ah, so."

"Then," the old one went on, "she will light the candle. That is the signal." He saw the movement up in the castle. "Now you watch."

And that is what happened. In the soft darkness, the Duchess of Bamboo Island, clad in a silk kimono, came from within the castle, took a match, struck it, touched it to the wick; and as the candle flared in the night the eyes of the nobility, gathered in the courtyard below, turned to observe.

Other eyes were watching, too. Down in the archway leading from the royal enclosure to the Courtyard of the Dukes, Colonel Henderson, who was posted as a lookout, saw the flame, and turning, called softly to General Mosby Winthrope, "There it is, sir."

"Fine. Fall in," Mosby gave the command; and as senior officer present, he surveyed the formation lined up there in the Courtyard of the Dukes. First was the King, wearing his best sport jacket. Next came Elwood, carrying the red pillow with the fraternity pin; and flanking Elwood on one side was General Scheick, while General Winthrope himself would be on the other. Immediately behind them were Colonel Henderson and Lt. Colonel Seymour, heading the other officers of the command, who were lined up two by two. Seeing that everything was in order, Mosby asked, "Are you all ready, King Kenji?"

"I'm all set, Mr. General," the King replied and his voice betrayed his nervousness.

"Good." Mosby faced the formation and said, "Gentlemen, light your candles."

Immediately matches and cigarette lighters flickered, and all along the column candles burst into flame.

Mosby walked over, took his place beside Elwood and half turning his head, called softly, "Forward . . . march!"

The column moved out behind the King, their faces solemn in the candlelight. They passed through the arch leading to the royal enclosure. Then Mosby raised his hand; and their song, drifting out on the night, reached the girl standing on the improvised balcony. "Sweetheart, sweetheart, sweetheart," she heard, and her eyes glowed in the flame of the flickering candle as she watched the King coming toward her.

Down in the courtyard, the Viscount of Kunigami, also hearing the words, whispered, "Mr. Yamaguchi, what song is that?"

"That is the sweetheart song of Lambda Beta Theta."

"Ah, so." The Viscount nodded, not understanding, but agreeing, it was a pretty song. And seeing the girl's eyes, he smiled and said, "Isn't it wonderful to be young on a night like this?"

His thoughts were shared by others. The Queen Grandmother could only wish that she had known of this custom years and years ago, out in her home village of Little Koza. While up on the improvised balcony behind the Duchess of Bamboo Island, Mrs. Scheick and the members of her Investment Club looked down at the officers, whose heads were thrown back in song, and tears glistened in many an eye.

"Yes, it is wonderful," the old historian said, and watched as the column, reaching the foot of the castle, spread out and formed a semicircle just behind the King, who stood looking up at the girl. Then they began another song. "What song is that, Mr. Yamaguchi?" the Viscount whispered.

"That is the fraternity Panhellenic Serenade."

The Viscount didn't understand that either, but he knew it must be one of the King's favorite songs, for the King was standing with his eyes closed and his face wreathed in a smile as he heard of Sigma Chi, and Kappa Sig, and the rest. This was just like being back at old Cambridge with his fraternity brothers around him. Then the women behind the Duchess broke into the sorority Panhellenic Serenade. They sang of Delta, Delta, Delta; and Delta Gamma; then there was silence. There was quiet, and it was the King's turn.

As those behind him began to hum softly, the King raised his head, looked at the Duchess, then he sang. He sang the song about God making the ivy twine, about God making the stars to shine. And while the original song told about her eyes so blue, the King changed it, because her eyes weren't blue. He sang because God made her eyes so brown, because God made her, she would wear his crown. And then it was over. For a long moment the two of them, the girl on the balcony and the boy below, could only look at each other and smile, then slowly the King turned to the red pillow to take the fraternity pin, and Yamaguchi Kiei, the old historian, began to chuckle.

"Here's the surprise," he whispered to the Viscount, and the Queen Grandmother was chuckling, too. "Now listen. Here is the famous whistling chorus." And like the Queen Grandmother, he wet his lips, preparing to join in.

"Your Majesty," General Winthrope spoke softly. "Would you mind waiting a moment?"

"Waiting?" the King questioned.

"Yes. We have something special prepared."

"You have?"

"Now just stand there." Mosby raised his hand, brought it down; and Yamaguchi Kiei, the Queen Grandmother, and both the Dukes of Tatami and Beancurd Islands, along with the officers of the command, began to whistle. They began to whistle "On, Brave Old Army Team."

"Well," the King said. "Well." And he shook his head, in pleased delight.

Then they sang the chorus, with the staff coming in with a special arrangement which General Winthrope himself had given it; and with a final flourish of whistling they ended up.

"Well," the King repeated. "Well. I thank you, gentlemen."

The officers were beaming, proud of their surprise. Then once again they grew solemn, for now was the moment. The King walked to the red pillow, held by Elwood, and took the fraternity pin. He looked up at the Duchess. She looked at him. Then slowly turning, she left the balcony to meet him within the castle.

As Elwood watched them in the night, a realization came to him. He realized that Dorothy Landridge, who lived down the street back home, was a darn cute kid. He cocked his head in thought, and as he did so, he heard his uncle whisper.

318

"You know, Mosby," General Scheick whispered, "youth is a wonderful thing."

"It certainly is, Pug."

"I wonder," General Scheick went on, "if my obligation isn't to youth."

"What do you mean, Pug?"

"Perhaps I should go back home to Youngerville, and maybe give the coach a hand with the high school football team."

Up on the balcony Mrs. Scheick, all in white, stepped forward, blew out the single candle in signal, and Elwood whispered, "Uncle Matt."

"I think I ought to help out with the physical conditioning," General Scheick went on. "Teach them tension exercises. Show them how to break boards."

"Uncle Matt," Elwood whispered again. "Aunt Caroline just gave the signal. The King and the Duchess are together."

"I think that's what I'll do." There was a look of dedication on General Scheick's face. "Because we can't let the youth of America get soft."

"Uncle Matt, can't we blow out the candles?" Elwood pleaded. "It's the custom to leave them alone in the dark."

"The custom. Oh, yes." General Scheick turned to General Mosby Winthrope, the senior officer present.

"All set, Pug?" Mosby asked.

"All set."

Mosby faced the semicircle. "Gentlemen," he whispered the command. "Candles . . . out." And the soft darkness closed in over the ancient Castle of Tamagusuku.

But out in the chain the other Islands were aglow. From Goat Island in the far north to Cherry Blossom Island in the south, the villages were ablaze with light. And out on the China Sea the sailors were shaking their heads in wonder. For by every almanac and every guide the tide should be ebbing now. It should be withdrawing, retreating. Yet it wasn't. It was surging and sweeping, running full and strong toward the Land of the Lighted Lanterns.